T0248423

Advance Praise for
GO TO HELL OLE MISS

"While globalism and the mass-market have long tried to genericize us all, regionalism has remained a dynamic and steadfast force—and especially for those who hail from the South. In this spirited debut novel, we see a 1970s-era Mississippi family in high relief and high dudgeon. Jeff Barry deftly captures the idiosyncrasies, the conversational quirks, the deeper strains of melancholy, and the darker impulses of violence that most lifelong Southerners know all too well."

—HAMPTON SIDES, *New York Times* bestselling author of
Blood and Thunder and *Ghost Soldiers*

"A must-read for fans of Southern lit, Jeff Barry's novel exquisitely captures the South and its complications of family, faith, hopes, and dreams. It's a first novel of literary depth that makes a mark. His characters spring to life and keep the pages turning because we know them and can't forget. Barry's detail is rich, the literary voice strong."

—DAVID MAGEE, author of National Bestseller *Dear William*

"Rich with imagery of the Deep South and just the right dose of faith to make it real, Jeff Barry's very well-written debut novel is a must-read for lovers of Southern literature."

—RON HALL, #1 *New York Times* bestselling author of
Same Kind of Different as Me

"There's a perfectly good story behind this memorable title, and curious readers will enjoy finding it as they sort through the complicated dynamics of the big, messy Southern family at the heart of this winning debut. You'll recognize these people. Hell, you may even find yourself in these pages. Jeff Barry relishes the pastime of good banter and storytelling. Reading his novel reminded me of a bygone time and of eavesdropping on the grown-ups with their colorful ways of tiptoeing around (and often steamrolling over) the truths and assumptions found in all families."

—JAMIE KORNEGAY, author of *Soil*

"One-part Tim O'Brien's *The Things They Carried* and two-parts Richard Grant's *Dispatches from Pluto*, Barry's book overlies the ways soldiers carry war home and carry home into war. With a pitch-perfect cast of characters, it's a colorful tale of family and all its messy incarnations—humor, loyalty, revenge, conflict, acceptance and, ultimately, unconditional love."

—**MOLLY CROSBY,** author of National Bestseller *The American Plague*

"Truly great storytellers make the reader feel as if the story is one she has lived. In *Go to Hell Ole Miss*, Barry writes with authenticity, humor, and subtlety to bring Mississippi hill country in the 1970s to life. The protagonist, Big John, is as brilliantly flawed as Odysseus, and following him on his journey as he works to right his own wrong is entertaining and engaging. Perhaps most importantly, this novel offers a much-needed meditation on Southern masculinity."

—**COURTNEY MILLER SANTO,** author of *Three Story House* and
The Roots of the Olive Tree

"Jeff Barry's novel is rich with veins of lore interconnecting all things and peoples Southern. His title demonstrates the natural intelligence a POW conveys to the next captured warrior of his nationality and origin. Such a message to a captured fighter in a lonely shed can save a life because it points toward home where springs hope.

Southern readers will love the rivalry his title points out. His characters are dramatic and faithful to the culture, ways, and influences bred in Southern families and communities. Its truth is that people in the South often do not address violence directly, nor even express love openly. So much emotion is held inside, safe, to protect one's soul. The Southern experience often hides in shadows below the level of the conscious mind. Finding that truth in Barry's first novel is a labor of love. When I think of Barry, I think of Slide."

—**SUE WATSON,** journalist with *The South Reporter*

"I fully endorse Jeff Barry's debut novel. *Go to Hell Ole Miss* is a pleasant and enjoyable read about a man and the love he has for his daughter and the people around him. Barry's book tackles race through the eyes of the friendship, offering a welcome respite from the divided nation we find ourselves in today."

—**JAMES ARMFIELD,** book scout with Alcon Entertainment

GO TO HELL OLE MISS

a novel

JEFF BARRY

GREENLEAF
BOOK GROUP PRESS

Published by Greenleaf Book Group Press
Austin, Texas
www.gbgpress.com

Distributed by Greenleaf Book Group

For ordering information or special discounts for bulk purchases, please contact Greenleaf Book Group at PO Box 91869, Austin, TX 78709, 512.891.6100.

Design and composition by Greenleaf Book Group and Kim Lance
Cover design by Greenleaf Book Group and Kim Lance
Cover image used under license from Getty Images / Robert Thorley

Publisher's Cataloging-in-Publication data is available.

Print ISBN: 979-8-88645-155-9

eBook ISBN: 979-8-88645-156-6

To offset the number of trees consumed in the printing of our books, Greenleaf donates a portion of the proceeds from each printing to the Arbor Day Foundation. Greenleaf Book Group has replaced over 50,000 trees since 2007.

Printed in the United States of America on acid-free paper

24 25 26 27 28 29 30 31   10 9 8 7 6 5 4 3 2 1

First Edition

To Dot Dot, Pops, Beverly, and Alice

PART I

FEBRUARY 1971

BIG JOHN SAT AND LEANED AGAINST the concrete wall of his cell. The bench was hard and the wall cold, but he was thankful for his new home.

The farmhouse he'd treasured for twenty-five years hadn't felt like home for the past two weeks. Every sight and smell made him long for the lost. The pictures on her bedside table, her wheelchair in the den, her rocker on the screened-in porch. The scent of perfume lingered on her clothes. Her pillow smelled of death. Had his huge white cat, ornery Black Angus bull, or favorite woodpecker made a sound since her last breath? If so, Big John hadn't noticed.

A few hours ago, he'd lifted the bloody bat from his knees, handed it to the sheriff, and called it *evidence*. When the sheriff asked about the body, Big John shrugged and said, "Did what I had to do."

Had he done enough?

1

Slide

BIG JOHN KNEW MORE SHAKESPEARE THAN anybody else in Hope Springs, Mississippi. Seven words.

My uncle was proud of the line he'd stolen from a smart Yankee in a German prison camp during World War II. Hailed as the camp genius by guards and POWs alike, the fella must've doled out more than seven words. Not that it mattered. Big John needed only three—*prince, darkness,* and *gentleman*—for the hell on our home front that year.

Big John blamed himself for losing sight of his Shakespeare when it counted. I blamed a drunk on a couch, for Big John would've seen what was coming if all he'd been worried about was the man his only daughter was going to marry.

— ✻ ✻ ✻ —

ANOTHER BOTTLE HIT THE WALL AS I skirted the den. I didn't flinch. I would've been scared two years ago. Sad or mad last year.

I stopped at the doorway to study my deddy and our den. A spindly beard coated in drool. The bony right hand with a loose grip on a bottle. Eyes that told a story I didn't want to hear. Shaggy carpet littered with broken glass. A busted lamp and shredded wallpaper that fared better than what had been our television. The room's lone survivor was a light bulb hanging from a cord in the ceiling, probably the only thing Deddy couldn't reach or hit with a bottle.

"Slide!" Momma called out in a booming drawl that still made me flinch. She opened the kitchen door and peered out. "I just got off the phone with Big John. He's up and on the way to get you. This here's no place for a fourteen-year-old boy."

"Shouldn't I stay with you?" I asked, hoping she'd say no.

"You heard me, Slide. Pack enough for a month and don't forget the Sunday clothes you wore last time you stayed at the farmhouse."

I rummaged through the dresser Deddy had built from the scraps of his construction jobs, shoving church clothes and other hand-me-downs into a duffel bag. Stretching out on my bed, I pondered how long it would take Big John to reach our house. I figured he'd thrown on his overalls and boots, hurried to the end of his gravel drive, and climbed into the truck his daughter had named when she was my age: Life Lesson Larry.

Though Larry remained a mystery, I'd endured more life lessons on God and girls and guns than any number provided by ninth-grade math. I once made the mistake of asking Big John why he preached about guns but didn't own one, only to receive a sermon on good and evil that taught me not to ask again.

Had Larry covered the mile of Highway 5 and taken a left onto our street? Within minutes, the rattles of the old pickup answered my question.

Momma opened the door as Big John crossed our porch.

"Sorry to wake you," she said. "Especially on your birthday."

"Couldn't sleep anyhow," he said. I stepped onto the porch, duffel bag in hand. He gave me a weak nod and turned to Momma. "Ethel, where's my brother?"

"In the den," she said. "You'll hardly recognize him."

We followed Big John down the hall. He stopped at the doorway and swallowed hard. He pulled his bandana from a back pocket and wiped sweat from his forehead.

It never seemed to bother Deddy that he'd been a cook in a war nobody wanted while his brother had flown a B-24 bomber in a war that saved the world. A prison camp in northern Germany cost Big John sixty pounds but gave him a lifetime of memories. A kitchen fire in southern Vietnam gave Deddy nightmares six years of liquor couldn't drown.

"Flat out of his mind," Momma said. "Slobbered and slurred all yesterday about a mansion he paid cash for, one of those antebellums near the square. God knows we barely make rent on this place. Annabelle left him this go-round, the poor old dog. She's blinder than a baby mole these days, but her nose still works."

"Ethel, how long's he been like this?" Big John asked.

"Started Friday night after one of those dreams," she said. "Took the longest to slap him out of it. Then he squirmed in my arms and bawled like a toddler until daylight. No telling what he saw and did over—" She glanced my way. "War's even hell on the cooks, I suppose."

"You hidden the guns?" he asked.

"Did that years ago. Not that it matters." She pointed. "Damn carpet's got enough glass to slit every neck in Mississippi."

Big John started for the couch. He cleared a spot on the floor, sank to his knees, and nestled his elbows into the puddle under Deddy's chin. My hero wasted a long hug on the sorry excuse I had for a deddy.

Big John was a soggy mess by the time he reached the doorway.

"All we can do is hope and pray," he said.

"Hope?" She looked Deddy over. "Here I am married to a man named Cash in a town called Hope Springs. Tell me the Lord ain't got Him a sense of humor."

"Come on, Ethel."

"How'd you make peace with such madness?"

"Every war's different. We beat Hitler and the Japanese and came home to parades. Cash hit the ground nearly twenty years late for my war."

"His war'll never end, I reckon."

"It will someday." He draped an arm around my shoulder and half carried me to the front door. "We'll be happy to have Slide. Long as it takes."

"He'd rather be with you than his own daddy."

"Damn right," I said.

Big John stooped, holding me at arm's length. "Your deddy needs you, and you need him."

He straightened up and set his sad eyes on Momma. "When my brother comes to his senses, make sure he knows I'm here for him."

"Even Cash knows that," she said.

"Well, I haven't been lately. My girl's gonna marry one of these two boys, and it's all I've been thinking about."

"She's your daughter," Momma said. "Your only living child. Who could blame you?"

✶ ✶ ✶

JOHNSTON STREET, NAMED AFTER A CONFEDERATE general who'd died at Shiloh over a hundred years ago, was dead quiet except for the creaks and groans of a truck that acted older than its owner. With Big John chewing his bottom lip like he was about to cry, I turned and looked out the window.

Whoever had drawn up the antebellums in town had died off by the time the houses on my street were born. They all looked the same besides a different shade of brick here and there. The roofs were flat enough to steady an egg and low enough to keep one from cracking if a strong wind helped it along. The front porches were no bigger than the two bedrooms joined by a bathroom made for kids and skinny grown-ups like Deddy.

I rolled down my window as Big John turned east onto Highway 5. I listened for the crickets, frogs, and cicadas that made summer nights in Hill County bearable, but all I could hear was the wind whistling through the truck as it bounced toward the ninety acres of paradise I called home.

Big John pulled off the highway and through the gate he never left open. He switched on the brights for a better view of the pasture on our right and the pecan grove on our left.

"I hope none of my Black Angus got out," he said. "They'd be hard to see on the blacktop."

"What about the cattle guard that's been on your list since you retired? Must be on the same list as your fences and gates."

A giant hand circled a scrawny arm. "Been waiting on some muscles to show up. Feels like my wait is over."

I laughed and opened the door. "I'll start with the gate."

I'd closed the gate and hopped back in before I noticed Aunt Shine waving from the end of the gravel drive. With every wave, the headlights lit up her long, white hair.

"The very love of my life," Big John said. The sound of tires crunching gravel filled the night air. "Why am I so lucky, so blessed?"

Lucky or blessed, I had no answer and didn't offer one.

"Slide, about time you got here," Shine said, as we rolled to a stop.

She opened my door and gave me a hug.

"Do I smell peaches and cinnamon on your apron?" I asked.

"Maybe," she said, squishing my lips into a tight circle she always had to kiss. "Maybe not."

She took my hand and led me through the yard, up the porch steps, and into the den.

"Aunt Shine, why are you up?"

"Big John's tossing and turning over Pearl sent me to the kitchen and gave me a head start on his birthday dinner," she said.

I followed her into the kitchen and made a beeline for the table.

"Is this for me?" I asked, bowing to Shine's cobbler.

She giggled, eased an arm around Big John, and pinched his side. "Who else you think it's for? These love handles certainly don't need it." She scanned the kitchen as if searching for her Griswold skillet. "Slide, you wouldn't mind sharing a few bites with Pearl, would you?"

Pearl darted from the pantry for a hug that covered my cheeks with silky brown hair. Sinner's truth, I was mad at God for making Pearl six years older and my first cousin to boot. Course, none of that mattered to our kin from Arkansas. Family might've been fair game in a state that named its school after a wild boar, but the Mississippi branch of our tree had standards.

"Who have you been pestering lately?" she asked.

I pondered the truth but landed on a lie. "Nobody."

"Still making straight As in your sleep?"

"We haven't had any tests yet," I said, glad I didn't have to give Pearl an update on the nerd she had for a cousin.

She stepped back, smiling at her deddy. "Happy birthday, old-timer." Big John reached for a hug but got a poke in the belly. "Driving eighteen-wheelers for a living and rocking on a porch for a hobby must do that to a fella over the years."

He chuckled. "You saying I'm fat?"

"Of course not, just tall and beefy like a bear on its hind legs." Pearl kissed him on the cheek. "I love you, Daddy."

"I love you too, darling. Y'all have a good time in Memphis tonight?"

"Myles loved those ribs," she said, glowing at the mention of his name. She pointed at my bowl. "And he adores Momma's peach cobbler. Slide, you're lucky I kept him to one serving."

"Sorry I missed him," I said. "He's the best boyfriend you've ever—"

Myles bolted from the pantry and grabbed me by the shoulders.

"I outfoxed you again," he said. "Moved my truck around back when I heard you were on the way."

"A fire truck's hard to hide," I said, thinking of the shiny red pickup that made Big John's look worse than every scrap of steel littering the junkyard in Oxford.

"Start acting right and he'll take you on a ride sometime," Pearl said. She winked at Myles. "The back seat has plenty of room for long-legged boys."

Momma, the worst cook in at least one state, came to mind as I wolfed down the world's best cobbler and watched Myles's face turn red. Momma swore on the family Bible he could sell condoms to the pope without breaking a sweat. If that didn't send me from the kitchen at a trot, I'd hear that Myles had the looks of a movie star—Robert Redford was her standard pick—to go with a wallet thicker than King Solomon's. Sounded sketchy to me, but anything that took her mind off Deddy couldn't have been the worst sin in the Good Book.

Big John cleared his throat. "Myles, I hear you liked the Rendezvous."

"Best ribs this side of the Mississippi, Mr. Jackson."

"Son, how many times do I have to remind you to call me Big John?"

"Sorry, my parents are sticklers for manners," Myles said, flashing a line of white teeth that should've made Big John think twice about his crooked yellows.

Big John pulled a rag from a drawer, wiped at Deddy's leftovers, and looked my way. "Slide, you're bound to be tuckered out. Let's head on up to your room."

Myles glanced at the clock above the back door. "Goodness, Slide. It's three in the morning. I'll see you at church in eight hours. Then we'll have us a time at Big John's birthday dinner."

"I hope so," I said.

Myles put a hand on my shoulder and stared through me with his warm blue eyes. "Your father will make it through this valley. The same God who looks after the sparrows will take care of him." I'd seen plenty of dead sparrows but nodded anyway. "Meanwhile, lean on this wonderful family of yours. And know you have a friend in me."

Myles. I couldn't put a finger on it, but something about Pearl's latest suitor was different. From a pat on the back to a corny joke, Myles knew how to make me feel like his best buddy and only brother all bundled into one special package.

Pearl wrapped an arm around his waist. "Slide, let's help my man to his truck. He's scared of the dark."

He tucked a strand of hair behind her ear. "Whatever you say, Boo-bear."

Shitfire, Myles wasn't perfect after all. Baby talk and *Boo-bear* made a bad mix in my book.

We filed through the back door and down the steps to Myles's pickup. Pearl locked her hands around his neck, planted a long kiss, and slapped him on the bottom as he got behind the wheel. I turned for the house, wondering why the hell I hadn't stayed in the kitchen.

—✳ ✳ ✳—

BIG JOHN STOOD BY THE BED as I slid under the covers. He knelt and bowed his head. I wasn't high on prayer but didn't mind his. His prayers didn't ramble from one eternity to another with strange voices and long words other grown-ups thought God made a big to-do over. They didn't take forever to start either.

"You praying or not?" I asked.

"Afraid I don't have it in me tonight." He grunted to his feet. "I love you, Slide. So does your deddy. Try and get some sleep."

His shoulders filled the doorway as he paused and looked back. "Slide, when have you been the happiest? What comes to mind?"

"A couch," I said. "I'm sorry Deddy ruined your birthday."

He walked back and sat on the edge of the bed. "Having you here *makes* my birthday. You got that?" I nodded. "Now toss me a happy."

A happy? Staying with Big John and Shine would be one. Playing with Annabelle in her puppy days would be another. I was five years old when *Santa* left her in a kennel under the Christmas tree. We wrestled in the yard the whole summer. By September she could plant her paws between my arms, pin me down with her chest, and go to town with a tongue that felt like worn-down sandpaper and soft-warm butter all at once.

"Annabelle," I said.

"Your Annabelle's quite a dog."

"Best yellow Lab ever. Best dog."

"Course I'm more of a cat person, but—"

"Nobody's perfect," I piped in.

Snowball was meaner than a bobcat and would've passed for one if not for his long tail and bushy white fur. He liked only one person, and only one person liked him. Big John acted like Queen Elizabeth had honored us with a visit whenever his cat sauntered in from another hunting trip.

"You'll come around," he said.

"And Shine?"

"She's also got some maturing to do," he said with a smile. "Tell me about Annabelle's puppy days."

"She loved nibbling my ears with those baby-sharp teeth."

"Can't blame her for that part of the equation. The good Lord didn't stop with that brain of yours. He was mighty generous on those ears."

"Aren't you funny?"

He grinned. "I suppose Annabelle had her puppy breath back then."

"Now it smells worse than what slides out of her bottom."

"My, oh, my. We might as well call it on that note."

"Not yet, Big John. You haven't told me your vote."

"My vote?"

Now that Pearl was looking to settle down, she'd narrowed the field to two. Hank had been in the driver's seat before he'd joined the Marines and headed off to Vietnam, but now he was in the back seat if not clinging to the bumper. It made sense to me. Folks were more likely to confuse Hank with Deddy's toolbox—not much to look at but always ready for the next project—than Myles or Robert Redford.

"Hank's tough," I said.

"He's tough all right. I tried talking him out of signing up for a war that didn't make sense to begin with. Here President Nixon's bringing troops home, and the boy goes charging off into battle."

"Go with Myles. He's nicer than Hank. And richer. Ten of your trucks and five of Hank's wouldn't match the price of his ride."

"Myles is in the car bidness. I'm sure he gets a deal on whatever he wants. Slide, you know better than to talk about folks and their money."

"How about diamonds?" I asked. "Hank's saving for a ring and plans on popping the question when he gets back, right?"

"I don't know, Slide."

"I bet you do know."

He sighed. "I've been dreaming about Pearl's husband ever since she was a baby. Maybe that's all there is to it. Or maybe it's the way my brain works. Once I get to stewing on something, I'm like Annabelle gnawing on a bone. I can't let it go."

"So who's your pick?"

His eyes darted up and down the bed. "Either boy's fine with me." He kissed me on the forehead and stood. "I'll see you in the morning."

PART II

B IG JOHN STILL BLAMED HIMSELF FOR the death of his baby boy, and the fear of losing his girl had haunted him since the second she was born. He'd fretted over her every move as a child. And as an adult.

Women were the sunrise of Big John's world—glorious and beautiful and beyond. Though he'd come to believe women were stronger and smarter than men, he'd lived in a land where men were supposed to protect their "weaker vessels," as the Good Book said.

Big John had done more than protect his headstrong daughter. He'd not only introduced her to the man he was now pushing her to marry, a man with money and manners and religion to boot, he'd picked the very spot on the farm where he wanted them to build a house and raise a family.

Would she toss him aside like she'd done with so many of her suitors? Big John knew the danger of hope, but he hoped anyway.

2

Slide

AT DAYBREAK, MY EYES SHOT OPEN like Deddy's after one of his dreams. My only nightmare was missing coffee-talk.

Big John and Aunt Shine spent the first part of every day on the porch. I could've done without the coffee, not to mention the ten minutes they read the Bible to each other, but the way they talked and teased, even after twenty-seven years of marriage, filled a hole that stayed deep and lonely at my house.

The lovebirds had more than coffee and talk brewing on the porch that morning. I was crossing the den when I saw Shine standing over Big John. Her hands were flying through the air, his rocker dead still. He seemed to be looking everywhere, from the pecan grove on his right to the far pasture on his left, but at the woman he worshiped.

"Mind your own damn business!" she yelled, loud enough to have made a heifer in the next county stand up and spit out her cud.

I heard steps and glanced back to see Pearl strolling my way, her sleepy green eyes and messy hair pretty as ever.

"Bet I know why Momma's yelling," she said.

"Sounds more like my momma than yours," I said.

We inched closer to the half-open door.

"One day Hank's stepping over a spider," Big John said. "Next day he's itching for a fight."

"I see those ears took another vacation," Shine said.

"Myles has a clean mouth. He knows the Bible cover to cover. Heck, he's even got my girl back in church."

"*Our* girl."

"Shine, what else can you ask for given the boys Pearl's run with?"

Pearl shook her head, her eyes still pretty but no longer sleepy. Shine rubbed her temples. A woodpecker, not to be outdone, sounded off on the dead oak in the front yard.

Three years ago, a bolt of lightning killed the tallest tree on the farm, ended Big John's nap, and sent the war hero racing into the house. Shine laughed for a week but said the tree had to go once the leaves turned brown. Cutting down the big oak meant the burial of a loved one for Big John. And change, which he never welcomed. Dead limbs were littering the front yard by the time Shine's demands landed on Deddy's ears. To Shine's chagrin and a woodpecker's delight, Big John convinced his brother to spare the bottom half of the trunk.

Big John pointed at his blue-ribbon woodpecker. "Shine, isn't Ole Red a beauty?"

"Now you've gone to naming birds?"

"Only Ole Red."

"Where's your cat when I need him? Or is he afraid of feathers these days?"

"Honey, when's the last time you watched a woodpecker peck?"

"When's the last time you watched a grown man bang his head against a stump?"

Pearl lit out through the door and ran to the edge of the porch. "Get out of here!"

"Why'd you scare Ole Red off?" Big John asked.

"The shit-for-brains wakes me up every morning," Pearl said. "I'm almost as tired of that bird as I am of you." She marched to a stop next to his chair. "You were fine with Hank before Myles moved here. Now you're writing Hank off. Why do you think that is?"

He shrugged. "I don't know, Pearl."

"Praise the Lord," Shine said. "You're finally making sense." She sat and took hold of the only dress shirt he owned. "You're a smart man, Big John. But your brain was muddled over Pearl before Cash hit the bottle again."

"And now it's scrambled and fried," Pearl said.

"Myles hasn't been here a full year," Big John said. "And he's already one of our top givers."

"He told you that?" Pearl asked.

"Lord no, he'd never mention such a thing. Sheepish as he is about money and that bidness he's building on the county line."

"How do you know what Myles gives?" Pearl asked, firing the question that was on my mind.

"Well, I am a deacon. Not to mention Brother Sam's good friend."

"So much for the verse on the left hand not knowing what the right hand is up to," Shine said.

"Not a tough choice, ladies. Myles is our man."

"Stay out of this or you'll live to regret it," Pearl said, her finger inches from Big John's nose.

"Amen," Shine said.

"I want Pearl close," he said. "Right here on this farm if I have any say in the matter." He pointed. "Shine, wouldn't that hill looking over Cookie's pond make the perfect spot for their house?"

Big John studied his wife, perhaps hoping the mention of her best friend would lighten her mood. Cookie was tall, black, and had little patience except when it came to fishing.

Shine held up her arms as if asking God for help. "These are the times that try women's souls."

"*Men's* souls," he said. "Shine, you've heard me quote Thomas Paine enough to know the words by heart."

Shine laughed. "You sure it wasn't Benedict Arnold? I thought he was your hero from the Revolutionary War."

"Go ahead and laugh," he said.

"Laughing beats crying or killing," Pearl said.

Big John fumbled through the right pocket of his Sunday pants. How the navy-blue polyesters had room for a dime was a mystery to me, much less a pocketknife. He opened the blade and went to digging under fingernails that had every dirt dauber in Mississippi licking its chops.

"The military will keep Hank on the move for who knows how long," he said.

"Who said anything about the military?" Pearl asked.

"Big John, it's hard to believe you're knocking Hank for serving his country," Shine said. "You of all people, the man who keeps one American flag at the road and another on the edge of this porch. Both flying year-round. The war *made* you, Big John."

"Myles's bidness is here. He'll be hard-pressed to leave."

"What makes you think *I'd* want to stay?" Pearl asked. Big John didn't answer. "At least tell me why you've stayed in Hope Springs."

"Pearl, you know this farm is a mile or so past the town limits," he said.

"And you know that's not what I meant."

He rocked back and folded his arms. "Pearl, where you going with this?"

"Well, Cuz's Diner is one of the only stores on the square that's still open, but there are five churches within cursing distance. Don't get me started on our town's *glorious* Confederate history."

"You're right, Pearl. And wrong."

"Wrong? What people call history in Hope Springs amounts to a few nonevents from the Civil War. Plus the lynchings of black people who didn't mind their manners."

Big John's body jerked back like he'd been smacked with a bat. He slumped forward, elbows on his knees and hands under his chin.

"I'm sorry, Daddy. I didn't mean to bring that up."

Bring what up? I wondered, as Big John pulled his bandana from a back pocket. He wiped his eyes and reached for her hand.

"Pearl, I suppose you've heard of the yellow fever epidemic that struck our parts in 1878?"

"You told me."

"Most everybody left except for the priest and six nuns who stayed behind," he said. "They gave their lives caring for the sick. Wouldn't you call that history?"

She nodded, kissed his hand, and grinned. "Daddy, I oughta know better than to argue history with you." She turned for the den. "But you have to admit there's more churches in this town than cute boys my age."

He chuckled. "I don't recall you having much trouble in that department. A passel of boys has knocked on the door of this farmhouse."

Pearl gave me a playful shove on the way to the steps and her room.

Shine patted Big John on the arm. "I'm glad y'all ended on a better note." She stood. "But Pearl's right. You do need to stay out her affairs."

"I'm her deddy," he said in a firm if not irritated tone that caught me off guard. Shine cocked her head, apparently surprised as well. "It's my job."

"Your job is to love her and leave her be."

"Simple math, Shine. The answer is Myles."

"Enough of your damn math," she said. "And English."

She tromped across the porch and stopped at the door, narrowing her eyes before moving on to the fakest smile in southern history. "Morning, Slide. Have a seat and I'll get your coffee."

— ✶ ✶ ✶ —

BIG JOHN FORCED HIS OWN SMILE as I crossed the porch. I rocked until I got tired of acting like everything was A-okay.

"What was that about?" I asked. He raised a brow that needed a barber. "We can start with *damn*. Either one."

"Shine's been slipping a little here lately," he said. He leaned back, looking me over. "No wonder you're so bright beyond those fourteen years."

"I'll be fifteen in four months. Old enough to drive in this state."

"I'd wager it has more to do with your smarts, plus spying on grown-ups, than a driver's license. How long were you nosing into our bidness?"

"Long enough to know you weren't leveling with me last night."

He sipped his coffee. "Not much to it, Slide. A little grown-up talk."

"If it's okay for grown-ups to lie, why do kids have to tell the truth?"

He stared toward the gate like he expected company. Shine rushed out and handed me a steaming cup of cream and sugar.

"How's it going today, Aunt Shine?" I asked, as if I didn't know.

"Fair to middling," she said. "I'll let you men enjoy the fresh air while I get ready for church."

Get ready for church? Who needed three hours to dab on some makeup and throw on a dress? Not Shine.

Big John started rocking after the door closed. I studied the zipper boots he polished every Saturday night while tapping his foot and humming along to *The Lawrence Welk Show*. The boots were older than the pants that supposedly fit back in his courting days.

"Slide, see my pear trees on the edge of the pecan grove?"

"All three," I said.

"My pears'll be ready for these beauties any day now." His mouth opened wide to show a set of teeth that was better left hidden. "Lucky for me Deddy couldn't afford braces when I was growing up in the Great Depression. Those pears are mighty sweet, but they're hard too. Straight teeth wouldn't have the angles to cut through those jessies."

"You should get some pointers from Myles," I said. "On teeth and clothes." He quit rocking. His smile disappeared. "What is it, Big John?"

"Myles," he said.

"He seems perfect for Pearl. What's wrong?"

"Nothing like that. What he said about your deddy crossed my mind. Last night, remember?"

"I remember how much better Myles made me feel, though I'm not sure about the sparrows."

"He said your deddy will make it through this valley."

"This valley? Add them up and we're talking the Grand Canyon."

"Have you seen the Grand Canyon?"

"What do you think?"

"Well, I have, and it's no match for what Cash is going through. Been through."

"I wish you were my deddy."

"Slide, every kid's Santa pulls a no-show at some point."

"You haven't."

"That would be for Pearl to answer," he said in a way that said coffee-talk was officially over.

* * *

PEARL STAYED IN HER ROOM FOR the next two hours. Big John forgot his wife's name. *Honey* and *darling* had crossed his lips a thousand times before Shine glared up from her corn bread batter and told him to "quit blistering my ears."

Shine ignored his *oohs* and *aahs* over her Sunday dress as we loaded up for the short drive to church. For some reason he must've thought a hundred yards of gravel and a left turn onto Highway 5 would give new life to a worn-out word.

"Darling, doesn't it feel like we're in a tunnel?" he asked, peering up through the windshield. "Those limbs are thicker and longer than most trees." He pointed from one side of the road to the other. "How old you think these oaks are? Hundred years?" Shine stared straight ahead.

Live trees in the rearview, Big John decided to give dead people a shot. "I've found tombstones from the 1840s in there," he said, as we drove along the north edge of the Hill County Cemetery. "No telling how many poems I've scratched sitting against this iron gate next to the road. The words on those tombstones give me ideas and—"

"Pull over and we'll let you spend the rest of your birthday scratching on poems," she said.

I understood why Shine was fed up with Big John's meddling in Pearl's affairs. That said, wasn't it time to ease up on her man? I thought so, but after two *damns* and a truckload of silent treatment followed by a fiery offer to drop Big John off at the cemetery, I kept my thoughts to myself.

Far as talk went, Life Lesson Larry might as well've been a coffin until Big John pulled into the parking lot, parked, and pointed at the cross in the front yard.

"Shine, you remember what Deddy said about not keeping a score-card," he said with a chuckle.

Another bad idea, I figured. Though hardly an expert on the ins and outs of marriage, I considered myself a real pro at reading grown-ups until Shine smiled.

"He told *me* that," she said, opening her door. "For damn good reason."

As we made our way through the lobby and down the aisle toward the front of the sanctuary, I realized Big John had been right about one thing that morning: Shine was definitely slipping. Three *damns* on a Sunday, one at church of all places, would've made Momma proud.

A deacon who looked older than Adam started the service. The announcements might've made the highlight of his century, but the strand of gray hair plastered across his shiny bald head kept my attention through most of the prayer requests. By the time he got around to the menu for Wednesday night supper, I'd moved on to Big John's tie.

"Bill's Five and Dime oughta have a tie that reaches the belly button of a man who's six-three on a short day," I said. "They might have one without those stains from years of Shine's Sunday dinners."

He leaned in to whisper in my ear. "Stains are memories, my boy. Some good, some bad. The stains on my tie are all good."

I nodded. What else could I do? From Shine's cooking to Big John's stories, Sunday dinners at the farmhouse were my favorite memories.

The first hymn was winding down when Myles and Pearl snuck in. Her long black dress made a perfect match for the pinstriped suit he'd probably bought at a fancy department store in Memphis.

"You and Myles fit right into the family pew," I said, scooting closer than a first cousin had a right.

"Smart-ass," Pearl said with a grin.

"Nice place for a wedding."

She landed an elbow that pushed me against Big John. His stern look might've worked if not for the eyes that said he was happy to have his girl in church instead of at Sardis Lake drinking beer and listening to Black Sabbath with Hank.

I was picturing Pearl and Hank singing along to Ozzy Osbourne when "Great Is Thy Faithfulness" cranked up. Then all I could think about was Myles. He knew every word and sang even louder than Big John. My uncle would have to wait on heaven to carry a tune, but Myles was already singing with the angels far as I could tell.

Brother Sam stepped up to the pulpit after the Lord's Prayer and Scripture reading. "Brother Sam ain't exactly Billy Graham in the preaching department," Momma had said back in our church days. While it was hard to argue with her on that count, Sam was still my favorite preacher. He didn't drown his coal-black hair in Crisco. He didn't point his shoulder out of socket sending every soul to hell with every breath. And he knew Big John well enough to have the collection plates rolling before the belly of his biggest deacon was howling for mercy.

As we stood for the last hymn, Pearl grabbed my hand and pulled me past Myles. She didn't stop until we got to his pickup.

"Don't ask me why Myles locks his doors," she said, searching her purse. "He's paranoid for some reason."

"Never heard of anybody being robbed at church," I said.

She took the keys from her purse. "I make him hand these over. He's usually the last one out after sweet-talking every sinner in that sanctuary." She opened the door. "Let's wait inside. You can ride home with us."

"You think he'll mind?"

"He misses his brothers," she said. "Acts like you're one anyway."

One of Myles's brothers. I was too proud to soak up the smell of a new truck.

Pearl found a song she liked, raised her arms, and danced in her seat until a red-faced Myles yanked open the door. He jumped in and reached for the door handle. The door was headed for a slam when he held up, glancing at the churchgoers filing out. He eased the door shut, turned off the radio, and drove off without looking Pearl's way or acknowledging his *brother* in the back seat.

"What's your problem?" she asked.

"You know," he said.

"Forgive me for missing a hymn, *Daddy*."

"Maybe you should listen to him."

"Had my share of that this morning."

"He's like any good father," Myles said. "Wanting the best for his daughter."

"What he thinks is best."

The way Pearl said *thinks* said she wasn't over the argument on the porch that morning. Wasn't over a lifetime of having a mother hen for a deddy.

I pondered how Big John had ended coffee-talk. The tone of his voice as he'd said, "That would be for Pearl to answer." What was her answer?

3

AUNT SHINE, THE BOSS OF SUNDAY dinner and more, took her place at the head of the table. The birthday boy sat to her right, close enough for a slap when he reached for his third helping in five minutes.

Big John and I sat across from Pearl and Myles while Brother Sam and his wife, Sandy, held down the other end of the table. Sandy's one line of the afternoon—"I'd rather be part of Sam's rib than women's lib"—gave Sam plenty of leeway for bragging on Shine's cooking.

"These pork chops don't need a tooth or a knife," he said. "Your candied yams and fried okra would make a glutton of John the Baptist."

"Keep on preaching," Shine said.

"This corn bread doesn't need butter or your muscadine jelly to stretch every belt at the table," Sam said. "I pray you don't have dessert waiting on us."

Myles grinned. "The prayer of a righteous man availeth much," he said, quoting a verse I remembered from my Sunday school days.

"Myles, I'm afraid our preacher just proved how righteous he is," Big John said. "Shine saves her Mississippi Mud for my birthday. Chocolate cake and melted marshmallows topped with homemade fudge."

Sam pushed back from the table. "Better slow down before it's too late."

"If it's anything like her cobbler, you'll be glad you did," Myles said.

Sam smiled. "Myles, I can't believe this makes the first time we've broken bread together."

As food ran a close second to money in a preacher's book, I didn't believe it either until Myles nodded.

"Sorry I've been so busy and haven't reached out," he said.

"That's on me," Sam said. "Big John tells me you're in the car business."

"Yessir."

"You buy and sell used cars?" Sam asked.

Myles picked at his plate. "That's the gist of it."

"Quit acting like you did something wrong and tell Brother Sam about your business," Pearl said.

Myles folded his napkin and set it back in his lap. "We buy banged-up cars, mostly from Memphis, then fix them up and sell them to used car dealers in Memphis and Birmingham."

"None to these lots around here?" Sam asked, a puzzled look on his face.

Myles shook his head. "The dealers in those larger cities want all they can get."

"Big John says your family has similar operations in Biloxi and Saint Louis," Sam said.

"My father and younger brother run the business back home. My older brother handles Saint Louis."

"Big John's been a gold mine of information," Shine said. "Sam, he must've forgotten my rule on discussing business at the dinner table. Else he would've cut you off by now. Isn't that right, *darling*?"

Big John mopped his mouth with the back of his hand. "Honey, I've told Sam your rule so many times I'm embarrassed he forgot."

"Shine, he's never mentioned it while jawing about some business idea he's mulling over," Sam said.

"Call me if he gets a notion to try one," she said. "Business is *not* his strong suit."

Sam laughed and turned back to Myles. "Tell us about your family. Any sisters?"

Myles froze like he'd been shocked with a cattle prod. I couldn't tell whether he was mad or fixing to cry, but something in his face scared me.

"It's all right, Sam," Pearl said. "You didn't know." She took Myles's hand and smoothed his fingers with her thumb. "Myles has two brothers and now only one sister. The youngest, Holly, died a few months before he left Biloxi. She was sixteen. You can see he's not over it."

Myles bolted from the table.

Pearl waited for the bathroom door to close behind him. "Holly went for a walk on the beach one afternoon. Two weeks later Myles and his younger brother found her in a shed outside of town. What was left of her anyway. They never found the monster. Figured it was a drifter."

I sat back and stared at my lap, hoping to settle my nerves. I thought about praying but decided Brother Sam or Big John was a safer bet. The stone-faced preacher looked ready for revenge on whoever had killed Holly. Big John wiped tears from his cheeks. He looked me over, nodded, and I was no longer afraid.

Nobody moved or mouthed a word until Miss Cookie busted through the front door. Without a knock of course. Her face would've been beet red if any color besides deep black had a chance. Every skinny inch of her six feet looked ready to explode, especially the eyes locked on me.

"Watch it, Slide," she said. "Yo mouth is fixing to write a check yo butt can't cash. Don't lie to me, boy. Where's my fishing pole?"

Cookie knew I loved pranks. Problem was, she seemed to have forgotten she was the only grown-up I never messed with. My butt was fixing to cash in on a quick dash for the back door when Big John stood and pointed at the empty chair next to Sam.

"Cookie, we saved you a seat," he said. "I'm sorry you didn't make it for—"

"Big John, don't you act a fool with me! You know we don't quit church the second our bellies go to growling."

A toothpick searching for leftovers couldn't hide his grin. "A good pole is hard to find. Sure hope it wasn't your favorite."

"Damn straight it was."

Only Cookie got away with cursing at Sunday dinner. Course she'd never bought into how everything worked in our parts. Men were expected to curse Monday through Saturday if the ladies weren't around. Women like Momma were allowed a bad word or two when their men stayed drunk for days on end. Cookie cursed by her own rules. A single breath was apt to start with *Lawd* and end with *damn* or *shee-it*.

Shine wasn't about to let her man have all the fun with her best friend. "Cookie, you know what Job says: 'The Lord giveth, and the Lord taketh away.'"

"The Lawd ain't got nothing to do with my fishing pole."

"Why is one pole such a big deal?" Shine asked.

Cookie studied the empty chair next to Pearl, but she didn't ask about Myles.

"Big enough to switch the hide off somebody's ass," Cookie said, glaring my way.

Shine peered through the window. "I see two poles propped against the porch."

"I use three. Number three was the best ten feet of cane the Lawd ever thought about making. That pole's caught thousands of fish in my pond."

My pond didn't raise a brow. Nobody wet a hook in Big John's acre of muddy water without Cookie's permission, and nobody went back. First-time fools landed on the shallow end where cows waded in to cool off and relieve themselves of excess fescue. If the sound, smell, or sight of shitting cattle got old, the squatters had a first-rate view of Cookie catching fish from the deep end by the levee.

"Thousands?" Shine asked. "Well, I'll declare. I knew men liked to stretch the stringers. Never heard it from the ladies."

"Thousands, Shine. And you know it."

"Doubt it's anything my cooking can't handle," Shine said. "Have a seat and I'll get you a plate."

Cookie didn't budge. "Line to cork and hook, I had it rigged just right. Weights too."

Big John tapped his huge knuckles on the table. "Tell you what, Cookie. Let's pay Harry's Bait Shop a visit. Harry owes me for hauling a load of life jackets and other gear back in my trucking days. Didn't charge him a dime. He'll give us a deal on a new pole." He scanned the table. "Come join us, Slide. Sam, you mind checking on Myles?"

"I will," Pearl said. "A little road trip might do him some good."

I trailed the grown-ups into the den and put my back against a wall that was a safe distance from Cookie but close enough to the bathroom for spying.

Pearl gave the door a light tap. "Myles, you okay?"

"I'll be right out," he said.

Shine was filling Cookie in on Myles's sister when he stepped out. His eyes were wet. His cheeks were swollen like they'd met a fist the size of Big John's.

He pulled Pearl into his arms, burying his face in her hair. A long minute passed before she leaned back, ran her fingers across his cheeks, and gave him a tender kiss on the lips. She whispered in his ear, then led him by the hand toward Big John's truck.

I followed, watching Myles's every step and wondering what was on his mind. The last time he'd seen Holly alive? What he'd seen after opening the door of that shed? Was it really a drifter or maybe someone he'd known?

4

I CRAWLED OVER THE DUSTY SEAT AND joined Myles in the back of the old truck. While Big John got behind the wheel and Cookie climbed in on the passenger side, Myles kept staring at the back of her seat. I couldn't imagine having a brother or a sister, much less one killed by a drifter, but I'd been around enough grown-ups to know a goofy question could help.

"Myles, what's your guess on the color of this clunker?" I asked. "Dusty white or rusty red?" He forced a weak grin but didn't answer. I leaned forward. "Look at all these Dr Pepper cans and Snickers wrappers on the floor. A crowbar's hiding in here somewhere. Let's hope Big John learns how to use one before he's sixty."

"My, you're going tough on the ole fella," Big John said. "Reckon I'll ease on down the road and enjoy the ride."

Big John turned right and headed east on Highway 5. His right hand found its place at the top of the steering wheel, so he could lift a finger to greet every truck and tractor coming our way. His slab of a left arm hung out the window and wouldn't move until called upon in praise of some pasture or pond no different from the others we'd passed.

We'd covered two miles in five minutes when Cookie pointed to her right. "Myles, I grew up in that house. Daddy built it with his own hands. Momma had a garden there on the left. Nice place when I was a chile."

"Yes ma'am," Myles said, as if he were to blame for the sunken roof, busted windows, and head-high weeds.

A few minutes later we came to the farm, which often got a rise out of our driver, though he never mentioned the thousand acres or white picket fences. Big John saved his jealousy for cows. The hundreds of cows of every color were no match for the twenty or so pure Black Angus roaming his ninety acres. He didn't care about the color of people, but cows were a different story. Why? Another question for the mystery books, I figured.

After a twenty-minute drive that should've taken ten, we rolled into Harry's parking lot. Parking pile more like it, or whatever Harry called the hodgepodge of packed dirt, gravel, and asphalt he'd assembled over the years.

Big John got out, closed his door, and peered into the truck. "What else can I get y'all?"

"All we need's the pole," Cookie said.

"Nobody up for a Snickers or Dr Pepper?"

"I'd take a MoonPie and Coke if I hadn't eaten two pieces of Shine's Mississippi Mud," I said.

"Myles?" he asked.

"No, thanks."

Big John sulked across the lot and stopped at Harry's iron door. "Cookie, need any line or hooks?"

"Nope."

"Weights?"

He moped into the store after she answered with a hard stare.

"Surprised he didn't ask about corks," Cookie said. "The clown acts like he's carrying the whole world on his shoulders."

"Reminds me of Abraham," Myles said. "A real patriarch."

"Shee-it, don't tell him that. Big John's only got one chile anyhow. One girl, that is." Cookie whirled in her seat and looked Myles in the eye. "Yo Abraham has been acting a fool over Pearl getting married, and you ain't even asked her yet. Have you?"

Myles blushed and looked away.

I didn't know much about Abraham, but I knew Harry's Bait Shop had no more business in a beauty pageant than Big John. The concrete blocks longed for another round of mortar and paint. Both windows were too skinny for a fat possum but lined with bars for reasons maybe Harry could explain.

The ugliest building in Hill County kept me from noticing the muddy pickup stopped for gas in front of us. I didn't see the man until his fist pounded our hood. He looked about Myles's age, somewhere around twenty-five. Ridges of muscle jutted from a tank top that needed a wash to go with an extra size or two. His jeans were no cleaner than the finger now inches from Cookie's raised chin.

"Who the hell do you think you are, sitting in the front seat with a white man and boy in the back? You uppity nig—"

"Get outta my face!" she yelled, slapping his hand before the N-word made it through the window.

The man lunged and grabbed her by the neck. She slapped and clawed but couldn't budge a finger.

Myles scrambled over the seat as Big John ran out and hollered at the redneck. The man spun around.

Big John slowed to a fast walk. "What's going on here?"

The redneck answered with a roundhouse right that sent Big John straight to the ground. A grimy boot was heading for ribs when Myles swung the crowbar. The man collapsed.

Cookie and I ran up as Myles hoisted the crowbar for another blow. Big John crawled on top of the man and lifted an arm like you'd expect from a momma begging for her boy's life.

"Get off, Big John," Myles said, his voice cold and steady.

Cookie reached up and took hold of the crowbar, but Myles didn't let go.

"Good job," she said. "Let me have it." He didn't. "Myles."

She wrestled the crowbar from his hand.

"He's alive," Big John said. He wiped at the blood on the man's shoulder. "Lucky for him this took a good bit of the blow before the crowbar glanced off and clocked him above the ear." The man started coming to. "Myles, open his tailgate for me."

Myles opened the tailgate and let it fall with a loud thud.

Big John reached down with one hand and gripped a fistful of jeans, belt, and T-shirt. As if toting Cookie's bucket before she'd loaded it with a stringer of fish, he hauled the man to the pickup and eased him into the bed.

He sat up, rubbing the side of his head. He scowled and leaned to stand.

Big John held up a hand. "Not so fast."

The man slapped it away and stood. Myles stepped forward. Cookie followed with the crowbar. The man sat.

"Y'all let me have a word with this fella," Big John said.

Cookie stepped back, but Myles held his ground.

"Myles, I've got this," Big John said. Myles took a deep breath and backed away. Big John faced the redneck. "Son, the lady you attacked is my wife's best friend. My friend too." He craned his neck, scanning the tags on the truck. "Pike County's a good four hours from here. I don't know what brings you to these parts, but don't let me catch you bullying folks around here again, particularly the ladies. You got that?"

"Get out of my way," the man said, scooting to the edge of his tailgate.

Big John stayed put. "Did you hear me?"

The man glanced at Myles, then glared at Big John. "Yeah, I heard you."

The redneck staggered around his truck, slammed the door, and drove off.

—✶ ✶ ✶—

I STARED AT THE BAIT SHOP as we pulled out of the parking lot. Little more than a rectangle of blocks. *Simple math*. Big John had been right that morning. It didn't take a smart Yankee to know Myles was richer and nicer and better looking than Hank, but who would've guessed he was tougher?

I put a hand on Big John's shoulder. "How's the lip?"

Big John wiped his mouth with the back of his hand. "Hard to hurt a pretty face like mine."

Cookie turned in her seat. "I'm proud of you, Myles."

"Me too," Big John said. "No telling the shape I'd be in if you hadn't shown up."

Myles doubled over, burying his face in his hands.

"What's gotten into you?" Cookie asked.

"I snapped when he hit Big John," Myles said. "The man at my feet became the monster who murdered my baby sister."

"The man deserved it," she said.

"Thank the Lord y'all stopped me."

"Not *y'all*," she said. "Big John. I grabbed the crowbar after it was too late anyhow."

Myles straightened up and faced the window. "I have no patience for a man who mistreats a woman."

"I'm starting to like you," she said with a smile.

A smile? Cookie's smiles were like hope in Hope Springs. They didn't show up very often, and they never hung around for long. Maybe a second in this case.

"You were there when it counted," she said.

Big John pulled off the road and shifted into park. "Let's pray for that fella."

"Already told the Lawd what I think of that no-count," Cookie said. "And where I hope he ends up."

Big John looked in the rearview mirror.

"No way," I said, for I never prayed out loud and didn't plan on starting with that dirtbag.

"Sorry," Myles said. "I can't right now."

Big John pulled onto the blacktop.

"Why don't you pray," Cookie said. "It was yo idea."

"I suppose this isn't the time," he mumbled.

"Thanks to that redneck, your lip's prettier than your hood," I said, hoping to cheer up our birthday boy.

"My hood?"

"The pothole near the front on Cookie's side," I said.

He slapped the top of the steering wheel. "Looky there, Slide. We got us another memory."

"This truck is long on memories and short on smooth," I said. "Myles, y'all have any deals on bodywork or paint?"

"Well, my fellas in the warehouse could work on it."

"I appreciate the offer," Big John said. "But Slide'll tell you that bumps and bruises build character in trucks. And boys."

Bumps and bruises. Character. I studied the man who had always been my hero. Big John hadn't tucked tail and run, but he'd walked up with arms in the air and gotten decked before he knew what hit him, then squirmed on the ground like a worm on a hot sidewalk as the redneck closed in. What if Myles hadn't been there?

Big John parked at his spot next to the porch.

"Guess I'll mosey on down to the shed and piddle a while," he said. "Y'all tell Shine for me."

"I'll tell her," Cookie said. "Then I'm heading to my pond." She turned my way. "Time for me to drown a few worms before I drown something else."

She made a beeline for the house while Big John made his way toward the shed. I tapped the top of the seat, waiting on Myles. Manners might've been one of his many strong suits, but they weren't one of my few. That said, I let grown-ups go first.

"After you," I said.

He sighed and put a hand on my shoulder. "Slide, I'm sorry you saw me act that way. There's no excuse. Pray for me when you pray for that man." He climbed out before I could help with excuses or lie about praying.

As Myles crossed the yard, I found myself hoping I'd be like him one day. And wondering how the same person could be so gentle and tough.

— ✳ ✳ ✳ —

I LEANED AGAINST THE HOOD, WAITING on Cookie and thinking of Mr. Brand. Whenever my old Sunday school teacher wasn't scratching

EVILution on the chalkboard or calling Charles Darwin the devil incarnate, he was frantically shoving the fruits of the Spirit down our throats. Patience was Mr. Brand's favorite fruit.

Not Cookie's. While "drown something else" left little doubt what a fishing pole and redneck had done to her morsel of patience, the slam of the screen door left zero doubt.

She flew down the stairs, lunged for her fish bucket, and squinted my way as she rounded the porch. The call of her name did no better than a friendly wave.

She'd marched to the edge of the yard by the time I caught up.

"You got a minute?" I asked.

"I still got *two* poles no thanks to you," she said, not missing a step.

"I wanted to ask you about Big John."

"Never took much sense to know men never had much. Boys too, I reckon."

"I thought he was a war hero," I said. "Now I'm worried he's a chicken."

She dropped her bucket and slapped both hands on her hips. "He is a strange bird. But he ain't no chicken."

"Well, he wasn't much help back there." Bulging eyes darted from me to her pond. She snatched the bucket and took off. "Cookie, wait."

"I got a story for you," she said. "Long as you don't interrupt my fishing."

I followed her downhill to the contraption Big John called a gate, which amounted to three half-rotten sticks of cedar and two rusty strands of wire.

"Piece of shit," she said. Her long fingers hurried through the two-bit rope holding the gate to a fence that was supposed to be barbed wire. "I told Big John a hundred times to quit knotting this up." She eyed the fence. "One of those black cows leans the wrong way, and this'll all be on the ground." She finished and threw the gate open. "You close it."

I trotted past the barn and up the hill to find Cookie sitting on her bucket with a pole under each foot. Two corks floated in water that looked and smelled like cow patties. Her Prince Albert can was packed with worms stout enough to send even Myles running for cover.

"Where's the can of snuff nobody's supposed to know about?" I asked.

Her eyes told me to shut the hell up and sit down. I searched the ground, found a clean patch of fescue between two well-baked cow patties, and plopped down Indian style.

She stared at the corks like they'd done something wrong. "Fish ain't biting nohow."

"Patience helps," I said.

"You gonna listen or smart off all day?"

I planted both hands behind me and leaned back, waiting.

5

Cookie

LIKE COOKIE TOLD THE BOY THERE in the yard, Big John was a strange bird. The bird even had a black man for a friend. A best friend. Her daddy.

When she was a child, they spent every Thursday night smoking and joking at the same table. The *same* table. Some evenings at the farmhouse. Some at her family's place down the road. They ate supper, played cards, and drank whiskey until her momma or Shine put an end to their foolishness. This was before Big John poured his whiskey down the drain—Shine sent him to that Billy Graham deal at the Crump Stadium in Memphis—and before what happened to Cookie's sister.

"Slide, this all went down the year after Big John got back from the war," Cookie said. "1946."

"How old were you?"

"Well, I'll be forty next—"

"Only forty?"

The lines on the bones of Cookie's cheeks were deep and hard, but Slide had no business questioning her age. The willow tree on her left was too far to cut a switch before he ran off. She stared until he squirmed.

"I was right at fourteen when this happened," she said.

"Same as me."

"Which oughta be old enough to hush up and listen."

"I hear you, Miss Cookie."

"Hearing ain't listening."

She looked the boy over to see if he was ready to put those floppy ears to work. Men and boys used half an ear on their good days, but the look on Slide's face said it was time for her story. She began:

Back then I was a girl who would do anything to tag along with her daddy. Even work, or least act like I worked while I spied on the man who might as well've been God to me.

Big John didn't bother with fences or cows in those days. Cotton ruled the roost, and a dirt road ran from the blacktop to a fuel tank in that field near the barn.

Daddy was checking the fuel one Friday afternoon when a squad car zoomed in and slammed on the brakes. When Sheriff Mathis and two deputies jumped out, Daddy told me to hightail it to the farmhouse and find Big John.

I banged on the door until Big John came high-stepping it from the kitchen. Scared and breathing too hard for words, I pointed at the field. He hoofed it to the bedroom, stormed out with a double-barreled shotgun, and told me to stay put. Course I never have minded too well.

By the time we made it down the porch steps, those deputies had hog-tied Daddy across the tank. One was raring back with a belt when Big John sent a barrel of buckshot over their heads. The deputy dropped his arm but not his belt.

"Back off!" the sheriff hollered, as Big John charged his way. "This man raped a woman in town, a—"

"He's lying," Daddy called out.

"A *white* woman," the sheriff said. "We got proof."

Daddy went to cussing and growling and pulling at the ropes.

Big John stuck his shotgun under those chins the sheriff

was so proud of. "Touch Elijah with that belt and I'll blow the sheriff's head off," he told one deputy. "Clean off."

"Don't worry, Sheriff," the deputy said. A smile eased under the fuzzy blond mustache he was trying to grow. "He's only bluffing."

Mathis had a better view of Big John's eyes. "He ain't bluffing, boys. I promise he ain't bluffing."

"Untie those ropes and I'll take my finger off this trigger," Big John said.

"Do it, boys," Mathis said.

They cut Daddy loose. He straightened out, clenching his fists and eyeing the deputy with the belt.

Once Big John lowered his gun, Mathis found the bones in his back. "Drop it, Big John. You're in deep shit for sticking those barrels up my throat. The law around here don't play."

Big John raised his gun to a belly that could've held a bushel of beans on a hungry day. "Sheriff, I'm not half as concerned about your law as you oughta be over how close I am to pulling this trigger and splattering your dinner from one end of this field to the other." Mathis glanced from the gun to the man staring him clean through. "Now tell me again why you're here."

The sheriff pointed at my daddy. "He raped a white woman, like I said."

"Another white lie that's all black," Daddy said, gritting his teeth.

"She swore it was him," Mathis said.

"Elijah would never do such a thing," Big John said. "Sheriff, what proof have you got?"

"The woman swears she scraped the hell out of his back."

"At what time does she *claim* it happened?" Big John asked.

"Last night around ten."

"Elijah and I played cards until midnight last night. Like we do every Thursday night."

"Have him take off his shirt," Mathis said.

"I won't *have* Elijah do anything. He'll do it if he has a mind to. I'm liable to use this other barrel if what I see came from a belt."

My daddy ripped off his shirt to show a back full of muscles and a stripe wide as that belt. And that was when the hatchet hit the chicken in the neck. Almost did, anyhow.

Big John was raising his gun when Daddy yelled, "Stop, Big John! They ain't worth it."

The sheriff threw up his hands and stepped back. "We'll head on and forget all this."

"I've a mind to use this load of buckshot on you and the two shells in my pocket on your deputies," Big John said. "Get out of here before I change my mind."

At that, all three of those badges bolted for the car. The sheriff hit the gas and left a cloud of dust so thick I could barely see brake lights as he slowed at the highway. Well, I reckon more than dust was clouding the view. My eyes were filled with tears of pride. Lawd, I was proud of my daddy. And Big John.

"Part of me was itching for you to pull that trigger and let me have a go at those deputies," Daddy said, staring a hole in that tank. "More than a part."

Daddy's fire simmered down when he saw Big John looking more dead than ready to kill. Daddy rushed over and helped him to the ground. Big John took a breath he couldn't let go. He blinked hard and closed his eyes. I went to crying, afraid my daddy's best friend was fixing to die.

A few minutes passed before Big John was able to talk. "Elijah, how 'bout we talk to the Lord?"

"Have at it," Daddy said, sounding like me this afternoon. "Man willing to jaw with the Lawd after that oughta do the praying."

Big John struggled to his feet and gazed across those fields like he'd never laid eyes on cotton.

"Lord, help the sheriff and his deputies see man and not skin," he said. He looked Daddy and me over. "Keep Cookie and Elijah from the hate I just felt." He dropped his head and kicked at the ground. "I got no idea why You sit back and watch all the hate and bloodshed in this world, but I remember the promise I made the night those Germans locked me all alone in that shed. I knew the bombs of my B-24 had missed the factory and landed on a village filled with women and children and old folks. Lord, You heard my vow to never kill again. And You know how close I just came to breaking that vow. Don't let me go there again."

He turned to Daddy. "I hope it'll be different one day."

"I doubt it," Daddy said. He laid a hand on Big John's shoulder. "I sho' thank you for what you did."

"I'm the one who needs to thank you."

"Thank me?"

"You saved me," Big John said. "The sheriff's a bully, not a crook. He'd have let you go once he saw there were no scratches on your back. But I would've killed at least one man if you hadn't stopped me. Would've died in the electric chair or spent the rest of my days in the state pen at Parchman." He wiped a tear. "Thank you, Elijah."

With that Big John took off running. He stopped in the middle of that cotton, eyed this pond for the longest, and ran straight to that oak tree yonder. Strange really showed up when he sent the gun sailing and yelled like a madman until it landed in this here water.

The bird stared a while longer, then strolled to the porch and eased into his rocker like he'd been piddling at the barn all day.

"That was my last gun!" he called out. "Good thing she didn't float!"

Cookie finished her story and looked down at the glow on Slide's face. "So Big John's not a chicken after all," he said.

"Just strange," she said. "Here we are twenty-four years later, and I still don't know which bird will show up. I got a good idea on Myles. Big John'll keep you guessing."

"No guessing to it this morning."

"What you talking about?"

He grinned and got to his feet. "Never mind, Miss Cookie. Gossiping is a bad sin in the Good Book."

"Sit yo ass back down."

The boy did as he was told.

"Big John and Shine were arguing on the porch," he said.

"About Pearl again?"

Slide nodded. "She joined the party."

"Big John's been smitten with Myles from the get-go. Pearl's apt to marry Hank to show her daddy who's in charge. Hank's a good boy most of the time, but his boozing and temper remind me of the man I married."

"You were married?"

"Married a fool named Billy soon as I hit eighteen. We were done picking cotton and ready to get the hell outta Mississippi. Saint Louis had more jobs than our part of the world, so we headed thataway."

"How long were you and Billy—"

"Not long. The man who tried his luck beating on me didn't try again."

"What happened?"

"Don't you worry about that."

"Did you kill him?"

"Boy, what did I say?"

"I'm sorry."

"You don't look sorry." Cookie studied her corks. "Big John needs to shut his trap."

"Shine and Pearl tried to shut it."

"Trying ain't doing."

6

MANY A TIME COOKIE ASKED THE LAWD what would've gone down in 1971 if Big John had pulled that trigger in 1946. The Lawd never gave the answer she wanted, but that was all right. Cookie knew what to do with a snake—put a hoe to that head. Else he'd slither off, join up with a bigger devil, and leave you wishing there was blood on that hoe.

Even Victry, smart as he was, got it wrong on where the snake raised its evil head that year. Cookie was twenty years old when she went to raising the boy. His daddy was fat and rich but no-count with raising children, and Cookie wouldn't call the woman who brought Victry into this world a momma on her kindest day.

His soft voice reminded Cookie of Myles. Hands too, though neither of Victry's hands would've known what to do with a crowbar.

The soft in Victry's skin drove him to New York City, of all places. Fact was, he never took to the way things worked in Mississippi. Wouldn't even slide a hook through a worm. Whenever Cookie did take him fishing, seemed like they ran into one snake after another. He'd stop at every last one and ask what kind it was and such.

"They all highland moccasins," she'd tell him. "They all straight from hell. And they all need killing."

Soon as she got a good grip on her hoe, he'd go to begging. "No, Cookie, please. Please let it go."

* * *

COOKIE AND SHINE WERE SITTING ON the farmhouse porch when Victry pulled up to the gate. Shine jumped up and went to waving, but

Cookie kept her seat. She'd been griping for the past fifteen minutes and was in no mood for such nonsense.

Shine looked her way. "Still moping, I see."

"My own boy hasn't made *one* of my birthdays since he finished college four years ago," Cookie said. "He gets a long weekend for Labor Day and shows up for Big John's."

"He missed Big John's by six days. It was last Sunday, as you might recall."

"I recall Victry calling me on Monday morning to say how awful he felt for missing Big John's. And how excited he was to fly home and surprise the old man."

Shine laughed and slapped her hip. "When did you start caring about birthdays, even your own?"

Shine had a point on that count. Every day was the same to Cookie. Least it had been, until Victry's call.

"The Lawd is a jealous God," Cookie said, trying to hold back a grin. "Reckon I can act like Him on occasion."

"How many times has Victry offered to buy you a first-class ticket and put you up in one of those fancy hotels?" Shine asked, opening the screen door as Victry drove up.

"He knows I'd rather step on a snake than set foot on a plane."

Hugging was like crying in Cookie's book—a waste of time. But the sight of her best friend hugging her boy put a smile on Cookie's face. She trotted to the door, hustled down the stairs, and ran their way.

"Enough," she said.

She wrapped her arms around Victry and squeezed until they were both out of breath. She stepped back to look him over.

"I was here for Easter five months ago," he said.

"Five months and six days," Cookie said.

"Victry, they must be rationing food in the Big Apple," Shine said. "Leave it to the Yankees to forget World War II ended twenty-five years ago. Turn sideways and you won't need to open a door in this farmhouse."

Cookie took him by the arm and led him to the porch as Shine followed behind.

"Victry, you're bound to be hungry," Shine said.

"Maybe later," he said. "Travel steals my appetite."

"Let's sit and talk a while," Shine said.

He waited on the ladies to sit, then settled into the rocker between them.

"How was your trip?" Shine asked.

"The flight was wonderful," he said, winking at Cookie.

"Boy, don't start with me."

"Where do I start?" he asked, no doubt pondering the best way to irritate Cookie. "Perhaps the old farmer driving a tractor on Highway 77 was the highlight of my trip. His burnt, white skin. Eyes red from sun but not hurry. Left cheek bulging with tobacco. Wooly gray beard stained brown with its juice."

"Nothing special about a white man on a tractor," Cookie said. "I seen enough of that combo for one lifetime."

He chuckled. "Neil Armstrong landed on the Moon last year. Would our farmer's first step in my city of eight million have been different?"

Cookie shook her head. Victry's brain had traveled thisaway before landing at Harvard and settling in New York City.

"No different from yo first *and* last steps in Hill County," she said. "Lost."

"I can't argue with you there. But I'm glad to be here now."

"Least you making up for missing Big John's birthday. I get a card or a call if I'm lucky."

"Aunt Shine, I hope you and Big John will forgive me for not being here Sunday," Victry said, smiling at Cookie.

Shine sighed. "Probably for the best. Big John had a rough one." She glanced at Cookie. "As did your real mother."

"Cookie told me."

"She tell you about Myles's sister?" Shine asked.

Victry slumped back in his chair. "I can't imagine."

"Me neither," Shine said.

"Myles seems like a great guy," he said.

"Sure does," Cookie said.

"I hope Big John's prodding and prying doesn't run him off," Shine said. "And Pearl, for that matter."

"I would love to see Pearl while I'm in town. Is she here?"

"Myles took her shopping in Memphis," Shine said. "We didn't tell her you were coming. You know how Pearl is with secrets."

"I remember. Is Big John in the house?"

"Victry, where does my baby go when he gets tired of moping on this porch?"

"The shed."

Shine nodded. "I guess Cookie told you about Cash?"

"Yes, ma'am."

"Slide's staying with us for the time being. But with Big John stewing nonstop over Pearl and now Cash, I'm sending the boy to y'all's house for a night or two. Pestering your daddy and sister should keep him busy for a while."

"Is Slide there now?" Victry asked.

"He's with Big John, keeping my man distracted until you show up." Shine giggled. "Victry, I guess Big John knew what he was doing when he played God and made y'all blood. Cousins-in-law or whatever you call it didn't suit him." She stood and pointed toward the den. "Started in that very room on your first birthday. Let's see if I can remember the story."

"You ready for the old folks' home if you can't remember every word," Cookie said. "Us too, the times you told that story."

They followed Shine into the den.

Victry took a long breath through his nose. "The smell of stained wood. A smoke-blackened fireplace. My aunt's last meal."

Shine pointed. "Big John was sitting next to Cash on this very couch. You'd left that chair by the fireplace and taken a few wobbly steps before Big John scooped you up and set you in his brother's lap. Cash was around ten at the time and had no idea how to hold a baby. Might as well've been juggling a dozen eggs between his bony arms until Big John steadied him with one hand and patted your head with the other." Shine raised her hands. "And then came the words from on high: 'Victry, this is your Uncle Cash. Your flesh-and-blood uncle, just like me.'"

"And so it came to pass," Victry said.

"Made no difference that Big John was only related to you by marriage," Shine said. "From that moment his little brother was also your flesh-and-blood uncle."

"As if preordained from the foundation of this world," he said.

Cookie eyed the carpet, ready for this foolishness to end.

"Years later Big John did the same with Slide and your daddy," Shine said. "Slide calls him Uncle Lore to this day. Calls you and your sister first cousins without a second thought."

"Which we are. Thanks to Big John."

Shine laughed. "Victry, I'd like to see your Yankee friends make sense of our family tree. Just tell them to go with uncles and cousins and be done with it."

7

Slide

THE SHED WAS NO MORE CHEERFUL than its owner. The dim bulb, which hung from a cypress rafter, reminded me of Deddy and our den. The bulb barely lit the picnic table Big John called his workstation. The only light on the dirt floor came from the sun as it slipped through cracks in the two walls not attached to the barn. The only sound in the dark shed? The grind of steel on rock.

Big John couldn't oil a hinge or change a bulb—Shine had turned those chores over to Deddy years ago—but he could sharpen a knife. If not asking me questions or responding with life lessons Larry would envy, he enjoyed talking to the *pretty* blades as they slid across the thin layer of oil on his whetstone. He whispered to Sweet Betsy, his favorite pocketknife, in the same voice he used while cradling his cat or cooing over a baby.

Not this Saturday. Without a word, Big John sharpened Sweet Betsy and returned her to the right front pocket of his overalls. When I asked if Betsy was named after an old girlfriend, he reached for another knife. He gave me a stern glance when I asked if his pecker had fallen off. Another after I wondered out loud if I'd go to hell for lusting over a girl's boobs.

I moved on to more serious matters. Did Pearl and Myles break up? Had Deddy taken a sober breath all week? Both questions were answered with blank stares.

I closed my eyes but couldn't close my ears to the back and forth of blade and stone that made sweet music of Ole Red hammering away on a dead stump. Though I loved Shine like a momma instead of an aunt, was her little surprise worth this? I'd asked myself that question a thousand times by the time the door opened.

"Victry, my boy," Big John said. He wrapped an arm around Victry and lifted him off the ground. "You're a scoundrel for sneaking in on me like this."

"Surprised?" Victry asked.

"Just what I needed," Big John said. "My two boys in one shed."

He eased Victry to the ground and asked about his trip.

"Cookie didn't like my answer," Victry said.

"Only you and Shine can keep her happy," I said. "Besides your little sister when she's acting right."

Victry laughed. "Big John, I'll give you a different answer."

"Keep it simple," I said. "Short words and shorter sentences. I'm still not over your sermon on the *beauty* of Big John's gate from your last visit."

"Simple and short," Victry said. "The airport in Memphis. My rental car. Lamar Avenue. The county line." He smiled. "Traveling southeast on Highway 77, I beheld a world with more grass and cows than concrete or people, fences of wood and wire amid old barns and quaint churches, abandoned sharecropper shacks within a whisper of the iron gates and paved drives of country estates and—"

"That'll do for now," I said.

"No time for the square, or countless streets named after Confederate generals?"

"Nope."

"Nothing around here ever changes, does it?" Victry asked.

Big John stared at his table. "No, I guess not."

"How's Pearl?" Victry asked.

"She's doing all right."

Victry turned my way. *Must be Deddy*, I mouthed. He nodded.

"I'm sorry," he said. "I know your brother has been in a bad place."

Big John blinked but didn't respond.

Deddy had wrecked Big John's birthday and was now on the verge of ruining our surprise party. I thought of the pranks I'd played on Big John. Victry had joined me on several occasions.

"Time for an emergency," I whispered. "A project in the handyman department."

Victry slapped his hip. "Big John, I forgot! I just noticed a missing wire in the fence near the farmhouse. I hope your cows aren't already stomping through Shine's yard."

"Lands alive," Big John said. He reached for the rope looped around a nail he'd managed to drive, albeit at a curious angle, into the shed wall. "Lead the way, boys. Shakespeare must've busted a hole in my barbed wire this morning."

Why Big John had named his bull Shakespeare was a question worth asking. "Barbed wire this morning" wasn't. Knit together by more rope than wire of any kind, Big John inspected his fences once a year at best.

Victry and I jogged up the hill, scanning the fence which separated the pecan grove from the yard. Fences on respectable cattle farms in our parts had four tight strands of barbed wire fastened to metal posts. Big John's were lucky to have two strands of sagging wire to go with a stretch of frayed rope he'd tied to secondhand cedar posts.

"Victry, how do we choose?" I asked.

"Quite a quandary," he said.

I pointed. "A fat heifer wouldn't lose a hair on this hole, and her calf could step right over without breaking stride."

"Perfect."

Big John trotted up, panting like Annabelle in her ball-chasing days. He squinted at the hole as if facing such a task for the first time. He pulled the pocketknife from his overalls and held it high.

"'Give me six hours to chop down a tree and I will spend the first four sharpening the axe,' Abe Lincoln used to say." He gazed at his prized possession. "Sweet Betsy will make warm butter of this rope in no time." He handed one end of the rope to Victry. "Take this to the post behind you and hold her tight. Yessir, we'll show ole Shakespeare who's boss."

Big John dropped to a knee. The blade in his hand was hard to see, but it was sharp. A proud grin crossed his face as one rope became two. He tossed the extra piece over his back, reached for the other, and fished a lighter from his pocket. He held it to the loose ends, then looked up with a smile. The smile faded to a frown when he saw Victry.

My cousin was gasping for air like he'd just finished a race if not a fight. His eyes were fixed on the yellow weeds at his feet. When Big John asked what was wrong, he gave no sign of hearing a word.

Big John hurried his way. "What is it, my boy?"

Victry steadied his breathing and cleared his throat.

"The Rope," he said. "With each stroke of your knife, the tiny strands scattered in all directions, fled as if desperate to escape. The flame of your lighter melted them back into place." Victry studied the rope in his hand. "Into their rightful place under the rule of one rope. The *Rope*."

I shook my head, wondering where the hell this was going. Victry could find a maze in a straight line, and his *Rope* was a maze to begin with.

"Bring it down to earth," I said.

"I think he's referring to what drives the bus in our parts," Big John said.

"The twisted white strands of religion and race," Victry said. "Worshipping the outside of the cup while ignoring the *inside*. Offering warmth to those who obey, flame to those who stray." He sighed. "The Rope chained millions for hundreds of years." He looked at Big John. "How many white churches in this land opposed slavery? Or stood up to Jim Crow over the next hundred years?"

"Not enough," Big John said.

"Six days have passed since The Rope wrapped its fingers around Cookie's neck. Will it ever change?"

"We got a long way to go," Big John said. "But it has changed."

"I have trouble seeing it. You and others have seen but stayed. Why couldn't I?"

"It's how God made you," Big John said.

"I don't believe in a god who wouldn't make a blade for this rope."

"Do you believe I love you?" Big John asked. "Just like you are."

Victry nodded. Tears filled his eyes and rolled down his cheeks.

Big John pulled the bandana from his back pocket. He wiped Victry's face, kissed both cheeks, and pulled him in for a long hug.

—✳ ✳ ✳—

THE BLAME.

Blame was a game that knew no end in our parts. Victry blamed The Rope for what he called "the scourge that strangled our homeland." We were all "simply clay in the hands of a master," he said. The Rope was all he needed.

Cookie, wanting no part of Victry's convoluted way of thinking, cursed Big John for not shooting the sheriff in a cotton field in 1946. And Big John never forgave himself for forgetting what mattered when it mattered.

I suppose they were all right. And wrong. Half-wrong anyway.

PART III

BIG JOHN GLANCED AT THE BAT propped against the corner of his screened-in porch. He didn't own a gun but figured a bat would do the job if a man threatened one of his ladies.

He rocked back and closed his eyes, listening to the loud purrs of the cat in his lap, the distant bark of a squirrel in the oaks along the highway, the bobwhite whistles in his overgrown ditches and fencerows. Perhaps the smell he'd always loved but never been able to describe would settle his spirits. Was it the blend of new grass and old hay? Of cow patties, new and old? The aged wood of his rocker? It wasn't the overalls, T-shirt, or boots he wore six days a week.

He counted holes in the screens, stopped at twenty-seven, and smiled at the thought of his beloved bride. *Twenty-seven years*, Big John thought to himself. *And she's still putting up with me.*

Decades of joy brought minutes of relief. Consumed with the fate of his daughter, he stared at the splinters and chipped paint on the floor.

8

Slide

THE OLD HOMESTEAD WAS TOLERABLE WHEN my favorite cousin was in town. Victry might've been embarrassed that the house we rented around the corner would fit into the dining room of their antebellum with room to spare, or that General Grant had cherry-picked their mansion for a winter vacation during the Civil War, but his sister wasn't.

Two years and ten inches should've given me the right to boss her around on occasion. Only Miss Cookie told Salt what to do, and nobody could make her shut up. "The good Lord plumb forgot that girl when He went to doling out shy-bones," Big John had said more often than I cared to hear.

On Sunday afternoon, Salt was lying about stealing Cookie's fishing pole while messing with her hair and smiling in the mirror of an antique dresser when I heard her deddy snoring downstairs. I eased down the spiral staircase, peered into the den, and found myself admiring Mr. Brand's EVILution. What else could explain the creature lounging in a leather recliner? Uncle Lore's bald pate, no-show neck, and bulging belly made the perfect match for a penguin that stood five-and-a-half feet on its tiptoes.

He didn't budge when I stomped in and plopped down on the couch. I pinched my nose, wondering why the smoke from his last cigar didn't help with the stench watering my eyes.

"Hellfire, Uncle Lore. How many servings of beans and cabbage did you have for dinner?" He kept snoring. "You working on your second or third nap of the day?"

I took one of Big John's Snickers bars from my pocket and let it fly. Bull's-eye.

Lore bolted awake and grabbed his crotch. "Slide, you little shit-head!"

"I thought you liked candy bars. Hope I didn't disturb you."

"Hope, my ass."

"Any words of wisdom for your number one nephew?"

"I've got some wisdom for that shit-eating grin of yours," he said, sharing a short middle finger before sliding the Snickers into his shirt pocket. "How come you're not playing with Salt?"

"She's worshipping herself in the mirror."

"Women like those mirrors. Girls too, I reckon."

Lore studied his pocket, perhaps pondering his next snack. He smacked his lips while looking me over.

"You are a smart little whippersnapper," he said. "I'll give you that. Along with all the learning you get here on my couch, must be the time you spend on the porch listening to Big John." A grin from below crossed his cheeks. "You oughta be one helluva a listener, courtesy of your Uncle Orman."

"*Great*-uncle," I said. "He certainly wasn't good."

Orman Slide Jackson's picture from Momma and Deddy's wedding left no doubt who'd given me the world's biggest ears, not to mention the skinniest neck and pudgiest Adam's apple. Worse yet, I'd been set for the best name in southern-boy history, Buck Stonewall Jackson, until Orman stormed into the hospital at the last hour and demanded naming rights. Momma supposedly gave it her best shot before she went under. Problem was, the sterile old mule signed Deddy's paycheck every week. The check was no fatter than my neck, but it was a check.

"Slide, you oughta be ashamed for giving ole Orman such a hard way to go. He left you that 20-gauge shotgun he retired after a lifetime of missing quail."

"What advice did you have in mind?" I asked, not wanting to give Lore the pleasure of waxing my ears with Orman for the next hour.

In wonder if not worship, Lore gazed at his row of mounted bucks on the far wall. "Boys like you and Victry got plenty of book smarts. But y'all tend to forget what Momma always told me: 'Sonny Boy, your *I do* is way more important than your *IQ.*'"

"She told you that a lot?"

"Near 'bout every day."

"That never worried you?"

"Worried me? Hell, Slide, worrying's for sissies. Uncle Lore ain't got time for nonsense. He's a bidnessman."

I had a notion to dig further into Lore's *IQ* and his *I do*, not to mention why he referred to himself in the third person on a regular basis. Instead, I moved on to more pressing matters.

"Who's Pearl going to marry?" I asked.

"What do I know?" he asked in a way that swore he knew it all. "She's ready. Guaran-damn-well-tee you that."

"But she's only twenty."

He sat up and stared as if I'd never heard of corn bread or country ham. "Shit, Slide, don't let the ladies fool you. Five to fifty take your pick. They're all either thinking about, itching to, or downright panicking to walk that aisle. I'd bet my left nut Pearl's somewhere between itching and panicking as we speak."

Cocksure as Uncle Lore was in the marriage department, I wanted to ask about the woman he'd married. Cookie had named her Misry for a reason, though even Cookie had no explanation for how *that woman* could be Shine's sister.

"You willing to bet that nut on Hank?" I asked.

"Would have, before he signed up for Vietnam. The boy ain't brilliant if he thought Pearl wanted a war hero like her deddy. A family bidness stretching from the Gulf Coast to the Missouri River is more her style. Fine manners and all, Myles booted him right out."

"You saying Hank's a goner?"

"Pearl's a looker," Lore said with a grunt. "But the girl's got a mind of her own. I wouldn't lay money."

——— ✳ ✳ ✳ ———

THE SOUND OF MY FOOTSTEPS ON GRAVEL didn't keep me from hearing the commotion on the porch. I couldn't tell whether Pearl or Shine was yelling, but I knew it wasn't good news for the big man sitting between them.

Only Snowball seemed to notice when I let the screen door slap shut. He gave me a sour look, tucked his huge white head into Big John's lap, and started purring. I crossed the porch and sat.

"I wish the cat had stolen your tongue instead of your ears," Shine said, glaring at Big John. "Why don't you join Snow*man* on a hunting expedition? Today. Bring a rabbit and I'll make a stew."

I wanted to laugh but settled for a grin, thanks to the look on Shine's face. She called Snowball the wrong name when particularly irritated with his servant. Speaking of Big John, he nearly cried when the killer dropped a bird or rabbit at his feet instead of a rat or snake from the barn. The only animals this uncle hunted were the mosquitoes that slipped through one of the holes Snowball had scratched in the porch screens while sharpening his claws.

Big John ran his fingers through his master's fur. "Hank hasn't been to church in years. But he loves that Budweiser."

"Budweiser beats the liquor you were fond of before Billy Graham and the Lord got hold of your hide," Shine said. "Thank God I had Elijah to keep you in check until then."

"We're not getting any younger, Shine. Who'll push our wheelchairs if Pearl's off chasing Hank?"

"Nice to know this isn't about you," Pearl said.

"Never trust a fella who tries to convince you he's worth trusting," he said.

"What's that got to do with anything?" Pearl asked.

"Everything, from what my deddy said. I lose track of the times Hank said I can trust my daughter in his hands."

"*Your* daughter," Shine said with a scowl.

"I remember two of Deddy's lines on trusting folks, judging 'em if you will, and that's one."

"You've got the judging down pat," Pearl said.

Big John crossed his legs. "Hank doesn't stand when a lady enters the room. He glances my way before he opens Pearl's door."

"Pearl is *here*," Pearl said.

"I doubt Hank opens the door when I'm not around," he said.

"Now you're judging the boy's heart," Shine said.

"Hank's a used pickup," he said. "Myles will give our girl the extras she's always wanted. Fancy clothes, nice vacations, a big house."

"I'm sure that will make me happy," Pearl said.

"Won't hurt."

"Not as much as listening to you," Pearl said.

"Myles has the get-up-and-go you want in a man."

"In a *man*?" Pearl asked.

"You know what I meant," he said.

"Get up and go your own self," Pearl said, turning for the den. "Maybe it's time you *un*retire and hire on with one of those trucking companies out of Memphis. Longer hauls the better."

Shine giggled. I chuckled. Big John rolled his eyes.

Pearl reached for the door and ducked at the buzz of a hummingbird a few feet from her head.

I scanned the eight hummingbird feeders Big John had hung under the eaves of the porch. Summer brought waves of his favorite bird to the secret recipe of sugar and water he bragged about but wouldn't even share with his wife or preacher.

"Pearl, did you know my little angels are the only birds that fly backward?" he asked.

"You've gotta be the only man in Mississippi who cottons to cats and hummingbirds," she said.

"I bet you didn't know they weigh less than a nickel and can fly five hundred miles across the Gulf of Mexico without a stop."

"I wouldn't if you hadn't told me five hundred times."

"Most of my gorgeous little dive-bombers are humming on back to Central America as we speak."

"As you speak," she said.

Pearl didn't slam the door like Cookie was apt to, but it was loud enough to make her point.

Shine reached and plucked a hair from Big John's ear. He pulled away, puckering his lips like he'd bitten into a green persimmon.

"My used pickup," she said, taking his hand. "Who had to borrow ten dollars from the Red Cross for a marriage certificate. Lord knows where you stole the money for my puny ring and our one night at The Peabody hotel in Memphis. You were poorer than Job's turkey."

"I didn't know Job had a turkey."

"Smart aleck."

"Myles is a brand-new Cadillac," Big John said. "And a good-looking boy to boot."

"My Lord. Bragging on Myles's looks might be the dumbest thing you've said this month."

"Hank drives a forklift at the lumberyard in Byhalia. Or did anyway."

"Let's pray he graduates to eighteen-wheelers when he gets back from serving his country."

"Pearl never has taken to my particulars. What I did to make a living. What I wear. The way I love this farm. But Myles is everything I'm not."

"And Hank's like you, Big John. Hardly the prettiest picture on the porch, I'll admit, but a soldier boy who acts tough to cover the lamb under his wool. Hank's gold under that skin."

She got up and left.

Big John was fiddling with the suspenders on his overalls when the Black Angus bull let out a roar.

"Slide, look at Shakespeare pawing the ground and pushing on the fence. Temper of his flared something awful when I moved his heifers to another pasture. I doubt he feels a barb on that wire."

"Why'd you name him Shakespeare?"

"'The prince of darkness is a gentleman,'" he said in a proud drawl. "Tell me that bull's not the darkest creature God ever made. Though Shakespeare himself would be hard-pressed to call my ole boy a gentleman."

"I'd be hard-pressed to call you and Shakespeare the smoothest pair on the planet."

"Albert Brown, our undisputed camp genius, used that line on presidents and preachers he didn't like."

"You and that Yankee spent over a year in a prison cell. Why didn't he teach you more than one line?"

"Who said I only knew one?"

"You're welcome to prove me wrong."

"Another line or two will come to me one of these days. I know more Shakespeare than anybody else in these parts anyhow."

✳ ✳ ✳

MY DAY TOOK A BAD TURN when the phone rang that night. Shine beat Big John to the kitchen and picked up on the third ring. We stood in a circle as she listened.

"Great news, Ethel," Shine said, handing me the phone.

"Slide, your daddy's off the couch," Momma said. "Time for you to come home."

"You sure?" I asked.

"That's why I called."

"Why don't y'all ever come to the farmhouse? You could visit a while and—"

"Slide, you know what a homebody your daddy is." She sighed. "Cash is like his big brother in one way, I suppose."

I was fixing to tell Momma I had less interest in seeing Deddy than eating whatever she'd cooked for supper. Big John's smile changed my plan if not my mood. I told Momma I'd be waiting and hung up. I glanced at Big John, an arm around Shine and happy tears in his eyes, and felt like a turd for being so selfish.

"You and Myles were right," I said. "Deddy made it through this valley. I hope it's the last."

Big John leaned down and looked me in the eye. "Hope is dangerous but good, my boy. Just like God."

9

Cookie

COOKIE'S EX-HUSBAND CAME TO MIND AS she listened to the phone ring. Besides busting Billy's head wide open, Cookie never had much use for the telephone. Especially when she was sitting down for her one meal of the day.

She'd fried up a fat bream and was forking its tender white meat off the bone when the phone sounded off. She picked it up with a "Yeah."

"You should've been there today," Shine said.

Cookie knew something was wrong when Shine didn't ask about her day. Every day was the same for the most part, but how Cookie loved the sound of her friend's giggles when she griped about babysitting Salt and her daddy.

"You all right?" Cookie asked.

"Better now that Big John's gone to bed. The knucklehead was all mouth and no ears this afternoon. Even carried on about how handsome Myles is."

"Lawd have mercy."

"Tonight he waited up until Pearl got home, so he could spout off another sermon on how *blessed* she is to have Myles courting her."

"Let the clown waste his breath. Pearl's hardheaded like you."

"That's what worries me, Cookie. His jabbering is liable to backfire. Myles has been a godsend for our daughter."

"From the little I've seen to what I've heard, Myles sounds like a catch. Hang tight, angel. I'll do some checking to make sure we ain't missing something. Meantime, don't fret over Big John. We'll set him straight if need be. Bye."

— ✳ ✳ ✳ —

THE SUN HAD TROUBLE BEATING COOKIE out of bed. She'd be done with her Scripture and coffee by the time it showed up for work. Sun did what it did every day, and so did Cookie.

Every now and then she'd fish at first light. Her bream were finicky before the sun warmed the water, but the red worm hiding her hook would fool a bass looking for breakfast, and those cats never wore a watch.

First Saturday in October, a cool snap had a button on the mouth of every fish in Cookie's pond. Least the sun was doing its job. Edge of that red ball made a million rainbows on the wet grass at her feet. Soon as it cleared the hill on her right, the pond lit up with more colors than the coat that almost got Joseph killed. All kinds of orange and yellow and red.

Only the Lawd could make a show out of this muddy water, but two hours of pretty sun and dead corks were enough. Cookie was on her way home when she found Big John leaning under his hood, like he could tell the engine from his butt.

"What you working on?" she asked.

"That you, Cookie?"

"I reckon so."

"My truck's got an extra tick in her this morning," he said.

"*Her?* You calling that bucket of bolts a woman?"

"Sounds like her old self idling but makes all kinds of noise when those wheels go to spinning." He shut the hood and stretched his back, grunting like he'd been on his knees picking cotton all day. "Thought I'd swing over to Myles's place and see what he can find. Fella sure knows the car bidness."

"Can't you fix a rattle?" She chuckled. "Where's the crowbar you so handy with?"

"Aren't you in a smarty mood today?"

"Smarty. I got better words for tending to Salt all week and not catching a fish all morning. Fact is, seeing you under that hood has my mood on the mend. I'll go with you."

He scratched his melon with one hand and tapped the hood with the other. "Cookie, you know the fish'll start biting now that it's warming up."

"I know you know less about fish than cars, if that's possible."

She set her bucket next to the porch and climbed in.

He frowned. "Suit yourself. I'll run in and let Myles know we're on the way."

⁎ ⁎ ⁎

ANTSY TO FIGURE OUT HIS PROBLEM, Cookie's driver made it to the county line in less than fifteen minutes. Big John pulled off the highway and rolled to a stop as Myles waved from his tailgate.

"I'm glad y'all made it," he said, as they got out.

"Same here," Big John said.

"See if you can help this man with his rattle," Cookie said. "It's got him all shook up. Like you and Pearl but to a different tune."

Myles blushed and set his eyes on the hood. "Any idea what it is?"

"Carburetor or transmission would be my guess," Big John said.

Almost feeling sorry for her friend, Cookie turned to hide the grin spreading across her face. She stepped back, pointing at the tall fence with a heavy steel gate and razor-sharp wire across the top.

"Myles, what's all this about?" she asked. "Reminds me of the state pen in Sunflower County."

"We've had trouble with break-ins. People must think we're mining gold instead of repairing old cars. Most of our work's done in the warehouse out back."

"Fence is so tall I can barely see it," she said. "Metal roof tells me how big it is."

"Carburetor or transmission?" he asked Big John.

"I'm afraid so."

"Well, let's take it for a spin," Myles said, reaching for the keys.

Myles had three wheels on the highway when Big John cried out, "There she is. Y'all hear it?"

"Afraid not. Can you, Cookie?"

"Nope."

"I see y'all winking at each other," Big John said, crossing his arms.

Myles pointed toward the front wheel on the driver's side. "Is that it?"

"Yes!" Big John hollered.

"Listen to you," Cookie said. "Sounding more like Salt opening a Christmas present than a grown man."

"Now I'm tracking you," Myles said, turning for the shop.

He squatted next to the tire, tapping on the hubcap. "Big John, you mind handing me your crowbar?"

"Sure thing. Let me find her."

Big John rummaged through the back and came out with the crowbar Myles had used on the man at Harry's. Myles needed two seconds to pop the hubcap and solve the problem.

"Here's your rattle," he said, dropping a pebble into a fat paw. "Must've picked it up somewhere between your farmhouse and the gate."

Big John was peering at his pebble when a racket from hell cranked up in the warehouse.

"Sorry about that," Myles said, not missing a beat. "Truckload of banged-up cars from Memphis has my men working overtime. Let me show y'all the shop." He opened the door and followed them inside. "Not much to it besides my desk and these two bays."

"My, you run a clean operation," Big John said.

"The cars are in good shape by the time we move them here from the warehouse. Our mechanics give them a final look over before they're shipped off to the dealers."

"Where they at?" Cookie asked. "I don't see a car."

"They're working overtime to catch up."

"I sure am proud of you," Big John said. "You've built quite a bidness in no time. I got no idea how you keep up with it all."

"Well, we only do business with people we trust," Myles said. "We don't waste time, won't waste time, on contracts and paperwork. Everything is done on a handshake. Everything. And that does help."

→ ✳ ✳ ✳ ←

BIG JOHN WAS BACK TO HIS usual ways on their drive to the farmhouse. Right hand on the wheel. Left arm out the window. His speedometer hadn't worked in years, but Cookie guessed they were bumping down the road at twenty miles an hour.

Myles hadn't seemed worried about his business, and he sho' didn't have a daddy to worry about. The boy was already part of the family from Big John's seat at the table.

"You oughta see the smile on yo face," she said.

"I think we've found the man for Pearl," he said.

"We? You found him. You introduced 'em. And you've been a nagging hen ever since. I reckon he's yo man as much as Pearl's." She sighed, looking out the window. "All good except two things. I see the first but not the second."

"Cookie, what are you talking about?"

"Let's start with the one I *can't* see—Myles's family."

"Well, I only know what I've heard from Myles and Pearl. His older brother, Duke, reminds me of Cash. Duke had a rough go in Vietnam, but now he's in Saint Louis running their biggest operation."

"You don't know squat about business. Or Saint Louis."

He tapped on the wheel. "Cookie, are you coming to my funeral?"

She leaned against the door and looked Big John over. Her daddy would slap his knee when his friend got happy on liquor and asked crazy questions. These days, Big John acted a fool when he was drunk on himself, happy or sad.

"Tell me about Myles's people in Biloxi," she said.

"Well, they're good church folks," he said. "Good stock."

"*Stock*? You talking cows and horses or slaves?"

"You know what I mean."

"How they handling what happened to Holly?" He stared ahead. He whispered Holly's name. "Big John?"

"Losing baby James to pneumonia nearly killed me," he said. "Took Shine four years to talk me into trying again, and I was a wreck every time Pearl got a runny nose." Tears filled his eyes and rolled down his cheeks. "No telling what they've been through with poor Holly."

10

Slide

I WAS GRIPING TO BIG JOHN ABOUT another boring week of school when a car skidded to a stop near the highway. Pearl bailed out of her two-door Pontiac, threw the gate open, and hopped back in. She slammed on the brakes to keep from ramming into his truck, then jumped out and sprinted to the porch.

He bolted to his feet. "Darling, where'd you get that cut?"

"Sit down," she said. He sat. "Number one, it's not a cut. Nicked my forehead on the shower door this morning."

"A shower door?"

"Number two. I'm not your darling. And three, I've made *my* decision." She leaned down and narrowed her eyes. "I'm marrying Myles. Because he's nothing like you."

The news Big John had all but arranged had been delivered with a stick upside the head. A bat more like it. He didn't look mad, but I was.

Pearl straightened up, pulled a letter from the back pocket of her jeans, and dropped it in his lap.

"From Hank," she said. "Responding to a note I sent a while back. I was afraid he'd snap and go looking for a bullet if he didn't know where I was leaning beforehand." She sighed and took a seat. "I want you to read it."

I wanted Big John to meet his daughter's eyes, rip the letter to shreds, and hurl the pieces onto the floor. He bowed his head and went to reading.

Dear Pearl,

I should've written the second I finished your letter. I'm sorry I didn't. I pray every night I'm not too late. You're probably shaking your head at the thought of me praying, but I've seen enough men die to give it a shot. Will it last when I get home? Your guess is better than mine.

My commanding officer thinks our platoon will be part of the troop withdrawals next spring. Please hold off on this Myles fella until I get back. How well can you know a newcomer to town? Can his months touch my years? Give it some time, Pearl. Please.

I love you with all I've got. With all I'll ever have.

Your Hank

Big John sank back in his rocker, staring at the letter. He looked up with Shine's I-told-you-so stamped across his face.

"I'm sorry, Pearl. So sorry. Hank's a fine boy who tries hard and tells it like it is. I know he loves you." He wiped a tear. "My heart skipped a beat when I thought about you and Myles getting married. You and Shine warned me to keep it to myself, but I didn't listen. I blew it."

To my surprise, Pearl climbed into his lap and hugged his neck. "It's okay, Daddy." She smiled. "You weren't trying to be a pain in the ass."

I was glad Pearl had picked Myles but still not over the way she'd treated Big John. I got up to leave.

"Slide, get Momma for me," she said. "We'll tell her the news."

I made my way across the porch, glancing from one door to the other. *Take the screen door*, I told myself. *Let Pearl get her own momma.* Instead, I tucked tail and struck out for the kitchen.

"What do you want?" Shine asked, looking me over like I was another pan to clean.

"Pearl needs you," I said. "She's on the porch."

The two women spent the next eternity hugging and squealing before taking their seats.

"When's the big day?" Shine asked.

"No idea, Momma."

"Middle of April when the dogwoods and azaleas are blooming?" Shine asked.

"Perfect," Pearl said.

That was all I could stomach for one day. Little did I know what the next week would bring.

PART IV

BIG JOHN SAT ALONE ON THE dark porch. Still haunted by the sounds of joy and celebration from the women he loved, the father felt no joy. Only sadness and shame, for he'd acted like a stubborn and foolish child while treating his daughter as one. For months. No, years. He deserved Pearl's anger, her words as well: "I'm marrying Myles. Because he's nothing like you."

He walked to the edge of the porch, staring but not seeing. He pressed his forehead against the screen. Myles. Why didn't he ask Big John for his daughter's hand? It was certainly the custom in their parts, especially with men like Myles. Had Pearl kept him away?

Cookie's words came to mind: "All good except two things. I see the first but not the second." They discussed the *second*, Myles's family. In Big John's grief over James and Holly, he forgot to ask about the *first*. What had Cookie *seen* in Myles?

Big John turned for the house but found himself straining for his rocker. He sat, trying to slow the shallow breaths that delivered no air. He felt a chill that brought sweat, and he didn't know why.

11

Cookie

COOKIE PICKED UP ON THE TENTH ring. "Who's dialing my number at this hour?"

"Big John."

"I'd cuss you for calling if it wasn't such a big day for the big man."

"I guess so," he said.

"What's behind the gloom in yo voice? I figured you'd be shouting for all the world to hear that yo Pearl was getting married."

"Part of me is, I suppose."

"The other part's found something to bother yoself and everybody else over."

"Well, on our drive back from Myles's shop, we never got around to what you saw in him that had you worried. Remember?"

"I doubt it amounted to much."

"What was it?" She didn't answer. "Cookie?"

"Nothing to it, I reckon. Now leave me alone and go on to bed."

"But—"

Cookie hung up before he could ask again. She leaned against the kitchen counter, pondering what she'd seen—felt more like it—the day she met Myles.

After filling her bucket with a mess of fish, she trotted into the farmhouse and caught Pearl and Myles smooching on the couch. They were sitting up with their clothes on, so Cookie didn't mind. Myles did. Pretty face of his turned redder than hers was black.

Pearl didn't miss a beat acting like Cookie had picked the perfect time to meet her new boyfriend. Instead of waving from his seat like Hank, Myles got to his feet with his hand stuck out and bent the right way to meet a lady. A white lady.

"Miss Cookie, nice to meet you," he said, his voice high and creaky like Victry's.

"You too," she said, shaking a hand that felt too soft for a man in the car business.

He tried one of those one-armed hugs Victry got away with when Cookie was in a good mood. Myles backed off when she nodded for him to stay put.

"Pearl talks about you all the time," he said.

"*All* the time? Was she *talking* when I opened the door?" The look on Myles's face made Cookie go easy on the boy. "You better watch this girl. She's hard to catch and harder to keep."

Pearl laughed and patted on the couch. "Over here, Myles. It's best to keep a safe distance from Cookie."

Myles. Not counting Big John, Cash, and her Victry of course, Myles was the only white man who'd acted like her skin wasn't black. So what if his hands were soft? He was the boss man after all.

Cookie picked up the phone, realized she didn't care to listen to Big John fretting over Myles's hands, and dialed another number.

— ✳ ✳ ✳ —

COOKIE DIDN'T CARE FOR SLEEPING ANYMORE than sitting or hugging. She'd asked the Lawd why He'd needed rest on the seventh day, and why He'd put sleep in Adam's bones—she knew enough about men to know it hadn't started with Eve—but never heard back on either count.

Victry didn't sleep much better than Cookie did, but he tried. One night he'd shower and shave and read a while. Next night he'd turn on the tube and watch the news as if all the mess in this world would soothe his spirit. A few times he'd straggled in late from work, walked straight to bed, and tried sleeping in his suit and tie.

Victry's routine never changed when Cookie called and woke him up. Their routine, that is. He'd wrestle with the phone before mumbling a hello that would've made anybody else feel sorry for him. She'd ask what tricks he'd tried, then tell him to talk to the Lawd for a change. He'd go to pouting like Salt before making all kinds of racket fighting the covers and messing with the light. When he griped about the time, she told him the Lawd set his clock too—Victry just didn't know it yet. By then he was awake enough for one of those lines that sounded like he was giving a speech to the president.

Cookie had no time for such foolishness on this night.

"You listening?" she asked.

"Cookie, what time is it?"

"I asked if you were listening."

He sighed. "Your supposed disdain for the telephone belies the truth that you use it whenever you want."

"You ain't talking to that crook in the White House. I got news, Victry. Big news."

"Let me get some water."

"I ain't got time for yo water tonight. We got a wedding on the way!"

The phone went quiet for a few seconds. "Pearl and Myles?"

"Sho' nuff."

"I thought Hank was in the picture."

"Pearl wanted a man she could touch, not to mention one with money and looks. I been figuring on Myles for a while now."

"Why didn't you tell me?"

"That's what you get for moving to Sodom and Gomorrah."

He snorted. "My prophet has a telephone."

"You lucky I ain't close enough to put it to good use."

Victry chuckled like he always did with that line. "Have they set a date?"

"You'll get one of those fancy invites white folks waste money on."

"When is the wedding, Cookie?"

"April."

"And Big John?"

"He ain't got a say in the matter."

"You know what I meant."

"He is acting a little strange. That's Big John for you."

"It happens," Victry said. "We get what we want and then feel a let-down. A void we can't explain."

"I can explain it a lot better and cheaper than whatever big city shrink you talking to these days."

"Not the time for another lecture."

"What about you, Victry? You don't sound too excited."

"I'm not sure why."

"Well, I reckon Myles's Bible will crack clean in two if they put it off any longer. No reason to wait with them cooing and petting like dogs in heat."

"Oh, Cookie. Only you and perhaps my father would use mating dogs to celebrate such news."

— ✳ ✳ ✳ —

COOKIE DIDN'T KNOW WHAT TO THINK of Shine's call. The giddy tune of her voice sounded like the first time she'd told Cookie about Pearl and Myles. Only this time Shine wanted Cookie to join her on a "fun little day trip" to a doctor's office on Union Avenue in Memphis.

Shee-it. Shine knew doctors were right behind white sheriffs in Cookie's book. She also knew what Cookie thought of Memphis before Martin Luther King Jr. was killed a couple years back. Too many people, not to mention crazy-ass streets like Union Avenue.

"What happened to yo sawbones on the square?" she asked. "The old kook try a little too much *inspecting* on the last visit?"

Shine giggled. "Dr. Saunders sends his patients to Memphis for a thorough examination when they turn fifty. I'm a year late as it is. Tomorrow morning, you coming or not?"

"Big John forget how to drive?"

"I could use a break from the man who acts like the bride-to-be one minute and mother of the bride the next."

"I hear you."

"I also thought it would be nice to talk over my girl's wedding with my best friend."

Cookie hung up and stared out the kitchen window, thinking back on the night she met Shine. Big John brought her to Elijah's house on the second date, looking for a nod on the woman he'd fallen in love with. Cookie chuckled to herself. What kind of a white man wanted a black man's okay on anything, much less a woman? A strange one.

Cookie smiled, remembering how she'd liked Shine from the start. Her smile disappeared the second she thought of the minute she first loved Shine. Elijah hadn't been dead a full day when Cookie opened the door to find Shine with supper in her arms and tears in her eyes. She brought supper every night until Cookie's momma told her to stop.

Like and love came easy with Shine. *Best friend?* That started the day after Cookie left Billy on the floor and bused home from Saint Louis. The evening a white woman walked straight into her kitchen, set a tray of food on the counter, and gave Cookie the first hug she'd felt since the night her daddy died.

Shine. A lovely lady inside and out. Even more lovely than her sister was evil.

— ✳ ✳ ✳ —

LORE'S CADILLAC ROLLED UP TO COOKIE'S house at eight o'clock that morning. She opened the door and took a long look at the woman behind the wheel.

"If you'd rather sit on a barbed-wire fence for the next hour, we'll run back to the farm and steal Big John's gentle ride," Shine said.

"This'll do," Cookie said. "Lore can drive his *work* truck to the *plantation.*"

They cruised down Highway 77 and into Memphis, chatting about the wedding. From Pearl's dress to a rehearsal dinner at the farmhouse, Shine had a ball.

Until she turned onto Union Avenue, that is. Her eyes went to darting every whichaway. She wiggled in the seat like she was sitting on a hot skillet.

"What's wrong?" Cookie asked.

Shine let out a deep breath. "I lied to you last night. We're going to see the doctor about my cancer."

Cancer. Cancer in her Shine. Cookie didn't blink for the next five minutes.

"How bad is it?" she asked, as they pulled into the parking lot.

Shine nodded at the building. "We'll know soon enough."

Cookie glared at the fancy glass doors, the shiny red brick, the sign on the Mid-South Cancer Clinic.

"Does Big John know?"

"I've been lying to him too. He thinks I'm planning a Chi Omega reunion with my sorority friends from Ole Miss."

"I should've known," Cookie said. "But should've ain't worth a shit."

Shine chuckled. "How were you supposed to know?"

"Something told me you were lying after Big John's birthday dinner when I found you stretched out on the bed, saying you'd pulled a muscle clearing the table. You never had problems with yo back. I'd have caught on if I wasn't so riled about that white man at the bait shop."

"Nothing you could've done," Shine said. "Let's see what the doctor has to say."

Shine checked in at the front desk while Cookie headed for the empty chairs on the back wall. She passed an old man wiping his eyes. She sat and watched other folks gazing at the floor like they were counting their days. She didn't feel their pain. Only Shine's.

For the next hour, Shine flipped through magazines. She held Cookie's hand a while, then rested her pale white hands in her lap and closed her eyes. Shine's face was full of peace. Cookie's wasn't.

A round lady in a nurse's uniform walked in, studied the clipboard in her hand, and called, "Shine Jackson." The nurse led them to one of those piddly-ass rooms doctors used to give people news they didn't want to hear.

Minutes that felt like months had passed when the doctor strolled in and gave Cookie a funny look.

He nodded at Shine. "Mrs. Jackson, how have you been feeling?"

"About the same."

"What do those papers in yo hand say?" Cookie asked the doctor.

Shine put a hand on Cookie's knee. "Doctor, my friend Cookie—"

"What do those papers say?" Cookie asked again.

⋆ ⋆ ⋆

CANCER. DEEP IN THE BONES. THREE to six months.

Cookie was too angry with the Lawd to talk to Him or anybody else. The Lawd could've sicced the devil on those deacons who killed her daddy instead of one of His angels. Instead of her angel.

Shine's cancer turned Cookie's world upside down. It tore Big John's clean through. He'd spent the past year worrying about Cash and Pearl. He spent those next few weeks moaning and groaning like Job after the devil had given him those boils and such.

⋆ ⋆ ⋆

COOKIE WALKED INTO THE FARMHOUSE AND found Big John, Shine, Pearl, and Myles at the dinner table. Every plate except Big John's was half-full. His baked chicken, mashed potatoes, and string beans hadn't been touched.

"Hey, Cookie," Pearl said. "I was about to tell Momma and Daddy that I decided to put the wedding on hold."

"Like hell you are!" Shine hollered. "I don't care whether I'm in a wheelchair or a hospital bed. I'm living to see you get married."

"No, Momma. It's too much with you . . ."

Pearl couldn't finish that line, but her momma could. "With me *dying*?" Shine tapped a fork on her plate until Big John looked up. "This isn't some dream we'll snap out of. Not a one of you's had the spine to admit the truth." She turned with strong but begging eyes. "Even you, Cookie."

Cookie looked away, then nodded. "The road to dying is lonely enough without going it alone. It's time we all listen to the song the Lawd is singing."

"Don't call it a song," Pearl said. "It's a death wish."

"But it is a song," Shine said. "A hymn. Can't y'all hear it? I'm going home to see Jesus and baby James."

"What about me?" Big John asked.

"You?" Shine asked. Her grin took the edge off the scowl Cookie had been wearing since they'd left the doctor's office. "Leave it to a man to worry about his own hindquarters while the bones of his wife rot away."

Big John kept staring at his food.

"And leave it to a dying saint to make light of her bones and her man's butt," Cookie said.

"Let's have a Christmas wedding," Shine said, a smile on her pretty face.

"But Christmas is less than two months away," Pearl said.

"We better get to work," Shine said.

"Let's do it," Myles said. Pearl's eyes told him to shut his trap, but he kept on. "I'll tell my folks. They can't wait to meet y'all."

"Christmas it is," Shine said. She struggled to her feet. "I need to rest a spell. Big John, get the dishes. We'll start tomorrow."

12

Slide

WATCHING BIG JOHN OVER THE NEXT forty days was worse than the falderal of planning a wedding. I never saw him eat a bite of Shine's pumpkin pie or leave the small wooden chair by the fireplace in his den.

A fire on Thanksgiving Day was more than a tradition in Big John's book. It was an American duty if not one of Thomas Jefferson's inalienable rights I'd studied in eighth grade. But the fireplace was dark and dead that Thanksgiving. Same with the cold days of December. The only life Big John seemed to notice was the lady who hummed one happy hymn after another while she went from a cane to a walker.

✳ ✳ ✳

BY THE TIME CHRISTMAS EVE ROLLED AROUND, Big John's Sunday clothes said he hadn't eaten much more than Jesus during His forty days in the desert. Big John's face said he wasn't looking forward to meeting Myles's family, much less the rehearsal dinner in two hours.

I looked Big John over, pondering my chances of cheering him up. Slim to none, I figured, and slim had left Hill County over a month ago. I tried anyway.

"I see you finally let Shine have a go at those eyebrows," I said. He kept staring through the screens. "The hedge clippers you never use must be worn slap out."

The porch was dead quiet until Myles wheeled Shine through the door. I jumped to my feet, fixing to cry at the sight of Aunt Shine in a wheelchair.

"Got this for the wedding," she said, smiling my way. "Brand-spanking new. Why bother with a walker when I have this beauty?"

Pearl closed the door. "Slide, I know what you're thinking. But if Momma can be happy, we can at least try. Right, Daddy?"

Shine wheeled over and elbowed Big John in the arm. She waved a hand in front of his face, then pinched him on the cheek.

"Stamp a smile on that frown," she said. He stared toward the same field that had held his gaze for the past thirty minutes. "Well, you better before Myles's folks get here. I expect them any minute now."

Gabriel might as well've floated down with his trumpet at full blast when the Lincoln Continental passed through the gate.

"Here they are!" Shine yelled. "Y'all welcome our new family while I hold down the porch. You too, Big John. Get up."

We walked up as the driver got out.

"Hey, brother," Myles said. He gave the man a one-way hug and turned our way. "Y'all meet Shad."

I'd thought Big John and Deddy were an odd match until I met Myles's brother. Shad nodded but didn't say a word or shake a hand on his way to the trunk.

"My father's in one too," Myles said, as Shad pulled out a wheel-chair. "He goes by BM. Myles Sr. and Big Myles got too confusing around the house. Don't ask me why the second son was named after his father."

Shad opened BM's door while Myles helped the two ladies from the back seat. Myles's sister, Betty, had pale skin that showed no sign of seeing the sun. His momma, cursed with the Christian name of Opa, wore a blue dress that made Big John's tie look spiffy. The ladies said "hello" and "nice to meet you" before stepping back and dropping their chins.

BM apologized for the rest of his family living too far away to make the wedding on short notice. I wondered about Myles's brother in Saint Louis, as BM hugged Pearl and rattled off a sermon on how blessed Myles was to have found such a beautiful bride.

"Such a nice evening and all, I thought we'd visit on the porch a while," Big John said. "Shine's waiting on us."

Myles and Shad lifted their deddy's wheelchair, carried him up the steps, and rolled him toward Shine.

"You must be Shine," BM said. "You might be even prettier than your daughter."

"I heard that," Pearl said.

"Now I see where Myles gets his charm," Shine said, grinning at BM.

I sat in the far rocker while the grown-ups found their seats. All but Shad anyway, who stood next to the screen door as if on guard duty. BM sized up the scene like he owned the porch if not the whole farm.

"I gotta confess one thing," he said. "Our Mississippi clan is a tight bunch, but there's lots of Yankee blood running through these veins. Opa here is a southern girl, but I was born in Chicago. Momma's folks came from Ireland and Deddy's from Italy."

Big John nodded but didn't smile. For some reason he'd forgiven the Germans but still held a grudge against the Italians for their fence hopping during the war.

"So there you have it," BM said. "I'm a Yankee from the cradle but not to the grave, thank the good Lord."

Everybody laughed except Myles's brother. Still standing by the screen door in a suit that should've been a size or three larger, Shad looked like a bowel movement was fixing to get the best of him.

"In 1948, my deddy bought a small repair shop on the outskirts of Biloxi," BM said. "I got into the bodywork and resale side of the bidness after he'd gone on to heaven. Thank the Lord it took off from there. Otherwise, we wouldn't have an operation in your county. Or a wedding to celebrate!"

"Amen," Shine said.

With blood and business in the rearview, BM was ready for war.

"Thought I'd seen the worst of it in the Bataan Death March," he said. "Then the Japanese broke my legs and locked me in a shed where I couldn't sit up straight or stretch out. I hobbled with a cane for twenty years and have called this wheelchair home for the past five."

Myles studied his watch and cleared his throat.

"Hate to break up the party," he said. "But we'll be late if we don't hurry."

"We'd hoped to have the rehearsal dinner here at the farm," Big John said, glancing at Shine. "So little time and all, my brother-in-law was kind enough to offer the Country Club."

—✳ ✳ ✳—

BIG JOHN LIFTED AUNT SHINE FROM the wheelchair and eased her into his truck. She groaned, shifting her weight on the springs of the worn-out seat.

"Their fancy Lincoln would be a smoother ride," he said. "Or Myles's new pickup for that matter."

"I'm here now," she said. "Y'all get in."

Shine was humming "How Great Thou Art" when Big John parked next to the curb at my house. The silver Lincoln and red pickup rolled to a stop behind us.

No more comfortable at the Country Club than church, Deddy had been dead set on following us to the rehearsal dinner. A week in the wilderness all by his lonesome was a party to the man who became a mole when people, especially strangers, entered the equation.

No stranger to comfort or people, Momma trotted out and gave our caravan a wave that jiggled the buckets she had for bosoms in a way that must've broken every law in town.

"Your mother looks pretty in that baby-blue dress," Shine said.

"She bought it at a garage sale at one of those antebellums near Lore's house," I said. "Deddy griped about the price for a week."

"That's a man for you."

Shine sang her favorite hymn—"It Is Well with My Soul"—as our caravan pulled out. Though little seemed well in Big John's soul, he smiled when she squeezed his hand.

"Mighty nice of Lore to host the rehearsal dinner," he said. "And the reception for that matter."

"There's a kind soul under Lore's bark," Shine said.

"How long has Uncle Lore been a member of the Country Club?" I asked.

"He's a lifelong member," she said. "Like his daddy and granddaddy. You've been there."

"Dragged with Salt," I said. "Lore can't hit a tennis ball over the net without sailing it to the stars and back, though I'm sure every shot's a winner in his mind. The men's bar is Lore's salvation."

Shine laughed. "Or the locker room. I've heard the man struts around with a towel dangling from his neck like he's got the biggest dipper in the three-county area instead of the smallest."

"Shine Delilah Jackson," Big John said, sounding like a momma scolding her child.

"The Lord's truth," she said. "And Lore's of course. All the same to the man who reportedly should wrap his towel tight as a girdle."

Thanks to Momma and Cookie, plus Shine and Pearl when they were in the right moods, I was no stranger to outspoken women. That said, no one was supposed to talk about peckers in our parts. Everyone did, of course. Boys bragged and lied and dreamed. Men too, I figured. Salt mentioned tallywhackers when she wanted to make me blush. Now even Shine had joined the party.

"I sneak into the men's bar when I get tired of Salt," I said, eager to move a long way from a short pecker.

"Slide, you oughta know better," Big John said.

"Damn right," Shine said, playfully patting his shoulder. "Kids are strictly forbidden in the men's bar."

"With all the smoke and whiskey flowing, nobody notices," I said. "Lore lights up cigars and sips Wild Turkey, telling stories until he's too tipsy to put one line in front of the other."

"A house with Misry will do that to a man," she said. "Big bucks only travel so far, I suppose. Not far enough for living with my sister."

I wanted to shout "amen!" though "living with" would be a stretch. Misry stayed on the far side of the Old Homestead and hardly ever showed her face.

"Will Misry be there tonight?" I asked.

"Lord no," Shine said. "Not after all the dirt she's thrown at Pearl through the years, not to mention the way she's treated her own children. Plus Cookie and, let's leave it there for now, Slide."

"Good idea," Big John said.

"So who's coming?" I asked.

"Everybody from Big John's birthday dinner a few months back," Shine said. "Plus Victry, Salt, Lore, and Myles's folks." She pointed ahead. "Look, Sam's pulling in."

We followed Sam's Buick through the gates, crossed a span of brick pavers, and parked.

Myles hopped out and waved. "Sam, y'all come meet the family."

Sam's wife fiddled with her hair and makeup as he hurried to the Lincoln.

"Brother Sam," BM said. "What a blessing to lay eyes on the Shepherd who's opened his doors for my son."

"I'm proud to call him a friend," Sam said.

Once Myles made sure everyone was properly introduced, we crossed the parking lot and headed for the dining room.

— ✳ ✳ ✳ —

SHINE MIGHT'VE BEEN THE BEST AUNT a boy could hope for, but a quick glance at the nameplates left no doubt that seating arrangements were *not* her strong suit. Sitting across from Momma and Deddy was tolerable. Between Salt and Lore was an outright disaster.

I ducked as Lore hollered my name and sent what amounted to a full salad sailing over my head.

"Gravity's been working for generations now," he said, peering at the

94

mound of lettuce and cheese, soaked in what appeared to be Thousand Island dressing, on the green carpet.

"Nearly took my head off," I said.

"Be grateful you're skinny and quick. Have a seat, my boy."

"Don't you and Salt want to sit next to each other?" I asked.

"Shine's the boss," Lore said. "She knew Uncle Lore and Salt would keep you in line."

I sat and took a sip of tea that was no longer sweet. I choked, spat a mouthful of pepper into my glass, and glared at the smirk on Salt's face.

"Turd," I said.

"Aunt Ethel, did you hear what Slide called me?" Salt asked.

Momma grinned, took a big gulp of water, and swished it around in her mouth until every sinner this side of the Mason-Dixon had time to haul ass for higher ground. "Salt, I'm depending on you and your daddy to teach my boy some manners."

While I'd never cared for speeches, Salt had me aching for the toasts that were supposed to bring our dinner to a close.

Big John once said he'd rather fly another B-24 bomber into a hailstorm of German fire than speak in public. I'd found it hard to believe until he staggered to the podium and gazed at the crowd like he was facing a firing squad. He fumbled through the front and back pockets of his polyesters. His wide eyes raced across the room before landing on Shine. She giggled and half whispered for him to "try the inside pocket of that sporty blazer you wore to our rehearsal dinner."

He fished a scrap of paper from his blazer, unfolded it, and tried to read.

"I first want to thank Lore for sharing the Holy Springs—" He blinked and cleared his throat. "For sharing the Hope Springs Country Club with us this evening. Now I'd like to say something about my lady."

He stared at Shine. He looked down, chewing his bottom lip. His whole body was shaking by the time Myles went over and guided him to his seat between Shine and Pearl.

"Mind if I say a word?" Myles asked.

Big John didn't respond.

"Of course you can," Shine said.

Myles gave Big John's shoulder a light squeeze and walked back to the podium.

"I grew up in a church that recited the Lord's Prayer every Sunday," he said in a calm voice. "I've said 'Thy will be done' a thousand times. How often have I meant it? The truth is, I'm usually more interested in my will than God's."

"Amen!" Cookie hollered, not giving the first damn she was the only black person in the room besides the waiters in white suits. "Right there with you, Myles."

He nodded. "In Romans 8:28, Paul tells us that 'all things work together for good.' Not some things but all. Do we understand why God allows so much suffering? No. But we can trust that He is in control. And good." Myles scanned the crowd. "We also have each other. Whether brothers and sisters in blood or marriage or the Lord Jesus, we're all one family." He looked to his right. "Big John, I love you like a father. And you, Shine, you are my second mother." He smiled, wiped a tear, and found the only dry eyes in the room. "Pearl, the woman of my dreams. You're beautiful, inside and out, and I can't wait to be your husband."

The room was dead still as Myles returned to his seat.

Shine pointed toward the podium and whispered in Big John's ear, "You can do it!" I wanted to cry out, but my hero shook his head. Like that day with the crowbar, Myles had come through when it mattered. And Big John hadn't.

I was chatting with Victry when Shine wheeled up and reached for his hand.

"Victry, I asked Myles to push my wheelchair down the aisle at the wedding," she said. "I know I asked you about this earlier. Do you mind?"

Victry leaned down and kissed her on the forehead. "Of course I don't mind."

She glanced back toward her table. Pearl had one arm around her deddy's waist and the other across Myles's shoulder.

"Something tells me Pearl will need all the backing she can get," Shine said. "And that starts with her husband. I just told Myles he's one of our own from here on out, and tomorrow I'd like to show him."

13

IF EVERYDAY WEDDINGS WERE SUPPOSED TO be accompanied by angels dancing in the church rafters, I figured a wedding on Christmas Day would have them parking cars and handing out bulletins. The only angel I saw was in a wheelchair. White hair to wet and happy eyes, Shine glowed as Myles pushed her down the aisle.

The weeping mountain of a deddy wouldn't have made it through the double doors if not for the bride. After a series of starts and stops and tugs on Big John's arm, Pearl steered him to the front of the sanctuary. Then what? Did he answer Sam's question and give his daughter away like other southern fathers? No, he turned and gazed at the guests until Pearl led him to the empty seat next to Shine.

I shook my head, wondering why a man who'd survived the Germans and stuck a shotgun at a sheriff's throat couldn't finish a toast or get hold of himself at a wedding.

Sam knew Pearl well enough to skip the verse on wives submitting to their husbands. He didn't even guarantee the bride and groom a waltz through Disneyland for the rest of their days. Instead, he must've been preaching straight to Momma when he compared being a wife to plowing hard ground with a drunk mule.

✶ ✶ ✶

I THOUGHT ABOUT UNCLE LORE, AUNT SHINE, and Mr. Brand as Deddy pulled out of the parking lot and joined the long line of cars heading for the reception. Strange thoughts, I admit, but better than what I'd seen from Big John at the wedding.

It took a sharp axe to pierce the scaly bark of Uncle Lore's skin, but maybe Shine was right about the "kind soul" below. Her cancer got his attention. When Cookie mentioned Shine's worries about planning the reception and having the farmhouse ready for the rehearsal dinner, he listened. Hell, he even offered to help. *Mr. Brand was wrong*, I told myself. *Evolution is true after all.*

From valets in white tuxedos to candles along the wide brick path and porch steps of the Old Homestead, Uncle Lore had done his part. It wasn't his fault the reception was worse than the rehearsal dinner and wedding put together.

Standing in the foyer next to Shine's wheelchair, Big John was a nervous wreck. While Shine lifted a hand to greet everyone from Mayor Hipp to Judge Reynolds, Big John could've filled buckets with the sweat that poured from every pore. Both sleeves of his blue blazer were drenched when Salt snuck up and burped in my ear.

I turned, glaring at her smocked dress and pink bow. I was reaching for the bow when Cookie appeared, staring at me with those eyes I'd seen after *Salt* had stolen her favorite fishing pole.

"Where did you come from?" I asked, wondering how I'd missed the tall black woman in a white dress.

"You think I'd let Babygirl outta arms' reach with all these strangers roaming the place?"

Victry strolled up as I was planning my escape. He stopped behind Cookie and peered around her shoulder. Her mad eyes moved to the tall glass easing toward her lips.

"Southern Comfort," he said with a smile that was more than happy. "Want a sip?"

She pushed the glass away. "How many you had?"

"I lost count at four."

Cookie reached for the glass, but Victry was sober enough to step back and take a swig.

"Slide, have you seen the open-aired tent in our backyard?" he asked.

"No, but I'm ready," I said.

"The tent's bigger than our house," Salt said. "It has Christmas lights and a bar with all the Shirley Temples a girl could drink."

"And enough liquor to keep the drunks happy," Cookie said, staring at her boy.

"Plus a dance floor," Victry said. He studied his drink and grinned at Cookie. "Maybe you'll like the band."

Cookie lightened up when she saw Pearl. "Look at that girl shaking the floor." She pointed at Myles. "Her man might as well stop embarrassing hisself."

"Perhaps dancing is one thing he cannot do," Victry said.

"Reckon we'll find out soon enough," Cookie said. "He's part of the family now." She turned and eyed Victry. "Speaking of family, who you seeing these days?"

"You know I won't discuss such matters," he said.

"You got a girlfriend?"

"Is that a different question, my dear mother?"

"Go ahead and be that way."

He smiled. "If only you knew Cary."

"Cary?"

"Wish I could tell you more."

"I ain't playing yo games," Cookie said, as she took off for the house.

I was draining my third Shirley Temple when the band finished its last song. Lore strutted onto the dance floor and let out a whistle that silenced the crowd.

"Ten o'clock!" he roared. "Everybody to the front steps. Time for these lovebirds to get on with their bidness at The Peabody hotel."

—⋆—⋆—⋆—

VICTRY WASN'T THE ONLY ADULT WHO enjoyed his share of whiskey at the reception. I'd never seen Momma so tipsy.

Deddy hadn't taken a sip at the party, but he was lucky a squad car didn't spot his truck on our drive home. He struggled to keep it between the lines as Momma pinned him against the door and slurred in his ear. I stared out the window, cursing the thin wall that separated the two bedrooms in our house.

I went straight to bed, hoping to fall asleep before the music started in the next room. Hope didn't help. Before long Momma was making enough noise to keep the whole neighborhood awake.

I turned on my side and buried an ear in a pillow. I shoved a second pillow against my other ear. Still no luck.

"I got two choices," Momma had said during one of Deddy's bouts with the bottle. "Lie to myself or think about something else."

I thought about the wedding and reception. Big John the baby. Shine the angel. Salt and her antics. Victry's happy drinks and mad momma. And Pearl and Myles as they danced. Sinner's truth, I had trouble keeping my mind off whatever was going down in a dark room of a fancy hotel in Memphis.

I didn't wait long to find out.

PART V

MERRY TEARS IN HIS EYES, BIG John watched the new-lyweds dodge rice as they dashed down the steps of the Old Homestead. For the next half hour, he held Shine's hand while they said goodbye to the last of the guests.

He was reaching for his keys when Shine said, "Let's dance, baby boy. How those big feet can shuffle is a mystery to me, but you're the best I've held."

"Honey, I'm sure the band has packed up by now."

"I'm always a step ahead of my man," she said, smiling. "It's been arranged. 'You Made Me Love You.'" He nodded, remembering their favorite song from the forties. "And you still do, Big John." She lifted her arms. "Carry me."

She hugged his neck as they made their way to the dance floor.

"Shine, how are we going to do this?" he asked.

"The course of true love never did run smooth."

He cocked back his head, more than a little confused.

"Nine words," she said. "Maybe you don't know more Shakespeare than anyone else in these parts." She kissed his ear. "Just set me down and hold me up."

And so they danced. Hand in hand, cheek to cheek, they made slow and tender circles without saying a word. None were needed. Big John was dancing his last dance with the love of his life, and he savored every moment.

Big John slept better than he had in a long while, but he didn't know why. Second thought, maybe he did.

After they'd returned from the reception and gotten into bed, Shine lay in his arms, whispering in his ear about the first night of their honeymoon at The Peabody. The elevator ride with two ladies he recognized from Hope Springs. His pleasant hello. The slanted eyes and raised noses which said the soldier boy and his *loose* woman were up to no good. His wide eyes and red face. The nervous tip of his hat. The rain of rice upon his shoulders and the elevator floor. Their faint nods and half-smiles. Shine's words as they stepped off the elevator: "Sorry you missed out on another round of gossip, ladies."

Shine then recounted the scene he'd caused in their hotel room. They were soon to be "joined together," as the preacher had said. In two single beds? He dialed the front desk, tapping his fingers on the bedside table until the man picked up. "This is Second Lieutenant Colonel Jonathon Jackson," Big John said. "And I am not spending my wedding night in a single bed. Bring up a queen and make it quick."

Before drifting off to sleep, Shine teased the *warrior* who hadn't been able to walk down an aisle without his daughter's help, much less find his seat. She prayed out loud, tugging on his chest hair as she asked God to finally do away with the blue blazer her man had sweated through at the reception. She giggled, recalling the look on his face when Lore made his grand announcement about the lovebirds and "their bidness" at The Peabody.

Big John woke at daybreak. For the better part of an hour, he watched his sleeping bride. He didn't even cry. He kissed her softly on the cheek, eased out of bed, and slipped on his clothes before tiptoeing to the kitchen.

Though reportedly one of the few men in the Magnolia State who helped with the dishes and laundry, Big John wasn't much of a cook. That said, the nonhunter was mighty proud of his hunter's breakfast: fried eggs, sausage, and toast. Sometimes he forgot to flip Shine's eggs— he preferred sunny-side up—but he always remembered the tablespoon of cream and the teaspoon of sugar she liked in her coffee.

She was sitting up when he opened the door.

"Not as sneaky as you think," she said.

He crossed the room and gently set the tray in her lap. "I didn't mean to wake you."

"Breakfast in bed," she said with a smile. "I should die more often."

14

Slide

I WOKE UP AND TROTTED INTO THE kitchen to let Momma know I was heading to Big John's for coffee-talk. She waved me off, said they'd be tuckered out after the wedding, and told me to wait until at least one o'clock.

I was skipping up the gravel at one o'clock sharp when a car screeched to a halt at the gate. I figured someone had borrowed Pearl's car until she darted out and sprinted for the gate.

She was fumbling with the chain as I ran up.

"Let me help," I said, wondering why she wasn't on her honeymoon with Myles.

"Back off!" she hollered. Her black eye backed me up a step. "I can open the damn gate."

She finally gave up and told me to open it. Without so much as a thank you, she hopped into the Pontiac and slung gravel with all the might those puny tires could muster. My hands were shaking like Pearl's by the time I started for the house.

Big John and I stepped onto the porch at the same time. Pearl was sobbing on his shoulder when Shine hobbled out on her walker. She rubbed Pearl's back, limped across the porch, and worked her way into a rocker.

"Y'all have a seat," she said.

Pearl sat. Big John kept staring through screens. I leaned against the front door, wishing I'd closed the gate and gone home.

Shine patted his rocker. "Sit, Big John. Now."

Pearl got up, led him across the porch, and sat in his lap.

"I see your eye," Shine said. "What else?"

"Nothing else, Momma."

"Who did it?" Big John asked.

Pearl cleared her throat. "The creep Myles has for a brother."

Pearl leapt to her feet as Big John bolted up from the chair.

"Where's Shad?" he asked.

"Simmer down, big fella," Shine said. "And sit back down while you're at it. Let me handle this."

He sat but didn't simmer down. The knuckles on his big hands turned white as he gripped the sides of a rocker that didn't rock.

"I was too excited about the wedding to give it much thought," Shine said. "But Shad bothered me from the get-go. Suppose I wrote it off to him being one of those quiet types."

"He is quiet," Pearl said. "He's also mean. And jealous of me and Myles."

"I never understood why Shad drove y'all to Memphis," Shine said. "Myles can afford a chauffeur."

"Shad acts like my husband needs a bodyguard."

"Last night I watched you floating down the steps of a mansion on your way to a luxury hotel in Memphis," Shine said. "Now you're a mess, and your husband is nowhere in sight."

"He's following Shad to Biloxi."

"Why did Shad beat you up?" Shine asked.

Pearl circled the porch. "I guess it wasn't that big of a deal."

"Not a big deal," Big John said, clenching his right fist.

"Let her finish," Shine said.

"I was tipsy leaving the reception. Had a few more drinks on the ride to The Peabody and another round at their snazzy bar in the lobby. I had a terrible headache this morning. Myles was downstairs looking for aspirin when Shad banged on the door."

"And?" Big John asked.

"Shad told me to hurry the hell up and get ready for our flight. After I let him know what his pounding on the door did for my hangover, he barged in, griping about the *drunk* his brother had married. I lost it and went to yelling and pushing him toward the door. He reared back and hit me and stormed out."

"Shad is bad news," Shine said.

"Myles will take care of him," Pearl said, turning my way. "I'll stay here until he gets home tomorrow." She smiled as I opened the front door. "Aren't you the gentleman?" I nodded but didn't feel like smiling. She looked back at her parents. "I sure like our house by the way. Myles has it leased for another six months and plans on buying us a big antebellum in town this summer."

Pearl crossed the den with nearly a skip in her step. I closed the door.

"I don't like it," Big John said.

"What's there to like?" Shine asked. "Our girl just landed on the wrong end of a one-day honeymoon."

"Something's not adding up," he said. He lumbered to the edge of the porch. "The way Pearl was sitting in my lap gave me that feeling I used to have when she'd cozy up with a lie on whatever trouble she'd gotten into at school. Or out drinking with the boys."

I made it to the gate in record time, only to set a different record from the gate to my house. I'd stop and stare at the blacktop or sidewalk, trying to make sense of the past two hours. The past twenty-four hours. The past few years for that matter.

"Something's not adding up," Big John had said. Nothing added up to me. What did Pearl's drinking with the boys in high school have to do with a black eye from her honeymoon? Why did Pearl seem excited about leasing one house and buying another when her husband was running his brother out of town? And Shad. Would he stay in Biloxi? If not, how would his face hold up to Big John's fist?

Well, at least I knew one answer. Or thought so anyway.

15

In no mood for another dose of Salt's antics, I was wandering the third floor of the Old Homestead when I turned the corner and came face-to-face with Misry. I stepped back, staring at her curled lip and wondering why I hadn't stayed downstairs. The fact that I hadn't seen her in over a year was no excuse for daydreaming my way toward the den of Misry.

She leaned closer and stuck her nose in my face. "Have you been drinking?"

"No, ma'am," I said, wanting to kick myself for saying "ma'am."

She straightened out. "My father never drank or touched a cigarette. He was a godly man."

"Must've been," I said. "He raised Aunt Shine."

Misry narrowed her eyes and showed her teeth. I expected a slap instead of a smile.

"I overheard Lore and Cookie talking about Pearl," she said. "'A man reaps what he sows,' as the Lord says. And so does a woman."

With that, Misry turned for her room.

Thanking God I'd survived the wicked witch of Hope Springs, I hustled down the steps and into the den.

"Have a seat, my boy!" Lore called out. "Where you been?"

"Had a run-in with your wife," I said.

He snorted. "Misry send you to hell with a Bible in your hand?"

"And Pearl," I said. "Sounds like you heard about her honeymoon."

"Sure did. What's the latest on that Shad fella?"

"Myles took him to Biloxi."

"Needs a bullet in the brain if he shows back up. If Myles can't set him straight, and our slow-footed sheriff won't do his job, Big John'll have to do the honors."

"He'll need a gun for that bullet," I said.

Lore shook his head. "Big John's smart when it comes to talking history and philosophy and such. But throwing a perfectly good shotgun into a lake? His *last* gun? Shit, tell me that ain't a one-way ticket to Whitfield."

"Whitfield?"

"You know, Slide. The funny farm near Jackson."

"You're funny, Uncle Lore. You'd fit right in."

He leaned back, locking his hands across his belly. "I hear they're building a new wing for the juveniles in our state. Ones who have trouble respecting their elders."

"Then you and Salt can both go."

He laughed. "Tell Big John I'll loan him a deer rifle, though I'd have to teach him to shoot the dern thing. Or better yet have Cash give him a few lessons. Your deddy was a crack shot in the day."

My deddy. The boy who'd outshot every grown-up in Hill County. The man who'd threatened to shoot himself on more than one occasion. Truth was, the threat of Uncle Lore butchering another hunting story while bragging on himself in the third person beat listening to him brag on the deddy I'd never known.

"Tell me about your deer season," I said. "I hear you're the wiliest woodsman these parts have ever seen. Surely a soft-stepper like you outfoxed at least one trophy buck this season."

"One big boy down and another to go, Lord willing."

"Didn't the season end last week?"

"Lore ain't worried about the letter of that law," Lore said. "Deer season's always open at the plantation. Second rut's hitting on all cylinders as we speak, and Lore's on the verge of outsmarting a buck that's been roaming the place since you were in diapers."

Playing dumb with uncles never got old. "What's the rut?"

Lore raised his arms, staring as if I'd taken Robert E. Lee's name in vain. "Hell, Slide, sprouting boy like you's bound to know about the rut." I shrugged. "Listen here, son. The rut's when the bigguns let their peckers do the talking. They go to chasing the ladies and plumb lose their minds. And that's when your Uncle Lore enters the picture."

"And the second rut?"

"Damnation," he said, forgetting I'd asked this question a dozen times. "Second rut's when those yearlings come into heat. You know, the young does weren't bred the first time around. The ole bucks really lose it on those darlings."

"Hardly seems fair, Uncle Lore. Lounging and napping in a tree 'house' with a high-powered rifle. You call that hunting?"

"Shitass!" he yelled, as I bounded from the couch and took off.

→ ✳ ✳ ✳ ←

THE NEXT MORNING, I FOUND MYSELF in a pantry the size of my bedroom, awed by the mounds of Twinkies, Suzy Q's, and other goodies Lore and his daughter demanded on an hourly basis. I turned at the fast and fiery steps in the kitchen.

"Boy, get outta there," Cookie said.

"I was looking for a snack," I said.

"You ain't got time for a snack. You're going fishing."

Fishing? Cookie knew I was like Big John in the fishing department.

"Thanks for the invite but—"

"It wasn't an *invite*," she said. "Be waiting at the door when I get back."

Twenty minutes passed by the time she dragged Salt, wearing a bow big enough to cover an eagle's nest to go with a dress that cost more than every thread in my closet, into the foyer.

"Slide, quit scratching that ass and get with it," Cookie said, as if I hadn't been waiting by the door. "Time's a-wasting, and my fish are a-biting."

We lit out from the Old Homestead with Cookie's bucket and poles hanging on for dear life. My steady jog struggled to keep up, but two blocks on a warm winter morning proved more than a struggle for Salt.

"Hold up!" she kept hollering.

Cookie ignored her until we reached the highway. "Hurry yo ass up, Salt. Get those legs to moving or get left."

With Salt on her last leg and Cookie on her last nerve, Myles drove up at the perfect time.

"Y'all want a ride?" he asked.

Salt decided she wasn't dying and ran our way.

"Might take you up on that," Cookie said, glancing at her baby.

Salt stood on her tiptoes and stuck her face through the window.

Myles chuckled. "Those cute little cheeks are redder than my truck."

"'Little' cheeks," Cookie said. "Try chubby if you wanna be an honest man. Lawd knows how I put up with this girl."

"Oh, she's all right," he said.

"You chillun hop in the back," Cookie said.

The rushing air from a rolling truck and its open windows felt cool to me. Not Salt.

"Sure is hot today," she said. "I wouldn't mind a milkshake."

"I made you a breakfast that would fill yo daddy's belly," Cookie said.

"Feels like forever since I've been to Smith Drugstore for a milkshake," Salt said.

"Try every Friday afternoon since you been old enough to remember," Cookie said.

"Best milkshakes ever," Salt said. "You had one, Mr. Myles?"

"Not yet," he said, pulling up to the gate. "I've heard Mr. Smith makes a dandy."

"I reckon you here to see Pearl?" Cookie asked.

"No ma'am. I had a meeting on the other side of the square and was on my way to the shop."

"You supposed to be on a honeymoon," Cookie said. "And here you worrying about work?"

He draped his arms over the wheel and sighed. "This first year has been crazy. Pearl wants me to get the business straightened out, so we can spend more time together."

"Good idea," Cookie said. She pointed toward the farmhouse. "Pearl ain't used to a man working hisself to death."

Myles grinned. "Should I drop y'all off at your pond?"

"Sounds great," Salt said.

"Nope," Cookie said. "Babygirl needs to use those legs every year or two. Slide, get the gate."

I closed the gate and climbed back in.

"Drop us off at the farmhouse," Cookie said.

"Mr. Myles, I'd love a ride to Cookie's pond," Salt said. "We've been walking all day."

Cookie mumbled what sounded like a mixture of Lawds and bad words before telling Myles to drop us off at her pond.

He turned left off the gravel, rolled downhill toward the barn, and drove up to the pond. Cookie rushed to the back for her gear, then jogged to the open door and tossed her bucket onto the ground.

"Get yo asses outta this truck," she said. "You chillun want a switching?"

"You'd never touch me with a switch," Salt said. "I know that."

"I don't," I said.

I scurried across the seat and got out. Salt didn't.

"Get yo butt to moving," Cookie said.

Salt shook her head. I did the same for a different reason, for anybody else would've been in deep doo-doo.

"Well, I do need to catch me some fish for supper," Cookie said.

"Why don't you stay and let me take them?" Myles asked.

"I thought you had work to do," Cookie said, squinting at Myles.

"Truth is, I could use a break."

"I like you, Myles. But I don't let Babygirl outta my sight unless she's in the house. Never *thought* of her riding off with any man besides her daddy or one of those uncles."

"I understand," he said. "Have to be careful these days."

"Cookie, those fish aren't going anywhere," Salt said. "Come with us."

"Already told you I ain't going."

"Let us go," Salt said, even more persistent than spoiled.

Cookie looked Myles over. "Have 'em back within the hour. You hear?"

"Will do," he said. "Don't worry, Miss Cookie. They're safe with me."

Cookie snatched her bucket and took off as if every last fish was fixing to jump out and sail on to heaven. She stopped at the pond, tossed her gear onto the ground, and reached into her Prince Albert can. She eyed a huge red worm for a solid ten seconds before deciding the poor beast was worthy of her hook. Then she stared our way until the truck was out of sight.

—✳ ✳ ✳—

"MISS COOKIE IS SOME WOMAN," MYLES said, as he turned left onto the highway.

"She only talks a big switch," Salt said.

"Maybe for you," he said, winking at Salt. "I wouldn't bet on that for the rest of us."

As we drove into town, I sat back, glancing at Myles and wondering why such a fine fella had moved to such a crummy place. My favorite part of Hope Springs was Big John's farm, and it was *outside* the town limits.

"Business must mean the world to you," I said. "Why else would somebody like you move to Hope Springs?"

"Well, I do live out in the county not far from the shop," he said. "What makes you say that, Slide?"

"I'll tell you when we get to the square."

Truth was, I didn't know where to start. Victry and his rope? The Rope explained why he'd gone to a Yankee college and moved to New York City. Did it answer Myles's question?

While I still believed in God and didn't fret over it all like Victry did, I had plenty of questions about the way things worked in the buckle of the Bible Belt. Why was the color of a person's skin such a big deal? Why did preachers send you to hell for drinking when Jesus had turned water into wine? Did we need a church on every corner?

We had five churches within cursing distance of the square, from what Pearl had said, but I knew of seven. First and Second Baptist.

United and United Front Methodist. The Presbyterians, Episcopalians, and Catholics must've felt lonely with only one to choose from, but they'd have company soon as the next jittery batch of Holy Rollers got fed up with the meatloaf at Wednesday night supper.

"I can stomach y'all's church on occasion," I said, as we passed another steeple. "Brother Sam is all right, but those other preachers are a bunch of slick-haired goofballs nagging nonstop for money and fighting over the same sorry pool of sinners."

Myles parked in front of the courthouse. "Goodness, Slide. I didn't know you felt that way."

"This square is nearly as dead as the Johnny Rebs buried in our cemetery. All but two of the decent stores are closed. Momma swears the diner and drugstore are barely hanging on."

"What does Ethel say about Pierce Hardware and Bill's Five and Dime? They've been around for a hundred years."

"My deddy used to work at the hardware store. Mr. Pierce is a nice man. He put up with Deddy's bottle long as he could."

"I know it's been hard on you."

"Deddy brings it on himself. Counts his curses with the best of them."

"My older brother reminds me of your father," Myles said. "Duke was a wreck after Vietnam."

"For six years?"

"Long enough to—" Myles closed his eyes. He scanned the square, then pointed. "Ever tried Mr. Wei's pizza at the Dungeon?"

I studied the sign with its red arrow pointing down the steps. "The chubby old Chinaman knows his pizza."

Salt giggled. Myles didn't.

"Slide, do you use the N-word?" he asked.

"No. Spent enough time with Big John to know better."

"That's what I thought," Myles said. "Has he told you about the history of this town?"

"More than I'd care to hear. Big John knows his history."

"Where did he learn it all?"

"He never went to college besides a stint at Southwestern before pilot school. Says he took a liking to history in prison camp and has been interested ever since. He's read every marker from here to the cemetery. Even reads the tombstones. Don't ask me why."

Myles put a hand on my shoulder. "Have you heard of Pascal, by chance?"

"Is that a milkshake?" Salt piped in. "Mr. Smith's always coming up with new ones."

"Afraid not," Myles said. "Blaise Pascal was a Frenchman who lived in the sixteen-hundreds. Mathematician, scientist, and inventor, among other things."

"Where is this going?" I asked.

"Slide, when I was your age, my Sunday school teacher often quoted the man."

"Mine was too high on Darwin."

Instead of the laugh I expected, Myles placed his hand on his heart as if singing the National Anthem. "Pascal wrote about a 'God-shaped vacuum' we all have right here. A hole only God, not money or girls or anything else of this world, can fill."

"You're sounding more and more like Big John," I said.

"I'll take that as a compliment," he said. "But, Slide, I want you to see the sun while you're young. If not, you're liable to grow up and see nothing but clouds."

"Easy for you to say. You've got the prettiest wife in town. And more money to boot."

"I'd bet the Old Homestead somebody has more money than I do," he said, turning to Salt. "You ready for a milkshake?"

"A chocolate milkshake," she said.

Myles checked at his watch. "We better get them to go. I'd hate to find myself on the wrong end of Cookie's switch."

16

I CLOSED THE GATE AND RAN DOWN the gravel with only one thing in mind: Aunt Shine's New Year's Day special. Loaded with lard and country ham, her black-eyed peas had warmed the first day of every year I could remember. Shine hadn't cooked in weeks, but maybe she'd coached Big John into making a pot.

I stopped at the end of the gravel drive, scanning the fields and peering down at the barn. Where was Big John's truck?

I opened the front door but didn't make it inside.

"Big John's not here," Shine said, waving me off from the couch. "Wait for him on the porch. Or go on home if you like."

I'd never imagined Shine kicking anyone out of her house, much less me. I stepped back and closed the door. Porch or home? Shine had given me a choice.

I sat but didn't rock. The only happy place I'd known felt like the trunk of the dead oak in the front yard. I closed my eyes, dreaming of a world with black-eyed peas, a healthy Aunt Shine, and a jolly Big John.

I studied the floor until the thrill of splinters ran its course. I looked out across the farm. The deep greens of summer were long gone. Cows moped along like they knew they'd be steaks and burgers before supper hit the table. A lonely barn still begged for a new metal roof and another coat of red paint.

Nothing sounded right either. Snowball hadn't killed every bird on the farm. Why couldn't a cardinal sing one song to cheer a boy up on a cloudy winter day? Couldn't Ole Red fly over and pound on the dead tree for a while? All was dead quiet until a dove mourned a tune that reminded me of Deddy and his bottle.

Big John rolled up to the gate and got out. Shine opened the door.

"Slide, help me with this walker," she said. I hurried to her side. "Take a gentle hold of my arm and walk beside me."

I felt the pain jolting through her body as we shuffled to the chair Big John had packed with pillows to ease the pressure on her bones.

"Should I give y'all some time alone?" I asked.

"You've already decided against that. Besides, if anyone can brighten Big John's day, it's you."

He parked, plodded up the steps, and crossed the porch without looking my way or giving his bride the sweet kiss I expected. He plopped down in his rocker.

"Pearl's eye any better?" Shine asked.

"The swelling's down," he said.

"And?" she asked.

"I'd been there a minute tops when my girl planted a big kiss on Myles and looked at me like I'd been the one hitting on her. Said she had an errand to run. Errand on New Year's Day, my foot."

"So that's why you're in such a surly mood? *Your* girl didn't give you the time of day. What's new?"

"Not much, I reckon. At least Myles has Shad far off and under control."

"Imagine having a brother who beat your wife and ended your honeymoon."

"Myles wouldn't stop apologizing. I feel sorry for our boy."

She looked Big John over. "You have that same look in your eyes."

"Can't say why," he said. "But I left their house with the same feeling I had last Saturday when Pearl was in my lap."

17

Cookie

ONE THING KEPT TICKLING COOKIE'S GUT—MYLES'S hands. They were skinny and soft like a white lady with one maid for cleaning and another for cooking. Made sense with Victry, but a man in the car business? Even the boss man?

Those hands worried Cookie enough to take Myles fishing, which said a lot coming from her. More people, more problems in her book, especially when it came to fishing. Talk and tangled lines did little for her stringer and less for her patience.

—✳ ✳ ✳—

THE MOODS ON THE PORCH SURPRISED Cookie, though white folks were good at acting good when life was bad. Shine had been a real pro with her cancer. Myles could do the same, Cookie figured, but not the rest of this bunch.

Pearl was petting her man like a girl who'd found a new puppy instead of a wife with a smudge of black still showing under her eye. Slide wore a grin that told Cookie to keep an eye on her fishing poles. Big John held his bandana in the air like Cookie was liable to do with a three-pound bass. The man was acting a fool, but he wasn't acting.

Myles stood and offered his seat as the screen door closed behind Cookie.

"Not much for sitting unless I'm fishing," she told him. "You ready?"

"Hold on a second, Cookie," Big John said. "I was just telling our fellow travelers that a bandana might not make you happy, over the long haul anyhow, but it will do most everything else. Anything you'd care to add?"

"See if a tight knot will seal those lips for a while," Shine said. "A long while."

Big John reached for the little notebook he kept in the front pocket of his overalls when Shine hadn't hidden it in the house. He scribbled with the mechanical pencil she'd bought after he'd given up on sharpening everyday pencils with his pocketknife.

"Lip-sealer makes number thirty-five on the list," he said. "Yessiree Bob, a bandana's the most versatile raiment known to man."

"Raiment?" Pearl asked. "Where'd you learn that word?"

"He must've been a Sunday school teacher," Myles said, rubbing the back of Pearl's neck while she played with his pretty blond hair. "Mine used to beat the word to shreds."

"Maybe that's it," Big John said. "Hard to keep track of everything I've picked up on through the years."

"I'd kiss the cat to see you pick up that rump and track it into the house," Shine said. "Or better yet, the shed."

Big John smiled at his lady. "Martha Washington was a wife beyond compare. Who knows if ole George could've whipped the Brits without the bandana she gave him?"

"Where'd you get the damn thing?" Pearl asked. "Pink, of all colors."

"Darling, you know pink's my favorite. And surely you know a bandana beats the stew out of a baseball cap except when it comes to keeping the sun or rain out of your face."

"I didn't know caps had stew," Shine said. "Try one for supper tonight."

"Try using a cap for a flyswatter or place mat," Big John said. "Much less a napkin."

"The fool in this man is a-growing by the day," Cookie said.

"Amen," Shine said.

"My dear ladies," Big John said. "With a bandana you can—"

"Wipe your bottom," Slide said. "Next time you get stranded in the national forest without your standard two rolls."

Pearl giggled. Shine didn't, but the spark in her eyes lied about the frown on her face.

Big John cracked a smile. "Boy, I haven't stepped foot in those woods since your deddy left me for dead some twenty years ago."

"My favorite uncle could use a bandana," Slide said. "Uncle Lore's always in a bind at his plantation. Too many pines and not enough oaks."

Big John went to scratching in his notebook. "In honor of your favorite uncle, I'll add toilet paper to the list. Now we're at thirty-six. No telling where we'll end up."

"What about stuffing a girl's bra?" Pearl asked.

Pearl's bosoms didn't need any help, but her husband and daddy sho' did.

"Pearl," Myles said, blushing and fidgeting in his seat.

"Pearl *Deborah* Jackson," Big John said.

"Don't forget us boys," Slide said before Big John could get hold of himself. "A bandana would make one helluva package enhancer."

"A what?" Big John asked.

"Ease one into the right spot and it would do wonders for making a boy's package look bigger," Slide said.

"That's it," Big John said, hopping to his feet.

"Nice sending you to the house for a change," Pearl said, as he hoofed it across the porch.

Everybody but Myles was howling when the door shut behind the pink bandana.

* * *

COOKIE HAD PLANNED ON BAITING MYLES'S hook like she'd done for Victry or Salt the times she'd made them go, but Myles brought his own pole and bait. He had two bream on the stringer before her third cork hit the water.

"Should've put you in the shit spot," Cookie said, pointing to the shallow end where she sent everybody else who showed up at her pond.

"I'd hate to outcatch you," he said, grinning her way.

"I wouldn't hate to send you back to the house."

He smiled. "These worms from Harry's Bait Shop put yours to shame."

"Keep on talking, boy. We'll see."

He was slipping another fish onto the stringer when a big catfish took her line and wrapped it around a stump. Damn stump had cost her hundreds of fish, not to mention hooks and corks.

Myles waded in like he was the Lawd fixing to walk on water.

"Get outta my pond!" Cookie shouted. "Snakes'll eat you alive." He kept wading. "You wasting time, fool. Cat's long gone by now."

"Almost there," he said, listening no better than most men.

She remembered those hands and how snazzy he always looked. "You see the color of that water. Looks and smells like cow shit for a reason."

"Hold your pole up and keep the line tight."

"I know what to do with my pole and—"

In a flash he grabbed the line with one hand, dove headfirst into those muddy waters with the other, and popped up with the biggest cat Cookie had ever seen. Much less caught.

She griped when he insisted on carrying her poles and bucket to his truck. Griped again as he fetched a strange-looking knife from under the driver's seat and went to cleaning their fish. He wouldn't let her slice a belly, chop off a head, or pop a scale.

Myles's hands were soon covered with blood, but they no longer worried Cookie.

18

COOKIE KNEW A WEDDING AND A black eye had eaten most of the strength cancer hadn't already stolen, but she wasn't ready for the sound of Shine's voice on the phone that evening. She mumbled half of Cookie's name and started over, then tried again.

"Why you calling, angel?" Cookie asked.

"Big John."

"What now?" The line went quiet. "Shine?"

"You mind stopping by after church tomorrow?"

"Fine by me. I'd planned on fishing anyhow."

—✳ ✳ ✳—

COOKIE LIKED THE BACK ROW BECAUSE she liked the first hour of Jeremiah's sermons but not the second. Jeremiah was still preaching at two o'clock when she slipped out the back.

She closed in on the farmhouse porch, caught Shine's nod that said Big John wasn't ready for whatever she'd had in mind, and veered left for the pond. Cookie's stringer had six bream and two cats when she heard a crash at the gate. Pearl scrambled out of her Pontiac and stole one glance at the car and another at the gate. She crawled under the fence and took off for the house.

She was wailing on her momma's lap by the time Cookie got to the den. Shine didn't seem to care that her bones were fixing to snap with Pearl's every move. Cookie did.

"Get up, Pearl," she said.

The girl scooted over and turned around, showing blood from a swollen lip and busted nose that made red of her white shirt.

"Where's Shad?" Big John asked, staring into the fireplace.

Cookie couldn't see his eyes but knew they were melting brick.

"It wasn't Shad," Pearl said, wiggling her butt too much for Cookie's liking. "It was Myles."

Big John spun around, looking stuck between what to believe and who to kill. There was no stuck on Cookie's brain. Myles had passed her tests without a hitch.

"You got some explaining to do," she said.

"I had a feeling you were lying to us," Big John said.

"I didn't lie about the honeymoon," Pearl said.

Big John pressed his lips together, eyeing his girl. "And the afternoon you stormed in and tossed Hank's letter into my lap? The cut on your forehead from the *shower door*."

"Also true," she said. "I drove out to Sardis Lake and drank Budweiser where Hank and I used to watch the sunset. Only this time I was stewing over telling you about marrying Myles. I went back to his place and took a shower. I wasn't outright drunk, but close."

"Was Myles there?" he asked.

"No, he was at work."

Big John walked to the couch and leaned in. "I smell liquor on you now." She folded her arms, glaring his way. "Darling, I'll do whatever it takes to protect you, but you gotta level with us."

"Forget it!" Pearl yelled.

She hopped up and raced for the door.

Cookie grabbed her by the wrist. "The long arm of my law ain't playing no games. Sit."

Pearl sat. Big John reached under the couch and pulled out a bat.

"Don't have a gun," he said in a smooth and steady voice. "But this'll do the job."

"No!" Pearl and Shine yelled at the same time.

They kept hollering while he plowed through the door like Cookie's daddy the night her sister had come home from working at a white man's house.

Big John was cranking the engine when Cookie caught up.

"I'm all for you cracking somebody's skull," she said. "First we gotta know whose skull needs cracking."

"My head keeps pointing at Shad," he said. "My—"

"Yo gut is playing with yo head right now. No telling how many wrong turns that gut has taken through the years. Good times and bad, mine never has told a lie." Cookie heard steps and reached back for Pearl's arm. "Now my gut is saying this girl is mad at her man and ain't coming clean with us."

"Cookie's right," Pearl said. "It wasn't Myles."

"I'm fixing to find out," he said.

He tore off across the yard before Cookie could snatch his keys.

They trotted up to find Big John standing at the gate. Bent their way and wedged against the Pontiac, the man knew he was in a pinch.

"Pearl, give me your keys," he said.

"They're in the house," she said real quick-like. She jumped into his arms. "Daddy, I love Myles."

Holding his baby hit the strange in the man.

"I'm sorry, Pearl," he said, whispering in her ear.

Big John had turned soft. Cookie wanted answers.

"Let's head on back to the house," she said.

＊ ＊ ＊

PEARL TOOK A SEAT ON THE couch between her momma and daddy. Cookie guarded the door.

"Straight," she said. "You hear me?"

Pearl nodded, staring at her knees. "An hour or so after Myles left for work, Shad woke up and—"

"I thought Shad was in Biloxi," Big John said.

"He drove in for a meeting at the shop yesterday afternoon. Spent the night drinking and womanizing before showing up at our house." Pearl turned, gritting her teeth and glaring at the floor. "I didn't like Shad before he hit me and ruined our honeymoon. Now I'd like to kill the bastard."

"I do like the fighter in you," Cookie said. "Hang on to that and you got a chance."

"Back to what happened today," Shine said.

Pearl took a deep breath and blew it out. "Shad stumbled in from the guest bedroom, looked me over like I had no right to be watching TV in my own den, and knocked over a lamp on his way to the refrigerator. He was reaching for a beer when I slammed the door and caught his finger. He whirled and hammered me with the back of his hand, then grabbed his beer and left."

"Where'd he go?" Big John asked.

"Myles figured the shop or some woman's house. He's looking for him now."

Big John walked to the window.

"Makes more sense than anything else I've heard," he babbled to himself. "But who knows? Why would she lie about her own husband?"

"Because she's mad and in love," Cookie said. "Add money to the wash and guess what comes out? A fat load of dirty laundry."

"I just told y'all the truth," Pearl said.

"Sure changed that story after I grabbed my bat and headed for the truck," Big John said.

"Like Cookie said, I was mad at Myles. I've been mad. I knew from the start how much that business meant to him, but I'm sick of my husband being gone all the time." She leaned forward, eyes on her feet. "After he left to find Shad, I poured a drink to settle my nerves, then another. With every sip I got more upset. With *Myles*. For always making excuses for his asshole of a brother. For letting him sleep off a hangover at our house. And for leaving me to check on work. Again. Truth is, I blamed Myles for not being there."

"He should've been there," Shine said.

Pearl sighed. "But I shouldn't have come over here blaming my husband. I'm sorry."

She hugged her momma and got up like she was on her way out.

"Big John, I need a ride home," Cookie said. "You coming too, Pearl. I ain't done with you."

— ✶ ✶ ✶ —

COOKIE LED THE WAY, DOING HER best to ignore the racket of big feet and leather boots on hard gravel. Her best wasn't good enough. Big John could wake a dead possum, she was thinking when her fish came to mind.

The Lawd must've needed that day of rest before He made possums and coons, much less given them noses that could smell the dead a mile off. The thought of those scoundrels gobbling up a mess of eight fish was almost enough to send Cookie thataway. Almost. The Indian summer they had for a winter had something worse stirring from their holes.

"The sun's calling it a day," she said, turning to Big John. "You'll need a light to find my bucket."

"Cookie," he said, as if the name were news to her. "It's too long of a walk. Nearly dark for that matter."

"You think I'm giving my fish meat to yo possums and coons? Or walking dark ground with all them highland moccasins crawling every whichaway? You gotta be joking."

"But it's January."

"And seventy degrees."

"Guess you don't mind if I get bit."

"Ain't a thing for you to worry about, Big John. Those devils'll hear yo three hundred coming a mile off."

"You expect me to gather up all your gear?"

"Shee-it. Get my lines outta the water so the cats don't steal my poles, then load my stringer in the bucket and meet us at the gate."

Big John wasted five minutes whining like Salt did when Cookie made her carry a dish to the sink. The man stamped those chubby hands on his hips, stomped his boots in the gravel, and blew one excuse after another until Cookie and Pearl sauntered off.

Pearl sat back against the gate while Cookie stood, taking in the pinks and blues of the sunset. Her daddy would sit on his porch and brag about these colors like he'd never seen them before. "Tell me there ain't a God," Elijah would say. The colors made no difference to Cookie, but oh, how she loved seeing her daddy so happy and full of peace.

Big John wandered up, handed Cookie the bucket, and waited on a thank you while she slid between two strands of wire the man called a fence. Pearl followed.

"What's yo plan?" Cookie asked.

"Don't have one," he said, scratching his melon and staring at the gate.

"Try and hop it, Daddy."

"Or ease through that no-count fence like we did," Cookie said.

"Glad y'all are having fun," he said.

He moseyed to the fence and stared longer than a cow had a right.

"I reckon you stuck," Cookie said.

He aimed his flashlight at the car. "She looks okay besides the bumper. Pearl, back her up and give me room to bend this gate into shape."

The fool can't bend steel, Cookie told herself, as the car eased back toward the highway. Then she remembered one stout arm hauling one limp redneck across Harry's parking lot.

Sure enough, Big John gave a few shoves that made the gate look silly. "Nothing to it, ladies," he said with more than a touch of pride.

"Daddy, I knew you could do it."

"Just had to show Cookie a thing or two," he said.

Cookie let the mood stay light as they passed through the square and crossed the tracks. With Big John scrunched behind the wheel of Pearl's piddly-ass Pontiac, it was hard not to.

It was time for business when they pulled up to Cookie's house. She turned and looked Pearl over, balled up in the back seat with arms around her knees.

"Pearl, what makes a man beat a woman is like the cancer in yo momma's bones," she said. "Only the grave's got the cure." Cookie waited on the nod she didn't get. "You heard about Billy?"

"No ma'am."

When the girl said "ma'am," Cookie knew it was time for her story.

"Pearl, the biggest fool I ever acted was running off with Billy soon as I hit eighteen. We moved to Saint Louis right after the wedding. No money to rent our own place, we moved in with Billy's cousin and some painted-up woman that joker was living with.

"I found work cleaning and cooking for a white lady. Billy liked my job. Gave him a full day to lie around on the couch and spend my money on booze and worse.

"He'd been drinking the day I got back from work and found him cuddling on the couch with that woman. After I'd told those no-counts what I thought, Billy shot up and knocked me flat. Stood there cracking his knuckles and licking the corners of his lips, a little smile on his face.

"I glanced around the room and spotted a telephone on a table by the couch. I got to my feet, mumbled I was sorry for smarting off, and kept my mopey eyes on the carpet as I walked past him toward the phone. I picked up the handle like I was making a call. He was mouthing about his baby calling home when I swung with all my might. Whacked that handle across his ear with my first blow and cracked his nose with the second. Lawd, what I'd give for another sight of Billy wiggling on the carpet, squealing and bleeding like a stuck hog.

"I headed straight to the station and caught a bus. Decided on the way home I was done with men. My daddy walked on water. Yo daddy's a fine man. Most men are good when they wanna be good. And most women hang around until it's too late.

"Listen up, Pearl. I was young, and I was dumb. Dumb enough to marry a good-looking, sweet-talking boy like Billy. Don't play around with this, girl. Besides trusting in the Lawd, best thing I ever did was bust the hell outta Billy's head and leave the first time he hit me.

"Every hour of every day, some woman's telling herself, 'This time will be the last.' Next minute she's covering the man's ass and blaming her own self. Lots of those women wind up dead or wishing they were."

Cookie watched and waited, wondering if her words were sinking in.

"I know you both love me," Pearl said. "So does Myles."

19

OOKIE DIDN'T SLEEP MUCH THAT EVENING. Nothing close to the five hours she was used to. She kept asking the Lawd about lies and truth, Pearl and Myles and Shad.

The Lawd might've been listening, but He didn't mumble a word until daybreak. Well, it could've been one of His angels. Maybe the one who told Joseph to get the hell out of Bethlehem before Herod got hold of baby Jesus.

The voice was clear as could be: "Get up, Cookie. Big John needs you. Now."

Cookie's everyday walk, a run for most folks, put her at the gate in fifteen minutes on most days. She doubted it took ten that morning.

—✳ ✳ ✳—

COOKIE LOPED UP AS BIG JOHN was opening his gate. She asked where he was going but got no reply. The fool must've known she'd ask again.

"I appreciate your help yesterday," he said. "But where I'm going is no bidness of yours."

"You interested in what the Lawd just told me?"

"Nope."

She told him anyway, then climbed in and closed the door.

"Cookie, get out of my truck."

She leaned out the window, looking him over. The man acted a clown more than she cared for, grouchy when hungry or sleepy, even angry on occasion. But never rude.

"I see strange has paid you another visit," she said.

He cranked the engine, pulled through the gate, and shifted into park. "Your seat better be empty by the time I've closed the gate."

She was still chuckling as he turned right onto Highway 5.

"Where we going?" she asked. No answer. "I'd say old men were hard of hearing if the young ones listened."

"Myles's shop," he finally said.

"He'll be there at this hour?"

"Always is, from what I've heard."

"What's yo plan?"

"The Socratic method," he said. "Part of it anyway. Learned it from Albert Brown, the genius in our prison camp. You interested in the details?"

Cookie didn't know whether to cuss Big John, ask the Lawd what He'd gotten her into, or heed her momma's words and keep her loose tongue in the barn. Cookie listened to her momma for a change.

"I'll be asking questions," he said. "Trying to catch Myles in a lie. I also plan on acting like I think it's him."

"I don't think it is."

"Neither do I, but maybe it'll help us figure something out."

"Maybe yo fat paws will have claws for once."

The big gate was closing behind an eighteen-wheeler loaded with cars when they drove up to Myles's shop. He got up from his desk and headed for the door while they waited in front of Big John's truck.

"Big John, Miss Cookie," he said. "Surprised to see y'all so early."

"My daughter's been beaten twice since you married her," Big John said, glaring at the boy. "Anything you need to tell us?"

Myles stepped back, squinting at Big John. "Are you accusing me of beating my wife?"

"Should I?"

"You want the truth?"

"Why do you think I'm here?"

"The truth is, Shad lost his way when Holly died."

"You're blaming everything on your brother?"

"No," Myles said. "I should've seen this coming the first time."

"Then why was there a second time?"

"Because I gave my brother a second chance. I screwed up, Big John. I'm sorry."

"You oughta be."

Myles looked down, kicking at pebbles. He squatted, picked one up, and held it high.

"I'm the same man who fixed your rattle," he said. "And I've taken care of my brother." He handed the pebble to Big John. "Now we need to address Pearl's drinking and temper."

"My girl's always pushed the limits. She's never run into this."

"It was there before we married," Myles said, looking Big John in the eye. "You had to know."

"I know my daughter."

Myles nodded. "Pearl and Shad are a bad mix."

"You're comparing that louse to my daughter?"

Myles shook his head. "This is tearing me to pieces, Big John. We all want what's best for Pearl. And this marriage I'm trying to hold together."

"How do you explain the cut on her forehead *before* the wedding?"

"I wasn't even there, but somehow I'm the bad guy?" Big John tossed the pebble over his back and crossed his arms. Myles raised a finger. "Wait right here." He ran into the shop and came out with a Bible that must've weighed ten pounds. "My father gave me our family Bible when I moved. Hold it and I'll swear I've never—"

Cookie whirled at the sound of dogs barking and growling up a storm behind the tall fence she'd been worried about a few months ago. "Trouble with break-ins," Myles had said.

"Sorry," he said. "We keep the dogs out at night and haven't locked them up yet." He eased forward and rested a hand on Big John's shoulder. "Your own brother to your wife and only daughter, the way you've held up is beyond me."

Big John stared at his shoulder until the hand was gone, then turned for the truck without a word. Cookie did the same.

She let a mile pass, maybe two. "I got no idea why the Lawd told me to get up and come yo way." He rolled his eyes. "How come you white folks believe the Lawd quit talking right after He gave us the Word?" He reached for the pink bandana and blew his nose. "All right, tell me what you think happened back there."

"You and the Lord will figure it out," he said, shoving the bandana into his back pocket.

"Drop me off at the damn house."

"I'd rather you come back to the farm. Shine'll want to know everything. Can't say I'll be much help."

"The Lawd must be speaking to *you* now," Cookie said. "Except for my Victry, I can't remember the last time I heard a man mouth those words. Probably 'cause there ain't a last time." His eyes darted from one side of the road to the other. "What you thinking, Big John?"

"Myles either told us the truth or lied with it. I'm not sure which."

* * *

COOKIE HAD EXPECTED TO FIND SHINE on the porch or in the den, but she hadn't left the bed, from what Cookie could tell. Big John sat, took his lady's hand, and rubbed her neck. Cookie stood by the door, wanting to cuss and trying not to cry.

"How you feeling, angel?" she asked, though pain was written across every wrinkle on her best friend's face.

Shine smiled. Cookie looked away, chewing her lip.

"You're not going to cry, are you?" Shine asked. Cookie didn't answer. "Where did you come from, anyway? Don't tell me you've given up on work and fishing."

Cookie walked to the foot of the bed. "The Lawd woke me up and said Big John needed my help. I got no idea what the Lawd was thinking, but I rode with yo man to see Myles."

"Albert Brown and William Shakespeare," Big John said, as if both men had just strolled into the room.

"What the hell?" Cookie asked.

"Albert called it the three-step dance," Big John said. "Lying, playing the victim, and shifting the blame. Said he'd first seen it from this preacher who'd been caught fooling around with a woman in his church. When lying didn't work, the preacher played the victim and carried on about all the gossip and *false* accusations leveled against him. Step three, the preacher got his church buddies to form a committee and investigate the whole deal, then worked behind the scenes to make sure they pinned it on Albert's deddy. The poor fella ended up killing himself."

"Myles let his brother take the blame today," Cookie said. "Wife too. Nearly cried over the marriage he's trying to mend."

"He also blamed himself for letting his brother loose," Big John said.

"I reckon it all depends on whether Myles was lying or not," Cookie said.

"He was," Shine said. "It came to me this morning."

Big John smacked the side of his head. "Albert tied his three-step to Shakespeare. 'Thou protesteth too much,' or something along those lines. Albert said the guilty will rant and rave in a way that tells you they're lying. Myles didn't."

"'Something's not adding up,'" Shine said. "You remember those words, Big John?"

"It does the more I've thought about it. Shine, you saw how they were acting on the porch while I was playing with my bandana."

"Would've told Pearl to head to the house, their house, if I wasn't taking Myles fishing," Cookie said.

"I suppose y'all are also sold on yesterday's bloody nose and busted lip," Shine said.

"The way Pearl flipped from Myles to Shad kept me up last night," he said. "And sent me to Myles's shop this morning. Not saying I'm *sold*, but I feel better now."

"You're making this too complicated," Shine said. "It's *simple math*, Big John."

He turned. "Cookie, you heard Pearl when I couldn't get through the gate: 'Daddy, I love Myles.' How do you explain that away?"

"Hard to do," Cookie said. "Though it could be the same ole story. Girl meets boy and falls in a love and a lust bright enough to blind the eyes and clog the brain."

"A *gentleman* came along and treated our girl like a lady," Shine said. "Smooth as Myles is, I bet he's got Pearl believing everything is her fault. Probably believes it himself. At some point a con man buys his own lies."

"Two sides to every story," Big John said.

"A truth made a lie if there ever was one," Shine said, reminding Cookie of Big John's last words in the truck. "From thought and word to deed, there's a mark on every slate. But that doesn't mean every situation has two sides to it. Not of what matters. Were there *two sides* to the story on Albert's daddy? Is Myles's face battered and blue like Pearl's?"

"Shine, we both know our girl's been fudging with the truth ever since she could talk."

"There's no excuse for hitting a woman," Shine said. "You of all people should know that."

"We don't know who did what," he said. "My money's on Shad."

Cookie nodded. Shine didn't.

"Dying helps a person see," she said.

"You might have a different take if you'd been there," Cookie said.

"I might," Shine said. "Myles is that good."

PART VI

BIG JOHN HAD LISTENED TO SHINE that morning. "Quit stewing and take the next step," she'd said before he took off for Myles's shop.

Big John didn't listen that afternoon. "Don't do it," Shine told him. "You'll do more harm than good."

Big John barreled past the secretary and into the sheriff's office, looking for answers. Minutes later he barged out, wanting to kill.

He drove for hours, to New Albany and Oxford and Memphis. The road had been a god in his trucking days. War in Germany to hell on the home front, the miles helped him heal. The road, his god, was no help that day.

He pulled up to his gate, for once relieved by the sight of the dark house.

20

Cookie

COOKIE ANSWERED THE PHONE WITH A growl.

"Shine might be right about Myles," Big John said. "I dropped in on Sheriff Mathis yesterday afternoon."

"You expected *him* to help out? That afternoon in a cotton field with my daddy must've slipped yo mind."

"I wasn't looking for help, Cookie. I wanted to see where Mathis stood on all this. To hear his voice and watch his eyes."

"And?"

"With Myles's shop in Hill County, I assumed they knew each other. Had no idea they were good buddies."

"Mathis told you that?"

"Sat back with boots on his desk while I told him the gist of my concerns. Then he sat up, leaned across the desk, and whispered, 'Big John, I'll deny every word I'm fixing to say, but know this. One, I got a long memory. And two, I consider Myles a good friend. We drink whiskey and play cards on a regular basis. Like you and Elijah used to.'"

Cookie threw the phone against the wall and slammed the door on her way out. She stopped on the porch steps and tried to steady her breathing. Tried.

Sheriff Mathis, the name above all names that boiled her blood. *Let the dogs forget and the saints forgive*, Cookie told herself. From a belt on Big John's farm to a rope at her house, Sheriff Mathis was a name she would never forget. Never forgive.

She took a seat and did her best to ignore the men sitting on porches and tilting bottles, smoking and joking like it was payday. She watched the children running through dirt yards and jumping over potholes the town called a street. Their shouts and squeals brought Cookie out of herself.

"Cookie," the voice said.

"I'm doing fine now, Lawd. I got these chillun to listen to."

"Who made them?" He asked.

"You showed up to ask me that?"

"No. I want you to remember My good when you're looking at the bad."

"Hard to do, Lawd."

"I never said it was easy."

"Who did?" she asked.

No answer, which was fine by Cookie. She was ready to finish her call with Big John.

He picked up on the first ring.

"Keep going," Cookie said.

"You okay?"

"'Elijah' crossing the sheriff's fat lips was more than I could bear. But I cooled off a touch. Tell me what else Mathis had to say."

"Well, after that part on your deddy, he told me not to expect any help from the sheriff's department. Said Myles was a fine man who'd given one of his deputies the money to cover the medical bills for his girl. She'd gotten bad sick and seen a doctor in Birmingham."

"Help folks and you hook 'em. Preachers know that trick. Legit ones like Sam and Jeremiah don't use it. Our Jeremiah preaches too long and eats too much, but he's the same in good times and bad, even when his own ass is on the line. Also fesses up when he messes up. Imagine that for a man."

"Cookie, we're not talking about preachers right now."

"I am," she said. "Watching those chillun and talking with the Lawd lifted my mood a notch."

The sound of hairy nostrils taking a long breath filled the phone. "What's the Lord's number, Cookie? I'll give Him a call."

Big John's smart lip showed up at the strangest times. Least the bird hadn't acted a fool since he'd asked Cookie to his own funeral.

"White folks never learn," she said. "Go ahead."

"Well, Mathis went straight from his deputy's girl to mine. Said Pearl was on her own and no saint to begin with. Also said Myles wasn't surprised when I *ambushed* him at his shop."

"What did you say to that?"

"Asked questions and acted like I knew, same as with Myles yesterday morning. First asked the sheriff where he stashed the money Myles was paying him to look the other way on whatever bidness the boy was running behind the walls of his shop."

"I bet that sent the sheriff's chins to jiggling."

"Mathis jumped up from his chair and said he had better things to do than listen to me attack his character. I stood and leaned across the desk. Our faces nearly touched when I asked how much he got paid to let Myles get away with beating on my girl. He was either too riled or rattled to answer."

"The sheriff's a bully not a crook," Cookie said, recalling what Big John had told her daddy in a cotton field that day. He sighed. "Anyhow, sounds like Myles had the sheriff sold before you got there."

"I'm afraid so."

"What about Myles and his whiskey?"

"He told me he'd never taken a drink."

"I reckon Myles ain't straight if the sheriff's spouting the truth," Cookie said. "He could be lying for his brother with half a tongue and keeping his ass in Biloxi with the other."

"Who knows? Mathis and Myles to even Pearl."

"I don't know what to believe," Cookie said, realizing those words had never crossed her lips. "But we can't wait around, Big John. Lots of women wind up dead or wishing they were, like I was telling Pearl the other night."

"Let me talk it over with Shine and sleep on it," he said. "We gotta find a way, some way, to flush the truth out of Myles."

— ✳ ✳ ✳ —

COOKIE WAS LEAVING FOR LORE'S HOUSE when Big John knocked on her door. She wasted no time asking what he was doing.

"I wrote a poem," he said, like it was the normal thing to do.

"A what?"

"A poem."

"Man's beating on yo girl, and you standing here jawing about a poem?"

"I was too worked up to sleep last night," he said. "Finally got up around three o'clock and made a pot of coffee. Sat down at the kitchen table and was taking my first sip when it hit me. Next thing I knew, I'd scratched it all out on a napkin."

"You sipping coffee or smoking dope?"

He flashed a grin she wanted to slap. "'Trust your instinct to the end, though you can render no reason.' I owe that beauty to Albert and Emerson."

"Shee-it. You better off talking Shakespeare with that sheriff than wasting time on a poem."

"Wrote my first to Momma when I was in prison camp. For Mother's Day. Maybe this will be my last."

"Well, I reckon it won't hurt long as you keep it to yoself."

"Too late," he said. "On my way here, I stopped at the square and dropped her off at the *Hill County News*. Bought a full-page ad for tomorrow morning."

"Shine know about this?"

"Thought I'd talk it over with you first." Cookie shook her head. Strange had now taken a back seat to crazy. "I named it 'The Bride' and put Myles's name in there. Also mentioned his sheriff buddy. Comes on mighty strong, I'll admit, but I'm hoping it'll show us what Myles is made of. What have I got to lose?"

"Sho' ain't a brain," she said, closing the door in his face.

Most daddies did one of three things when a man whupped on their girl. They either looked the other way, tucked tail and ran like a stray mutt, or tried talking it out until it was too late. Cookie's daddy went for blood that first go-round.

It took more than a strange bird to scratch out a poem.

— ✳ ✳ ✳ —

THE NEXT MORNING COOKIE FOUND LORE slurping his coffee and slapping the newspaper. He'd spread the *Hill County News* across the breakfast table and was carrying on like Ole Miss had won a football game. He wasted a full minute bragging on "our dern poet" before she told him to read it while she fried four eggs and loaded the skillet with enough bacon to feed a whole football team instead of one man on his first breakfast of the day.

The Bride
He's one helluva con, the best I've seen.
Draping wool over eyes, making nice of mean.
Myles played so well, this deddy for a fool.
His smile so slick, his words so cool.
Cried it wasn't his fault, did nothing wrong.
Busted lip and nose, sang a different song.
Who knows what's up, behind the walls of your shop?
Crooked sheriff in the pocket, makes you hard to stop.
The posse's got your back, but my horse is strong.
And when I do catch up, your hide won't last long.
Guess you think I'm soft, a Teddy Bear of fat.
Another bruise and you'll see, Deddy Bear has a bat.

Damn poem was the talk of town that week, both sides of the tracks. Some thought Big John had gone mad. Others said he was a hero. Everybody knew he was in one helluva bind.

21

Slide

I TURNED FIFTEEN A FEW DAYS AFTER Big John's poem made the *Hill County News* a bestseller for a day. January 10, 1971, should've been my best day ever. A driver's license in the back pocket of a Mississippi boy went a long way with the girls, and a long-nosed kid with big ears and a name like Slide needed all the help he could get.

My folks hadn't said a word about "The Bride." No surprise on Deddy. But Momma? She'd answered every question with a direct order to march straight home after school.

I didn't know what to think of Big John or his poem. Was *Deddy Bear* any better with a bat than a crowbar? Did *Teddy Bear* have claws, or had Big John gone soft in his old age? I'd heard Cookie's story about him sticking a shotgun up the sheriff's throat some twenty-five years ago. But not five months ago, I'd watched Big John hit the gravel of Harry's Bait Shop and lay there without a fight. The redneck might've killed him if not for Myles.

Myles knew how to use a crowbar, and that did have me worried. Was he on the warpath over Big John dragging his business and name through the mud?

Momma wouldn't say who'd been invited to my birthday party at the farmhouse that afternoon, but as grown-ups in our parts had the irksome habit of inviting even cousins and in-laws they hated to family gatherings, I figured Myles had made the list. Would he come?

Would Pearl?

— ✴ ✴ ✴ —

WE'D MADE IT HALFWAY DOWN THE gravel drive when Deddy hit the brakes and rammed the gear into park. He threw his door open, lit out through the pecan grove, and fell to a knee at his brother's feet.

Propped against his favorite pecan tree, Big John didn't look up when Deddy yelled his name. Deddy grabbed him by the shoulders and shook until Big John raised his chin.

I figured Big John was in bad shape when he didn't call to sing "Happy Birthday" like he'd done every birthday I could remember. I never imagined this.

"Scoot over and drive us to the house," Momma said. "You're old enough to crunch fifty yards of gravel without wrecking this spiffy ride of ours."

Momma was trying to make light of a heavy load, but I could tell she was every bit as rattled as I was. The smack of her everyday voice had simmered down to a scratchy drawl that sounded like a girl with a bad cold.

— ✴ ✴ ✴ —

THE WHEELCHAIR WAS FACING THE FIREPLACE when we stepped inside. Momma grabbed my arm and held me in place. I stared at the pretty white hair and sagging head. Shine didn't stir when I said her name.

"Shine!" I cried out. No response. My aunt was dead. "Aunt Shine!"

She lifted her head and let out a laugh. "Slide, you're not the only practical joker in this family. Come get me and we'll have us a party."

Momma let go of my arm, but I couldn't move. I was still frozen in place when she parked the wheelchair at my feet.

Shine held out her arms. "You better give me a birthday hug before I send Ethel for a switch. Fifteen whacks plus one to grow on will loosen you up a notch."

I cried, hugging my aunt with all the might I thought her weak bones could handle. I straightened out and wiped my eyes. Her eyes were bright and beaming. Shiny. How could a person be sunny in the middle of a storm? I wondered. Storms, more like it.

She smiled. "Thought I better one-up you while I had the chance."

I took off for the bathroom. I leaned against the sink, rubbing my eyes and gazing in the mirror. Had Myles done the same after Sam asked about his sisters?

I walked back into the den to find Uncle Lore, Salt, and Cookie circled around Shine's wheelchair.

"Big John better get himself together and straggle in before I make one of y'all push a wheelchair through a pecan grove," Shine said.

"Cash ain't the first person I'd choose to cheer a fella up," Momma said.

"What the hell is Big John doing out there?" Cookie asked.

Shine grinned. "Strange birds have their ways."

"Slide, my boy," Lore said. He picked me up for one of his all-belly bear hugs. "What are you now, twelve?"

"He's only eleven," Salt said. "I'm twelve."

After Cookie had given me one of her quick one-armed side hugs, we all lingered in the den, trying to make small talk while waiting on the men outside. Nobody mentioned Pearl or Myles.

Twenty minutes or so passed before Big John followed Deddy into the house. Hands at his side, Big John squinted at the door as if wondering how to close one until Shine reminded him of my party.

"Oh, happy birthday," he mumbled without saying my name or looking my way.

"Big John, go freshen up and get out of those nasty overalls," Shine said. "We'll get the cake and ice cream ready."

He trudged off toward the bedroom.

A birthday boy's head start was a big deal when it came to sharing food of any kind, much less sweets, with Lore and Salt. I'd finished my cake and moved on to ice cream when they strolled up with plates that appeared to hold another gallon of ice cream and at least one more cake.

Cookie marched over to *Babygirl* and preached hell on the evils of overeating. Salt grinned with every bite. Her plate might as well've been licked clean by Annabelle by the time Big John lumbered into the den.

"You look ready for your own funeral," Shine said.

Everybody laughed except Big John. With a face stiffer than his zipper boots and tighter than his polyester pants, he walked to the little chair by the fireplace, sat, and stared at the dark bricks.

I was opening my first present when the door opened.

"There's our girl!" Shine called out. "Come have a seat."

Pearl closed the door, squinted at her deddy, and made her way to a folding chair next to the couch.

"Happy birthday," she said.

I nodded and forced a smile.

How many presents did I open? Who gave me the button-down shirt and khaki pants? Did I ever say thank you? No idea.

That said, I had no trouble remembering three other questions that raced across my mind as I fumbled with boxes and wrapping paper. Why had Big John been sitting in the pecan grove? What was Pearl thinking? And where was Myles?

22

Cookie

IN COOKIE'S EYES, THE BIRTHDAY PARTY was everything a boy could ask for. Except fun.

Slide had sweated through his last present when Pearl stood, glared at her daddy, and jutted her chin toward the porch. Maybe Cookie should've waited on an invite to join their little party. She didn't.

Backed up against the screen closest to the door, Big John would've been standing on the moon if he'd been able to. Pearl was in slapping range but didn't need a hand. The ice in her eyes beat whatever a slap could do.

"Why have you been ringing my phone off the hook?" she asked.

"Well, I just wanted to check on you," he said, looking surprised she'd known it was him.

"Your poem is all the *checking* I need."

"What did Myles say about it?" Cookie asked, aiming to take the heat off Pearl's daddy and learn something about her husband.

"He's too mad to talk," Pearl said. "Hardly ever around anyway."

Big John straightened up and leaned forward, no longer looking confused or sounding scared. "Where has Myles been?"

"Where do you think? At the damn shop."

"He hasn't mentioned my poem?"

"I think he's past words. Thanks to you."

"Darling, I'm sorry if—"

"Don't start that again," Pearl said, her finger an inch from his nose. "I'm leaving before I lose my temper. Don't call me again."

With that she hoofed it to her Pontiac and drove off, leaving Cookie with two questions. One, what in the Lawd's name was Big John thinking every time he tried Pearl's number? Two, why had he been sitting by himself in that mess of trees he was so proud of? Problem was, he didn't look up to answering one simple question, much less two hard ones.

✳ ✳ ✳

COOKIE USED THE PHONE SHE HATED to call Shine seven times over the next four days.

Shine hadn't seen Pearl and wouldn't talk about Myles. When she'd lie about feeling the same as the day before, Cookie told her to take the pills Big John had gotten for her pain. Shine would fuss about him spending money on medicine she'd sworn she wouldn't take, then say Cookie had more important things to worry about. Another lie.

The morning Shine called and asked her to stop by the farmhouse after work, Cookie didn't wait on work. Lore could eat both breakfasts at Cuz's Diner after he'd gotten Salt up and off to school.

Big John was sitting by the fireplace when Cookie opened the door. In Shine's wheelchair. She gave the man a long stare and headed for the bedroom.

She eased up to the door and peered inside. Shine, stretched out on the bed with her eyes closed, had hidden the pain longer than any man and most women, but the wrinkles and bones of her face could not tell a lie.

Cookie walked in and whispered her friend's name. As Shine sat up, her body went to twitching every whichaway. She caught her breath and mumbled a "Hey."

"Take 'em," Cookie said, pointing at the pills next to the glass of water Big John refilled every time she took a sip. "Yo man is right about one thing."

"Was he sitting in my wheelchair?"

"Sho' nuff."

"At least you didn't catch him dialing Pearl's number."

"He up to that again?"

"Dozens of times since y'all's talk on the porch. He must think I've lost my hearing too."

"A dead armadillo could hear him *reaching* for the phone," Cookie said, hoping to lighten her lady's spirits.

No hint of a smile crossed Shine's lips. "He usually picks up and puts it right back in the cradle. But I've heard him twirling the dial before hanging up."

"I know you asked him about it."

"Said he was calling Cash, but I doubt that. Someone's always at their house."

Shine had a point. Cash had been working long hours, using their one set of wheels. Ethel, no fan of walking, hadn't let Slide visit the farmhouse since the party.

"Any word on Pearl?" Cookie asked. Shine looked away. "Shine?"

"She's been stopping by every night."

"You told me Pearl hadn't shown her face."

"She's been parking at the gate and sneaking up to the porch after Big John's gone to bed." Shine pointed at the stack of letters on her dresser. "Leaving notes on how much she loves me and hates herself for not being here."

"My Lawd."

"She finally broke down and came in yesterday afternoon. Ignored Big John and walked straight to this bed. She wouldn't discuss Myles. Couldn't talk much anyway. She held my hand and soaked it with tears like I'd just taken my last breath."

"Yo girl has a tender heart under her sass."

"I hope she forgives her daddy one day."

"I'll see to that."

"Cookie, even you can't make a person forgive."

Shine looked her over with a love strong enough to kill. Cookie dropped her head, fighting back tears.

"Don't start," Shine said, a cry in her own voice. "Not you."

Cookie nodded, working to get hold of herself. "Why did you call me today?"

Shine glanced at the bedside table. "I won't take that medicine because I need my mind until the end." She rested her head on the pillow. "Cookie, before I die, Big John is going to make me a promise. And I want you to hold him to it."

"What promise?"

"About Myles," Shine said.

But she wouldn't say anything else.

⋇ ⋇ ⋇

COOKIE HAD SLAMMED HER FRONT DOOR more than once since the night her daddy died, but never like today. She stomped from one end of her den to the next, telling the Lawd what she thought of Him putting cancer in Shine while her sister strutted from one prayer meeting to the next.

Misry. The last time Misry *fired* Cookie must've been ten years ago. Victry was right at sixteen and Salt nearly three when Misry strolled in from one of those meetings, Bible in hand, and accused Cookie of stealing. Knowing the children needed a woman in the house who didn't treat them like wasted breath, Cookie had put up with more of Misry's evil tongue than she cared to admit. But when the woman called her a "no-good nigger," Cookie marched straight to the den.

"Lore, wake up!" she hollered.

"Tell Cookie she's fired," Misry said, running up to his recliner.

"What happened?" he asked, wiping sleep from his eyes.

"Let's stick with today," Misry said. "The dress I'm wearing for tomorrow's Bible study hasn't been ironed. Your bird dogs wouldn't eat the breakfast she cooked this morning. Now I can't find the china tea set you inherited from your mother." She pointed at Cookie's bulging eyes and clenched fists. "And she stole it."

"Lore, I ain't taking this shit," Cookie said. "You got a decision to make. Now. Either fire me or tell this woman to get outta my face. For good."

He leaned back in the recliner and folded his arms.

"Who'd you say inherited that china?" he asked Misry. "Not to mention the mansion you've lived in for over twenty years." He pulled a cigar from his shirt pocket and propped it in the corner of his mouth. "While we're at it, who signs Cookie's check every Friday?"

"What exactly are you saying?" Misry asked.

"I'm saying Victry and Salt need a real momma. Besides telling 'em what pathetic little sinners they are, you might as well've forgotten their names the second they were born. They need Cookie."

"The devil is in you," Misry said.

"Save it for the faithful," he said. "You got most everybody at your church fooled, I suppose. You make one helluva righteous cheerleader for the folks who buy your bull. Not us."

Misry stormed over and stuck a finger in Cookie's face. "This is all your doing!"

"You a miserable woman," Cookie said, slapping the hand away. "*Misry* is yo name from here on out."

Misry fooled the fools. Had Myles fooled them all?

Cookie stretched out on the couch to ponder that question. Was Shine right about Myles?

Before and after the wedding, Cookie had done her best to see through the smoke. Speaking of smoke, she'd never smelled it on Myles's clothes or breath. Same with that liquor the sheriff mentioned. She wouldn't have minded a pouch of Levi Garrett in a back pocket or a can of Copenhagen in a front—Hank could water a whole pasture with his spitting—but there was none to be found on Myles. Or in his truck, which she rummaged through one evening while he was helping Shine with the dishes.

Cookie paid no mind to the way he doted on Pearl. Any man could act right to get where he wanted on a woman. A man who took a woman to church for the first time she had a say in the matter? Cookie couldn't remember one of them.

A white man who treated her like a white woman, a lady to boot? Myles made number four on that list. Those hands made number one when it came to catching and cleaning fish.

Skin to Scripture, Myles was smooth. But passing Cookie's gut took more than smooth. Her gut saw two colors, black and white. Had no use for that color in the middle. Gray was a cold rain that froze you bone-deep but didn't make snow to give you hope.

What color was Myles where it counted? Cookie had missed by a hair but never a whole man. Was Myles the first?

Nope, her gut was still pointing at Shad.

23

COOKIE WAS ARGUING WITH LORE ABOUT fixing his third sandwich when the phone rang. He picked up and said "Hello." He listened, his whole body stiff as the dead. He mouthed Shine's name and handed Cookie the phone.

Pearl was in the hospital. Cracked ribs. A punctured lung. Teeth knocked out. Cuts and bruises all over and Lawd knew what else. The poor girl still hadn't come to.

Shine wanted Cookie at the hospital. Cash too, and they both knew why.

—✳ ✳ ✳—

PEARL DIDN'T NEED PALE SKIN TO show what had gone down. Cookie's would've told this story of black and blue. The girl was out cold with bandages on her face and tubes in her arms. A sheet covered the rest. She looked worse than what Shine had said.

Big John sat in a chair next to the bed, holding her hand. Cash walked over and put a hand on his brother's shoulder. Big John didn't look up. His chin was too low to see Cookie standing across the bed. She cleared her throat and said his name.

She said his name again, this time a touch louder. He raised his head and set his blurry eyes on his girl.

"What did the doctors say?" Cookie asked.

He slumped forward, gently rubbing Pearl's hand against his cheek.

"They say she'll live," he said. "But probably won't be able to have children."

Was Pearl raped? Cookie asked herself. Big John was too shaken up to cry, much less handle that question.

"Any word on Shad or Myles?" she asked.

Big John couldn't answer. Or didn't want to? She'd never seen Cash cry, but now the boy was wiping his cheeks. Too mad for tears, she stared at Pearl while thinking of Shad.

Cookie wanted answers but decided to wait. Shine's broken bones and heart didn't need to be alone. Cookie said a quick prayer, starting with Pearl and ending with vengeance. Cash knelt and wrapped his arms around his brother.

They left Big John in the same chair, holding the same limp hand.

— ✳ ✳ ✳ —

"THEY'RE BOTH GUILTY," CASH SAID, AS they drove toward the farmhouse. "Shad and Myles."

Cookie leaned against the door, looking him over. Reading Cash was no problem on most days. Every day for that matter. But he didn't look sad or lost as he pulled off the road, cut the switch, and met her eyes.

"Why do you say that?" she asked.

"I never liked either one."

"You didn't exactly know either one."

"I met Shad at the rehearsal dinner. I watched him at the wedding and reception."

She could see why Cash didn't care for Shad. Who did?

"And Myles?" she asked.

Cash propped his elbow on the steering wheel and gripped his chin. "Myles reminded me of this major in Vietnam. He'd pray with the camp chaplain one minute, cozy up to his colonel the next, then send his men out to kill or be killed, before moseying into his tent for a nap. And the man knew how to cover his ass when the time came. Nothing was ever his fault."

"What made you see Myles in that man?"

"I don't know, Cookie. Ethel says I find thunderstorms on a bluebird day, and she's right. I figured it was another misguided hunch of mine. Big John and everyone else thought Myles hung the moon."

"You right on that count. Pearl was hardly the only one in love with him."

"I should've said something."

"You think Myles nearly killed his wife?"

"I didn't say that, Cookie. He's probably dealing with Shad as we speak. But if nothing else, Myles has been lying for his brother, and that makes him responsible."

✳ ✳ ✳

COOKIE WALKED INTO THE HOUSE AND LOOKED BACK, waiting on Cash. Feet on the porch and eyes on his feet, he asked if he could drive her home and come back to watch over Shine. Said it was the least he could do for everything she'd done for Slide and his brother. The way Cash stood there all stiff and sweet like almost changed her mind. But Shine's last breath was a-coming, and Cookie wanted all she could get.

Watching Cash drive away, Cookie had to admit she was proud of the boy. He'd been sober and sound until Vietnam grabbed him by the throat. Now he was off the bottle and back at work. Working hard, too. She chuckled to herself, wondering how the best handyman in Hope Springs had come from the same momma and daddy as Big John.

She sat on the couch and rested her eyes a spell, but there was no rest in her spirit. Not with Shine in the next room.

That night was the second longest of Cookie's life. Shine would groan in her sleep until the pain woke her, then turn from one side to the other, searching for a spot that didn't hurt so bad. It broke Cookie's heart clean in two.

✳ ✳ ✳

AT SEVEN O'CLOCK THE NEXT MORNING, Cookie heard tires crushing gravel. Figuring it was Cash, she kept her eyes on the photograph by the fireplace. Fresh out of pilot school, Big John looked trim and almost handsome in his military suit. The man was puffed with pride no doubt, but not with himself. His wide eyes and big smile were locked on the cute little bride under his arm. His Shine.

The screen door didn't make a sound. Neither did the porch floor that whined with the wind. Cookie didn't hear the front door open, much less the steps heading her way. She flinched when the man said her name.

She looked up, shaking her head and thinking of the racket Big John would've made, and told Cash to wait there while she checked on Shine.

Cookie opened the bedroom door and flinched for the second time in two minutes, but the grind of a crooked door on thirsty hinges hadn't stirred Shine. Lawd, it lifted Cookie's spirits to see her friend resting easy for a change.

One glance at Cash told Cookie his spirits needed a lift as well. "What the hell you been doing?" she asked. "Those hinges on Shine's door already busted one of my eardrums. You know Big John can't use a can of oil. Didn't Shine put you in charge of looking after this place?"

A shy little smile touched Cash's lips. "Sorry, Miss Cookie. Guess I've been loafing on the job."

"Loafing. Here you working twelve-hour days on paying jobs and won't even say so. Hell, yo brother's got more excuses than time if that's possible."

Cash wasn't much for words, but he sounded like Victry on the first part of their drive to the hospital. Wouldn't stop asking how Shine had slept, and so forth.

"You a good man," Cookie said.

"No, I'm not," Cash said, quick and firm-like.

"I know about yo bottle."

"That's not half of it."

"I know about Vietnam."

"No, you don't," he said. "Nobody does."

Ethel was always on Cash for letting folks slide on paying for work he'd done. The woman really hit the roof when he'd go back to the same house and fix something new without taking a check for the old. The boy who couldn't say "no" had said it twice in less than a minute. Said it like there was no doubt in his mind.

24

COOKIE OPENED THE HOSPITAL ROOM DOOR to see Big John standing at the foot of the bed. His wide back kept her from seeing, but not from hearing, his girl.

Cookie left Cash at the door and walked to the side of the bed. Pearl kept moaning like she was trying to come to. Her eyes cracked open a few times. She passed out, breathing like a bride ought to.

"How'd it go last night?" Cookie asked. "Big John?"

"Not good. Ribs nearly killed her when she moved or struggled to breathe with that hole in her lung. Nightmares kept waking her up. She'd gaze at the ceiling and conk back out."

"She say who did this?"

He shook his head. "I'm glad she didn't stay awake long enough to see me bawling like the day James died."

Pearl's body gave a twitch at the name of the brother she'd never known. Her eyes opened, circled the room, and landed on her daddy.

"What are you doing?" she asked. "Where am I?"

He hurried to her side. He swallowed and tried to clear his throat.

"The hospital," Cookie said. "Go on back to sleep now."

He leaned and propped his cheek against Pearl's good ear.

"I love you," he whispered. "Love you so much."

She didn't nod or say a word.

Cookie expected tears when Big John straightened out, but his eyes were clear and hard.

"Pearl, tell me who hurt you," he said.

"She can't handle that right now," Cookie said. "Let her rest."

"I can talk," Pearl said.

Cookie shouldn't have been surprised—Pearl was tough and a woman to boot—but she was.

"All right," Cookie said. "Give us a quick rundown."

"I lied and lied and lied," Pearl said. "It was Myles every time."

Myles. Every time. The woman who didn't like to sit took a quick seat. Cookie eyed the bed and the girl in it, and felt a fool for trusting a devil more than an angel.

"Tell me about this time," Big John said.

She looked down, then up at her daddy's heaving chest. She met his eyes.

"Myles had been in a terrible mood since your poem hit the paper, working daylight to dark and acting like I'd never been born whenever he was around. That morning I decided I'd had enough. Went to the shop and found him on the phone arguing about a shipment of stolen cars he'd been expecting. He glanced up, saw me standing at his desk, and slammed the phone without a word. He ran over and grabbed my arm and didn't let go until he shoved me behind the wheel of my Pontiac. He followed me home and—"

"Myles did this to you because of that?" Big John asked, gritting his teeth.

"Let her finish," Cookie said.

"Myles acted like he'd simmered down once we got home. In that high-pitched everyday voice of his, he said he was hungry and asked what I'd overheard." Pearl sighed. "When I told him *stolen* was the only word that mattered, he jabbed me with his finger and shouted that I'd better learn to stay out of his business. I slapped his hand and pushed him away." Pearl tilted her head and closed an eye like that would help her see what no woman wanted to see. "He took off his belt and started whipping me. I kicked and screamed until he threw me on the ground and pounded me with his fists. I must've blacked out at some point."

Big John whirled and slammed both palms against the wall.

"Daddy, this is between Myles and me. He's pretty much kept his temper in check until now."

"Pretty much," Big John said, clawing at the wall with his fingernails. "Until now." He turned. "From the cut on your forehead to a black eye to a busted lip and bloody—"

"Pipe down," Pearl said, glaring at her daddy like a poem had broken her bones.

"That poem only sharpened his fangs," Cookie said. "The wolf was there all along."

"You don't know him," Pearl said.

"I know you blind like the women I warned you about," Cookie said. "You hear a word of my story on Billy?"

"Myles always has a plan," Pearl said, again showing no sign of hearing Cookie's words. "Part of him comes unglued when he loses control of that plan. All of him gets angry. The poem. My surprising him at his shop. Going off about stolen cars, then slapping and pushing him. None of it fit his plans, and he exploded." She looked away. "Maybe we can work something out."

"Too late for that," Big John said.

"But I still think—"

"You ain't thinking," Cookie said. "Let us do that for a while."

"Stay out of it, Daddy," Pearl said, almost crying. "Please."

Big John's eyes were now darting every whichaway. He trotted over to Cash and whispered in his ear. Cash answered with a locked jaw and cold eyes. Big John walked back to the bed and sat. He pulled out his bandana and wiped his face. He nodded.

"Okay, Pearl," he said. "Okay."

Pearl studied her daddy for a good while. She made half a smile, leaning forward until the pain stopped her. She eased back and closed her eyes.

Once she'd drifted off to sleep, Big John figured it was time for a pity party. He went to blaming himself for the deaths of his best friend in the war, his only son, and Cookie's daddy before carrying on like he'd put Shine on a deathbed and Pearl in a hospital bed.

"Pearl has every right to blame me," he said. "From pushing her to marry Myles to the poem, I deserve it all."

Cookie pointed at the bed. "The man who did this deserves it all. Myles needs killing before he kills yo daughter."

"Cookie, you saw me chuck my only gun into the pond after I nearly blew the sheriff's head off. You remember my vow to the Lord."

"You were ready to kill ten minutes ago." He shrugged. "There is a time to lie, Big John. And kill."

He stretched his legs and stared at his boots. "Pearl will be in this hospital for another two weeks. She'll be safe here."

The look on his face said he had no more to say. Fine by Cookie. There would come a time for talk. And vengeance.

"Cash, we need to check on Shine," she said.

"Big John, why don't you come with us?" he asked.

"I hate to leave my girl by herself."

Cash walked over and gave his brother's arm a gentle squeeze. "Let me stay with her."

Big John watched Pearl's every breath like it was her last.

He stood. "Call me if anything changes. I'll be back before dark."

"I'll stay the night if you want," Cash said.

Big John hugged his brother and mumbled "Thank you."

—✳ ✳ ✳—

HOSPITAL TO TRUCK, BIG JOHN DIDN'T say a word. Neither did Cookie, for the eyes of Cash had her full attention.

Big John was pulling out of the parking lot when she asked what he'd whispered to his brother. The worst liar this side of the grass answered with a line of mumbo jumbo about thanking Cash for staying with his girl. Cookie couldn't help but chuckle.

"I also wanted his advice on something," Big John added, as if Cash had opened his mouth.

"Advice on what?" she asked. "Planting that garden you never get around to?"

"When's the last time you planted a garden?"

"The last time I *said* I was going to. Never."

"Let it go, Cookie."

"I let those deacons go. I ain't doing it again."

"Told Cash I might need his help with Myles."

"The last thing yo brother needs is to get mixed up in this."

"He's got another side."

"Vietnam," she said, thinking back to her talk with Cash not two hours ago. "Cash ain't a killer, but he will kill. Will you?"

Big John sighed. "You mind if I spend a little time alone with Shine?"

"Good idea," she said. "Time alone with you takes an angel. Not me."

PART VII

BIG JOHN KNEW HARDSHIP AND DEATH. He didn't know babies. No more than a cold, he'd told Shine. James died within a week.

What had Big John learned over the years? Last summer he assured his wife the pain in her back was nothing but the aches and pangs that came with the years. It was too late by the time she snuck over to see a doctor in Memphis.

As Big John held his lady's hand, he cringed with every bolt of cancer that poured through her body. He didn't beg her to take the pills she'd refused so many times, but he did beg.

"You knew," he said. "You knew it was Myles." She nodded. "Please forgive me. Shine, please forgive me."

She forgave him with a gentle tug of his hand, a kiss, and a question: "What did your daddy say about not keeping a scorecard?"

He cried on her shoulder, and then he did reach for the bottle of pills. Shine turned her head, said the broken but living body of his daughter was more important than the dying bones of his wife, and asked him to leave.

He drove back to the hospital, realizing his time alone with an angel, with his angel, had lasted fifteen minutes.

Rage. Guilt. Despair. When not staring out the window with clenched fists or sitting by Pearl's bed with face in hands, Big John stood next to his girl, watching and listening and weeping.

Before that night he couldn't imagine why his childhood friend had killed himself. The Marine had survived two years of torture in a Japanese prison camp but lasted only six months in Hope Springs. Big John would never take his own life, but now he understood.

25

Cookie

COOKIE STEPPED INTO THE ROOM, GLANCED AT PEARL, and looked away. The tile. The walls. The ceiling. All cold and gray, like the girl in the bed. Myles had turned the prettiest girl in Hill County into a mess who reminded Cookie of her daddy that night.

Big John looked as dead as her pond that cool October morning before Myles fixed his rattle. Cookie felt sorry for her friend, though feeling sorry didn't hold much water in her bucket. From Ruth and Mary to Jesus and Dr. King, living and dying never had been easy. Never would be.

"Pearl any better?" she asked.

"The heart of the matter is the heart of the matter," Big John said.

"What?"

He blinked a few times, then shook his head. "Only doubt I had came the time Myles was showing us around his shop. One desk. No filing cabinet. Two empty bays, both clean as the top of his desk. It all seemed strange given the scale of his operation."

"I remember, Big John."

"When Myles mentioned doing everything on a handshake, my deddy's words came to mind: 'Never trust a man who won't put any and everything into writing.' But they were gone in a flash. I'd already bought everything Myles had to sell. I couldn't wait to lead Pearl down the aisle. I was itching for grandbabies. It was all about me, Cookie. And look what it's done. Look what I've done to my only girl."

"Blaming yoself won't pull us outta this hole."

"But I'm her deddy."

"Help folks and you hook 'em," Cookie said, remembering her words to Big John after he'd left the sheriff's office.

"I'd rather not listen to another sermon on preachers."

"This sermon's on *you*. Myles got Pearl outta the party and into a church. He helped her, for a time at least, and he hooked you. Me too, I suppose."

"I'm the one who urged her to marry the man."

"Myles ain't the first wolf dressed like a sheep, but he is the best I ever seen. Anybody with eyes can see Misry coming. Too late when Myles shows his fangs."

"I knew Pearl was in love. Called myself looking Myles over."

"I let him drive off with Salt and Slide for a damn milkshake."

"I could ramble all day on what a prince I thought Myles was. He covered lots of ground without leaving a track. Like a ghost, I reckon."

"More like a devil. From whupping that man at the bait shop to diving into my mucky pond after a fish, Myles had the rough edges to keep those shiny teeth and pretty hands from looking too slick."

"I catch myself thinking this must be a terrible dream."

"Pearl's tubes and what's under those sheets ain't a dream," Cookie said.

"Imagine if Myles had been a general with an army behind him. Or a preacher with a church believing he walked on water."

"Who gives a flip about generals and preachers when the man has a sheriff watching his back?"

Big John answered with a long and loud sigh that said he was done talking. With him blowing smoke about generals and such, Cookie was done listening.

Wasn't long before Cash opened the door and wheeled Shine into the room. Only Cash could've lifted her precious body out of bed without breaking every bone she had left. And only a momma could act so cool when times were so bad.

"Big John, what's on your mind?" Shine asked.

"I halfway sided with the man who'd blackened and bloodied my girl's face," he said, rambling like Shine had been there all morning. "Who blamed Pearl and fought back tears with that family Bible in his hands."

"Myles had us all in the dark at some point," Shine said.

"Sundays at church. Our farmhouse and screened-in porch. The rehearsal dinner."

"What's your point?" Shine asked.

"Myles walks into a room, and every last person looks his way without a second thought. Without a *first*. Something reaches out and grabs you by the collar and gives you no choice but to like him. And trust him. They say Teddy Roosevelt had it. I know President Kennedy did." Big John pointed at the bed. "Thank God they didn't use it for this."

Generals, preachers, and now dead presidents? Cookie glanced at Shine as Big John hurried to the window like he expected to see Myles waving from the parking lot.

"Crazy thing is, most of what Myles said was true," he said. "From Pearl's drinking and temper to everything he'd done for her, he painted the perfect picture for whatever tale he was selling."

"That picture's got us in a bind," Cookie said. "Especially with Mathis on his side."

Big John listened that go-round. "Even if Mathis were straight, Pearl would have to file a report and stay the course. Hard to see either one happening, the way she's been vouching for Myles."

He trotted to the bed and eyed his girl for the longest.

"What are you thinking?" Shine asked.

"I'm gonna kill that boy," he said.

"By golly, you're not!" Shine hollered. "I'll be in heaven, and you'll be in jail."

"Time for a reckoning," he said. "Past time."

"No, it ain't," Cookie said.

"Did I hear you right?" he asked, glaring at Cookie like a stranger he didn't care to meet.

She was glad to see his brain moving in the right direction. Myles had to be put down. But not yet. Shine's last days would be full of pain but free of this worry.

"We'll find another way," Cookie said. She turned before having to come up with another lie. "Let's go, Cash. Shine needs to get on to the house and stretch out."

Hospital to farmhouse, Cash did his best with a truck that had fewer years but more miles than Big John's. Every bump on the road seemed to hurt him more than Shine.

Skinny and strong like wire, Cash picked her up without a hitch, but his soft and easy steps jolted Shine like she'd been punched in the ribs. Broken ribs. Liked to have killed her when he laid her in bed. She tried a "thank you" but didn't have the strength. Neither did Cookie.

26

Slide

DEDDY AND COOKIE TOOK TURNS WATCHING the farmhouse that weekend. Not counting a quick trip to check on Pearl each day, Big John spent every second prowling from Shine's bed to the den.

On Sunday night, Deddy came home with a grim look in his eyes. Grim even for the man who frowned at good news. I wanted to ask but couldn't. Momma asked every question except *the* question.

When she finally asked if Shine had much longer, he glanced from one kitchen cabinet to another as if wondering whether Momma had found every bottle he'd stashed through the years. He shook his head and left.

Momma reached out and brought me in for a long hug. "Are you okay, Slide?"

I kept staring at patches of vinyl on the kitchen floor, wishing I'd followed Deddy through the door and headed for my room. A boy my age wasn't supposed to cry in front of his momma. But it was too late.

— ✳ ✳ ✳ —

WHEN DEDDY SHOWED UP AT SCHOOL the next day, I stood and shoved the rest of a turkey sandwich into my lunch box. We hurried outside and through the parking lot. His shaky hands were fumbling with the keys when I asked about Shine. The man who could hear a blink acted deaf. I didn't ask again.

Big John was pacing the porch when we drove up. He was gone by the time we made it to the front door. At the roar of Lore's Cadillac racing up the gravel drive, Big John darted from the bedroom.

Cookie stepped out and gave a slow wave for Lore to head on. She strolled around the edge of the porch, took the stairs one at a time, and eased the screen door to a close.

"You barely made it," Big John said. "Shine's breaths are farther apart and carry a raspy sound that tears me to pieces."

"How's her spirit?" Cookie asked in a calm if not soothing voice.

"Better than mine."

"I didn't ask about you."

"She came to an hour ago." He looked away. "She knew it was time."

"Happens at the end," Cookie said, as we followed her into the den. "Y'all wait here while I spend a few minutes with the best friend I ever thought about having."

Cookie had been in the bedroom maybe two minutes when she called out, "Shine's coming to!"

I'd planned on staying in the den until Deddy took my arm and led me into the bedroom. My first glance made me wish I'd stayed put. Shine was going to heaven but looked like she'd already been to hell.

Cookie's dark fingers held a gray hand that looked alive compared to the face. I'd never seen the bones of Shine's cheeks look ready to burst through skin I could see through. The pink and puffy lips that had given me a thousand juicy kisses had withered to scaly lines that were now purple and blue. Her once-bright eyes were cloudy and buried in dark holes. Only her hair looked the same.

"Shine, this here's Cookie. Cookie Kate."

"Hey, Cookie," Shine whispered. She looked around the room. "You too, boys. I wish Pearl could be here."

"Rest easy while I stroke this pretty white hair and talk with the Lawd," Cookie said.

Shine nodded and closed her eyes.

"Lawd, You know what I think of You sending my lady through this valley," Cookie said. "But You are her shepherd, amen, good times and bad, living and dying. You also a jealous God, amen, and I reckon You got tired of waiting and wanted this angel right there by Yo side. Now You a-coming, Lawd, and her pain'll be a-going." She stared out the window. "These pastures I'm looking at are dead, dead-brown and ugly, but my lady's fixing to walk the greenest pastures You ever made. These valleys, these shadows of death, they hurt, Lawd. But our lady has nothing to fear 'cause You walking her every step of the way to that far-off land with the stillest of waters. Amen!"

Shine flinched and looked up.

"Cookie, you're in charge of these brothers from here on out," she said, her eyes now clear and strong. "Cash will be right behind me if he goes back to drinking, and Slide needs his daddy." She glanced at Big John. "This cancer has eaten my bones, but it's broken my man's heart. Cookie, I'm leaving it to you to make sure he keeps this promise. Get over here, Big John."

He sat and took her hand.

"You can't beat Myles," Shine said. "He's too slick and too mean. You're a sad husband and a mad daddy but a teddy bear under that fur. He'll kill you or have that brother of his do it."

"Shine, I was just thinking about our honeymoon," Big John said, as if changing the subject or time itself would heal his bride. "Our first night at The Peabody and how you begged me to make do and push those single beds together. My, what a boondoggle." He pulled her hand to his cheek. "Not the smoothest start, but our years have been this soldier boy's dream. You're the love of my life."

"I love you too, Big John. But you're not cut out for this. Myles is a con man without a conscience. You'll be dead, and he'll cover and blame his way out."

"The man put my daughter in the hospital."

"*Our* daughter. Who will be left to face her husband without a momma or a daddy. Promise you won't fight him."

"Honey, I'd do anything to take your place. But I can't let Myles do it again."

"It's all I ask," she said. "Give me your word." He glanced at Cookie and Deddy. Shine squeezed his hand. "Give me your word, Big John."

"I won't fight," he finally said. "I promise."

"You hear him, Cookie?"

"Loud and clear," Cookie said. "Now go on back to sleep, sweet lady. Big John's got one hand. I got the other. And the Lawd's fixing to have 'em both. He's coming soon, baby. Coming to steal you and yo pain."

Shine kept her eyes on Big John. After minutes that felt like hours, she slumped back on the pillow and closed her eyes.

Five minutes or so passed when a deep rattle came from Shine's chest. Then another. Then nothing but an open mouth.

"Lawd, is that You?" Cookie asked. Her eyes filled with tears. She stroked Shine's hand. She nodded. "Yes, Lawd, You came. Came and got Yo Shine. Amen." She looked across the bed. "She's gone, Big John. The Lawd's got her all to His lonesome."

He dropped Shine's hand and stared into the dark hole that had taken the place of my aunt's warm smile. He leaned in and pressed his cheek to hers.

The whole bed was shaking by the time we followed Cookie into the den.

—* * *—

DEDDY CRIED ON THE WAY HOME, but I didn't. I was too mad at God.

Cookie had said God wanted Shine all to Himself, which sounded plenty jealous to me. He'd already taken Big John's only son and two best friends, then sat around while Myles beat his girl to a pulp. Was it too much for a good God to let Pearl watch her own momma die?

What's more, He'd left Shine's sister. Next to Myles, Misry had to be the worst person He'd ever made. Why didn't God send her sorry ass packing for hell while He was whisking Shine away to those *green pastures*?

I couldn't sleep that night. I didn't stare at the ceiling or toss and turn. Instead, I crunched myself into a ball and lay there. For some reason, I gave prayer a shot before grabbing my blanket and heading for the one I knew would be there.

Annabelle kept snoring as I walked into the kitchen and spread my blanket next to her mat. Every few minutes her body would shake like she was having one of Deddy's nightmares. She might've been dreaming about wrestling with me in her younger days, for all I knew.

27

MY SOBER DEDDY DIDN'T LIKE CURSING, but Momma didn't give a damn. Not on our drive to the funeral home Wednesday night.

She cursed Misry for not bothering to stop by the farmhouse before her sister died. Momma was "shitfire sure" the Misrys of this world had an extra sense or two that kept them a step ahead of your everyday sinners like us. When I asked what Misry's sixth or seventh sense was planning, Momma swore the "damn witch" would show up at the funeral home to soak Shine's casket with enough tears to keep half the town and most of her church snowed.

Would even Misry do that? I wondered, as Deddy pulled into the parking lot.

The Heavens to Betsy Funeral Home had a name that reminded me of hell to go with a smell that reminded me of cat food and Lysol. I skirted the crowd, searching for Misry but finding part of Big John and all of Cookie. Except for the fistful of blue blazer she was yanking on, his top half was in the coffin. As I walked closer, I heard him crying Shine's name and saw him kissing her forehead.

"Get outta there," Cookie kept saying until he gave up and straightened out. She took him by the shoulders and turned his back to the casket. "We got us a long line of visitors. All you gotta do is say 'thank you.'"

Deddy and Cookie spent the next hour trying to hold Big John together until another well-wisher would step forward and praise Shine or ask about Pearl. After his third dash to the bathroom, Cookie marched over to a man standing in the corner. He nodded and stepped to the middle of the room.

"May I have everyone's attention," the man said. "The church service will begin at two o'clock tomorrow afternoon. Thank you and good night."

—✶—✶—✶—

SHINE'S FUNERAL WENT LIKE BIG CHURCH on a Sunday—we stood for a few hymns, sat for Brother Sam's sermon, and stood for one last hymn before filing out through the double doors. But it wasn't Sunday. Shine was in a coffin. Big John bawled from start to finish. And I wanted to.

Big John didn't cry or even blink at the Hill County Cemetery. He didn't seem to notice the slab of granite which held the only words Shine had allowed on her tombstone: "SHINE DELILAH JACKSON. BORN JUNE 4, 1919. DIED JANUARY 25, 1971." He just sat and stared at the flowers on her coffin like he wanted to open the lid and crawl in. Forever.

Sam read two of Shine's favorite Psalms and was inviting everyone to the farmhouse for the gathering when Big John leaned over to Cookie.

"I need some time," he said. "Time alone."

She stood and cleared her throat. "Hold on, Sam. This man needs time to hisself." She looked Big John over. "*And* time with his Lawd." She turned back to Sam. "Y'all plan on Lore's house for the gathering."

If Sam wasn't the first white preacher to have a black woman change his plans mid-sentence, he was definitely the second. Cookie had no more interest in making history than waiting on a preacher.

"Let's go, Cash," she said. "You too, Slide."

With Deddy holding one arm and Cookie the other, they pulled Big John through the cemetery. They yanked harder each time he stopped to look back at the coffin.

Nobody said a word until Deddy parked at the farmhouse.

Cookie leaned forward. "Listen here, Big John. I know you don't care about living right now. I felt the same way after Daddy got killed. But don't forget yo girl in the hospital. Not to mention these boys here. They all need you and love you with all they got. We'll leave you be long as you promise not to do anything stupid. You with me?"

She tugged on Big John's arm until he nodded.

28

Cookie

OOKIE'S BOY ALWAYS WONDERED HOW SHE knew it was him. She'd unlatch one dead bolt and go to cussing the one that never acted right, all the while ignoring Victry's questions from the other side. Had she been peering through the window in her den? Did she know the sound of his steps? The tune of his knock? Fact was, Cookie had known the light steps and soft knuckles for ten years but wouldn't say so.

She'd throw the door open and give him a quick hug before stepping back to read his brain. Was he fixing to test her nerves with another round on why a good Lawd would let so many boys die in a jungle or some other war? Did whatever junk he'd seen in the news have him in a mopey mood? Or was he wanting to talk about all the shit in their part of the world? The Rope, Victry called it. If so, the Lawd would have to loan Cookie somebody else's patience for the next few hours.

Second thought, she needed that loan on Victry's good days too. Days when he loved to brag on the place he hated on his cloudy days. The charm of the town square, the majesty of a magnolia limb, the warmth of a stranger. The grit and grind of a place and its people.

Victry knew better than to mention the wondrous history of our cemetery. Cookie had needed one minute and two questions to put an end to that foolishness. One, how many black folks were buried in *our* cemetery? And two, how many of those white folks had owned *her* people?

Shine had been in the ground little more than an hour when Cookie heard his steps. She went straight to the door, realized she'd forgotten to lock it, and eased it open. Her whole body was trembling by the time she let him loose.

"Been hoping we'd have some time to ourselves," she said. "I don't know what's gotten into me."

"You lost your best friend."

"That ain't all, Victry. Let's have a seat in the den."

He found his place on the couch. She sat in the chair next to the room's only window.

"Shine's passing hit me harder than I let on," she said. "And the sight of that box waiting to drop my lady in a hole took everything I'd smoothed over Daddy's grave and plowed it into fresh dirt."

"I've never been able to ask you about your father," Victry said. "I asked Big John once. He rose without a word and hurried to the shed. I can't remember him mentioning your father's name."

"Big John can't do it unless he's already breaking down over somebody who died."

"Would talking it over help?"

She took a deep breath and closed her eyes. "We're fixing to find out."

Daddy could've moved to Cleveland or Detroit or some other big city up North. He knew the white man's game but decided to play along the best he could, I suppose.

The game ended the night my sister got home from work with red in her eyes and blood on her clothes. Georgia lied and said she'd fallen down the stairs carrying a load of laundry, but Daddy knew.

Every eye turned his way soon as Georgia fessed up. Momma clawed at his shirt. I blocked the door. Daddy's eyes said it all when he busted loose with a hog knife in his hand.

I knew it was the death of my daddy. The white man

too, but I was wrong on that count. Daddy held back a touch and didn't kill that man, though he did make sure nary another woman would have to worry about the business between those legs.

When Daddy walked in with blood on his blade, Momma begged him to run. I shouted and slapped and tried pushing him out the door.

Granny went to mumbling, "You be wasting yo time, wasting yo time, ain't no other blood gonna do. Only my boy's gonna do."

Daddy hugged his momma for a long while, then did the same with Momma and me. He saved his last hug for my sister. Told Georgia nothing was her fault. Said a white man had crossed one line and he'd crossed another. She nodded but couldn't say a word.

Wasn't long before we heard the engines roaring our way. Daddy whirled and hollered for us to hightail it to the back and stay there until sunup. He met every eye until every head bowed.

I ran to the front window after the door slammed shut. And there was my Daddy, walking graveyard-calm toward those men. Head up, he must've eyeballed every last one of those deacons.

They knocked Daddy over and took turns stomping his head into the dirt. Killed him right quick from what I could tell. Don't ask me why they hung him from that big oak by the street.

He was swinging in the air before I made it back to where I should've been all along. We huddled and hollered the rest of the night. When daylight finally showed, Granny got her cane and told us to stay put.

Few minutes later I ran to the front. Granny didn't need her cane anymore. Her arms were wrapped around my

daddy's feet. Around her boy's feet. One old momma holding one dead boy, swaying back and forth, back and forth.

Momma staggered to the kitchen and called Big John.

Granny had just hobbled into the house when his truck
jumped the curb and skidded to a stop. He got out and
stared like he was under a spell. He cut the rope, held
Daddy like his own brother, and laid him on the ground.

"I want the names of every man who took part in this,"
he said.

"We don't know," Momma said, glancing my way. "Elijah sent us to the back."

Big John eased the rope from Daddy's neck. "It won't be
hard to figure out."

"There ain't nothing for you to figure out," she said.

"Elijah was my best friend."

"And he was my husband." Momma pointed from me
to the house. "And their daddy and son." She stepped over
Daddy's body and took hold of Big John's overalls. "Whatever you do about yo friend will tie a rope around the neck
of his family."

"I'll talk to Sheriff Mathis."

"You expect a white sheriff to help out? Elijah wouldn't
run because he knew there ain't no justice this side of the
Jordan."

"But—"

"No *but* to it, Big John. You won't do a damn thing.
You hear me?" He nodded real slow like. "Now take Elijah
into the house."

He picked Daddy up and followed Momma to the den.
She pointed at the couch. He stretched Daddy out and
looked up at Momma.

"Thank you, Big John," she said. "We'll call when it's
time for the wake."

I closed the door behind him.

What happened next was the first time, the only time, I saw Momma lose her nerve. She tilted her head from side to side, staring like she'd never seen the man on her couch. She held up her arms, shouting words I couldn't understand, then fell to her knees and crawled on top of Daddy. Momma spent the next hour wailing and hugging on the man she loved more than the rest of us put together.

Cookie opened her eyes, stood, and faced the window. She gazed at the big oak, her body stiff as her daddy's and tight as that rope.

She turned and looked Victry over. The tears and drooping shoulders she'd expected were nowhere to be found.

"How can you forgive those monsters?" he asked.

"Well, I got a ways to go on that. With Mathis and white juries watching their tails, those deacons left their hoods at home. I remember every face. See 'em in town from time to time, going to church and raising chillun like nothing happened. But they always see me coming. One stares right through me with those same killing eyes. The rest see nothing but feet as I walk up and find myself—"

The last deacon came to mind. June of 1969, Friday afternoon on a hot summer day. Salt was sitting at the counter of Smith Drugstore, slurping on her chocolate milkshake, when Cookie spotted the old man shuffling along the sidewalk. She told Salt to stay put and hustled his way.

"Cookie?" Victry asked.

"I find myself bending real low, 'cause they gonna see my eyes when I tell 'em how much I loved my daddy. How I watched 'em every hungry kick of the way. And how I still wanna kill 'em. Kill 'em all."

"They deserve no less."

"But before I'm done, they also gonna hear about my Jesus hanging on that tree of His, all the while forgiving the devils that pounded the nails in His hands and feet. They gonna hear that if my Lawd can forgive them Romans, and me too, I gotta try and forgive them for killing my daddy. They hearing me loud and clear, Victry. Loud and clear."

"You've forgiven more than I can fathom."

"I said *try*. I didn't say how far I'd made it down that road."

"I wouldn't even try."

"Because you living without Jesus."

"Maybe you're right."

"No maybe to it." Cookie nodded at the door. "Let's sit on the porch a while."

—* * *—

THEY SAT IN THE FLIMSY METAL CHAIRS that always felt like they'd fold but never did. Two men sat on a porch across the street, brown paper sacks in their hands. Quart bottles of Pabst Blue Ribbon, Cookie figured.

"Kittens become cats, and boys become men," she said. "Big problems in my book." She chuckled. "Victry, you men are good at carousing and sitting on that ass but not much else."

"Didn't Peter say you women are the 'weaker vessels?'" Victry asked, a chuckle in his own voice.

"Shee-it. Women have the babies, raise the chillun, and do all the work while you jokers get drunk, fill the jails, and moan on the couch when you get the sniffles. Else you're hollering hungry with a ham on yo back."

He smiled. "You sound better now."

"Reckon I am, Victry. Reckon I am."

"You had me worried."

"Save yo worries for Big John. The man was a mess after James died. Same with my daddy. And now he's lost Shine." Cookie stared at the patch of grass under the big oak. "I wonder if Big John would've finished the job if Momma hadn't backed him down. He wanted to kill those men all right, but would he have softened up when it came time to punch their tickets to hell? Same for Mathis the day Daddy ripped off his shirt and showed his back. Not a scratch from whatever white woman the sheriff said Daddy had raped. Only muscles and the mark of that belt. Big John was raising his gun when Daddy cried out. Would Big John have covered his cotton with the brains of that no-count sheriff?"

"It's hard to imagine."

"And hard to imagine what he'll do without Shine. The beat of his soul and the light of his eye is now a cold body in a dark hole. We left Big John on the porch not two hours ago. Left a heart cracked top to bottom, inside and out. Add Pearl in the hospital and there's no telling where he'll end up. The man's heart is like the rest of his body. Too soft and too big."

"How will he make it?"

"Only chance he's got is to lean on the Lawd, and that ain't easy when the Lawd's showing nothing but His back."

"I'm scheduled to fly back in the morning. Should I stay?"

"Nope. Only the Lawd's got the power to wade these waters. Problem is, the Lawd's got His own ways. Ways I don't like but gotta try and trust in. You best come to grips with that, Victry. Else you'll find yourself worn slap out and floating deep waters in a leaky boat."

"What I would give for your boat."

"Shee-it. The long arm of the Lawd is a reaching yo way. All you gotta do is take hold and hang on."

"I have you and Big John."

"Might work for a while, but we ain't God. Only He can fill the hole you trying to mend. Been telling you that for years now."

"How I've loved every minute," he said. "And how I love you."

"You know I love you, Victry."

She met his eyes until they grew edgy and moved to his lap.

"Is anyone checking on Big John?" he asked.

"I got Cash slipping around every few hours. Soon as Big John comes to his senses, we got business to tend to."

"Business?"

"With Myles," Cookie said.

"I know the sheriff is no help, but you must stay out of this."

"I tell myself I was too young when Daddy died."

"Is that why you're so determined to get involved?"

"Part of it, I reckon."

"What of the forgiveness you spoke of?"

"What I care about now is judgment. Judgment on Myles before he kills Pearl or some other girl."

"Cookie, you're a black woman living—"

"I know the color of my skin. Not to mention the color of this world I'm living in."

She hopped up and trotted to the spot in the yard where those boots had killed her daddy. She stared at the dirt, pondering the blood that had covered this ground so long ago.

"My fear died with Daddy," she said, pointing at the ground. "On this very spot." She looked up at Victry. "Understood?" He nodded. She walked back to the porch and sat. "Daddy's spirit is alive in me. If Big John won't do his job, I'll find a way."

"I'm not leaving town until you give me your word."

"Then stay," she said, wanting him out of town for the first time but hoping to call his bluff. "You a grown man."

Without a word he hightailed it to the kitchen. The phone was in his hand when she ran up.

"Victry, what the hell you doing?"

"Canceling my flight."

She yanked the cord from the wall. He leaned back against the sink and crossed his arms.

"Okay," she said, knowing her boy wouldn't leave until she told him what he wanted to hear. "I'll stay out of it."

Like a momma searching for a lie, Victry studied her face. "I have your word?"

"You got it," she said. "Now go." He didn't move, but he blinked long enough for Cookie to grab the phone from his hand. She held it like a club. "I reckon it's time you met Billy."

He grinned. They hugged. And he left.

— ✶ ✶ ✶ —

COOKIE TRIED A NAP UNTIL SHE remembered the last had been nearly thirty years ago while her daddy was working in a cotton field. She went outside to see if the fresh air and sounds of those children would do her some good.

In no time she knew why they'd stayed in the house. The Indian summer had passed into what Shine called "a fine winter day" that meant cold and dreary to most folks.

Cookie headed to the kitchen and heated up some coffee to warm her bones and roust her brain. She sipped and stared through her little window above the sink. Shine, sweet Shine.

Her cancer brought to mind something else Cookie hated—cotton. The damn weed had kept her people chained up and split up for hundreds of years.

Granny was a baby when her oldest brother, Roy, was shipped off to a plantation with too much cotton to pick. Years later Granny learned about the white man who'd looked Roy up and down before pulling back on the boy's gums like he was selling a mule.

"Good teeth," the man said. "This un'll bring top dollar. Load him up." He eyed Roy's folks like he was doing them a favor. "Y'all can stay put for now."

For now? Shee-it. Buses and bathrooms to farming red dirt no higher on sharecropping than the cotton black folks tried to grow, what about the next hundred years? What about Granny's boy, Cookie's daddy, who was killed in 1949? Time might've helped, but it had not healed.

Hate. Along with cotton and cancer, Cookie hated those snakes. Big John said the snake hiding in the grass was the worst kind. He was wrong, of course. She'd spot that devil no matter how tall the grass was, then find a hoe and see how long it lasted without a head.

The worst snake wasn't even in the grass. He just popped up from a hole, did his evil work, and slid out of sight before the poison got to running in the veins.

Myles needed a shovel and a hoe—a shovel to find and a hoe to kill. Would Big John use either one?

29

PROMISES NEVER HAD BEEN ALL THEY were cracked up to be. One lie, no matter the color, had the power to wipe out more promises than a banker or politician could make in a year.

"I'll stay out of it" was nothing but a lie to get Cookie's boy out of her house and back to the big city before moving on to her *business* with Myles. Cookie had no doubt it was time for Big John to lie on those promises he'd made to the Lawd and Shine, but first she had to get the man back on track. A little time to himself was okay. Too much, and the devil would dig a trench too slick and deep to climb out of.

Shine's grave was a day old when Cash called with the same news: "Nothing's changed, Miss Cookie. My brother's still slumped in his rocker, crying Shine's name and moaning to be in her coffin."

"He seen you snooping around?"

"No, ma'am."

"I'll go see what I can do with yo brother."

"Can I give you a ride?"

"Nope. A fast trot'll get my blood to flowing in the right direction."

"You sure?"

The beg in the boy's voice changed her mind.

—✳ ✳ ✳—

EYES TO SHIRT AND TIE, BIG JOHN looked like he'd spent a hundred years in a thunderstorm. There was no use wasting words on hello and such.

When Cookie told him to run into the house and clean up, he looked her over like she was Spock or one of those other clowns on the TV show

Salt was so crazy about. He kept staring when she said they needed to pay Pearl a visit.

"Worrying about yo girl above ground will take yo mind off the one below," Cookie said. He shook his head. "Big John, get yo raggedy ass outta that chair and into the house."

"I'm not ready," he said.

"Ready? Were you ready for Shine to die? For Pearl to get—"

"Go easy on him," Cash said.

She eyed the man who never interrupted a child, much less her. "Cash, what's *easy* about Pearl sprawled on a bed in the hospital?"

Something caught Cookie's eye when she turned back to Big John.

She pointed. "What you got there? Another poem?"

He rocked forward, squinting at the paper on the floor. "Reckon so. I scratched for a spell yesterday before the funeral and some more last night, trying to make sense of everything. Can't say it helped."

Cookie had no use for poems, especially Big John's, but she did want to know what was cooking in that melon of his. She handed it to Cash.

"Slow and loud," she told him. "Read."

Lady
My Lady's going in the ground today.
My Lady, she's going in the ground.
She's headed for a better place they say.
But my Lady, she's going in the ground.
The box to shut your sweet body alone.
Shine, you're going in the ground.
No more the smile I've always known.
Dear Lady, don't go in that damn ground.
This porch a place of gloom not cheer.
Sweet Lady, you're out there in the ground.
Our preacher just said there's nothing to fear.
My Lady, you're out there in the ground.

Other souls have trod this way for years.
But now it's you who's out there in the ground.
There'll come a day with no more tears?
If so then how, with you there in the ground?

Big John had ridden *ground* straight into the ground, but something clicked when Cash said the word the last time.

"The hospital it is," Big John said, as if he'd had the idea all along and invented the wheel to boot.

— ✳ ✳ ✳ —

COOKIE POINTED TOWARD THE CURB AS they turned into the parking lot. Big John pointed at an empty parking spot. When Cash pulled up to the curb and said he'd be right up, Cookie told him she'd call for a ride. Soft spirit to hard liquor, the boy was no part of the business she had with his big brother.

One look at Pearl reminded Cookie that white skin had its own problems, especially when it came to hiding a beating. Least she was awake this go-round.

"Hey, darling," Big John said. He took her hand like he'd done at the wedding. She yanked it away and stared him down. "Pearl, I'm sorry you couldn't . . . couldn't make your momma's funeral."

"So am I."

"Doctors say you'll be coming home soon," he said. "How you feeling?"

"Doesn't matter how I'm feeling. Uncle Cash stopped by last night."

"What?" he asked.

"Pearl didn't get to see her own momma die," Cookie said. "Or the funeral you mentioned. She had every right to hear about it."

"But why Cash?"

"I asked for him," Pearl said. "Cash is too honest to lie without acting fishy. I asked question after question and pressed harder when he tried dodging. I know everything now, including the promise you made to Momma. So does Myles. Called and told him myself."

Big John stepped back, his hand on his mouth.

"Why the hell did you do that?" Cookie asked.

"I don't know. Could be these pills I'm taking. Pain pills, sleeping pills, other pills. Or maybe I thought Myles would change."

"Fool woman," Cookie said.

"I still love him. Part of me does anyway. Or did. I'm not sure which."

"What did he say?" Cookie asked.

"Not much until I told him about Daddy's promise. Then he cackled and quoted some verse on wives submitting to their husbands. Said my next beating would be my last and hung up."

"Good Lawd."

"He'll never stop now," Pearl said in a cool and steady voice. "I'm dead."

"You're not dead," Cookie told her.

"I'm not coming back here." Pearl stared down the bed at her feet. "It's over."

"Exactly what are you saying?" Big John asked.

"You don't have a gun," she said, glaring at her daddy. "But I do. Hank gave me a pistol and taught me how to use it. Remember him, Daddy?"

"You made your own decision," Cookie said. "Yo daddy was no more than a nagging hen, and you know it. Shooting Myles ain't the answer anyway."

Pearl stuck a finger to the side of her head. "I'm talking about *me*. I'm ending it before Myles has the pleasure."

"Quit that nonsense!" Big John shouted.

"Like Cookie said, I make my own decisions. Living with Myles is no life at all. Neither is hiding out."

"I can't believe you're saying this," he said.

"There's no use arguing once my mind is made up. I'm like Momma on that."

"You'll stay with me at the farmhouse."

"Myles will be madder than ever. He'll find me, and you'll get caught in the middle."

Cookie needed to think this over.

"Enough for now," she said, grabbing Big John's arm. "Pearl, we'll see you in the morning."

"I can't leave her like this," he said.

"She ain't going nowhere until the doctor says so. Meanwhile, the girl needs rest. We'll use the phone in the lobby to call Cash."

"Cookie's right," Pearl said. "I am tired."

— ✶ ✶ ✶ —

COOKIE TOOK BIG JOHN BY THE ARM and led him down the hall. He stopped and turned, facing Pearl's door. Thinking of his girl with a gun, Cookie figured, or what Myles had said about the next beating.

"She's safe in the hospital," Cookie said. "From Myles and herself."

"But the picture of Pearl's finger at her temple is pulling me her way," he said.

"The grip of my fingers is pulling you thisaway."

"Cookie, I don't know."

"You will soon enough."

A white lady at the front desk gave Cookie the eye when she asked for the phone. The woman was looking at Big John like she needed his permission when Cookie took hold of the cord and pulled the phone her way. She made the call, and they went outside to wait on Cash.

"It's time we make a plan," she said. "For killing Myles."

"Cookie, you remember my promise."

"Myles does too, from what Pearl just said."

"Those were my last words to Shine. You're supposed to hold me to them, in case you forgot."

"Told Shine I heard yo promise, *loud and clear*. Never said I'd hold you to it. In case you forgot." He snorted and sighed. "Big John, I'll lie over Shine's grave to save Pearl's life. Will you?" He cocked his head and narrowed his eyes. "You don't have to lie anyway. You promised not to *fight*. Never said you wouldn't *kill* the man."

"You know what Shine meant."

Cookie tugged on his overalls. "Big John, these storms have clouded

199

yo brain, but maybe it can handle this. One, Myles ain't changing. Two, the law ain't helping. And three, like Pearl said, she's Shine once her mind is made up." Cookie tightened her grip. "Yo girl is gonna blow her brains slap outta her head."

He pulled away and went to walking in circles. Cookie held her peace.

"Afraid I have no choice," he said to her surprise. "Problem is, I got rid of my last gun."

"The damn gun's been littering my pond since I was a chile. Lawd, here I am arguing with the only white man in Hill County who doesn't own a gun."

"You were there, Cookie."

"And I was there when Pearl showed up with a busted lip and nose. Remember what you said after reaching under that couch?" He nodded. "Said yo bat would do the job."

"Don't have it with me."

Big John still wasn't thinking straight, but he was on the right track.

"Don't have a truck either, do we? Maybe that's why we're waiting on yo brother. We'll get the bat at yo place after Cash drops us off."

"Don't you dare mention a word of this to him."

"How does that jibe with what you whispered in his ear last week?"

PART VIII

IG JOHN STOOD IN HIS DEN, staring at his favorite photograph. The young pilot was proud of the new wings on his uniform but prouder of the new bride under his arm.

He sat and buried his face in his hands. His Shine. His Pearl. Two brides. One dead. One who'd rather die than face her husband.

He reached under the couch. Glancing from the bat in his hand to the photograph on the wall, three vows and one sheriff raced across his mind. His deathbed vow to Shine. Myles's promise that Pearl's next beating would be her last, delivered with a cackle and a verse. Pearl's headstrong vow to kill herself "before Myles has the pleasure." And Sheriff Mathis.

Should Big John give the sheriff one last chance to protect Pearl? Had Mathis protected Elijah? Had a damn thing changed since Big John's visit to the sheriff's office?

30

Cookie

DARK HAD SET IN BY THE time the truck pulled through the gate and took a left toward town. Toward Cookie's house. When she reminded Big John that Myles's house was the other way, he stepped on the gas.

She took hold of the bat and told him to turn around. He didn't. She popped him on the knee, not hard enough to do any good but hard enough to hurt. He rubbed his knee, jawing about what the law would do to a black woman and such.

"Already had this talk with Victry," she said.

"You should've listened."

"I got a deal for you. I'll stay in the truck and let you take care of Myles."

"You're not making this any easier," he said, turning onto her street.

"I'm not leaving this seat until Myles is dead." Big John shook his head. "Where you dumping the body?"

"The body?"

"I figured you were too worried about killing the devil to have thought of that. There's plenty of dark roads and deep ditches in these parts, so quit burning yo gas and my time." He pulled up to her house, cut the engine, and went to drumming his fat fingers on the wheel. "You still wasting time."

He waited a while longer, then turned around and headed the right way.

— ✳ ✳ ✳ —

THEY ROLLED TO A STOP IN front of Myles's house. Big John shifted into park and cut the lights, though the lights in the house were shining like Myles had nothing to hide. And nobody to hide from.

"Here we are," Big John said.

Full dark couldn't hide the dread Cookie knew was lurking inside her friend. Adding to his promises to the Lawd and Shine, Big John's every ounce fought against hurting, much less killing, anything bigger than a mosquito.

"We ain't here to buy groceries," Cookie said. "That man is evil."

Big John grabbed the bat and opened the door like he was in a hurry. "I'll be right back."

"Hold on a second. Tell me how you plan on pulling this off. You ain't exactly Cash when it comes to slipping around on the sly."

He planted one boot on the blacktop and tapped the floorboard with the other. "Myles can't hear very well from the noise at his shop through the years. He'll probably be sitting on the couch next to the television. It oughta be loud enough to drown me out."

Cookie did not like the sound of Big John's voice.

"He ain't yo son," she said. "You ain't Abraham strapping Isaac to the altar, and there is no ram waiting in those bushes next to Myles's house. Either that man or yo girl is gonna die."

"Myles won't know what hit him," he said, easing the door shut.

Bad ears and a loud TV did little to settle Cookie's spirits. Big John had tried sneaking up on her one afternoon while she was fishing, but wet grass from a heavy rain didn't keep the man from sounding like a bull chasing a heifer through a dry cornfield. She kept staring at her corks and letting the boy have his fun until he was close enough to pounce. When Cookie wheeled around and yelled "Boo!" she caught a glimpse of the only three-hundred-pound bumblebee, all flight and no bite, the Lawd had ever made.

She was praying hard when Big John busted through the door with a body draped across his shoulder. "Amen," she mumbled, as he crossed the yard. He opened the door and tossed Myles into the back seat.

Cookie couldn't see much in the dark. But she could hear. She whirled and bolted to her knees.

"He's breathing, Big John. Breathing!"

"Couldn't bring myself to kill him."

"What *did* you do?"

"Didn't need my bat. Myles must've thought I was bluffing on my poem. His eyes shot wide like I was the last person he expected to see. He was getting to his feet when I knocked him out with one blow to the chin."

"Knocked him out! What good's that gonna do? Damn, you lost yo mind."

"Can't argue with you there."

"This ain't the time for lukewarm," she said. "Give me yo knife."

"Don't have one."

"Yo pocketknife. Hand it over. I ain't too soft to slice this joker's throat."

Big John fumbled through the trash at Myles's feet, found a roll of duct tape, and wrapped his ankles and wrists.

"Who do you think we're dealing with?" she asked. He pulled onto the road. "Listen to me, fool. The Lawd looked the other way when Moses killed a man for no good reason. We got *reason* to kill."

"I broke my promise to Shine but can't break my vow to the Lord."

"Give me the knife."

"I couldn't do it back there. Can't let you do it now."

Cookie stared into the dark, pondering the mess they were in. The wrong bird had showed up at the wrong time, but there was no use wasting new words on an old fact.

"What's yo plan?" she asked. "Another poem?"

"We'll take Myles to Biloxi. I'll make sure he never comes back."

"You think he'll say 'thank you kindly' and mosey on down the road like the sweet boy we thought he was?"

"He'll listen this time."

"He'll listen when his ass is shoved in a bag and dumped in the ocean."

A while later Myles woke up groaning like Big John had broken every bone in his body instead of maybe one chin.

"Big John, give me yo lighter," Cookie said.

"I quit smoking after the war."

"You keep a lighter next to yo pocketknife."

"Why do you need it?"

"To see what he's up to."

"Can I trust you?"

"Not with a knife or anything that'll kill quick. Lighter won't do enough good to bother."

To keep Myles from working Big John with another lie, she stretched a wide strip of tape across his mouth. She eased the lighter under his nose. Big John might've trusted her with fire, but Myles didn't. The white in his eyes was drowning the blue.

"You a lucky boy," she said. "My daddy knew what to do with the likes of you, and so do I. Big John's expecting a miracle, but the only miracle I'm interested in is seeing if you can live with a throat cut from one side to the other." She moved the flame closer. "Big John *will* kill you the next time you set foot in Hill County. If he needs help, I'll see that it's done."

They were halfway to Biloxi when Cookie tried again.

"Big John, here's another one for you. King David had his own soldier killed 'cause he couldn't keep his eyes, and something else, off Uriah's wife. The Lawd still called the king a man after His own heart."

"The Lord also took a killer named Saul and turned him into Paul—a man who was willing to die for the same thing he'd been killing for."

"You think the Lawd's fixing to make another Paul?"

"Who knows?"

"Damn," she said, wondering where the hell this road was headed.

—✳ ✳ ✳—

AT MIDNIGHT THEY HIT THE OUTSKIRTS of Biloxi. Big John pulled off the road, switched on the light, and looked back at Myles.

"Cookie's right," he said. "From what you did to Pearl to what you made of Shine's last days, I should've taken my bat to your skull. But know this, Myles: so much as show your face in Hill County and I will kill you."

He yanked Myles across the seat and out of the truck, pinning him to the ground.

He stuck the pocketknife in Myles's face. "You're dead far as Hill County goes. Far as Pearl knows. If word gets back you're alive and well, you won't be alive and well." Myles nodded. "I got no idea what bidness your family is really up to, but I do know you're all good at keeping secrets. Keep this and you'll live."

He cut the tape from Myles's ankles.

"Nice of you to free those feet," Cookie said, as Big John got behind the wheel. "Why not the hands and mouth? You could've given the man a gun—if you'd owned one, that is—to see if those pretty white teeth were glowing in the dark before the bullet hit yo brain."

He cranked the engine. "We can't leave Myles helpless on the side of a dark road."

"We can leave him dead."

"We've had this conversation."

"You'll regret letting him live."

They drove off but not away, in Cookie's view, for the lights of the truck lit the road ahead but not the darkness behind. She assumed a sliver of Big John wanted to turn around and finish the job. She knew the bulk of the big man held on to the hope that Myles would change.

"What you got in mind if the Lawd holds off on Paul and keeps Saul in the ball game?" she asked.

"I'll tell Cash—only Cash—in case my plan goes south."

"*When* it goes south," she said. "Any other bright ideas?"

"Pearl's gotta believe Myles is dead. We know what she'll do otherwise. What's more, I'll take the heat that comes our way. I'm the deddy. And I'm white. You weren't here, Cookie. Truth is, I messed up letting you ride with me."

"You messed up, all right. Not with me, though."

"I know you're not worried about the law, but I'm afraid of what could happen to you in jail. And of what *will* happen to Salt without you around for a momma."

"You win," she said for the first time.

"Not a word. Even to Victry."

"Not a word, Big John."

They reached Cookie's house at daybreak.

"What time you coming by?" she asked.

"I figured you'd want to go."

"You figured right."

Big John checked his watch. "Let's make it nine o'clock. Pearl should be up by then."

31

FROM COOKIE'S SIDE OF THE BED, Pearl didn't look any worse that morning. Or better. Second thought, she was holding a glass of water in one hand and pills in the other. Cookie didn't trust doctors enough to trust pills, but holding a glass was a good sign.

Big John eased a hand onto Pearl's shoulder and asked how she was feeling. She washed down the pills, glancing from Cookie to the window and door. Every direction but his.

He turned to Cookie as if she was supposed to pull him out of this hole. Shee-it, was she supposed to lead the way on lying to his girl about a *dead* man he wouldn't kill? Did Big John think she was Moses hoofing it down the mountain with a new Word from the Lawd? Nope. Cookie was not Moses, and she had not seen the Promised Land.

Fact was, she didn't know what to do. The Lawd had His ways. Men had theirs. Women did too. And none of it was making sense.

"Feeling better except for this," Pearl said, tapping the side of her head. "Not sure if it's the pills or IV or what, but the nightmares won't stop. Only change is whether Myles uses his fists or belt."

"You don't need to worry about Myles," Big John said, real strong and quick-like.

"Like he'll keep his word this time," she said, no life in her voice.

"Won't have to keep his word," he said. "Myles is gone. Gone for good. And you're safe."

Pearl's eyes darted around the room, then narrowed on her daddy. "Tell me you didn't."

"My only girl's safe. My last lady's free."

"No, Daddy, no."

"Yes, baby, yes."

"But you promised Momma. On her deathbed."

"I promised Shine I wouldn't fight. There was no fight."

"You killed my husband!"

"Hush up, girl," Cookie said. "And quit glaring at yo daddy like he put you in this place."

"I wasn't about to stand aside and let you kill yourself," he said. "Or let Myles do it."

"What did you do?" Pearl asked.

One glance at Big John and another at Cookie must've answered her question. She stared at her lap, taking one fast breath after another. Her eyes settled on the tubes in her arm. She nodded a while, catching her breath, then looked at her daddy with eyes that said she was finally breaking through Myles's spell.

"What will you do now?" she asked. "Sheriff Mathis and Myles were buddies."

"Only you and Cookie know," he said. "I'll tell Cash later this morning. He's tight-lipped. Nobody else will have a clue. And nobody is saying a word. Never."

This had gone better than Cookie expected. It was time to leave before Big John found a way to undo what the Lawd had done.

"Let's give her some time to digest all this," Cookie said.

"The sheriff will know who did it," Pearl said.

"I'm sure he'll come around asking questions," Big John said. "He won't get anything from me. Won't find the body, either."

"What . . . what did you do with it?"

"No need for the particulars," he said.

"You gotta run, Daddy."

"I'm too old to start running from the law."

"You can't go to the state prison," Pearl said. "Parchman is pure hell. They'll kill you or worse."

"Won't be my first time behind bars."

"That was Germany!" Pearl cried out. "Nearly thirty years ago!"

✳ ✳ ✳

COOKIE WAS ON HER WAY TO church when the phone rang. A Sunday morning call never brought good news, so she let it ring and headed for the door. The phone cranked up again while she was fishing for the keys in her purse.

"I'm stepping down," Big John said.

"Good, whatever it is. You sho' ain't worth a flip on stepping *up*."

"I'm talking about church, Cookie. Being a deacon. I'm telling Sam this morning."

"Why in the Lawd's name are you worried about that right now?"

"Rumors will spread, and Sam can't have a deacon who might've killed a man. Or one who's not sure where he stands with the Lord anymore."

"We'll get to where you *standing* soon enough," she said with a growl. "See what Sam has to say if you want to. Don't bother me with it."

Cookie wrestled with three questions on her five-minute march to New Hope Mountain Baptist Church. Would Myles come back? If so, would Big John keep his word and kill the man? And three, could she put up with a long sermon that morning?

Jeremiah was a good man with bad habits. Besides starting too late and going too long, he was bad about preaching on the last thing Cookie wanted to hear. As the Lawd would have it, "Forgiving Yo Enemies" was the title of Jeremiah's sermon that morning. And afternoon, since he was still preaching when she got up and walked out.

The deacon called again at four o'clock.

"Cookie, I've got serious bidness to discuss," Big John said.

"Look who's talking *serious*," she said. "The same fool who kept a knife in his pocket when it was time for the sword."

"We've gone over this, Cookie."

"Who said I was done with it?"

"Back to what I was calling about. I couldn't tell Sam the whole story, but he wouldn't have any part of me stepping down."

"Sam ain't the first preacher with a screw loose."

"Well, thought I'd let you know I'm still a deacon."
"You ain't mean enough to make a good deacon, anyhow."
"Goodness gracious. Can't we talk it over?"
"We did. Bye."

32

Slide

DEDDY WAS BETTER AT WAKING A boy up than Momma. Way better. He didn't barge in, yank the shades off the window, or holler "rise and shine" at the top of his lungs. With Deddy I'd wake to a gentle hand on my shoulder. As the worries of the day were an hour or two away, an easy smile would cross his face before he whispered it was time to get up.

On Monday morning I woke to a firm grip and no smile.

"Myles is dead," he said. I threw off the covers and sat up. "Fingers will point to Big John, and sooner or later you're liable to run across some kid talking smack at school. We don't need you in the headmaster's doghouse, so shrug it off."

"Shrug it off? I couldn't be happier Myles got his due. Or prouder of Big John."

"Slide, we don't know who did what."

"When did Big John kill him?"

"Myles has been gone for the past day or so. Leave it at that."

"Leave it at that," not to mention the eyes behind those words, told me not to ask how I'd been kept in the dark until now. Big John would tell me anyway, I figured.

"I'll see Big John after school and hear all about it."

"Not today," he said. "My brother needs a spell to get his bearings."

A *spell* turned into a curse that made the longest three days of my life. The curse ended on Thursday morning when Momma gave me the go-ahead to visit Big John after school.

Deddy argued that his brother needed more time. She listened for ten seconds tops, a near record for the worst listener in town besides Uncle Lore, before waving him off and shooing me out the door.

—✳ ✳ ✳—

AT THE FIRST RING OF THE bell, I struck out from school and ran all the way to Big John's farm. I hopped the gate and didn't slow down until I noticed the empty rocker.

I climbed the porch steps, reached for the screen door, and froze. Propped against the far wall, Big John looked every bit as dead as Shine after her last breath. His eyes were closed. His mouth was open. I tried to scream but couldn't. When I managed to mutter his name, he blinked.

I raced across the porch and stopped at his bare feet. His gray whiskers were covered in drool. The pink bandana Shine wouldn't let him wear was wrapped around his head. Had Big John gone back to drinking? I didn't smell whiskey on his breath. His eyes were lost, but not liquored up like Deddy's.

"It's me," I said. "Slide." His chin bobbed up and down as he looked me over. "What are you doing on the floor?"

"Oh, I don't know," he said. "Figured I'd try something new. You gonna help me up or not?"

I pulled with all the might my hundred and forty pounds could muster. Besides a long string of grunts that covered the gamut from short and quiet to long and loud, success was in short supply.

He rolled to his right and ended up on his hands and knees. He straightened out, reaching with both hands.

"Let's try this again," he said.

The popping of knees and hips drowned most of the grunts as he staggered up.

"Big John, your overalls smell like they haven't been washed since the war. And they're bordering on baggy."

"Might as well sit a while," he said.

He shuffled across the porch and stopped at his rocker. A baby-like smile on his face, he rocked it back and forth as if inspecting the world's first chair.

He stared through the screens, then pointed. "Look at my ole bell cow leading her heifers across the field. I wonder why they never trained cows to ride."

"Like horses?"

He sat. "I should've gone into that bidness instead of trucking. Who in their right mind would climb a ladder to sit on the bony spine of a horse if they had the low-riding back of a fat cow to choose from?"

"Who in their right mind would think of such a thing?"

"Slide," he said, as if remembering my name. "I'd be a millionaire if I'd thought of this when I was a young man, but it's not too late for you. I'll be your first investor. I got rope in the barn and cows in the pasture. Take your pick and have at it. You won't need a saddle, soft and sweet as those ladies are." He searched for the notebook that wasn't in the front pocket of his overalls. "Dern, I was hoping to jot that down in case we forgot."

I rocked back to spy on the man now gazing at his cows as if they were wading in hundred dollar bills. The hobo who banged on the front door of the Old Homestead every few weeks came to mind.

"No need to worry," Lore would say. "It's our old friend, Mr. Greer."

"I ain't trusting no bum who introduces hisself as Samson or Pilate before settling on Greer," Cookie would answer, a sack in one hand and a cast-iron skillet in the other.

Names and numbers were up for debate, but Greer's story never changed. The fact that his skin was paler than Salt's did nothing to keep him from swearing on seventy-times-seven Bibles that his momma and deddy were full-blooded Cherokees who'd lived for *centuries* in the Old Homestead until Lore's deddy—Greer took the liberty of naming him Nathan Bedford Forrest—rode in with a cavalry and booted them all out. After pointing from Lore and Cookie to Salt and me, Greer rattled down his list of other guilty parties, from Mayor Hipp and Governor Williams to President Nixon.

Greer would end his sermons with the good news of coming judgment. He'd called the full council of the Trinity into action, and the verdict was unanimous.

"Get out while the getting's good," Greer would say. "If you think Pharaoh had it rough with them plagues and such, you ain't seen nothing yet. A vengeance is coming upon this house that'll make hell seem perky."

"Thanks for stopping by," Lore would say, handing over the sack of ham sandwiches and potato chips. "Have a goodun."

Greer would peer into the sack and smile like he'd gotten the whole mansion before hobbling off for the next house or train on his list.

In a matter of minutes, I'd gone from thinking Big John was dead to knowing he was out of his mind. With Pearl out of the hospital and a slew of maggots having a ball at Myles's expense, I hadn't seen this coming.

"What have you been up to?" I asked.

"Not much." He crossed a foot over his knee and dug between his toes. "Not much to do."

"I heard Pearl's feeling a lot better. Is she here?"

He looked around like he expected to find her lounging in a rocker if not skipping through a pasture or climbing a pecan tree.

"She was here this morning," he said. "Got tired of being around me for some reason."

For some reason? My eyes and ears and nose could think of a hundred reasons. What I would've given for Aunt Shine to have strolled from the house with a warm smile and hot pie. Those days were over, and so was mine. I was fixing to head off for whatever sanity my house had to offer, when I heard commotion at the gate.

"We got us a visitor," Big John said, slapping his leg as Sheriff Mathis waged war on the chain. "Let's see how long it takes him this time. Poor fella hasn't caught on to how I dummy-lock that jessie."

Mathis kicked the post, threw the gate across the drive, and waddled back to his car.

"The fall of man has created all kinds of jobs," Big John said. "Makers of keys and locks and safes. Soldiers and lawyers and sheriffs. Slide, think of the folks who'd be out of work if Eve hadn't nibbled on that apple."

"How do you know it was an apple?"

"Now don't go to blaming women, my boy. Eve might've been a step ahead of ole Adam, but one glance at history and another at the headlines will tell you who starts the wars and does the killing and such."

The squad car rolled to a stop behind Life Lesson Larry. Mathis lumbered up the steps and onto the porch to face the scraggly-toothed smile of my wacky-eyed uncle.

Big John fired off a round that would've sent all but the stoutest of lawmen running for cover. "Hhholaaa, Sinner Mathis. Buennnos tardy. Cooomo esteees? Adeeeyos."

Spanish was hardly my strong suit, but I'd learned enough from a Mexican buddy at school to know what Big John was doing to these eight words of my friend's language. The *H's* were loud and long, the *N's* hard and short, the *E's* sure and steady. Strung together, it was either the massacre of an existing language, or the Tower of Babel building a new one.

"Big John, you know I can't speak *Eye*talian. Cut the crap and let's get down to bidness."

"Hhholaaa, Sinner Mathis. Buennnos tardy. Cooomo esteees? Adeeeyos."

"Here we go again," Mathis said. Every chin begged for breathing room as he stared at the floor and swung his head. He looked up at Big John. "Time to get this over with, big fella. Tell me, did you kill Myles? Did . . . you . . . kill . . . Myles?"

"Hhholaaa, Sinner Mathis. Buennnos tardy. Cooomo esteees? Adeeeyos."

"Shit on a stick, I knew this would happen." Mathis leaned in. "It's been nearly a week since anybody's heard from Myles. His family thinks you murdered him, and I know you did. Hell, you don't even deny it. Just tell me where the body is and be done with it. The body, Big John. Where is it?" Big John answered with a smile that would've made Greer proud. "Well, screw a turtle if all you're gonna do is grin and talk *Eye*talian to me. I'll see you tomorrow."

"It's hard to start a fire in the rain," Big John said, ending the sheriff's torture with a new line.

I almost felt sorry for Mathis as he stumbled down the steps. On top of the sights and smells he'd endured, he'd been clubbed senseless with eight words from a babbling caveman.

I'd loved every second but was stumped by the way Big John had treated the sheriff. He never made fun of folks. Or let anyone else get away with it. Life and death had pushed him right over the edge, I figured.

33

Cookie

THREE CALLS IN ONE WEEK FROM the same person made two too many, in Cookie's book. Three too many if that person was Big John.

She picked up, held the phone to her ear, and knew right off who was clearing his throat. The handle was zooming toward the cradle when she realized this made the *fourth* time Big John had called that week. As number five would soon be on the way if she hung up, Cookie said "What?" as loud as she could.

"We got us a problem," he said.

"You called to say we got a problem?"

"A new one," he said. "Sheriff Mathis is a bulldog."

"Nice way to describe the man."

"He asked about you this afternoon."

"I told you Myles would talk! Told you to put that pocketknife to work. But no, you had to be the Shepherd instead of the shepherd boy. David didn't think twice about chopping off Goliath's head."

"No need to rehash that for the umpteenth time."

"All right, Big John. Tell me what yo bulldog had to say."

"Mathis strolled onto the porch like he was Brother Sam stopping by to check on me."

"I suppose you gave the man a hug and trotted inside to fetch him a sweet tea."

Big John sighed as if *he* were the one who needed an extra dose of patience. "Cookie, I played along to see what Mathis really wanted. Even kept my cool when he mentioned how hard it must be on you, close as you and Shine were."

"The thought of Shine's name crossing the lips of that crook burns me up."

"Me too. The sheriff doesn't compare to his buddy Myles, but he is smarter than I'd given him credit for."

"Playing dumb's gotten his ass outta more than one fix," she said, thinking back to her daddy. "Mathis is smart enough to know what he doesn't wanna know."

"Exactly. And when he can't get where he wants by acting tough, he'll try the good-ole-boy routine to see if he can whittle down your guard. Today he waited until the end to ask what you thought of Myles beating the tar out of Pearl."

"Mathis only knows because the man who is *alive* tipped him off."

"I don't think so, Cookie."

"Myles could do what he wanted with us in the pen."

"That's why I told Cash, just in case. But how could we go to jail if the sheriff knows Myles is alive? For what, one hard lick to the chin?"

"Plus yanking the man outta his house and hauling him off."

"Mathis has his sights on murder. He's badgered me about Myles's body until he's red and then blue in the face."

"It would be a stretch to charge you for killing the person he's talking to."

"As for Myles, why wouldn't he move on to making his money somewhere else?"

"Because he's a man. A mean and evil man who got beat up and run outta town by an old ox like you."

"Myles knows his cover is blown here. I'm betting he'll lay low."

"You and yo bets. I bet you need a new barn for all the cash you made betting on that man."

"Come on, Cookie."

"Anything else?"

"Don't be surprised if the sheriff comes snooping around your place."

✳ ✳ ✳

COOKIE HUNG UP AND WENT OUTSIDE to sit a while. In two minutes, she was back on her feet.

"Not a word," she told Big John after they'd left Myles on the side of the road. The time had come to stretch those three words, and Victry was a safe stretch for three reasons. One, he lived way the hell off in New York City. Two, he knew how to keep his mouth shut. And three, with Shine gone, he was the only angel Cookie had left.

Myles's name had just crossed her lips when Victry let out a long sigh.

"Al Gibson," he said.

"Al who?" Cookie asked, wondering where Victry's brain was traveling this go-round.

"Why didn't I see it sooner? Myles even looks like Al Gibson. Six-feet tall, blond hair, blue eyes. Gibson has been all over our news."

"And I care about the news, especially in that crazy-ass place?"

"He's a convicted murderer who escaped from a maximum-security prison in upstate New York."

"Crooked jailer packed him a lunch and opened the door," she said. "What's this got to do with Myles?"

"They say Gibson could pass for a CEO on Wall Street as easily as a small-town pastor in upstate New York. That you'll consider him a friend until the moment he slices your throat. He's been described as a sociopath, charming and cunning beyond belief."

"Sounds like Myles," she said. "Now listen up and I'll tell you why I called."

Victry didn't ask a question while she gave him the lowdown on Myles. Didn't say a word when she cussed Big John for letting Myles go. But he chimed right in on Big John's, "You weren't here, Cookie."

"He's right," Victry said. "You have to admit a black woman in the South would—"

"I ain't admitting shit. Not of what you and Big John got to say. Bye."

"Wait," he said before she could hang up.

"What?"

"The story of your father moved me. I'm mailing you a poem I wrote."

"Send it to Big John. *Poem* is the worst four-letter word in my book these days. Next time I hear it better be when I'm listening to Solomon or his daddy in heaven."

"Poem," he said with a chuckle.

"You mighty brave on this telephone. See what happens when you close enough to swat."

"Poem," he said again.

He laughed, a rare but sweet tune from her boy. She hung up, smiling for a change.

Change. As good change had a way of skipping town before the bills came due, Cookie's smile lasted maybe a minute. Al Gibson. A friend who'd slice your throat in a flash. A man who was charming and cunning beyond belief.

She found herself fast-stepping it back and forth from the kitchen to the den, cussing one minute and praying the next. What was Myles up to? Was he gone for good, as Big John had told Pearl? The Lawd wouldn't answer, but Cookie's gut wouldn't quit.

— ✳ ✳ ✳ —

CLUMSY BOOTS CAME STOMPING UP COOKIE'S steps on Saturday.

Mathis wasted five minutes on the game he'd played with Big John. Called her *Miss* Cookie and asked how she liked the neighborhood and so forth.

"Care to take a seat?" he asked, settling his fat rump into the chair she always used.

"Nope."

"Suit yourself, Miss Cookie. Doesn't sound like you're in the mood for small talk."

"Never am."

He leaned to one side like a man passing gas. "Well, what can you tell me about Myles?"

"He a bad man."

"Is or *was*?"

"You tell me. You the sheriff."

The sheriff's smile didn't hide the glare in his eyes. "Where's the body, Cookie?"

She almost got cute and asked where the *Miss* had gone, but there was nothing cute about a white sheriff sitting in her chair.

"Ain't got a clue," she said.

"I have reason to believe foul play was involved."

"Is that right?"

"I'd bet this badge you know why Myles's house had the lights on with the TV blaring and no sign of life," Mathis said, jabbing his thumb at the silver badge pinned to his chest. "And why his shop looks like a ghost town."

"You think I had something to do with it?"

"I wouldn't be a bit surprised if you knew what Big John did. It's mighty easy to determine the motive."

"Must be, if you figured it out."

He stood and leaned as close as his belly would allow. His breath smelled like cigarettes soaked in coffee, but she didn't look away. He gave his tiptoes a try, maybe hoping to make up for what the Lawd had left out.

"Withholding evidence on a murder case will put your black ass behind bars for years. You tracking me?"

"I was tracking when you hog-tied my daddy to a fuel tank." Cookie pointed at the big oak in her yard. "And when you let those deacons hang him."

"I didn't have a thing to do with that," he said, turning for his car. "I'm done with you for now."

She watched Mathis drive off to waste somebody else's time, then took a seat in the chair next to the one he'd warmed up. After a while, she cooled down enough to think over what he'd said. White sheriffs and juries didn't need the law to put a black person in the pen. Not in this land. Not for hundreds of years. Not in 1971.

She remembered what the Lawd had already sent her way. He'd call her home when the time came. There was no use fretting over her own hide or anything else for that matter.

Least, that's what she thought—until the next man knocked on her door.

—✱ ✱ ✱—

THE STEPS ON COOKIE'S PORCH WERE soft and light. The tap on the door reminded her of Victry.

Cash didn't look up when she opened the door. His shoulders were even lower than his chin. She stooped to study his eyes. They weren't sad like his everyday eyes, or cold like the ones she'd seen in the hospital. Just lost.

She put a hand on his shoulder and asked what he was doing on her porch. No answer. She tightened her grip.

"I just saw my brother," Cash said. "In jail."

"Jail! For what?"

"Killing Myles. Even without a body, the prosecutor apparently had the motive and evidence for a murder charge."

"What evidence?"

"Big John gave the sheriff a bloody bat."

"Bloody?"

"Big John told me he'd thawed out a steak and wiped the blood on his bat. Said he called it *evidence* when he gave it to the sheriff. So I guess they've got a confession, on top of everything else."

"My Lawd."

"I'd expected my brother to be a mess at the funeral. What I saw on the porch that night had me worried. The way Slide found him this week left me thinking he'd gone off the deep end. Now I don't think. I know."

"You wrong, Cash. Yo brother was protecting me. The sheriff's been on my tail the past few days. Big John figured he was getting too close and decided to strap the trouble on his own shoulders."

Cash nodded. "Like he always does."

"I reckon so."

"There's more."

"What you saying, Cash?"

"Pearl's gone."

"Gone where?"

"Big John found her note in his rocker this morning. Said she needed to get away for a while, didn't think he'd mind because he hadn't noticed her anyway. Said she was staying with a friend in Memphis until she got a job and her own place. She promised to touch base at some point."

Cash backed down the steps and stopped, staring under the porch like he was searching for that dark world of his. A step and a hop had Cookie waving a hand in front of his face.

She pulled on his shirt. "Listen, Cash. We can't have you hitting the bottle again. Big John needs you. Yo woman and boy need you." He gave a weak nod. "You hearing me?"

"I'm with you." He looked up and met Cookie's eyes. "All the way."

She spent the next hour thinking about Pearl. The girl left town when her daddy was barely hanging on. Cookie didn't like it, but she understood. Pearl had been through a fire and needed fresh air. Hell, Cookie had skipped town for less when she was a girl. She had no right to blame Pearl for leaving this place for a while. Or longer.

PART IX

Big John woke and sat up in his cot, feeling fresh and relieved. Surprised as well, for he'd slept a full night for the first time since the wedding. Course he'd managed a few hours here and there. The little chair by the fireplace, the couch, his rocker. Anywhere but the bed he'd shared with Shine.

Truth was, Big John didn't mind the Hill County Jail. It was certainly no match for Stalag Luft I. Mississippi winters were toasty compared to northern Germany, and jail felt more like home than the farmhouse. Maybe *home* was a stretch, but the heaven he'd called home had become a living hell. The smell of cinnamon on Shine's apron. The lingering scent of her body on their bed. The sight of her unused pills on the bedside table, the nightgown she'd worn the day of her death.

He fled to the porch but found no escape. The place he'd cherished reminded him of coffee-talk with Shine. Of Pearl's "Stay out of this or you'll live to regret it."

Regret. He stood, walking circles in his cell, pondering the truth of her words. And haunted by Cookie's "You'll regret letting him live."

One of Cookie's heroes, and one of Big John's, came to mind. Big John had lost count of the times the brave man went to jail, but he remembered Dr. King's Birmingham march. Folks who didn't take kindly to it locked him up to think things over. Dr. King did more than think. He wrote a jailhouse letter that spread like wildfire.

Two lines stuck with Big John through the years: "Injustice anywhere is injustice everywhere," and "Justice delayed is justice denied." In Dr. King's view, those looking to harm used *time* better than those aiming for good.

Would Myles? Big John still believed in hope, though he didn't know why.

34

Slide

THE ARRAIGNMENT HAD US ALL ON edge. All except Big John. He didn't seem to care that Sheriff Mathis was set on locking him up for the duration. Or that Judge Reynolds, according to Momma, was a die-hard Presbyterian who trusted more in what the Bible had to say about total depravity than what the law had to say about innocent until proven guilty.

I tried to forget Shine's cathead biscuits as I mulled over the rocks Momma had concocted for breakfast. But trying ain't doing, as Cookie said, and I found myself craving Shine's huge fluffy cushions of butter and flour as I wondered how Momma's bloodthirsty biscuits could soak up a pot of gravy or a jar of jelly and still taste like cardboard.

Taste. Maybe that was the problem. Misry might've had six or seven senses, but Momma had three. Three-and-a-half if you wanted to be generous in the hearing department. As Momma liked her own cooking, her missing sense of taste was not up for debate.

Speaking of debate, I'd once heard Victry arguing with himself on whether nature or nurture was to blame for the Misrys of this world. He'd ended up more confused than I was from the start. Momma called it *blood and upbringing*, though there was little debate on her brain. Misry to Myles, blood was a flood that couldn't be stopped.

I didn't know whether to blame nature or nurture for the problems in this world, but I had no doubt Momma's cooking had nothing to do with the plate Deddy hadn't touched. She must've sensed something along those lines. She didn't make him lie about her biscuits or ask what projects our jack-of-all-trades would be working on that week. For better or worse, she had another plan.

"Had a dream about Judge Reynolds last night," she said. "Cash, you should've seen the skimpy nightgown Reynolds was wearing when he eased into *my* side of the bed." Deddy glanced at her grin and went back to eyeing his plate. "I'll swear on the judge's Bible no fornication occurred, but I'd be the Jezebel of Mississippi and beyond to say the judge wasn't sitting mighty close when he rubbed my . . ." She waited. Deddy didn't look up. "My *hand*, Cash, you dirty-minded scoundrel." Still no luck. "Anyhow, thought you'd want to know the old codger promised to read every last verse on mercy and forgiveness before presiding over the arraignment this morning."

Momma laughed, maybe hoping it would spread like a yawn. It didn't.

"Try something else," I mouthed. She nodded, studied Deddy for the next minute or so, and gave Uncle Lore a shot.

"Cash, you know what Lore's been spouting all week? 'No body, no murder. Guaran-damn-well-tee you, ole Reynolds will reduce those charges to reckless endangerment.'"

While there was no telling how endangered Myles had felt when Big John got reckless with his bat, there was no mystery surrounding the wisdom of Lore's way of thinking. Without a word, Deddy shot up from his chair and took off across the den. He slammed the front door and went for a drive.

— ✳ ✳ ✳ —

THE COURTROOM WAS DEAD QUIET AS the star of Momma's dream strolled from his chambers and sat in a huge leather chair. Judge Reynolds adjusted his long black robe and rearranged the stacks of paper on his desk. He eyed the courtroom like he owned every plank of wood and speck of dark stain on the floor, walls, and pews.

The judge nodded toward the prosecution's table on his right. "Good morning, Mr. Pickle."

Mr. Pickle stood, bowed low enough to sniff a judge's hindquarters, and said, "Good morning, Your Honor."

The judge who had greeted Mr. Pickle in a pleasant tone was now glaring toward the defense table on his left. Reynolds showed no sign he'd ever laid eyes on Big John, much less attended the reception at Lore's house a few months back.

"Who will be representing the defendant?" Reynolds asked.

Big John stood. "I'll represent myself, Your Honor." He glanced at Dewey Pickle and looked back at the judge. "I don't have much faith in these county lawyers."

"Hire your own counsel."

"I'd rather not, Judge. The truth is the truth. I'll do the best I can."

Reynolds shook his head, staring at Big John. Then he read the charges, made sure Big John understood, and asked for a plea.

Big John cocked his head as if the question hadn't crossed his mind. "I'll need to think it over, if that's all right."

Pickle hopped to his feet. "Your Honor, the prosecution shall oppose all attempts on behalf of the defendant to plead not guilty by reason of insanity."

The judge leaned forward and peered at Big John as if *insanity* made perfect sense. Big John raised his hand.

"Proceed," Reynolds said.

"I'd rather stay in jail until the trial. A lonely cell beats an empty house."

"I don't allow bail in murder cases anyway," Reynolds said.

"Far as the trial date goes, sooner the better," Big John said.

"Your Honor," Pickle said. "Prosecution requests sufficient time to complete the search for the body and prepare for the trial."

Reynolds leafed through the papers on his desk, studied one, and said, "Two months or so will be sufficient. The trial date is set for Monday, April the twelfth." He pounded the gavel. "This court is adjourned."

Deddy had fingernails for supper that night, and not because Momma's meatloaf looked and smelled worse than what slid from a can into Annabelle's bowl every morning.

"My brother isn't thinking straight," he kept saying.

"That ain't it," Momma finally said. "All the man wants is to be with Shine. From this seat at the table, he doesn't give a damn anymore."

Deddy pounded his fist on the table. "No!"

He jumped up from the table and ran outside.

✳ ✳ ✳

THE NEXT FEW WEEKS GOT DOWNRIGHT boring after the fun of jail wore off. While Sheriff Mathis did his part by dropping in for more of the same questions, my crazy-eyed killer uncle was nowhere to be found. The jail's showers and clean uniforms had Big John smelling better than summertime roadkill and, despite my prodding, he refused to murder the sheriff with even one of the eight words he'd conjured up from the depths of Spanish hell.

On the last Friday in February, Cookie decided to join me to pay the jailbird a visit. She marched in and locked both hands on her hips, glaring down at Big John.

"Care to have a seat?" he asked, though he surely knew the answer. "Any word on Snowball? Cash is supposed to be feeding my pretty boy."

"Pretty as a possum's tail," I said.

He chuckled. She didn't.

"Big John, what business you got turning lawyer on us?"

"Cookie, you've known of my plans for weeks. Why now?"

"You ain't the only dummy in town these days. I kept thinking you'd come around."

"The same pot that pays Mathis signs the checks for those lawyers. They got the blood on my bat, anyhow."

"*Blood* on yo bat?"

"Let's get on with her, far as I'm concerned."

"Parchman is nothing compared to this jail. The killers behind bars to the devils holding the keys, the state pen is bad. It'll be yo grave, Big John."

"I'll be fine."

"Fine, yo ass. Sounds like you giving up. Damn fool."

232

Cookie was safely out of sight when Big John reached under his mattress.

"Got this from Victry," he said. "No telling the times I've read it."

He studied the letter again, wiping tears with the back of his hand.

"Wish I had my bandana," he said. He reached for a hug. "Happy birthday, Slide."

"Thanks, Big John. But my birthday was over six weeks ago."

"I was there but still missed it." He leaned against one wall while squinting at another. He nodded and turned my way. "Slide, I think you're old enough now to hear what happened to Cookie's deddy. Elijah was one of the finest men I've ever known."

By the time Big John finished his story, I hated those white men more than Myles. Big John must've seen it on my face.

"I want you to read Victry's letter," he said. "Out loud."

"What's it about?"

"Hate," he said. "And love."

I took the letter and started reading.

Dear Big John,

Most bow to the might of money, the tyranny of today, the fleeting nod of man. You don't. You didn't.

June 25, 1955. You skipped work to spend the day with me, just me. A ten-year-old boy with his uncle, his hero.

I remember the cheese plate and ribs at the Rendezvous in Memphis. Our stroll through the lobby of The Peabody hotel. A mad dash for Tom Lee Park and what you called the prettiest sunset on both sides of the Mississippi River. (You were right by the way, for as an adult I've returned many times. Overlooking the mighty Mississippi, I gaze at the giant golden ball as it hovers and then joins the unbroken plain of the Arkansas Delta. The untold shades of pink and purple, blue and gray, orange and red. All timeless yet passing in the swirl of an angry river, the drift of a lazy cloud, the glow of a flat land.)

"Can't miss the sunset," you kept saying, as we scurried down the bluff, crossed Riverside Drive, and trotted through the park. You glanced to your right and stopped.

"Never noticed that before," you said, pointing toward the monument near the river's edge. "They must've put her up in the last year or so."

You led me by the hand to the foot of the obelisk.

"Must be thirty feet tall," you said. "Solid granite."

You read the words carved in its stone: TOM LEE WITH HIS BOAT "ZEV" SAVED THIRTY-TWO LIVES WHEN THE STEAMER U.S. NORMAN SANK ABOUT TWENTY MILES BELOW MEMPHIS MAY 8, 1925.

"Tom Lee was a real hero," you said. "With a fine monument to . . ."

You paused, then read the four words you had missed: A VERY WORTHY NEGRO. Over and over you mumbled those final two words. You whispered Elijah's name. And then you wept.

We missed the sunset, and you said very little on our drive home. Now I believe I know why.

Last month Cookie told me the details of what happened to her father. To your best friend. To Elijah, a brave and noble man.

A renamed park and granite monument was a just tribute to Tom Lee. Yet the hero's color had been noted before the lives, most if not all of white skin, he saved. And a worthy hero had been labeled "Negro."

Big John, you knew what awaited the others. The ones deemed not worthy. For you knew Elijah.

Can I imagine removing the body of a best friend from

a rope? As a white man from the largest antebellum in at least one Mississippi town, can I stand in the shoes of Cookie or her father? Do I deserve a place in Tom Lee's boat? Of course not. Yet can I not mourn their rope, The Rope? I hope so.

Big John, I've always treasured your poems. As with the carved words on a tombstone, they bleed a grit and a passion which sparks the mind and smacks the heart.

Below are my tombstone words to the death of an age. And to the lives of Elijah and Tom Lee.

A Very Worthy Negro
Chiseled in stone, made the words commit.
To remember a hero, who just wouldn't quit.
Thirty-two LIVES saved, in brave and noble way.
A VERY WORTHY NEGRO, so very much to say.
"I call you by first name, whether young or old.
You best say Mister, just like you been told.
You're part of the family, the toilet's out there.
When riding a bus, sit you know where.
Live anywhere you want, with the other blacks.
Make damn sure to stay, that side of the tracks.
Get a drink of water, the spicket's outside.
Barely does work, bend over open wide."
Not much expected, of a Tom back then.
Except to know his place, all because of skin.
Words last forever, carved deep in a rock.
Mighty fine hero, yet of lesser stock?
Countless stand our heroes, strong and brave.
They often get famous, just enemies to save?
Enemy at first, sounds way too strong.
Hundreds of years, pretty damn long.
Still Tom on the river, he saw only man.

JEFF BARRY

Said to himself, "Gotta do what I can."
Small boat raging river, he knew the danger ahead.
Of pulling whitened panic, and then the dead.
Risked life and limb, though saving not his kind.
So many LIVES relieved, to color Tom was blind.
One has to believe, amidst the waves and fright.
Shade of Tom's hand, didn't have to be white.
Touching pale skin, my oh my what a tiff.
Until pale hit the water, and Tom had the skiff.
Worthy man higher, reaching from his boat.
Couldn't last forever, as Negro gives note.
Chains of a culture, The Rope straight from hell.
Colors more than flesh, stains souls as well.
Power of an era, to force-shape the mind.
Customs of an age, dark ties that bind.

I finished reading, then set the paper on the floor. I stared at the last page but saw only five words: "The Rope straight from hell."

✳ ✳ ✳

VICTRY WORE HIS FEELINGS ON HIS face. Did I? Had Big John seen hate? Did he read my thoughts as I stared at those five words from Victry's poem? If so, he got what I'd seen in Victry the day Big John sliced through a rope with a few strokes from his pocketknife. I was upset. I was mad. And I was confused.

I asked Big John lots of questions that weekend. He couldn't talk about Elijah and wouldn't talk about Myles, so we spent most of our time on God. And The Rope, of course.

"White deacons and Myles, you and Sam," I said. "Strands of the same rope. How do you tell them apart?"

"No idea, Slide. Wish I knew."

I asked Big John if he still believed in God, if he thought God was good, plus a host of other questions along those lines. He answered a third or so with some version of "No idea." He reminded me of Victry on another third—a puzzled look as he answered questions with questions—and Cookie on the rest.

"One helluva cluster," I told Big John, as I was leaving on Sunday afternoon. "Like the strands in Victry's rope."

"Well, folks who think they've figured everything out are often the ones who trouble Victry so much. It's okay to be confused, Slide."

I didn't sleep much that night, but I did figure a few things out. On where I stood, anyhow.

Victry's rope. The Rope. In Big John's pasture on Labor Day weekend, I'd watched Victry and wondered if he was half-crazy and half-right. Now? I'd seen enough to know Victry wasn't crazy, and I thought he was seventy-five percent right.

✳ ✳ ✳

BIG JOHN'S FOURTH WEEK IN JAIL was the worst.

A jailer was fumbling with his keys when Big John shot up from his cot. "Hey, Slide. How'd school go today?"

The hop in his step reminded me of the day he'd polished off one bowl of Shine's cobbler and was hightailing it to the kitchen for his second.

"How come you're in such a good mood?" I asked.

"Oh, nothing much," he said, sounding like Lore bragging on a trophy buck he'd ambushed in another "secret spot nobody knows about." We sat on the bench next to his bed. "But I did write us a little song this morning." He winked. "About your *favorite* cousin."

"You feeling all right?"

"Truth is, I haven't felt this sporty in ages."

"About a song you wrote?"

He jumped to his feet. "Slide, I wouldn't do this for just anybody, but you're such a fine boy I'll sing her for you. Might even add my prairie shuffle to the equation. Free of charge."

The prairie shuffle? Crap. I had barely survived the other time I was tortured with the dance Big John had invented in his drinking days over twenty years and a hundred pounds ago.

I was praying for a way out when the world's biggest ballerina sprang into action. With one hand reaching for heaven and the other shooting straight for hell, he dug a big toe into the floor and rocked in a slow-motion circle somehow balanced by the other foot dancing through the air with its own round of circles.

I thought the silent shuffle was torture until he started singing:

A little bit of Salt goes a long, long way.
Not too many folks got so much to say.
Toss a little bit here, a little more there.
Next thing you know Salt's everywhere, everywhere.
She might be short, but she's more than loud.
And when my girl's a-smiling, sky ain't got a cloud.
But if my Salt's not happy, the whole world knows.
You'd rather have a thorn stuck between your toes,
between your—"

"Okay, Big John! Okay!" I swallowed a throw-up burp. "I've got the picture. All of it."

"You're not getting jealous on me, are you?"

"Jealous as a preacher's pecker."

"Orman Slide Jackson."

"Well, I can think of a blue-zillion things I'd rather do than watch that shuffle and listen to you sing about Salt."

35

M Y LOUSY WEEK BOTTOMED OUT WHEN Deddy came home from work with a bottle in each hand.

Why did he pick that Friday? He'd been sober for six months. Not exactly sturdy as steel given the nubs Deddy had for fingernails, but steady enough through Shine's cancer, Pearl's stay in the hospital, and Big John's first month in jail. Then he'd up and decided to grab two bottles and head for the couch.

Cookie came by on Saturday afternoon. She cussed and preached up a storm but got nowhere. She pulled Momma aside on her way out.

"Ethel, you got no time to waste," she said. "Get yo ass to church tomorrow morning and find Sam."

"Church?" Momma asked. "We haven't been to church in ages. Besides, Cash hasn't listened to the first preacher since Vietnam."

Cookie pointed toward the den. "You think I'm talking about *him* going?"

"I don't know what I'm thinking. He's worse than ever. With Big John in jail and you not making any headway, I'm out of ideas."

"Only idea you need is to give Sam a try," Cookie said. "He loves Big John like a daddy and will do what he can for Cash. Love trickles on down thataway."

"I might have to."

"No *might* to it. You got to."

⋆ ⋆ ⋆

MY FAVORITE PART OF BIG CHURCH, the closing hymn, was wrapping up when Sam slipped through a side door and into the hallway he used to circle around to the back of the sanctuary. Though the hungriest of sinners snuck out when the congregation stood for the last hymn, Sam gave the rest of his sheep a "shepherd's hug" or at least the "right hand of fellowship" before sending them out to face a world full of wolves.

Momma had other plans. She nearly yanked my arm off as we hurried through the double doors in the back and took a sharp left through the lobby. She opened the door as Sam walked up. I couldn't tell whether he was more surprised to be ambushed at the end of an empty hallway or to see us at church.

"Good to see you, Ethel," he said. "You too, Slide."

"Fine preaching, Reverend," Momma said.

"Please call me Sam. Or Brother Sam will do. We're all part of the same family."

"Family is why I'm here. You know we haven't made church in a month of Sundays, but I need your help."

"What can I do?"

"Cash is in bad shape, Reverend."

Sam nodded my way. "Would Slide like to play in the gym?"

"He ain't too spiffy in the gym," she said. "He's seen and heard everything, anyhow."

"I understand. Tell me what Cash has been up to."

"Nothing but drinking liquor and throwing up on the couch. I've tried it all. Talking, yelling, begging. Even brought Cookie over for one of her sermons. Nothing's done a lick of good. Cash is different this time. I see it in his eyes. If the drinking doesn't kill him, something else will."

"I'll be there tomorrow."

"Goodness, Sam. I didn't expect a house call. You got all these regulars to look after here."

"But I have a lost sheep *there*. I'm a pastor first, Ethel. A shepherd. I'm ashamed to say I haven't been with your Cash. With our Cash." He pulled a bulletin from his back pocket and scribbled down his number.

"Here, call me at home if it can't wait until the morning. Otherwise, I'll be knocking on your door at seven o'clock sharp."

—✳ ✳ ✳—

I WOKE AT FIRST LIGHT, PONDERING why Big John bragged on his brother given half a chance. Not even half, truth be told, and not always with the truth. That said, nobody questioned his claim that Deddy was the best woodsman in Hill County when he was a boy.

According to Big John, Deddy was ten years old when he snuck off with a .410 shotgun and went hunting in the Hope Springs National Forest for the first time. By himself and without a compass. At thirteen Deddy made a longbow and arrows from hickory saplings. Used turkey feathers for fletching and small rocks from creeks for arrowheads. Hunted squirrels and rabbits in the fall, deer in the winter, and camped or fished the rest of the year.

The boy with no compass was now a sheep who couldn't find his way off the couch. Little did he know a shepherd was on the prowl.

Momma opened the door on Sam's second knock. He ignored her greeting and asked where Deddy was. Sam was halfway across the den by the time Momma caught up and grabbed his arm.

Love and *like* didn't like each other around our house, especially when Deddy was in love with his bottle. But Annabelle still liked him. He might as well've been a cherry lollypop instead of a smelly bum by the way she waited by his side to lick up the mess, and she might as well've been a wild-eyed wolf instead of a sweet old Lab when somebody messed with one of us. Especially Deddy.

Hands on his hips and fire in his eyes, Sam reminded me of Cookie as he watched Momma lead Annabelle into the kitchen. He stalked over and kicked the couch. Deddy's eyes cracked open, closed, and shot wide.

"Preacher?" he asked, as if he'd woken up at his own funeral.

"At least you're sober enough to see," Sam said.

"What are you doing here?"

Sam grabbed him by the elbow. "Get up, Cash. You're coming with me."

"Let go of me. Who the hell are you barging in uninvited and ordering me around?"

"I'm Brother Sam. I was invited. And from now on I'll barge in and order you around whenever I damn well please."

"Hellfire. Never heard a preacher talk like that."

"Get the hell up!"

"Quit pulling on me. And quit cursing. It ain't right for a preacher."

"I'll curse all I want, and I'm not letting go. Maybe it's time you learned what an ass-whipping from a preacher feels like."

"Sam, you got no clue what I can do to a fella."

"You've been drunk for days. I'll take my chances. I fought drunk before I got saved. Never fought sober, but I'm ready."

"All right," Deddy said. "No use whipping a preacher's ass, I reckon."

Sam helped Deddy to his feet, clamped a hand on each arm to hold him up, and stepped close enough to taste his breath. Deddy cocked his head, squinting like Sam needed a long stay in a short bin for loonies.

"It doesn't matter you're too drunk to remember this," Sam said. "You'll hear it again and again. I have two rules for you, Cash. One, from here on you'll be at church every Sunday morning, Sunday night, and Wednesday night. Drunk or sober. Two, whenever I stop by this house, you're coming with me."

Sam led him through the den and down the hallway.

Momma opened the front door. "Sam, whatever you have in mind is fine with me."

"I've called a place in Memphis," he said. "They'll do their best to sober him up. They don't allow visitors, but I'll try and keep you posted."

"No hurry on this end," she said.

Amen, I wanted to say.

We watched from the porch as Sam shoved Deddy into the Buick and drove off.

"Sam and Cash," Momma said. "Opposites will attract if you give 'em time to sniff each other out. Look at your daddy and me."

"You and Deddy? Shitfire, Sam's screwed from the start if that's how it works." Momma's eyes told me the hope she was holding onto didn't need killing. I winked and changed course. "Unless *attracting* amounts to whatever you and Deddy are doing when you keep me up at night."

"Watch it, young man," she said, trying not to smile. "We ain't bird dogs after all."

I spent the better part of the day thinking about hope, bird dogs, and Uncle Lore. The whole town knew he'd blown a working man's fortune on two pointers that ran for cover at the first crack of a gun. With no room for bragging and no hope for keeping his trap shut, Lore turned his attention to talking about the dogs of rival hunters. From then on, their gun-shy bird dogs flushed more quail than they pointed. Every deer hound chased rabbits. And the best coon dog in the county treed possums on good nights and cornered skunks on the bad.

Another round of malicious gossip in the bag, Lore would lean back with the saddest face and voice he could muster. "Reckon all we can do is hope for the best," he'd say before moving on to a well-earned nap.

Hope for the best made sense when it came to Lore and his bird dogs. But Momma and her opposites?

✶ ✶ ✶

I HAD NO IDEA WHAT THE folks in Memphis had done with Deddy over the past four days, but I knew a miracle when I saw one. Momma gave all the credit to Sam, and Sam gave all the credit to God.

Deddy had a hint of a smile on his face as Sam reminded us that church started in less than forty-eight hours. The preacher pushed it too far when he mentioned Sunday and Wednesday nights again. Once a week was enough for a sinner named Slide.

"How long does night church have to last?" I asked.

"Until your deddy is settled long enough to stick," Sam said. He grinned. "Then we'll leave it up to his own free will."

"Free will?" Momma asked. "I guess we'll learn about that in Sunday school."

"Sunday school?" I asked.

Sam wrapped his arm around my shoulder. "Slide, I don't recall Sunday school being part of the deal, do you?"

"No sir. You only mentioned those other three."

"You good at keeping secrets?"

"Fair to middling."

He winked at Momma and Deddy. "Off the record here, Slide, you won't find a single verse on Sunday school. Now don't utter a word of this around church, or every deacon except Big John will have my head on a platter before our next meeting is called to order."

—⋆ ⋆ ⋆—

BIG JOHN HADN'T BEEN ABLE TO help his brother. Neither had Momma or even Cookie. But in a matter of days, Sam had Deddy off the bottle, back to work, and taking notes in church.

The next few weeks wiped away the last of my doubts. From camping in the national forest to crappie fishing at Sardis Lake, Deddy and his preacher carried on like they'd grown up in the same playpen.

Sam pulled me aside after one of his sermons.

"Slide, I've never seen anything like the man," he said, shaking his head as if Lazarus had just strolled out of the grave. "Your deddy knows every hill and tree and critter in those woods. Every spring and creek and swamp. The out of doors comes so natural to him."

"Big John gives their grandpa Chester the credit," I said. "He was a full-blooded Chickasaw."

"You think Big John's serious?"

"Yessir. Ask him about Andrew Jackson and you'll learn right quick what he thinks of that president. Chester's grandparents were shipped off on the Trail of Tears. He never forgave Old Hickory, and neither has Big John." Sam nodded. "Chester's picture looks just like Deddy."

"Well, maybe that's it."

"Deddy didn't care for playing in the yard. His playground was the national forest."

Sam said amen like he was wrapping up a sermon.

Momma and her opposites came to mind as Sam walked off. She'd been right for a change. What had started with a fighting-mad preacher and a liquored-up loafer ended with two best friends. And one new deddy.

Sam called it redemption. I called it another miracle.

PART X

HOPE AND FAITH WERE A MIXED bag for Big John. At times, they meant the same. At others, they meant nothing at all. Now?

Faith. Big John had lost faith in God and man—his bride was dead, and the best man for his daughter had turned out to be the worst—but he didn't share those doubts with Slide. The boy's bright eyes and zippy voice spoke of a new faith in miracles, a preacher, and a father. Big John vowed not to kill the spark he saw in the boy.

Hope. The hope Big John found in a German shed lasted two years. Most had died with James, the rest with Elijah. Hope had returned when Pearl was born. Then Shine on her deathbed and Pearl at death's door.

Truth was, Big John had grown to fear hope before he landed in jail for the murder of Pearl's husband. Now charged with a crime he couldn't commit but wouldn't defend, he welcomed death or life in jail over his daughter knowing the truth.

36

Slide

MIRACLES. FOUR DAYS BEFORE THE TRIAL, a horde of manna fell our way when a stone-faced Uncle Lore showed up with a plan that made sense. He was all business from the get-go.

"I talked to Judge Reynolds today," he said.

"You *what?*" Big John asked.

"I ran into him at the Rotary Club and decided to ask a few questions. Me and the judge were in the same fraternity back at Ole Miss."

Big John sighed and shook his head. "And what did your fraternity buddy say?"

"I didn't say he was a buddy. Ole Reynolds can be a first-rate asshole."

I scooted over on the bench and nudged Big John. "That means they're best friends."

"Slide, keep your mouth shut and let the grown-ups finish their bidness," Lore said.

Big John held back a laugh but not a chuckle. I managed a firm but fake nod, then waited as Lore seemed to ponder, for the first time no doubt, his next words.

"Truth is, the judge didn't say much."

"Good," Big John said.

"What he did say was important. He said you're a fool for representing yourself. Means you gotta quit horsin' around and lawyer up."

"You've been talking to Cookie," Big John said.

"Big John, you're a smart enough fella, particularly when it comes to history and philosophizing and such. But lawyering ain't your department."

"What have I got to lose? Shine's dead. Pearl left town. I took care of Myles and didn't run from the law. I'll be all right."

"Not according to the righteous and almighty judge who'll be running your trial."

"Lore, you heard what I think of those county lawyers."

"That's why I went straight home, picked up the phone, and hired one for you. A real hoss of a lawyer from Oxford named Tex Simmons. With the trial only a few days off, I went ahead and gave Tex a rundown. Told him you'd done a whale of a job hiding the body and so forth."

Big John buried his face in his hands. "Lord."

"You can thank me later."

"There was a *d* on the end," I piped up.

"I know that, Slide," Lore lied.

"How do you know this Tex fella?" Big John asked.

"I've hired him to straighten out a few property lines on my plantation, if you hear what I'm saying. But land ain't his forte. Keeping outlaws like you outta jail is where Tex butters his biscuit." Lore smiled. "Face the facts, my friend. Sometimes you gotta scoop shit with a shovel."

"I can't let you do that."

"She's a done deal."

"Lore, you know I can't afford one of those high-priced lawyers."

"You won't be out a nickel. Won't hear of it. From all you've done for my boy, Victry, to doting on Salt to the time you spend with this here whippersnapper, it's the least I can do. Adding meat to that bone, I might be short in lots of places, but I'm tall when it comes to the pocketbook."

"I appreciate your offer, but—"

"My pines won't break a sweat on Tex's bill. Money does grow on trees, my friend."

"The time I spend with those children has nothing to do with money."

"I'm not talking money, Big John. I'm talking love. T-I-M-E is how *you* spell love. It's how we all oughta spell it."

Lore's jawing about money was one thing, but love? Had everyday manna taken a back seat to the Pearly Gates?

Big John looked my way. "I do love my children. Love 'em with all I got. All I got left."

"You treat 'em like your own," Lore said.

"They got fine deddies and all, but they're mine too."

"I knew you'd come around," Lore said, deciding the matter was settled.

Love and lawyers in the rearview, Lore stuck his thumbs under his belt and hoisted his britches. A quick hop jiggled his belly in directions that should've landed him in jail for at least one lifetime. He planted a stubby hand on my shoulder.

"Uncle Lore's proud of you," Lore said. "You sure are a sprouting devil." He spun around and banged on the door. "I'm ready, jailer, ain't got all day!"

Manna hadn't been gone five minutes when a preacher dropped in. Sam gave me a hug and tried stretching his arms around Big John.

"Good news," Sam said. "I've dealt with Judge Reynolds on behalf of my *other* wayward sheep."

Big John sat and stroked the whiskers on his chin.

"I don't remember any sheep this wayward," he said, grinning at his shepherd.

Sam frowned. "Reynolds is a hard man, Big John. But I have something in the works."

"Something in the works?"

"Could backfire, though I doubt we have much to lose at this point."

"Sam, what are you saying?"

"I'm betting a roomful of voters will remind the judge of his next election. Our church will have his courtroom jam-packed on Monday morning."

"Lands alive," Big John said. "Well, guess I oughta thank the Lord you're on our team and not the sheriff's."

"We all love you," Sam said. He pointed at the concrete floor. "You're a rock, Big John. The crew trapped in your B-24 knew it. Same with your family and friends and church."

⊹ ⊹ ⊹

ON FRIDAY AFTERNOON, BIG JOHN BOLTED up from the bench and ran to the bars. They shook and moaned as the big man pulled. It didn't matter where she'd been, or what she'd been up to. All this deddy cared about was seeing his girl.

The second the jailer turned the key, Big John threw the door open and took Pearl into his arms. Looking healthy and pretty as ever, she gave me a hug before I slipped out and headed home.

Momma was happy to hear about Pearl, but Deddy could find a cloud in the sunniest of skies. He gnawed on his nails and pestered Momma all weekend. She'd had enough by Sunday afternoon.

"Cash, I'm tired of listening to every worst-case scenario this world and the next has to offer," she said. "I ain't got the foggiest notion what Pearl's been up to in Memphis, but I do happen to know the trial starts tomorrow. And that we better have one helluva lawyer and jury to make up for Judge Reynolds and a bloody bat. Y'all go bother Big John a while."

⊹ ⊹ ⊹

DEDDY AND I WALKED UP TO find Pearl sitting in her deddy's lap.

"Just in time, boys," Big John said. "Lore's high-dollar lawyer will be here any minute."

Sure enough, within minutes Tex moseyed up to the door.

Whoever named our lawyer knew what he was up against. Tex's cowboy hat could've held bottles of Deddy's whiskey. His dark blazer held a waxy shine to match whatever Cadillac I figured he was driving. The rat's tail some called a tie did nothing to hide the sparkly shirt held together by gold cuff links and tucked into blue jeans that would've stood board-straight without Tex's long legs and snakeskin boots for company.

He strutted in and nodded at Deddy before resting his beady gray eyes on my nose. "Aren't you a sporty young bird?"

Bird? Back in sixth grade, the school bully had called me bird and said the beak I had for a nose would make a woodpecker jealous. When the girls giggled, I forgot how tough the bully was supposed to be and had landed a punch that left no doubt he was all bluff.

Big John looked tighter than his lawyer's jeans as Tex eyed Pearl with a series of closed-mouth grunts that reminded me of Lore imitating a rutting buck.

"You must be the daughter I've heard so much about," Tex said. "My, you're a fine-looking filly. Too fine, truth be told. Tomorrow I want a layer of dark makeup under those pretty eyes. And your left cheek, assuming Myles was right-handed."

He studied Pearl with another round of grunts that didn't notice the pretty eyes glaring his way. Big John was now clearing his throat on a regular basis. I didn't know whether to laugh or throw up.

"Listen to me, baby," Tex said, though listening didn't appear to be his number one forte. "Tomorrow I need a long skirt stretching past those knees." His eyes moved up a notch or two. "And for the love of God, wear a homely blouse that covers those darlings."

"Tex," Big John said, sounding annoyed but not surprised.

He glanced at Big John and turned back to Pearl. "Baby, I need you looking plain, bruised, and broken. Then all you gotta do is keep your cool and play along with ole Tex here."

"If I can keep my cool with you, I can handle whatever else comes up," she said.

"Tex, anything else?" Big John asked.

He strolled over to Big John and leaned in like he was telling a secret. "I'm proud of you, chief. You did what any deddy worth his salt would've done." Tex smiled. "Lore tells me you got a little Injun in those veins."

Big John narrowed his eyes. "My granddeddy Chester was a Chickasaw Indian. He wasn't a chief."

"I'm with you," Tex said in a way that said he wasn't. He squared his hat. "Big John, I'm worried about the judge. A real back-stabbing, Bible-thumping bullshitter if you ask me. But Lord willing, the blacks on the jury will begrudge the sheriff for all his shenanigans through the years. They're good church folks, the whites too, so we'll make a big deal of you being a deacon and all."

"I wish you'd keep the church bidness out of this," Big John said.

"Keeping you out of Parchman is my bidness. It's not an easy job, Big John. Thank God they haven't found the body, but you all but confessed when you referred to your bloody bat as evidence."

37

I TRUSTED OUR PREACHER. THAT SAID, AS Judge Reynolds took his seat and glared across the jam-packed courtroom, he didn't seem a bit concerned about his next election. Had Sam's plan backfired?

Instead of facing that question, I studied the man charged with putting my uncle in the pen. The size of Mr. Pickle's mouth and ears, along with the high-pitched bark I remembered from the arraignment, reminded me of the squirrels that made themselves at home in Big John's pecan grove. Tex and all his thunder would roll right over this critter, I figured.

Until Pearl was called to the stand, that is. She'd not only left off the dark makeup Tex wanted under her eyes and on her left cheek, she'd worn a skirt and a blouse that were far from long and homely.

"Mrs. Spettle, correct?" Pickle asked.

"I don't use his name anymore," she said. "Call me Pearl."

"Yes ma'am, whatever you prefer. You are the wife of Myles Spettle, correct?"

"I was."

"What do you mean by *was*?"

"You're prosecuting my daddy for murder and asking me?"

"Pearl, when was the last time you saw your husband?" Pickle asked, a hint of irritation in his voice.

"The last time he beat me."

"And when did this event supposedly take place?"

"Supposedly? I suppose you didn't bother to check with my doctors at the hospital?"

Pickle turned to the judge.

"Mrs. Spettle," Reynolds said, "you are to answer the questions and not ask them."

Pickle faced the jury. "The defense has presented no evidence, none whatsoever, that Myles Spettle harmed this lady." He stepped closer to the stand. "Pearl, do you believe Mr. Spettle was murdered?"

"I sure as hell hope somebody killed the man who tried to kill me. Who put me in the damn hospital and made me miss my own momma's funeral!"

The judge pounded his gavel to silence the crowd.

He lowered his forefinger to within an inch of his thumb. "Mrs. Spettle, I'm this close to holding you in contempt of my court. Understood?"

She met the judge's eyes, gave half a shrug, and nodded.

Was Tex as worried as I was? Pearl was acting everything but plain, bruised, and broken.

"Pearl, I was sorry to learn of your mother's death," Pickle said. "By all accounts, she was a wonderful woman who meant very much to you and your father. How would you describe his condition before her passing?"

"I was in the hospital and didn't see Daddy much."

"And when you did see him?"

"About like you'd expect."

Pickle walked to his desk and returned with a newspaper. "Pearl, were you in the hospital when your father placed his poem in the *Hill County News*?"

"No."

"Did you read it?"

"Yes."

Pickle held the paper in both hands, tilting his head as if reading "The Bride" for the first time. "The slander of Mr. Spettle and our high sheriff is certainly worth noting, but my question concerns the last five words of your father's poem: 'Deddy Bear has a bat.' Pearl, what do these words mean to you?"

She chuckled, leaned forward, and winked at the squirrel. "Means what it says, Dewey, wouldn't you agree?"

Pickle raised his hands as a wave of whispers crossed the room. To my surprise, Reynolds didn't pound his gavel or scold Pearl. He only gave her a stern look and told Pickle to continue.

"Pearl, your father's words, written for all to see, clearly show intent," Pickle said. "Did he speak of his plan to kill your husband?"

"Daddy never mentioned it."

"What did he mention?"

"I was too drugged up on pain pills to remember much of anything."

"What do you remember?"

"Well, I told my daddy that Myles wouldn't put me in the hospital again." Her eyes lit up. "Because I'd kill myself first. Never would've said that if—"

She slid back in her chair, staring at Tex. For some reason he nodded for her to continue.

She pointed toward the man sitting behind Pickle's desk. "You already know, don't you, Sheriff Mathis? You remember the feel of my daddy's barrel after you came to his farm and hog-tied his best friend to a fuel tank for nothing more than having black skin."

"Objection," Pickle said. "Your Honor, the witness has no right to bring such unrelated rumor into this case."

"Sustained," the judge said. "Mrs. Spettle, keep your comments to the proceedings at hand."

"That will be all, Your Honor," Pickle said, apparently smart enough to quit while he was ahead.

Tex stood. "Your Honor, I have no questions for Mrs. Spettle."

No questions? What was Tex thinking? Pearl hadn't just ignored his advice. She'd ripped it to shreds. Reynolds shook his head, looking confused as well.

"Next witness," he said.

"Prosecution calls Jonathon Jackson to the stand," Pickle said.

Big John lumbered toward the front like he was heading for the grave Cookie had promised at Parchman. He made his way up the steps in the outfit he'd worn to Shine's funeral—the tie, blazer, polyester pants, and zipper boots he'd also worn the day Myles and Pearl joined us in the family pew.

Memories of Big John's birthday flooded my brain. Myles's suit and the smell of Pearl's perfume. Myles's praise of Big John, the good father who wanted the best for his daughter. Pearl's angry but telling response, "What he thinks is best." Sunday dinner and Myles's tears over his sister, the tears he nearly shed after leveling the redneck at Harry's.

My dream came to an end as Pickle asked, "Mr. Jackson, do you have an alibi for the night Myles Spettle disappeared?"

"No, sir," Big John said.

"I see," Pickle said, gazing at the jury like it was their duty to hang the cold-blooded killer. "Mr. Jackson, did you kill Myles Spettle?" Big John stared at his lap. "Mr. Jackson?"

Big John wiped his eyes, looked up at Pearl, and said, "Did what I had to do, Mr. Pickle. Hope you'd have done the same."

Pickle smiled. "That will be all, Your Honor."

Tex stood. "No questions for Mr. Jackson, Your Honor."

Now I was really stumped. Lore's high-priced lawyer had let Pearl go without a question and done the same after Big John had all but told the jury he was guilty. Was Tex on Lore's payroll, or Pickle's? I wondered, as Sheriff Mathis waddled his way to the stand.

After a long sermon on how blessed Hill County was to have such a splendid sheriff at its beck and call, Pickle asked, "Sheriff Mathis, did Jonathon Jackson kill Myles Spettle?"

"There's no doubt in my mind. That poem proves his intent. What his daughter just said shows his motive, misplaced though it was. He has no alibi. And we have the murder weapon."

Pickle strutted to his desk and picked up the bat. "Sheriff, is this the weapon you found on the defendant's porch?"

"Not only on the porch," Mathis said. "In his lap."

"This very bat?"

"Except for the blood."

"The blood?"

"Looks to me like a good bit of the victim's blood has flaked off. Otherwise, you're holding the weapon Big John used to murder Myles Spettle."

"Thank you, Sheriff Mathis. That will be all."

About damn time, I said to myself, as Tex's cowboy boots pounded their way toward the witness stand.

"Sheriff, would you be so kind as to update the jury on the search for the body of Myles Spettle?" Tex asked.

"Mr. Spettle disappeared without a trace over two months ago," Mathis said. He pointed at Big John. "He did a good job of hiding the body. Haven't found it but we will."

"No clues?" Tex asked. Mathis leaned back and crossed his arms. "Sheriff?"

"None to speak of," Mathis said. "But we got Big John's confession splattered all over his bat. 'Evidence,' he called it himself."

"Evidence for what?"

Mathis stared at Tex like he was the idiot. "Why, murder, of course."

"Of course," Tex said with a smirk. "Sheriff, have you ever nicked one of your chins while shaving?"

"Objection!" Pickle barked.

"My question is pertinent to this case, Your Honor," Tex said.

"Objection overruled," the judge said. "Mr. Simmons, you may proceed as long as you do so in a civil manner."

"Yessir, Your Honor," Tex said, turning to the sheriff. "Sheriff Mathis, have you hunted quail?"

"Since I was a boy."

"Do you prefer pointers or setters?"

Mathis cocked his head, perhaps searching for a trap. Tex craned his neck as if waiting for the most important answer in trial history.

"Pointers," Mathis finally said.

"Thank you, Sheriff," Tex said. "After a long day of chasing quail through briar thickets, the tender snout of a pointer is covered in blood, agreed?"

"Well, I guess so."

"And the blood-stained pointer is alive, correct?"

"I'm not sure what you're getting at."

"Sheriff, you know exactly what I'm getting at. The shedding of blood is no proof, none whatsoever, that a death has occurred. Or even a crime committed. Would you not agree?"

"Well, I suppose so."

"Thank you, *Mister* Mathis. And while we're on the subject of evidence, tell me what kind of a bozo for a sheriff doesn't need a body in a murder case."

The judge pounded his gavel. "Order! Order in my court!" He waited for the room to quiet down. "Mr. Simmons, you will respect this court. And witness."

"My apologies, Your Honor."

Tex strolled toward his seat as if done with the sheriff.

Mathis was halfway down the steps when Tex whirled. "I'm sorry, Mr. Mathis. I almost forgot my last question."

The sheriff climbed back up and sat.

"Mr. Mathis, it appears we're in agreement on so much of this case," Tex said. "You have a bat covered with the blood of some creature. Dead or alive, we have no clue. Speaking of clues. Not only are we missing a body, I don't recall you mentioning any witnesses to this alleged crime. Or did I miss that part of the trial?" A purple vein popped up, ran across the sheriff's forehead, and looked ready to burst by the time Tex said, "That will be all, Mr. Mathis. I'm much obliged for your assistance. Much obliged."

Tex called his next witness to the stand.

"Brother Sam, tell us about your friend Big John," Tex said.

Sam turned and faced the jury. "As a shepherd of the Lord's flock for the past fifteen years, I've never had a finer deacon. Never met a finer man. Family, church, town, country. Big John has been a rock for so many for so long." Sam lifted his arms. "What evidence, real evidence, have we seen for this crime our Big John has been accused of?"

"Objection, Your Honor," Pickle said. "The witness is not to question the jury."

"Sustained," Reynolds said.

Sam nodded. "I've staked my life on a Shepherd who embodies the very meaning of forgiveness. And I believe with all my heart Big John would've followed his Shepherd given one ounce of prayer, one morsel of hope, that a crooked sheriff would protect his girl from the monster who put her in the hospital."

Pickle pounded his fist and yelled "Objection!" while Reynolds pounded his gavel and called for order.

"Objection sustained," Reynolds said, glaring at Tex. "Mr. Simmons, redirect your witness. Or I will."

"Your Honor," Tex said. "I have no further questions for Brother Sam."

Pickle wanted no part of Sam, but he gave one helluva closing argument. Cradling the bat like a baby, he made a martyr of Myles, Hill County's model citizen, while pleading with the jury to put my cold-hearted killer of an uncle behind bars for life.

"Members of the jury," Pickle concluded. "A murder case, much less a guilty verdict, without a body is admittedly rare." He paused, pointing the bat at Big John. "But rare indeed, if not unheard of, is a defendant with no alibi who so clearly provides the intent, motive, and evidence, if not confession, which proves his guilt beyond a reasonable doubt. Prosecution asks that you find the defendant guilty as charged. Thank you for your time."

Tex stood, adjusted his tie, and made his way to the jury box.

"Ladies and gentlemen," he said. "You've heard the sheriff's testimony—no body, no witness, no crime for all we know. And you've heard from Brother Sam. The fate of this fine father now rests in your hands. Thank you."

Was that a closing argument? A minute tops, I figured. All delivered in a voice that reminded me of the funeral director at Shine's visitation.

I studied the jury. Twelve faces. Eight white and four black. Seven men and five women. Not a glimpse of mercy on a single face. As the jury filed out, I lowered my head and wanted to cry.

The jury needed only fifty minutes—a bad sign given what I'd heard about quick decisions and guilty verdicts.

I'd read *To Kill a Mockingbird* in school that year. Scout's words—"a jury never looks at a defendant it has convicted"—came to mind as the jury filed back in, sat, and stared at their laps.

38

I SHOULD'VE SLEPT LIKE A KID THAT night. Instead, I smiled at the ceiling as I pondered reckoning, redemption, and my plan for Big John.

First on tomorrow's list? A full account of the glorious swing that sealed the deal for Myles's skull. Then I'd pester Big John until he caved on where the maggots were munching on the body. War would come next. Big John always said I was too green for the good ones. But now? From a bottle at home to a cousin in the hospital and a bat on the porch, I'd seen and heard enough to deserve a good war story.

— ✕ ✕ ✕ —

I RAN ALL THE WAY TO the gate and hollered Big John's name. Moving lickety-split for an old-timer in boots and overalls, he lit out across the porch and through the yard as I trotted down the gravel drive.

He stole the last of my breath with a long hug before carrying on about how thankful he was to see me again. When I reminded him of yesterday's trial, plus dozens of jail visits, he chuckled and worked his way up.

"Those visits meant the world to me," he said. "But there's something extra special about having you here at the farm."

We'd just settled into our rockers when the white blur from Big John's heaven and Cookie's hell darted from the pecan grove to the dead oak. He scampered across the trunk, peering into one hole after another.

"Isn't Snowball supposed to be smart?" I asked.

"Smartest cat this side of the Mason-Dixon."

"God gave the brains to Yankee cats, I suppose."

He grinned. "Snowball knows Ole Red uses that tree for pecking and hobnobbing instead of sleeping."

"What the hell's he doing?"

I expected a frown instead of a wink. "Sharpening his claws, Slide. Lord knows Snowball doesn't need the exercise. My boy's nothing but muscle under his gorgeous white fur."

A gorgeous cat was no part of my plan for the day. An about-face was sorely needed.

"Big John, tell me how you killed that sorry son of a bitch."

"My, oh, my. Looks like somebody strapped on his big-boy britches while Big John was behind bars."

"Crap. Did you pick that up in jail?"

"Pick what up?"

"Referring to yourself in the third person. God knows I endure enough of that from Uncle Lore. It'll rip me a new asshole if you join the crowd."

"Slide, how 'bout we make us a deal? You cut out the cursing, and Big John'll do his level-best in the third person department."

"Done deal," I said. "So how'd you kill him?"

"I'm not getting into the particulars," he said. "Truth is, I waited too long. With a posse covering Myles's tracks at the sheriff's office, he thought there was no stopping him."

"You stopped him."

"If only I'd seen Myles for the con artist he is." Big John cleared his throat. "Myles was a real pro at adding the perfect touch of truth to whatever lie he was painting. Topped it all off with religion and fine manners. Kind of like Shakespeare used to say."

"I haven't heard from him in a while."

"Can't say I'm at the top of ole Shakespeare's class. But I might surprise you with a line or two."

"I'm waiting on number two."

"I remembered another line here a while back. Part of one, anyway."

"Part doesn't count."

Big John stuck a pinkie in his ear and dug for wax. "Looking in that rearview, driving semis cross-country gave me miles of daylight for thinking, plus many a lonely night for reading and scribbling on poems. Add this stint in jail to thirteen months in Germany, and I oughta be one heckuva philosopher."

"Philosopher would be a stretch."

"I learned more in POW camp than anywhere."

"From Albert Brown, who taught you all that Shakespeare."

"'The prince of darkness is a gentleman.' I've lost touch with Albert since the war, but I'm betting he'd add Myles to that list."

"You must've run out of patience, with Pearl in the hospital and Myles on the sheriff's payroll."

Big John leaned back, tightening his jaw. "I gave Myles more than one chance."

"Where's the body?"

"No more on Myles. Understood?"

There was no misunderstanding the tone of his voice.

"Tell me about the war," I said.

"Fire away."

"Let's start with Hitler."

"Hitler?"

"How'd he get that far?"

Big John squinted at the floor, then pointed toward the barn.

"Slide, see the watering trough just outside the branches of my big oak yonder?"

"Yessir."

"It wouldn't take a teaspoon of the right poison in that water to kill every cow on this farm. One man can do a world of damage."

"But how?"

"Well, Hitler spent those first years turning himself into a dictator, ranting against the Jews, and mowing down whoever got in his way. After he'd cleaned house in Germany, he rolled those tanks through one country after another while most everybody sat back and watched."

"Nobody could do anything?"

"Maybe could, but wouldn't. Brits had 'em a puppy dog in charge, a retriever at that. Fella named Chamberlain who kept saying everything would work out over time. But time only grew the monster."

"Like Myles," I said.

"Abuse is abuse. Some are able to carry it further than others, but the same ole engine's at work."

"All Myles had was a sorry sheriff. Imagine what he could've done with soldiers and tanks at his back."

Big John wiped his forehead with the back of his hand. He sighed.

"Slide, anything else on the war?"

"You flew a B-24, right?"

"The Liberator," he said. "One whale of a bomber but not all that shifty. I suppose they did the job, but folks called 'em Flying Coffins for a reason."

"How many missions did you fly?"

"Shot down on the fourth."

"Did the Germans really lock you in a shed that first night?"

He nodded and grunted to his feet. "Slide, let's mosey on down to the barn."

Thanks to the hundreds of snakes that feasted on the millions of rats fattened up by the piles of spilled grain Big John never got around to tidying up, the barn was the last place besides Sunday school or hell I cared to visit.

"Too many rats and snakes," I said.

"Come on, *Cookie*. Snakes moved on after Snowball cleaned out the rats. The highland moccasins are holed up this time of year anyway."

"It's April, in case you forgot." He crossed the porch while I kept my seat. "Springtime."

— ✳ ✳ ✳ —

BIG JOHN WAS SMILING AT WHAT passed for a shed when I caught up. "Slide, isn't she pretty?"

"Pretty? The crooked roof's barely hanging on to the barn."

He fixed his hands on his hips in a way that reminded me of Lore gazing at his antebellum. "Another coat of red paint would do wonders for this darling."

"Would it help the walls I can see through?"

"Those cypress boards will be here long after I'm gone. Maybe you too."

"What does this have to do with your first night in Germany?"

"Loneliest night of my life," he said.

"Didn't everybody jump out together?"

"I knew my plane could blow any second after two of her four engines caught fire. Ordered the crew to bail out while I did my best to hold her steady."

"You ended up in a burning plane all by yourself? Big John, you were already my hero but—"

"Doing my job, Slide. Pack of others did the same but never made it home. They're our heroes."

"How far did you make it after they bailed out?"

"Not far. Three German fighters were closing in for the kill when I found myself over a dark blue lake that looked like it belonged in some other world. All of a sudden, they pulled up and flew away. I never saw 'em again. Had no idea why they'd backed off until I made it to prison camp and found myself in a serious interrogation with the American boys."

"Americans?"

"Germans planted spies in our camps, and your time on this earth was up if our boys figured you for a spy."

"They'd kill you?"

"Ways of war, Slide. Course they were able to sniff out a skunk in no time, so our visit went smooth enough. Toward the end I was telling them about the lake when this colonel piped in, 'Son, that lake saved your life. It's where the Germans are making heavy water for their nuclear program. Most heavily defended facility on the planet. You must've been flying so low they were late picking you up and couldn't risk you going down and tearing up the place. Lieutenant, you gotta be the luckiest man in the war.'"

"What a miracle," I said.

"But not the first."

"What happened after the lake?"

"Those Germans didn't need their bullets anyhow. I was closing fast on two thousand feet and knew my chances of the plane holding steady long enough to unhitch my gear, scramble out of the cockpit, and bail out were next to nothing. Somehow, I made it."

"Bet you couldn't wait to get out."

"Then my parachute wouldn't open. Kept yanking on the cord, but she wouldn't budge." Big John took a few steps, kicking at clods of dirt. "The strangest thing happened. I heard a voice saying, 'Don't worry, young man. I've got plans for you.' I know it sounds hokey, but my parachute opened right up. Wasn't long before I hit the ground with a thump that knocked off my boots. Buried my chute and ran for a patch of woods but didn't get far. Germans had seen the whole ordeal and come my way. They hollered and sent a few bullets over my head for good measure."

He turned. "Slide, they locked me in a shed like this one but a heap sturdier. It was a night I'll never forget. Feeling guilty for losing my plane, worried sick over the other nine boys in the crew, cold and missing my wife, I hunkered down and leaned against the wall. At daybreak my chin was dragging so low I had to work these eyeballs to their limits to see my feet. I didn't care to see any further. Couldn't bear to."

Big John stared at one shed while surely thinking of another. "Sun went to rising and sending beams of light through cracks in the wall I was propped against. Felt the sun warming my back, watched it light up my boots and inch its way up the far wall. And there it was: 'Go to Hell Ole Miss.'"

I walked to the fence, shaking my head. For years I'd been waiting on more than a bedtime tale filled with the skinny mice and cardboard for bread Big John had eaten in prison camp, and now I'd heard *the* story. I circled back to the shed.

"What a story," I said, wishing I had more to say.

"She's my best. Sure lightened my load knowing a fella from back home had walked my path. And had the gumption to slip a knife past those Germans and give our Ole Miss buddies a piece of his mind."

"A State fan!"

"A real flesh-and-blood Mississippi State Bulldog. Yessir, the good Lord was taking care of me. Tossing a pebble of hope my way."

Something told me to stop there. I didn't.

"What about your best friend?" I asked. "Why didn't God open Jim's parachute?"

"You heard this story?"

"Momma mentioned him a while back. That's all I've heard."

Big John looked me over. "I reckon you're leveling with me." He put a hand on my shoulder. "Let's head on back to the porch."

— ✶ ✶ ✶ —

BIG JOHN SAT AND CROSSED HIS arms. His rocker didn't rock.

"Sorry I ruined your day," I said. "Should I go home?"

"Fine right where you are," he said. "I like having you here."

I pointed. "I bet your Black Angus are happy spring is here. Look at all the green grass they're munching on."

He didn't seem to hear a word or see a cow. "Jim and I went to get our parachutes that morning. Man behind the desk handed one to him and another to me. Bad chute could've been mine. Should've been mine. Jim had two young children. Plus a momma who'd already lost her other child in the war. Along with Elijah, Jim was the finest fella I've ever known."

"Big John, we don't have to talk about it anymore."

"Can't promise I won't cry on you," he said, reaching for his bandana. "Talking it over is part of the healing, I suppose." He wiped his eyes and cheeks. "Back to your question, Slide. Why didn't God take care of Jim? I've searched high and low for an answer. Paul said everything'd work for the good if you loved God and so forth. What's good about Jim's parachute not opening? Others point to all the pain in the world and say it proves there's no God after all, but I don't have enough faith to believe everything just got here all by its lonesome. Bunch of other ideas fall somewhere in between. Problem is, none of 'em answer your question. My questions. Why were millions of Jews slaughtered by a madman? Why Jim and not me? And Pearl. Couldn't a *good* Lord have stopped my only girl from marrying that man?"

He rocked back and lifted his arms. "God, why did You look the other way while the bones of my dear lady rotted to the core? Why, why, why?"

Big John stood and staggered to the edge of the porch, staring ahead as I tried to forget what a swell job I'd done of turning one of his favorite memories into a nightmare. By the time he returned to his rocker, the upper edge of his T-shirt was soaked like he'd been working in the sun instead of crying in the shade. He muttered a few words I couldn't understand.

"Big John?"

"Can't blame my foolishness on God. Jim made a fine copilot, but he was terrified of jumping from those planes, even with sunshine and plenty of air under his feet. I forgot all that when I ordered him to bail out with the others. Took a fool not to know what would happen if he jumped from a burning plane without me by his side and with no room for error. His chute was probably like mine and only needed some finagling to open her up.

"I got back to the States and went straight to see Jim's momma in Earle, Arkansas. The lady should've cursed the bony fella standing at her door. Instead, she gave me a hug and told me to have a seat on the couch while she got me a cool glass of water. Small house had the feel of a place that hadn't been lived in for years. Shades pulled down over every window. Only light came from the kitchen until she handed me the glass and switched on a lamp. I cried enough for the both of us while she told me how much I'd meant to her son. We were standing at the door when I promised to name my first boy after her last. She broke down and wept all over my uniform.

"Jim's namesake, James. Our first and only boy. James died because I argued with Shine over how sick he was. Told her it was only a cold and there was no use wasting money on a doctor. Shine had every right to hold our baby's death against me until the day she died. But she never mentioned it.

"My lady would be alive if not for me. I kept saying her pain was nothing to worry about. Now Shine's gone. Gone for good.

"And I was the one pressuring my girl to marry Myles. Pearl would've married a soldier boy if I'd stayed out of it. Hank might've been off serving our country a good bit of the time, but he would've doted on my girl every chance he got. Instead, she's off to Memphis to fend for herself. Maybe gone for good.

"Jim. James. Elijah. Shine. Now Pearl. My only hope's that she'll know Myles is gone, and her deddy is right here waiting on her."

39

THE NEXT MORNING, I SWALLOWED AN egg that was supposed to be fried instead of scrambled and charred. I got away with easing my bacon under the table until Annabelle started crunching on what sounded like the bones of another squirrel she'd found in the backyard. Momma knew how upset I was over Big John and let it go.

I didn't pay attention to what the teachers said that day. I didn't glance at a girl. All I could think about was the sight of Big John raising his arms as he cried out to God.

I quit worrying the second I stopped at the gate and saw his rocker swaying back and forth. It was a sure sign Big John was in a jolly mood.

"About time you showed up!" he hollered, as I rounded the porch.

"Ran straight from school," I said.

"Not fast enough."

I was halfway into my chair when he reached and hauled me into his lap.

"Feels like years since I've laid eyes on you."

"You said that yesterday. Somebody's sounding like an old geezer."

I poked him in the ribs and got up. When I sat and turned his way, his smile was gone.

"Slide, I'm afraid I need to make amends for yesterday. Particularly there at the end. I had no bidness carrying on in front of you."

"No use apologizing, Big John."

"I don't want you thinking I've lost my faith. Might be wrestling with the Lord like ole Jacob would—" I followed his eyes to the gate. "Look who's coming our way."

"Marching," I said. "She forgot to close the gate."

"I doubt she forgot, by the way she flung that jessie open and took off."

Somebody was in serious trouble. Except for swearing and fishing, Cookie and the God of her Old Testament had plenty in common. They both knew when folks had screwed up, and they weren't afraid to let them have it.

The screen door slammed behind her.

"How's it going today, Cookie?" he asked.

She stomped over to his chair and slapped both hands on the bones of her hips. I hadn't seen her this mad since Big John's birthday dinner.

"I ain't interested in yo small talk," she said. "What I'm interested in is yo whys. *Why, why, why.* A grown man whining like Salt."

The big whiner turned to me.

"I only told Momma," I said.

"Big John, you got no business doubting the Lawd in front of my chillun. Salt or Slide. Mess with them and you messing with *me.* And don't give me lip about yo hard times. The Lawd's sent plenty of trouble thisaway too."

"I know, Cookie. I'm just boxing with the Lord is all."

"Boxing with *who?*"

"You know, boxing with God here and there."

"Shee-it, you gotta be joking. You might as well go racing down a wet pile of gravel in those zipper boots you so proud of. Go ahead for all I care. See how many rounds you make it boxing with the Lawd. Those chubby arms might work on Myles, but the Lawd'll whup yo ass before the bell's done ringing."

"Well, I was just telling Slide how sorry—"

"Good. Be sorry." She sat and looked him over. "I know where you coming from, Big John. You wondering why the Lawd ain't stopping all the bad in this world."

"Something along those lines."

"I'm with you on part of that."

"Part?"

"If the Lawd made everything from the stars to these chillun, He should've kept the boots of those deacons off my daddy. And yes, He could've opened yo friend's parachute and healed Shine's cancer. Don't get me started on the man yo daughter married."

"Sounds like we're in the same drifting boat."

"The Lawd best send me a log if that's the case. Or the whale that gave Jonah a lift."

"Tell me why you're so riled up," he said.

"Close them eyes, Big John." He knew Cookie well enough to keep one eye cracked like a kid during a long prayer at the dinner table. "Both of 'em. All the way." He obeyed. "Now open them holes that are wider than my fish bucket and near about as deep."

"Do what?"

"Come on, slowpoke. What's that hairy snout taking in?"

"I'm not sure what you're getting at."

"Reckon I'll have to make this a chillun's lesson," she said. "Look around and tell me what you see."

He pointed. "My red barn, your pond, the finest pecan grove in Mississippi. Don't forget my pear trees. And tell me those heifers in the far pasture don't make a pretty picture."

"Cows, Big John. Cows that do nothing but eat, chew the cud, and—"

"Shit," I said.

Her wide grin surprised me. His narrow eyes didn't.

"Big John, you don't mind 'em munching away on yo pastures," she said. "You'll even get off that rump and toss 'em some grain every now and then."

"Hard to beat one of those T-bones," he said.

"Listen to me, Big John. My people were chained up for hundreds of years and Jim Crowed for another hundred. It still ain't right. Tell me how a *good* Lawd lets all that happen."

"What are you saying, Cookie?"

"I'm saying you can't have steak without shit." She leaned his way. "Losing my daddy made me question the Lawd. Still does. But one look at this boy or my girl changes all that. There's glory, Big John, a heap of glory. Right here and right now. But guess what?" Her finger started with me and moved across the farm. "This here ain't enough to say the Lawd is good, 'cause there's more shit than steaks can shake a stick at." His blank eyes looked her over. "We just passing through, Big John. If you living for this world, you ain't living. For the Lawd to be good, there's gotta be a better place. A far-off land where my daddy is resting, and our Shine feels no pain." She stood and raised her arms. "And that is why I can say, why I can *shout*, the Lawd is good, good all the time! Amen."

— ✳ ✳ ✳ —

NOT LONG AFTER COOKIE HAD MARCHED back through the gate, I gave Big John a hug and headed for another supper's serving of Momma's hardship. From the porch to the edge of town, I mulled over Cookie's sermon. I'd never heard God and steaks and shit tossed into the same pasture.

I reached Johnston Street and froze at the spot where Myles had offered us a ride. Close to four months had passed since his family had gathered on the porch before the rehearsal dinner.

Now I knew enough to piece together the family Myles had really come from. Tainted blood, Momma called it. In her view, upbringing could hold it back a while, but blood would seep through the dam and bust it wide open and cover everything in sight.

Apples followed blood. "That business about an apple not falling far from the tree is hogwash," Momma would say. "Look at Victry and his folks. His apple fell from the farthest end of the longest branch of the tallest tree God ever made. It's all a mystery, I reckon."

Momma was right, I figured. It was a mystery. Little did I know.

40

Cookie

COOKIE HAD BEEN MARRIED TWO WHOLE days when she quit waiting on men to use their ears. Hell no, she didn't stick around to see if Big John was listening. "Have at him," she told the Lawd, as she left the porch and walked home. "You the patient One, not me."

Fact was, Big John deserved a little patience. Pearl had been heavy on his mind since she'd pulled him aside after all the hugs and kisses at the courthouse. She told him she'd gotten a job at a club in Memphis but didn't say what kind of club it was. She'd found a place to stay and was itching to head thataway.

He tried changing her mind until he must've remembered what a waste of words that was. When he asked where she planned on staying, she gave him a kiss on the cheek and a quick goodbye.

✕ ✕ ✕

BIG JOHN HAD BEEN BOXING WITH the Lawd for a week and some change when Cookie caught herself feeling sorry for the man. She would've gone to a doctor or one of those quacks if she'd trusted one.

She stopped by the farm on Friday. Instead of the moping and mumbling she'd expected, Big John was rocking away with eyes that were wet but happy. He gave an easy smile as she crossed the porch and sat. When she asked what was on his mind, he kept smiling but didn't answer.

Cookie had no use for a rocker. A chair was for sitting, not rolling back and forth on long strips of wasted wood. But sometimes you had to be a fool to fool one. She rocked and stayed quiet long as she could.

"Why you in such a good mood?" she finally asked.

"The Lord is good," he said.

"I been telling you that."

He pulled a letter from his pocket and held it high as she asked who it came from and such. "Go ahead with yoself. We'll see how long yo arm can stay thataway."

The man wasted five minutes switching the letter from one arm to the other before he set it in his lap and said it was from Pearl.

"You gonna read, or act a clown all day?"

"Oh, I don't know, Cookie. You look mighty antsy this afternoon. I'm sure you're itching to *try* and catch a bream or two."

She kept rocking like she had nothing better to do until he gave up and went to reading.

Hey Daddy,

I love Memphis and my job at this place called The University Club. It's kind of like Uncle Lore's Country Club without a golf course.

I work at a snack bar by the pool. The only men I have to watch are the old ones who hobble up for handfuls of Goldfish, and the middle-agers who try keeping their bellies from flopping over their swim trunks while they flirt and check to make sure their wives aren't looking.

I've moved into a backhouse that used to be the "servant's quarters" for this big house on Peabody Avenue. Mrs. Hood said she'd been praying for "just the right person" and knew right off I was her girl. She drives a little blue Mercedes like she's sixteen instead of your age. I call her Dot Dot, after the two quick honks she gives every time she pulls into the carport and says "hello" with that squeaky horn.

Dot Dot has three daughters of her own but acts like I'm her fourth. You'd like her a lot, Daddy. She's always talking about Jesus and bugging me to join them for church. After growing up around Misry and marrying Myles, I was skittish at first. It didn't take long to see she's a sweeter and softer (and whiter) version of Cookie.

Mr. Hood reminds me of you, Daddy. He's a real gentleman. Whenever I join them for supper, he stands when I walk into the room and waits until I'm seated before he sits back down. He doesn't talk much unless he's telling stories about bird dogs or the war. He flew a B-24, like you! He also loves giving me pointers on men (if only he knew). When I get up to leave, he stands again and gives a shy little grin that says a seat is always open for me at their table.

Dot Dot walks me to the back and says "love-you-bye" as I head out. She stands at the door like I'm a girl, her girl, catching a school bus until I wave from the backhouse.

The Hoods can't wait to meet you, Daddy. And I can't wait to see you!

Love-you-bye,

Your Pearl

— ✶ ✶ ✶ —

AFTER SEEING BIG JOHN'S HAPPY TEARS, plus nearly adding one of her own, Cookie went home and slept six hours that night. Six good hours.

She was on her third cup of coffee when the phone rang. "Give up, Big John," she said on the fifth ring. She picked up on number fifteen.

"What?" she said.

"Good morning to you, too," he said.

"What you want, Big John?"

"Is this Cookie, by chance?"

"This phone's fixing to bust one of yo eardrums."

"Remember Holly?"

Myles. The man, the devil, had sounded just like Big John. A chill ran through Cookie's bones. It kept on running until she was mad clean through. She wanted to throw her phone through a wall, but she needed to learn all she could about this man.

"I remember the pocketknife Big John should've let me use on yo neck," she said.

Myles cackled. "Don't you wish he'd had the backbone to hand it over?"

"What you calling about?" she asked, grinding her teeth. "Get on with it."

"Sure thing, Miss Cookie. Holly had a mouth like yours. A tongue we'd gone easy on for too long, truth be told."

"Only truth you know is what you can make somebody believe."

"Will you pipe down and let me finish?" Cookie didn't answer. "Dad called me at the shop and said he'd flipped his wheelchair chasing Holly through the house. Said he wanted Shad and me to lock her in the shed to teach her a lesson."

"Poor girl."

"Good church lady like you knows what the Bible says about sparing the rod and spoiling the child."

"I know what it says about evil."

"Always judging folks. I guess you forgot those verses."

"Where was yo momma in all this?"

"She kept her mouth shut. It's a crying shame Holly never learned that trick. Or Pearl."

"How do you sleep at night?"

"Very well, Miss Cookie. My conscience is clear."

"'Cause you ain't got one to be cloudy. Even after killing a sister and nearly killing a wife."

"Holly banged her own head on the concrete floor," Myles said, his breaths now fast and angry. "She killed herself."

"I reckon Pearl strolled into the hospital and decided to bang her own head on the tile floor."

"Pearl," he said, disgust in his voice. "I was bound and determined to teach my wife to shut up and stay out of my business. I'd planned on a good belt-whipping at some point. Nothing more, but—"

"Nothing more," Cookie said, cutting him off. "Maybe you are the angel we thought instead of the devil I'm thinking."

The fast and heavy beat of what sounded like knuckles on a table filled the phone. Cookie waited, expecting Myles to either blow up or hang up. The man fooled her again and went right on with his story.

"Not a week after that poem's in the paper, Pearl shows up at my shop. Unannounced. I look up from my desk to see her staring down at me like I was a boy who'd spat on somebody's grave. Then at the house she goes to mouthing off about stolen cars and treating me like a piece of trash. In my own house!" He sighed. "The woman should've known it was too much for a man's temper."

"Why'd you marry her in the first place? Love's got nothing to do with yo world."

"A businessman needs a wife," he said. "Though I doubted it would work for me. Same woman, same life, until death do ye part? Monogamy's such a New Testament thing, Cookie. I prefer your King David in that regard, but I decided to give holy matrimony a try and see how it panned out." He paused like he was waiting for Cookie to lose her cool. She held her cool and tongue this go-round. "Big John was certainly an easy sell. Plus a damn good cover to boot. War hero. Deacon. Adoring husband and doting *deddy*. The best uncle a boy could hope for. Father Abraham meets the Job of Mississippi meets the rock of Hill County. The hell with him."

"You married her because of him?"

"Not that simple, Cookie. Life has more than two colors, in case you haven't noticed. Black plus white equals gray to these eyes. Pearl's too, I assure you. Her looks and sass stirred my blood from the get-go. I also thought molding her into a good wife would be a fun ride. Would've been if Big John had minded his own business."

"A fun ride. Like yo Bible and church talk."

He snorted. "Believed it all until I got old enough to see that the hat Dad wore to church looked nothing like the one he wore at home. I was sixteen when this priest here in Biloxi got caught with a kid. Caught red-handed when the boy's father barged into the creep's office and beat the tar out of him. What did the church do? Filed charges against the father and shipped their priest to some faraway parish with other kids to *minister* to. The last seeds of my faith died on that rocky soil."

"Bad people don't make a bad God. Or excuse yo evil."

"Fooling the faithful is lots of fun," he said. "Though our folksy philosopher was hardly the challenge I'd expected. Besides acting the southern gentleman and treating his Pearl like a queen, all I had to do was fill the offering plate at church. A little faith and a lot of money go a long way in the Bible Belt."

"Why didn't you call Big John instead of me?"

"I tried before dialing your number. Big John started all this, by the way. He was all but on his knees begging me to marry his daughter. Then he had the gall to threaten me at my own place of business and put his poem in the paper. And you haven't helped matters, Cookie. Showing up at my shop. Sticking that lighter under my nose and talking down to me."

His daddy and Holly to Pearl and Big John and Cookie, everything was everybody's fault but his. She was listening to a con man gone mad.

"What else you got?" she asked.

"Tell Big John I'm done with his daughter, wherever she is."

"You won't be done with Pearl until you kill her."

He laughed. "You still don't know me very well."

"Who does besides the Lawd and yo devil?"

"Why would I lie about Pearl now?" He had a point, but Cookie didn't answer. "I was bored with Pearl before she pushed me too far one too many times. I taught her a lesson. I won. And I'm done. With her, at least."

"You didn't beat Big John."

"He won the last round, I'll admit. Who knows how our game will play out?" Myles chuckled. "I have eyes on the rest of you. My, didn't Sam work a miracle pulling Cash out of the gutter? I'd expected Slide to spend more time at home instead of trotting over to Big John's every day after school, though I'm not the least bit surprised you're walking Baby-girl to the square on Friday afternoons for those chocolate milkshakes. I bet she'd love another ride in my pickup."

Cookie hung up and called Big John.

—✶ ✶ ✶—

COOKIE WAS WAITING AT THE CURB when Big John drove up. She propped her elbows on the window and leaned in. He whispered Pearl's name.

"Myles said he's done with Pearl, 'wherever she is,'" Cookie said.

"Cookie, you know we can't trust Myles."

"He made it clear he's had enough of her."

"And you think he's telling the truth this time?"

"I do."

Big John shook his head. "You sound so sure."

"Sure as I can be with that man. Myles said he'd won that battle and was eyeing the next. Truth is what he makes of it, but I don't know why he'd lie about Pearl and admit to Holly."

"Holly?"

Cookie told him what Myles had done to his own sister.

Eyes wide and puffed out like a dead fish, Big John pressed his forehead against the wheel. "I wouldn't stop jabbering about Myles, his manners and money and Bible. I even took my girl to church to make sure they met. How, Lord? Why?"

"Is the Lawd in the mood for yo hows and whys right now? Was He in the mood for telling you why Jim and James and Daddy and Shine died?"

"I wish He gave a damn, is all."

"Last week's lesson," she said.

He stared through his busted windshield. "I'll call Pearl in case Myles is lying. She's been wanting to take a road trip with some of her Memphis friends. Now would be a good time."

"Sho' would."

"What else did Myles say?"

"Blamed everybody but hisself for what happened. Also said he had eyes out. Went right on down the line from Cash being off the bottle to Slide going to yo farm after school to me walking Salt to the square for a milkshake. I hung up after he mentioned taking her for another ride in his truck."

Big John's hands worked the wheel like he was driving his eighteen-wheeler down a curvy road. "Any chance Myles was bluffing?"

"I *told* you, Big John! Told you we should've chopped the head off that snake. Now we got Salt and Slide to worry about."

"Cookie, we have to get them away from here. With somebody who can deal with the situation if it does get out of hand. That means Cash. And I want 'em somewhere Myles and his clan don't know about. A place nobody, Pearl included, would have mentioned."

"That ain't easy. Close as Myles was."

Big John slapped the dashboard. "Humphrey's farm in the Ouachita Mountains of Arkansas. Middle of nowhere. I've been there many a time but still wouldn't be able to find it. My brother knows it like every other piece of ground he's stepped foot on. He'll take 'em to Humphrey's on a camping trip."

Cookie liked part of Big John's plan. Cash was cool when it counted. He was always patient, but no man could be expected to put up with Salt on a camping trip. The night air would have her nose running through one roll of toilet paper after another. Could even Cash handle the fit she'd pitch at the first sight of a daddy longlegs?

"Salt ain't sleeping in no tent," Cookie said. "And Lawd knows how many beasts will be out there waiting on my sweet baby. Well, my *baby* anyhow."

"We can't be worrying ourselves with that right now."

"That ain't all, Big John. The devil is hard to fool but harder to stop. If Myles does get wind of our plan, we can't have those chillun in the same spot."

"I'm not worried long as my brother's in charge."

"I am," she said.

Fact was, Cookie did like the mountains. Mount Arafat worked for Noah and that boat of his. Moses climbed Sinai for the Ten Commandments. Jesus preached a long sermon on one and fought the devil on another. The tree where He died was on a mountain, but He'd already planned the whole deal anyway.

"How far those mountains east of here?" she asked.

"The Smoky Mountains," he said. "We could let Slide and Cash go to Humphrey's and send Salt and her deddy to the Smokies."

"I didn't ask for a name. How far?"

"Well, I'd say eight hours or more."

"Not far enough. Not with Lore."

"Cookie, why don't you go?"

"I'm staying here to watch out for Myles. And to make sure you do yo job if he does show up."

Big John scratched his chin. "Lore's buddy owns a ranch near Eagle Nest, New Mexico, where they used to elk hunt every year. You're talking a thousand miles or more to the Rocky Mountains."

"That'll do. Long as we make it quick."

41

Slide

SUNDAY DINNER OPENED WITH A THUD when Momma burned the corn bread and concocted a new way of making fried chicken taste like cough medicine. Big John and Deddy took turns stomping on the Ninth Commandment that made a big to-do over lying. One brother would swallow hard and declare how delicious everything was while the other surely dreamed of Shine's Sunday dinners. I kept my trap shut until the store-bought vanilla ice cream hit the table.

"Thanks a bunch, Momma," I said. "This'll make up for—" Her eyes said it was time for my own whopper. "It was great, Momma. All great."

"And what was your favorite?" she asked.

"Your turnip greens," I said.

"That's news to me," she said. "A teenager who likes turnip greens."

Little luck with truth and less with lies, I decided to change the subject.

"Big John, you're not too old to remember our talk on Myles and Hitler the other day," I said. "Myles only had to con us. How did Hitler get a whole country to tag along?"

Big John pushed back from the table, stretched his legs, and studied the zipper boots that might've been in style when General Grant was smoking cigars and sipping whiskey at the Old Homestead. "Slide, you remember me talking about Albert Brown, I suppose?"

"Not in the last hour," I said.

"Albert called it the Devil's Troika. Don't ask me why he didn't call it a pitchfork with three prongs. The scoundrel had a ball throwing big ideas and newfangled words our way."

"There's a Yankee for you," Momma said.

"Troy *what?*" I asked.

Big John grinned, showing specks of corn bread that looked white next to his teeth. "Start with Troy and add the last part of Becca's name." The grown-ups chuckled. I deserved to finish every plate at the table for mentioning a girl at school who didn't know my name. "Slide, should we tell your folks about the little redhead you're sweet on?"

"I'd rather discuss the Devil's Troika."

Big John stared out the window. "Albert said it amounted to three hooks, prongs if you will, Hitler used to gain power and carry out his evil over the years: nationalism, populism, and sectarianism. Hitler promised to make Germany great again, get the working man back on his feet, and get rid of the Jews. He blamed them for the common man's problems."

"What's wrong with those first two? You're patriotic as they come, Big John. And you drove an eighteen-wheeler for twenty-five years. Sounds plenty common to me."

"Albert went into that too. How it's good to be proud of your country and look out for the working man. But when you add that *ism* to the equation and set your sights on some particular group of people, no telling where you'll end up."

"That couldn't happen here," I said.

"Lord willing it won't. The folks who founded this country set everything up to keep it from happening. But you never know, Slide. Might find yourself out of a job when a big-talking politician comes along tooting his own trumpet and promising to make our country great again—as if it wasn't great before he got there—and to put you at the top of his list. Be especially careful if he blames your problems on folks who are outnumbered and easy to pick on."

"I still don't understand how so many people bought into what Hitler had to say," I said.

Big John smacked the side of his head with his palm. "No wonder, Slide. I forgot the hay."

"The *hay*?" I asked.

"Albert said the job of the hay is to cover those prongs and keep folks from knowing what you're really up to. Amounts to either playing with the truth or outright lying to get folks to believe what you want. That's propaganda for you."

"And Myles," I said.

"Enough on him." Big John leaned forward with a sketchy-toothed grin that kept my eyes off his short-sleeved dress shirt and shorter tie. "Slide, how does a camping trip to Uncle Humphrey's sound? Starting tomorrow."

"What about school?" I asked, glancing around the table.

"Missing a little school won't be a problem for your brain," Big John said. "Humphrey's been bugging me to have you boys pay him a visit."

"I'm surprised he doesn't want you to add another set of greasy whiskers and overalls to the picture."

"My, you're giving your uncles a hard way to go," Big John said.

"Don't worry, Slide," Momma said. "We call Humphrey your uncle because nobody's sure where he does land on the family tree. Second and once removed ain't far enough, but that's Arkansas for you."

"Since when did a state or tree matter?" I asked. "Uncle Lore's tree doesn't touch ours."

"Amen," she said. "Except for Victry and sweet little Salt. They're welcome in our tree."

"Speak for yourself on Salt," I said. "Humphrey's still my favorite uncle. Can't think of a close second."

"I thought Uncle Lore held that title," Big John said.

"Lore's still number one in the ass-scratcher department," I said.

"Orman Slide Jackson," Big John said, frowning the best he could.

"But he's fallen to number two in the overall rankings," I said. "Thanks to Humphrey's church." I'd been to the Holy Saints of Mount Ida before Humphrey's not-so-better half, Aunt Elma, died from the appendix their preacher and snakes couldn't cure. "Doctors might be forbidden, but snakes are holy, and first cousins are fair game."

Even Deddy laughed at that one. Big John stood and stepped back from the table.

"Y'all stop by the farmhouse on your way out," he said, nodding at Deddy.

PART XI

B IG JOHN SPENT THE AFTERNOON ON his porch, enjoying the sights and sounds of spring. Shine's red azaleas along the front of the house. The pretty white flowers of the dogwoods scattered across green pastures. A whistle from a bobwhite in a thicket near the highway. The song of a cardinal in the tall hickory by the barn.

New leaves in distant trees blocked most of the sunset. Big John didn't mind. He'd shared a Sunday dinner with loved ones, and these past few hours had reminded him why this place was his home.

It didn't feel like home that night. He tried sleeping in his bed, in their bed, then Slide's little bed upstairs. He walked circles in Pearl's room, worrying about his daughter and fearing the man who was still her husband. He trudged downstairs for a restless hour on the couch before heading to his rocker to wait on the sunrise.

The sun didn't steal his gloom. His coffee brought memories of mornings with Shine, then death as he stared at her rocker. Maybe she was no longer alone, but he was.

42

Slide

MOMMA MELTED BUTTER AND CHEESE WITH the best of cooks. On most days, she even set the skillet on the stove without making a mess of her one meal nobody had to lie about—cheese toast.

On Monday morning, she left the skillet on the countertop, poured herself a cup of coffee, and took a seat in Deddy's lap. She gave him a wicked smile and started playing with his hair.

"That hunk of Velveeta cheese won't melt on its own," I said, in no mood for horseplay.

"You boys aren't in a hurry, are you?" she asked, nibbling on Deddy's ear. "I had something else in mind for breakfast."

"Y'all took care of that last night," I said. "While I cursed the skinny wall between our bedrooms."

Deddy turned redder than a woodpecker's head as Momma gave him a sloppy kiss on the lips and strolled to the skillet. She waited on the butter and cheese to melt before adding a cup of milk and a table-spoon of flour. I was panting like Annabelle by the time she poured the hot soup over two pieces of toast and sprinkled a dash of paprika for good measure.

After breakfast we loaded up and drove to the farmhouse.

Big John opened the screen door as we trotted up the steps. "Hey there, boys. Where y'all off to this morning?"

"You know," I said. "You set it all up."

He stepped back and looked us over with a warm smile. "Does me a world of good to see you boys taking a trip together." He reached with both arms and brought us in for a hug. "Let's have a seat and visit a few minutes."

"Sure thing," Deddy said.

Big John leaned back in his rocker. "Slide, y'all's camping trip reminds me of the day I followed your deddy into the Hope Springs National Forest for the first time."

"And the last," Deddy said.

"Sounds like you were a chicken, Big John."

"A big one," he said, easing his rocker back and forth. "I had no business in that wilderness. Hundred thousand acres of creeks and swamps, trees that never let the sun hit the ground." He chuckled. "I was a grown man of course, but the thought of my baby brother leaving me in such a godforsaken place scared the living daylights out of me."

"You're lucky he's not a prankster like me."

"And lucky he knew how to get us out of there."

"Chester must've saved his Chickasaw blood for Deddy."

"Every bit of it. Your deddy was at home in those woods. He jumped creeks and hopped logs and topped hills like he was exploring every room heaven had to offer. Which he was, I suppose. The frown he wore at the house was nowhere to be found. His young eyes were bright and steady instead of searching for something else to do. Or somewhere else to go."

We'd talked for ten minutes or so when Big John grunted up from his rocker. "Reckon I better cut y'all loose. You've got a long drive, and Humphrey's got a short fuse."

After another round of hugs, Deddy and I headed for the truck and the little trick we'd planned. He scooted over as I slid behind the wheel.

"Hold on!" Big John hollered from the porch. "What in tarnation are y'all up to?"

"Watch this, old-timer," I called out.

Gripping the wheel with one hand and thumping my chest with the other, I hit the gas and sent gravel flying in all directions. Proud enough to pop, I parked and got out to help Deddy with the gate.

We were walking back to the truck when Deddy looked back and froze. I turned to see Big John standing at the end of his driveway. In full salute. It was Big John's highest honor. His way of saying, *You're my man, Cash. I'm proud of you.*

Tears rolled down Deddy's cheeks. He stepped back and returned the salute.

"I love my brother," he said. "Love him so much."

✳ ✳ ✳

FROM A SPUR-OF-THE-MOMENT CAMPING TRIP TO a big brother's salute, I knew something was up. Not that I cared. For the first time I was going somewhere with a deddy I wanted to be with.

We crossed the Mississippi River at Memphis and landed in a world that made pancakes look hilly. God must've known what He was doing when He made the Arkansas Delta, but it was no match for the hills and creeks of Hill County. There wasn't a tree or cow in sight. Just one muddy field after another, except for a few sloughs and ditches filled with brown water and green moss that hadn't budged an inch in the past century.

One of Big John's overused lines—"It's good to endure a little hardship"—came to mind as I endured a long hour of Delta hardship between the river and Crowley's Ridge. Hundreds of feet tall and several miles wide, the ridge had trees and pastures like land was supposed to. The cows weren't Black Angus, which would've raised Big John's nose, but they were good enough for me.

In five minutes, we were back on the planet that was long on flat and short on mystery. Deddy's easy smile was a welcome sight, though I could've done without him slowing down to ooh and ahh over some ditch or field that looked exactly like the others we'd already passed.

The hills finally showed as we crossed the Arkansas River and looped around Little Rock toward Humphrey's farm in the Ouachita Mountains. I couldn't wait to get there. Not Deddy. The man who only ate when Momma was on his case had to stop in Hot Springs for what he called "the best ribs both sides of heaven."

Both? I'd missed that sermon, but heaven didn't cross my mind as we pulled into the parking lot of Bill's Barbeque. The windows and blocks made Harry's Bait Shop look fancy, and the bathroom on the left side of the building would've made Harry proud of the outhouse he'd installed in the 1800s.

Our waitress didn't help matters. Though Beulah appeared to have eaten Bill's ribs, she acted like she had no interest in sharing. Without a nod, much less a word, she scribbled down our order and marched back to the kitchen.

Deddy grunted like Tex after Beulah tossed our ribs onto the table.

"Um, umm," he said with every bite. "Slide, tell me these don't beat the pants off our ribs back home. Or Memphis."

We left Bill's and set off on the pigtail of a road that led to Mount Ida. The bumps and curves got me to thinking about the hunchback I had for an uncle.

"Deddy, where did Humphrey get the hump on his back?" He didn't answer. "Must be what happens when first cousins do more than kiss."

"Slide," he said, a grin in his voice. "Next subject."

"Okay. Why do you like Humphrey's farm so much?"

"Hard to narrow it down, Slide. The mountain of virgin timber on the east side. The creek on the west. The rolling meadow in the middle. What's your favorite?"

"It's all the same to me," I said. "As long as I'm with you."

—✳ ✳ ✳—

TALKING ABOUT HUMPHREY WAS EASIER THAN finding him. His cabin smelled like he'd dropped a number two and forgotten to flush. His once-green tractor, parked in the middle of a field between winding rows of cut hay, said he'd made a few drunken passes that morning before deciding it was a bit early in the year for bailing.

We honked and hollered but had no luck. With Deddy in such a sunny mood, I decided to have more fun at Humphrey's expense.

"Think he's off tending to his family tree?" I asked.

He looked away, a hand over his mouth. "Slide, let's pick out a campsite."

Deddy scratched long and hard on the perfect spot for a tent. The view, shade, and firewood were all matters of life and death. Sound was another biggie.

"Gotta be able to hear the bullfrogs and moving water," he said. "Problem is, the creek will drown out the owls and grasshoppers if we're too close."

The sun was setting by the time he settled on a patch of grass that looked no different from the others he'd snubbed his nose at. He pitched a tent faster than most people tied their shoes, so we had a smidgen of daylight for our fishing poles.

I followed Deddy along the edge of the creek as he searched through one canebrake after another. Every stick of cane was straight and green and an inch wide, but he studied each one as if a bream would do the same before chomping down on what our hooks had to offer. It was dark when he propped our cane poles on the side of the truck and said it was time for a fire.

Fire. Big John couldn't make smoke without a lighter and a week's worth of rolled-up newspaper, plus an hour of begging and praying. His little brother needed flint, steel, and the abandoned bird's nest he'd found by the creek.

In less than a minute, Deddy created fire. I'd watched every step but couldn't explain my deddy any more than fire itself. The shades of yellow and gold, black and blue. The flames that darted and roared in a strong breeze. The crackles and pops of dry logs, the steam and sizzle of wet. The hot air against my feet and legs.

"Gotta be just right," Deddy said.

"The fire looks great to me."

"Sure does, but I was referring to our poles. Nothing works like eight feet of cane, another eight feet of line, and one slip-shot weight set three inches above a medium-sized hook. Don't you remember?"

"Yessir," I said, though all I remembered from our last camping trip was a liquored-up Deddy and a passed-out Humphrey.

"Well, Humphrey's bound to have gotten home by now. He'll see the fire and stumble in before long. You ready for supper?"

I'd never understood why a cook in Vietnam never lifted a finger on the home front, especially given Momma's struggles in that department. On camping trips Deddy only cooked three meals: Pop-Tarts for breakfast, Spam for dinner, and hot dogs for supper.

"What's on the menu?" I asked, trying to keep a straight face.

"Take a guess."

"Fire-roasted weenies, potato chips, and marshmallows," I said. "What did you cook in Vietnam?"

He closed his eyes, then leaned back in his chair and stared into the dark. Sure enough, I'd asked the perfect question for driving my deddy back to the bottle. He only mentioned the war when crying in Momma's arms.

I picked up the branch he'd cut near the creek, switched his leg until he glanced my way, and asked if he was ready for supper.

He took the branch and held it to the fire. The green wood simmered in the heat. To my surprise, a smile eased across his face.

"Slide, it's gotta be skinny enough to pierce a weenie, long enough to keep your fingers from getting burned, and green or she'll snap." He laughed. "Then you'd have a real *dog-burner* on your hands."

The best thing about Deddy's jokes was that he never told them, but I laughed along the best I could. Whatever took his mind off Vietnam was a winner.

After we'd wolfed down our hot dogs and chips, he handed me the branch and tossed the bag of marshmallows into my lap.

"Your turn," he said, stretching his legs. "I'll sit back and enjoy the fire."

A campfire was one thing Deddy could sit back and enjoy. It made the perfect world for staring. And hoping.

—✳ ✳ ✳—

HOPE TOOK A TUMBLE WHEN UNCLE HUMPHREY stumbled into camp, plopped down in a chair, and nodded off without a hello. He didn't budge until we'd eaten half the marshmallows.

"Humphrey, you ready for a hot dog?" Deddy asked.

"You boys have at it," he slurred.

"We're done," Deddy said. "Got plenty of extras, though."

"Whiskey's my supper," Humphrey said, stroking his long gray beard. "It's good to see you boys. I've been wanting to warn y'all about them Romans."

"The Romans?" I asked.

"The damn Romans are set on ruling every corner of this wretched globe," Humphrey said. "They'll do it, if we ain't careful."

"Didn't the barbarians conquer them fifteen hundred years ago?" I asked.

"Not them Romans, Slide. The pope."

"I didn't know he'd put together an army."

"You don't get it, do you, boy?"

"Afraid not, Uncle Humphrey. Mind helping me out?"

"Well, the pope is . . ."

Leave it to Humphrey to pass out mid-sentence with such important matters at hand.

Deddy grinned. "Slide, you know better."

"I couldn't help myself."

"I'm sure you couldn't. Let's roast a few more marshmallows while Humphrey collects his thoughts."

The stars were bright by the time Humphrey came to, but his brain was still dull.

"I enjoyed catching you, catching up with you boys," he said. "Reckon I'll retire for the evening."

He struggled up and staggered off into the dark.

"Will he make it back to the cabin?" I asked.

"He'll be all right," Deddy said. "Black dark to blinding sun, no telling how many times he's stumbled into that cabin. Might stop for a nap, but he'll make it."

I sat back and soaked in the best night ever for camping. It was cool enough to hold off the mosquitoes but not cold enough to bother the hands of a Mississippi boy. The sky was clearer than Humphrey's moonshine, and the full moon was perfect for my favorite part of the trip—catching grasshoppers. Not just any grasshoppers, mind you, but the yellow-bellied monsters that doubled the size of ours back home.

We hardly needed a full moon and didn't need our flashlights. The giant bugs were everywhere. In no time our Prince Albert cans were jam-packed and ready for every scale in Humphrey's creek.

We headed for the tent and a little shut-eye. Momma fussed that Deddy slept like an old dog before Vietnam but a stray cat after. A tent was the only place I'd seen the old-dog part. The out of doors put my deddy right to sleep and kept him there.

— ✳ ✳ ✳ —

COOKIE'S BUCKET WOULD'VE BUSTED FASTER THAN Peter's nets as we waded down the creek with our cane poles the next morning. Bream and rock bass to smallies and largemouths, our grasshoppers were downright irresistible.

Deddy liked fish but loved snakes. Banks to creek, they were everywhere. What I would've given for Cookie to have seen the world's quickest hand jut out and grab one highland moccasin after another. She'd have popped every eardrum in the valley when he pulled the devils to his face for a closer look before dropping them into the water and smiling as they slithered away.

After a long day of fishing, we headed to the cabin for Humphrey's fried fish, hushpuppies, and sweet tea. Humphrey's Mason jar might've been long on moonshine and short on tea, but he had no trouble staying awake as he told us about a big-bosomed widow-lady who lived in Mount Ida. When the bragging shifted to a pretty sister in the next holler, Deddy cleared his throat.

"Those fish were mighty hungry today," he said. "Bass and bream."

Humphrey stared into his moonshine, a blank look on his face.

"What's wrong?" Deddy asked.

"I'm proud of you, Cash. I've never been able to whip the bottle."

"Well, I've got Ethel and our preacher to thank. Wouldn't say I've whipped it, though. Doubt it'll ever leave my mind."

"Most soldiers who come back from Vietnam with half of what you—"

"Most had it worse than I did," Deddy interrupted.

"I hear what you're saying, Cash. I'm proud of you, is all."

Deddy fell right to sleep that night. I stayed awake long as I could, ignoring the owls and frogs but tuning into the sound of each steady and peaceful breath. Humphrey wasn't the only one who was proud of my deddy.

✶ ✶ ✶

AT DAYBREAK, I WOKE TO THE racket of Humphrey busting into our tent.

Deddy bolted from his sleeping bag and grabbed the old man by the shoulders. "What is it?" Humphrey struggled to catch his breath. "Spit it out!"

"Ethel called," he finally said. "Big John's in the hospital. He might not make it."

"Slide, get in the truck," Deddy said, as if he'd expected the news.

43

W E RACED THROUGH MOUNT IDA, HOT SPRINGS, and Little Rock without a word. Deddy would always slow and look each way when crossing a river or creek, but he sped across the Arkansas River bridge at ninety miles per hour, his body stiff as a paddle.

I'd grown up around the wild-eyed dreams of war and the blurry-eyed slobbers from a couch. For the past month, I'd watched the raised hands and glowing face of a new man in the pews of a church. I'd never seen these eyes, this person, and I was scared.

I clutched the door handle with both hands as Deddy took a hard right into the hospital parking lot. He didn't slow down until we reached the curb by the front door.

Sam was standing outside Big John's room when we ran up. His button-down shirt and khaki pants were wrinkled and spotted with blood.

"Is my brother alive?" Deddy asked.

"Barely," Sam said. "The doctor said it could go either way."

Deddy slouched against the wall. He didn't move for a minute or more. He whirled and studied his only friend with those eyes I'd watched for the past four hours.

"Big John's blood?" he asked, pointing at Sam's shirt.

Sam nodded. "I helped carry him to the ambulance."

"Tell me exactly when you got there and what you saw from that point on," Deddy said.

"Well, I left the church at four o'clock yesterday afternoon. That would've put me at Big John's around—"

"Was the gate open?"

"It was closed and latched, like you'd expect. Big John's truck was parked in its spot at the end of the gravel, but he wasn't on the porch and didn't answer the door. I circled around back and found the ruts, deeper near the house like someone had gunned the engine taking off. I noticed a wide path where the grass had been trampled and figured Big John had pulled a bale of hay to the barn, until I walked down the hill and saw where the fence had been bowled over. The path ran straight up the hill and made a loop before heading back down to the barn."

"Dammit!" Deddy yelled. He stalked up and down the hall with his head swaying side to side. "I shouldn't have let Big John talk me into leaving town." He stopped a few inches from Sam. "What else?"

"I stood at the barn trying to piece it all together. I hollered Big John's name. Nothing. I'd decided to run back to the house and call Cookie when I heard a weak groan in the shed."

Sam stared down the hall, his bottom lip in a tight grip between his teeth.

"Keep going," Deddy said.

"Cash, my three years as a chaplain in Vietnam didn't prepare me for what I saw when I opened that door. Your brother's face was bloodied and battered beyond recognition. Lips cocked open like a dead man's. Overalls ripped to shreds. Layers of blood and dirt caked between whatever patches of skin he had left. An arm bent the wrong way at the elbow. A thick bone sticking out of his right leg. A—"

"Enough," Deddy said, reaching for the door.

"One more thing," Sam said. "The doctors are worried about brain damage." Deddy pounded the wall with the palm of his hand. "They're wrong, Cash."

"Why do you say that?"

"Big John wanted to tell me something. I saw it in his eyes."

Deddy pointed at the door. "Is Cookie in there?" Sam shook his head. "The bastards got her!"

"Cash, we don't know where she is."

"They probably killed her by now," Deddy said. "And I'm damn sure killing them."

Deddy opened the door and ran to the foot of the bed. Sam put an arm around my shoulder and guided me to Big John's side.

Not counting his eyes and mouth plus a spot on his left cheek and another on his left hand, Big John was wrapped in bandages that should've been white and dry instead of oozing with pink and red. The skin on his cheek reminded me of half-cooked sausage.

I couldn't cry and wouldn't pray. If God cared about the best man He'd ever made, why did this happen?

"Big John!" I yelled at the top of my lungs. I was clinging to the bed and still shouting his name when his eyes opened. He blinked twice. His eyes searched the room and found the man standing at the foot of his bed.

"Cash, they have Cookie," Big John said. "Myles said Slide and Salt were next. And—" He choked on a mouthful of blood. He swallowed. "Shad laughed when Myles said it. Find 'em, Cash. Make 'em tell you where Cookie is. Where her body is. Then finish the job I couldn't. Kill 'em, Cash. Myles and Shad. You know what to do."

My hero took a long breath that sounded like Shine's last, then closed his eyes for what I knew was the last time.

PART XII

BIG JOHN HADN'T SALUTED SINCE THE war. Hadn't planned to that morning, but there he stood, honoring his brother until the truck rolled out of sight.

He turned for the barn, full of relief and joy. Relief that Salt, and now Slide, were safe. Joy in the new life of a new man, his brother.

He emptied a sack of feed for his cows, watched them eat, and made his way to the house. He took a long nap in his bed, in *their* bed, and spent the rest of the day on the porch, rocking and often singing to himself. Johnny Cash and Charley Pride for the most part, though he danced his way to the den to the tune of "Blue Suede Shoes," wondering what Elvis would think of his boots and overalls.

At dawn, he made a pot of coffee and went to the porch. He rocked and sipped, taking in the new day. The glow of Snowball's fur as he stalked across the yard in the dim light. The faint outline of a heifer in the near pasture. The soft chirp of the first bird. The crow of a distant rooster.

He drank a second cup of coffee before strolling to the shed. Eight long months had passed since Victry's knock on the door. As Big John sharpened Sweet Betsy and his other knives, he looked forward to another talk with his nephew. "I don't believe in a god who wouldn't make a blade for this rope," Victry had said. The Rope was real, but the power of God to heal a daughter and change a brother was also real.

He walked the pastures, hands at his back and eyes on his beloved place. Gazing at the sky, he spotted a lone buzzard circling overhead.

"Not today, ole boy," he said with a chuckle. "Lord willing, not today."

He stopped at Cookie's pond, staring at the murky water until startled by the strike of a bass that must've ended the life of some poor creature. He moseyed back to the house and called Cookie. She had no interest in his report, much less his advice on trying a cricket or a minnow instead of a worm. She hung up after he promised to say a prayer she'd catch a bass for a change.

Big John grinned at the click, poured another cup of coffee, and headed to the porch. After a while, he nodded off to sleep.

He didn't hear the footsteps.

44

Cookie

FROM BOXING WITH THE LAWD TO going easy on Myles, Cookie had been riled at Big John since Shine had passed. Was she too hard on the man? Maybe. Men got mopey when the going got rough, and Big John had been wading some deep water. Swamps, more like it. Swamps with ten moccasins to every fish and more mud than water. But he'd kept on keeping on, which was more than Cookie could say about most men.

On Tuesday afternoon she decided to leave Big John with a soft word or two before proving what a bass would do to a worm. When he wasn't dozing on the porch like she'd expected, she figured he was either on the commode or scrounging around the kitchen for something else to eat.

She poked her head through the front door. "Big John, where you at?"

"In the kitchen, Cookie. Thought I'd fix us a batch of tea."

"*Us* yo ass."

He chuckled. "Sweet tea does wonders for a sour mood."

"Same old fool," she said, crossing the den.

She walked into the kitchen and froze.

"Sounded just like him, wouldn't you say?" She was listening to Big John but looking at Myles. His cheeks were hot and red, but there was no sweat on his face. "Excuse my manners, Miss Cookie. You remember Shad, don't you?"

She glanced at Shad but wished she hadn't. His T-shirt and muscles reminded her of the redneck at the bait shop. Same with the little pits and scars on his cheeks.

"Where's Big John?" she asked.

"Waiting on you," Myles said, this time in his own voice.

"You killed him."

Myles narrowed his eyes like a dozing cat. "Shad, tie her up."

Cookie landed a slap across Shad's ear that would've made most men think twice about coming for more. Not him. She was bone-strong and cat-quick, but he was bull-strong and had her nose on the floor before she went to cussing.

"Listen to you," Myles said. "A lady of the *Lawd.*" Shad tied her wrists in a tight knot. "Good job, baby brother. Take her out back."

Shad hoisted her up, followed her through the kitchen to the back door, and shoved her down the steps. She landed face down and half wanted to stay thataway, nose on the ground and eyes in the grass, but her daddy had eyeballed the devils who'd killed him, and Cookie would do the same. She got to her feet, glaring at Myles and Shad, then searching for Big John.

"O ye of little faith," Myles said. "He's here."

Shad hauled her around the back of Myles's truck.

"There's your man," Myles said. Big John was out cold. Blood ran through his hair and down his whiskers. They'd looped a rope around his ankles and tied the other end to the bumper. "He gave me no choice, Cookie. You of all people should know that."

"I know what evil is."

"I'd planned on killing him quick until he did something to set me off. Like his daughter did many a time. Must run in the family."

"Come and get him, Lawd. It's time."

"Damn you," Myles said, hissing like a wet log on a hot fire. "Damn both of you." He wiped spit from the corners of his mouth. "Shad, run in the kitchen and get some water."

Big John came to when Myles splashed the water on his face. "Here I am, Big John. Remember me? Your boy, Myles. Your prize for Pearl." Big John moved his eyes but not his head. Had they broken his neck? "Look who we have for company."

Big John whispered half of Cookie's name and mouthed the rest.

"Save yo breath for the Lawd," she said. "He came for Shine, and now He's a-coming for you."

"Enough of your damn preaching! Shad, hold Cookie right there. We'll give her a front-row seat."

With that Myles ran to his door, hopped behind the wheel, and cranked the engine.

⤙ ✕ ✕ ✕ ⤚

COOKIE FLINCHED WHEN THE ROPE PULLED taut and sent Big John bouncing and barreling through a barbed-wire fence near the barn. The sound of that engine roaring up the next hill reminded Cookie of the trucks that came for her daddy. Myles hit the top, wheeled around, and raced back down to the barn.

Shad took a tight hold of her arm and led her down the hill to Big John. Blood and dirt and torn flesh covered every inch of his face. A bone jutted from his leg. She watched the slow up-and-down of his chest.

"What about her?" Shad asked. "I bet she'd like a ride on the rope."

Myles squinted at Cookie for a good while.

"We'll take her with us," he said. "Might need her for insurance." He pulled a handkerchief from his back pocket and wiped sweat from his eyes. He smiled at Big John. "How fitting for our war hero to spend his last hours in a shed. Just like his first night in Germany. 'Go to Hell Ole Miss,' as I recall. Shad, I'll let you do the honors."

Shad untied the rope from the bumper, dragged Big John across the ground, and opened the shed door.

"Wait," Myles said, jogging their way. He dropped to a knee, snatched the pink bandana from Big John's overalls, and held it high like Big John had done that day on the porch. "I'm sure it's a sin to spit on the most versatile raiment known to man, but here goes." He spat on the bandana and rubbed it across what was left of Big John's face. "You'll be happy to know I'm done with your daughter. But I do have plans for Cookie. And Slide. And Salt." Big John let out a weak moan. "Pray on that while you die."

Shad laughed and went to pulling on the rope.

"I'm wondering if we should kill him now," Myles said.

Shad trotted toward the truck, a wicked grin on his ugly face. He ran back with the rifle, nudged the barrel under Big John's chin, and clicked the safety off.

Myles raised a hand. "Hold up, Shad. I said I was *wondering*. We don't need a gun sounding off before we drive a red pickup to the gate."

Shad propped his rifle on the shed, took a knife from his pocket, and unfolded the blade. "This won't make any noise."

"No, he'll be dead soon enough," Myles said. "Let's go."

45

A S THE FLASHY RED TRUCK PULLED onto the highway, Cookie's eyes burned a hole in the back of Myles's head. Part of her wanted to kill the man. The other wanted to cry for the man he'd left dying in the dirt.

Couple miles down the road, they came to the house Cookie had lived in as a child. The house she'd pointed out to Myles on Big John's birthday. The house she was now looking at for what had to be the last time.

Cookie knew she'd see her daddy before long. She wouldn't mention the busted windows and roof on the home he'd built, or the tree growing in the porch he loved so much. She couldn't wait to brag on the chimney, still tall and free as the man who'd walked straight into that mob of deacons.

Free. Her daddy had been free. Had she? "Yo tongue was born on the loose," her momma would holler as she chased Cookie around that very house with a switch. Cookie thought the rest had broken free the night her daddy died. But there was no freedom in fear, and when Myles told Big John he was coming after Salt and Slide, not one inch of her six-feet was free.

She glanced at the blond hair Pearl had played with the day Myles dove into those muddy waters and came up with a catfish. Glanced was all Cookie could do. The thought of Myles with those children sent her whole body to shaking. She found herself cold but covered in sweat, breathing hard but losing breath. She couldn't think or pray or get hold of herself.

What brought her out of that mess? How long did it last? Cookie didn't know, but in a flash, her fear was gone, snapped clean in two, and she was free. Free to leave even Salt in the hands of her Lawd. Free to face this devil and his brother.

She said the first thing that came to mind. "Evil is hard work. Ain't it, Myles?"

He turned and stared a while. Cookie had no idea what he was thinking. Never had.

"Business is business," he said. "Though it got mighty personal when Big John ambushed me in my own house and then gave me that John Wayne bullshit about never stepping foot in Hill County again. He backed me into a corner, Cookie. At some point a man's gotta do what a man's gotta do."

"Whatever works, I reckon. Smiling, beating, killing. All the same to you."

"Was I supposed to close my shop and flush all that money down the drain? Hide in a hole and let the old hillbilly run over me?" Myles stared out the window, cracking his knuckles. "It's not like we could've just roughed him up and let him go. Especially after that bogus trial of his. I wouldn't have a chance against his high-priced lawyer. Not to mention Sam spouting off to a rigged jury."

"So you had no choice but to rope Big John to the bumper of this truck and drag him across barbed wire and through a field until he was good as dead."

"Already told you—I'd planned on making it quick. A small turtle within three hundred yards is dead meat for Shad and his high-powered rifle. He propped his .30-06 on the gate, peered through the scope, and trained those crosshairs on the good-for-nothing dozing in his rocker. One shot and Big John would've died in his sleep. We'd have made it look like a robbery, let the dust settle, and gone back to making money. Now the sheriff will have to figure something out."

"I'm sure he will. He figured out how to look the other way when my daddy was killed. How to fill his pockets with yo money and let you get away with beating Pearl half to death."

"Mathis does what he has to. Being a sheriff's not an easy job."

"But you couldn't bring yoself to make it easy on the sheriff. Or Big John."

Myles slapped the top of his seat. "Big John's the criminal! *I'm* the one who was attacked and kidnapped and tossed to the side of the road like a piece of trash. I couldn't, wouldn't let that be his last glimpse of my face."

"You had to let him know you'd won."

"I always win. But even there on the porch, all I'd wanted was a blow with the bat for old times' sake before Shad put a bullet in his brain." Myles rubbed his hand across his lips. "The sight of his fat-and-happy face napping on the porch got my blood to boiling. I really snapped after my first blow woke him and he—"

"Bet I know what he did," Cookie said.

"He said he'd forgive me! Forgive *me* for what he started."

"Pride is what made the devil *the* devil," she said. "Ain't that funny?"

"Let me pull over and shut the bitch up," Shad said.

Myles eyed the floor, gnawing on his nails. "I think she'll settle down after a week or two in Holly's shed."

"Why don't we kill her now?" Shad asked.

Cookie leaned toward Myles. "Let the dog loose," she said, aiming for a bullet over a shed. "Yo brother's foaming at the mouth."

Shad banged his hand on the wheel. Myles nodded at his brother. Shad slowed, glancing from one side of the highway to the other. He stopped at a dirt road near a ditch with tall weeds on each side.

Myles waved him off. "No, let's stick with the plan. The shed will buy us some time."

—✳ ✳ ✳—

A FEW MILES LATER THEY PASSED the biggest cattle farm in Hill County. Cows colored every whichaway roamed far as Cookie's eye could see. Thick green grass, not a yellow weed in sight. Lawd, these fences were now shining in the sun . . . shining in the sun.

Shine. Big John had already busted the Pearly Gates wide open, Cookie figured. Now he was flooding those streets of gold with happy tears, hugging Shine so tight she couldn't stop praising the Lawd she had no more bones to break. Wouldn't be long before she took him to see James and Elijah.

"And I'll soon be heading thataway," Cookie said. "After a week or two anyhow."

Myles didn't say a word, but Shad was still cussing when Harry's Bait Shop came into view. Big John had been too soft with that redneck. And Myles, of course. Same with the sheriff. If Big John had pulled his trigger in the cotton field that day, they might've found a sheriff stout enough to have kept those men from killing Cookie's daddy, straight enough to have kept Myles out of Hill County and away from Pearl.

"Why'd you move here to begin with?" Cookie asked.

"Same reason I told you I'm done with Pearl," Myles said. "Part of it anyway. I get bored. Always have, puppies and girls to working for my father and living in Biloxi. I wanted a fresh spot to hang my hat. Along with making money, I like *new*. Moving gave me the opportunity for both."

"I reckon my question wasn't easy enough for you. Why Hill County?"

Shad's mean little eyes darted from his brother to Cookie. "How long are we putting up with her shit?"

"It's part of the game," Myles said, patting his hound on the shoulder. "Cookie, you don't know any more about business than Big John, so I'll make it nice and easy for you. We buy stolen cars for next to nothing and have them painted and spiffed up for the used car dealers, and we need a county with a cooperative sheriff."

"A crooked sheriff."

"Mathis was only part of it. Here's the idea, Cookie. One, we need a location an hour's drive from a big city with too much real crime for the law to bother with stolen cars. Memphis is right there with New Orleans in that respect. Two, we want that city in a different state from our shop. That way it's harder to track if they do get suspicious. And three, like our shop near Biloxi, our operation has to be outside the city limits, so we're only dealing with a county sheriff."

"When did Pearl see through yo bull?"

"Well, the first time she really got out of hand was on our wedding night. Truth is, I went too easy on her." He propped a leg on the dashboard and rubbed his knee. "Course, she didn't know the particulars of my business."

"Or that you'd kill her if need be. Plus her daddy and your own sister."

"Pipe down, Cookie. I told you I didn't kill Holly."

"I doubt that. I don't doubt what you did to Pearl and Big John."

"What they did to themselves. If not for his poem and her mouth, not to mention their prying into my affairs, I would've bought Pearl a nice house in town and given her a few babies to keep her busy. Who knows, the bride might've made a half-decent wife if Big John had stayed out of it."

"And you'd have gone on about yo business."

He chuckled. "Over time I would've joined the Rotary Club, served on a few boards, made a fine deacon for Sam. Maybe even a Sunday school teacher, not to mention an upstanding father and husband. Add them all up and you're totin' the best business card the Bible Belt can buy. A white man with money who checks those boxes can hide enough dirty laundry to fill half the antebellums in the South. Toss a good business plan and salesmanship into the equation and you have enough money to fill the other half."

"Money ain't filling yo hole."

"Filling my hole," Myles said with a snicker. "Shad, maybe the Buddhists are onto something. A reincarnated Pascal is blessing our back seat."

"Pass who?" Shad asked.

"Miss Cookie, you'll have to excuse our chauffeur. Shad had bitten off the heads of enough fish to earn that name before he turned ten, but little brother is hardly the theologian you and I are."

A strange thought crossed Cookie's brain. Whether it was Myles blaming everybody else or saying little brother, she didn't know.

"You remind me of the man who wouldn't stop kicking on Annabelle," she said. "That would've ended if Cash had caught him."

Myles snorted. "Cash. Vietnam's best cook meets a handyman who can't handle a bottle. I should let my older brother put that drunk out of his misery. Duke killed more people in Vietnam than Cash set a plate for."

Cookie nodded to herself. The less Myles knew, the better. Cash would be looking for war once he saw what they'd done to his brother. Maybe he'd track Myles down before the children got hurt.

"The sweet old dog decided she'd had enough one day and took a chunk outta the man's leg," she said. "The clown acted like the big bad wolf had mauled the very lamb of the Lawd. Course, he was a postman. Not a killer."

"Cookie, you know what the Bible says about an eye for an eye. Big John was a fool if he thought I'd let him get away with running me out of town."

"He was no fool except when it came to reading people. Always hoping for the best, even with you."

"Big John was no prince. He was so worked up about marrying his daughter off he forgot his own brother until the drunk was rotting away on a couch. Once Shine got cancer, the perfect father didn't give a damn about our wedding."

"Nobody except Slide and Salt said he was perfect."

Myles swung around in his seat. "Slide and Salt. Did I mean what I said about *yo chillun*? Are they next on my list?" He stared at Cookie for the longest minute of her life. He smiled. "I've got good and bad news. What do you want first?"

"What I want is to slice yo neck."

His eyes lit up. "Shad, hand me the pocketknife you wanted to use on Big John."

Myles opened the blade and held it to her face. He eased it back and forth across her neck.

"How does your faith serve you now, Miss Cookie? A crutch would've come in handy when you were warming my nose with Big John's lighter."

"The Lawd's more real than yo knife."

"What does Victry say to that?" Myles asked with a mocking grin.

"'Train up a child in the way he should go, and when he is old, he will not depart from it.' Isn't that what Scripture says? You must've done a glorious job with my fellow pilgrim in the faith."

Right then Cookie saw why she hadn't seen Myles. She'd heard the same sweet voice and seen the same soft hands as her Victry. The dark had been hiding in her light.

"Evil," was all she could say.

"My, you love that word. But if Victry and I are right, and there is no God, who's to say what is evil? Or good?"

"Victry's good comes from the Lawd whether he knows it or not. Yo evil comes from—" Myles cut her off with a laugh that boiled her blood. "Get on with it, boy. Do what you gotta do if you got what it takes."

"Uppity tongue of yours," he said, moving the knife to her mouth. "The Holy Spirit must be leaving this part of your sanctification to an unholy man." He slid the blade between her lips, stopped at clenched teeth, and eased the knife to her nose. "I have a better idea."

Cookie couldn't help yanking her head when he started the blade up her right nostril. The cut was too quick and clean to hurt until the blood poured into her mouth. Myles's eyes were so wide she couldn't tell whether he was surprised or happy. He leaned down, searching the floor at her feet, and came up with an oily rag. He stretched it across her nose and tied a knot around her head.

"Did that to yourself," he said. "Should've known I was joking."

Cookie wanted to spit blood all over his face. Instead, she swallowed hard and met his eyes. He turned, slumped down in his seat, and took a nap.

46

COOKIE SPENT A GOOD BIT OF the next few hours trying to forget the sermon she walked out of the day after they'd left Myles on the side of the road. "Forgiving yo enemies is a command," her preacher had said. "And hate is a sin."

Would Jeremiah forgive the men in the front seat of this truck? Would the Lawd? Cookie knew her answer, for she was still sinning when Shad pulled off the blacktop and honked twice at a big gate.

A man with a gun on his shoulder and three mean-looking dogs on a leash swung the gate open. Myles reached back and pushed Cookie down.

"This will be our little secret," he said, letting her up as they passed a big warehouse on the right.

They veered left onto a dirt road that wound through a patch of woods and ended at a small field. And there it was. Holly's shed. Cookie's shed. Steel door and roof. Block walls four-feet tall, a few gaps on each row. Breathing room, she supposed, more time for more suffering.

The truck rolled to a stop at the door. Myles got out and stood aside as Shad yanked her across the seat, cut the rope from her wrists, and shoved her onto the shed floor. She looked up to see Myles squatting at the door, a jug in his hand.

He tossed it in her lap. "Unless you give up like Holly and slam your hard head on the concrete floor, that water will keep you nice and comfy until I get back. Don't worry about our puppy dogs. Those monsters couldn't dig their way into this shed in a million years."

"I'm looking at the monsters," Cookie said.

There was just enough light to show the mad on Myles's face.

"Another nigger with an attitude," he said. "You're all better off than you'd have been in Africa. Always have been long as you did what you were told, kept a little garden like your mother used to, wasted your Sundays hollering in church, and kept your mouths buttoned up the rest of the time. What's there not to like about that?" He leaned in. "Your father had it coming, by the way. My good buddy the high sheriff said so himself."

"Go on back to hell where you belong."

A grin crossed his face. "And now for the news on Slide and Salt. The good news is that I lost my temper with Big John and said what came to mind. The bad news? Now I'm having second thoughts." He took a coin from his pocket, flipped it, and hid it between his hands. "Heads they live. Tails they die. Fair enough?" She scooted closer. "You don't need a lighter, Cookie. Trust me. Heads or tails?"

She kicked at his face, but he was too quick. He jerked his head back and stood.

"You wouldn't mind sailing off to meet *yo Lawd* in the sweet by-and-by, but you're not ready to put Salt and Slide on that plane. I'll need them to hold over your ass in case I do let you live."

Cookie's life was now a danger to the children. It was time for her to die. And quick.

"You ain't man enough to kill me," she said. "I ain't sure about yo mutt-for-brains brother. Cut the boy's leash and we'll see."

Her plan didn't work. Again. Myles slapped his leg and laughed while Shad eased the door to a close.

"She'll hold out and drink the water I was kind enough to leave," Myles said, as the padlock clicked into place. "I can't see her taking Holly's way out. She's stubborn like Pearl."

"Her eyes said that much," Shad said.

"Nose too," Myles said. "The nostril she nearly cut in half was still flaring when you shut the door."

— ✳ ✳ ✳ —

MYLES TOLD THE TRUTH ABOUT THOSE dogs. They showed up after dark, growling and sniffing and pawing at the wall. Cookie yelled and growled back until they went looking for somebody else to eat.

Dogs. Like the devils outside this shed, most dogs told you all you needed to about their owners. Annabelle sure did. She treated blacks like people. Didn't act like your best friend one second and bite your leg off the next. Unless you deserved it, that is. Cookie chuckled to herself, thinking of the postman.

Annabelle didn't have much time, stiff and old as she was. Maybe a year. A year after Slide would've lost a hero, and Cash a brother. Losing a dog sounded like no big deal in that light, but men and boys turned baby when their dogs died. So yes, Annabelle's passing did have Cookie worried.

The racket in that warehouse made Wednesday a long one. The night too. All kinds of sawing and grinding and Lawd knew what else. Cookie saved her water but not her cool. She rested but couldn't rest.

Might as well talk to the Lawd, she figured. "Lawd, You hung on that tree a while, a good while, but not as long as those criminals hanging next to You. You went ahead and let Yoself pass. Why not me? You know I'm ready to see Daddy and Momma, Shine, and even Big John. You too, I reckon. Make it quick."

Daylight was peeping through the blocks by the time Cookie decided the Lawd had no more interest in listening than doing what she'd said. The birds had another fifteen minutes or so before cranking up their tunes. The dogs weren't barking or growling. The shop wasn't rattling. Dead quiet never sounded so dead.

Then she heard a voice: "You in there, Cookie?"

"Lawd, You know where I'm at."

"It's me, Cash. You okay?"

She caught on that go-round. It hadn't been two full days since Myles had pulled this trick in Big John's kitchen.

"Get outta here!" she hollered.

"Same ole Cookie," the man said. "I'll be back directly."

The man hadn't been gone five minutes when what sounded like a bomb went off in the warehouse. Then one blast after another.

Few minutes later she heard a truck barreling across the field and skidding to a stop at the shed.

"Hold your ears," the man said. "I gotta bust this lock open."

When the door flew open, Cookie knew she'd been right the first time. The Lawd had come, and He'd come in the name of Cash.

He reached in and helped her out. She got to her feet but couldn't straighten her back.

"The dogs," she said, her mouth too dry for more than a raspy whisper.

She followed his eyes to the red on his axe and quit worrying about dogs.

—✳—✳—✳—

"WHERE'S MYLES AND SHAD?" COOKIE ASKED, as they sped past the flames of what had been a warehouse.

Cash pointed with his thumb. "In there. What's left of them. Nobody else had gotten to work. I would've been glad to kill them, too."

Cookie had heard about this Cash, caught a glimpse in the hospital when Big John whispered in his ear. Minutes had passed since she'd seen the man with a bloody axe who reminded her of what Revelation said about Jesus coming back on that white horse of His. Twenty-two years had passed since she'd seen these eyes—the eyes of her daddy before he made a steer of a white man.

They'd made it a few miles down the highway when Cash said, "I see your nose. Anything else?"

"Nope."

"I'm sorry you got caught in the middle of this."

"What's done is done," she said.

Cash nodded real slow-like, one eye open and the other closed. "Myles or Shad mention the Dixie Mafia?"

"Dixie Mafia?"

"Loose-knit gang of killers and outlaws. Headquartered in Biloxi, from what I hear."

"Salt's way off in them mountains with Lore," Cookie said, fighting another wave of fear. "Where's Slide?"

"Slide and Ethel are at Sam's house with his German shepherd and every gun known to man. That preacher doesn't play."

"And Big John?"

Cash took a deep breath. "In the hospital he came to and told me what happened. Was barely hanging on when I left."

"Hard to believe he made it that long."

"Don't ask me how. No telling the soldiers I watched die in Vietnam with half of what he's got. Young soldiers." Cash peered under the top of the wheel. "I can't speed and risk getting pulled over. We need to make it a hundred miles or more before I stop at a pay phone to find out if he's still alive. I'm not sure I can handle the news."

"Bad news might be that he is alive." He glared her way, then stared down the road. "What's on yo brain? Cash?"

"My brother," he said. "And Vietnam."

"Vietnam?"

"I only killed on command. Some of it had to be done. Some I'm not sure. None of it felt right, and it all still haunts me. But setting fire to Myles and Shad felt good. Mathis is next."

"No, he ain't."

"None of this would've happened if not for the sheriff. Your deddy would be alive if Mathis had done his job."

"Happened too quick for a good sheriff to handle," she lied. "Much less a no-count like Mathis."

"I'm sure he heard rumblings when that mob was coming together."

Cookie had heard tales of the Mississippi River changing its flow during an earthquake way back when. She didn't know the truth in those tales, but she knew Cash's blood was now flowing to kill. Might've been a good thing in the war. It had been good a short while ago. Now it was time for another earthquake.

"Leave my daddy outta this!" Cookie yelled. "And Mathis. He's a crook but no Myles. Or Shad."

"But—"

"No *but* to it," she said, sounding like her momma talking to Big John after he'd taken her daddy down from that rope. "The Lawd will take care of Mathis in due time. You need to worry about yo woman and boy and brother. You with me?"

"Okay," he finally said.

Her talk with the Lawd came to mind. She'd told Him to make it quick.

"Cash, how'd you find me?"

"Myles's deddy was bragging about their family compound at the reception. Said it was on the beach exactly a mile west of Biloxi. Also mentioned a guesthouse where Myles stayed when he came home. I found them this morning. Along with enough empty bottles to say they'd had quite a party. I'd tied them up before they came to. At first, they wouldn't tell me where you were. Acted like they had no idea what I was talking about."

"How'd you make 'em talk?"

"Gave them a rundown on Vietnam and said two more didn't make a page in my book. Myles caved after I pulled out my pliers and took hold of a finger. Blamed Shad and became my best friend. Even warned me about those dogs when I pulled up to the gate."

"Myles thought he'd con his way outta that fix?"

"Until he pointed toward the shed where you were. Then he saw my face."

"I'm glad he knew it was coming. The devil would've killed our chillun. I saw it in those eyes yesterday. Shad was right there with him."

"I know."

"Without a blink."

"Myles sure blinked when I hauled them into the warehouse and tied them to the bumper of one of those cars. He lost it when I came back and tossed the dogs into his lap. Didn't have much left when I lit the fire."

"How'd you do it all so quick?"

"Fuel tanks were all over the place. I poured gas on every animal, the three dead ones plus the other two. Also covered the cars to make sure they blew. Once I had everything ready for a quick getaway, I hurried to the shed to check on you. Then I rushed back to the warehouse. Could've used the axe like I'd done with the dogs. But after what Myles had done to Pearl and Big John and you, after what he'd said about our children, he deserved to suffer before he died. Same with Shad." Cash glanced out the window. "Did my best to make it look like an accident. Nobody will find much, but I'm sure they'll figure it out when they see you're gone."

"Myles said nobody else would know. Said it was our little secret."

"Let's hope he wasn't lying for once. I'll be ready if he was."

"What you said about that mafia has me worried."

"Maybe I'm just seeing the clouds again," Cash said. "Thinking Myles or Shad would've mentioned it to scare me into letting them go. That said, Myles was too scared and Shad too mad to do much thinking."

"Don't forget their older brother. The way Myles talked about Duke reminded me of you."

"I said I'll be ready."

— ✶ ✶ ✶ —

THREE LONG AND QUIET HOURS HAD passed before Cash pulled over at a phone booth on the outskirts of Meridian. He stared at the booth but stayed on his ass.

"You know Sam's number?" Cookie asked, though she knew Cash had dialed it many times since Sam had sobered him up.

He nodded and got out.

Cookie had no idea what Cash was hearing on the other end of the line. His head went from dead still to twitching every whichaway like a chicken when the hatchet came down.

He hung up, propped his elbow on the glass, and dropped his chin. She was fixing to get out when he turned for the truck.

He climbed in and turned the key, but he didn't drive. Couldn't drive.

"Tell me, Cash."

"Ethel just got back from the hospital," he mumbled. "She was mighty relieved to hear about you."

"Big John?"

"My brother's hour to hour. Or breath to breath."

Lawd, Big John was still alive. Bad news or good? Cookie didn't know what to think or how to feel.

"Who's watching over him?" she asked.

"Ethel said Victry got into town this morning. He's at the hospital now."

"Any word on Pearl?"

"Ethel called the Hoods last night. They said Pearl left for California two days ago. She's supposed to touch base when she gets there."

"Big John's liable to be dead by then."

Cash nodded, hugged the wheel, and went to blubbering.

47

Slide

OUR PREACHER, HIS MEAN-LOOKING SHOTGUN, AND his all-lick German shepherd were keeping Momma and me company when the phone rang. Sam bolted from his leather chair, shotgun in hand. He grabbed the handset and said "Hello." He mouthed Deddy's name.

I sprinted to the spare bedroom, slammed the door, and turned on the AC unit to make sure I couldn't hear the grown-ups in the den. Truth was, I doubted Big John's faith in his brother, in my deddy, to find Cookie. Much less kill Myles and Shad.

I sprawled facedown on the bed, hoping but not praying. A hand touched my shoulder. I didn't move.

"Cookie's safe," Momma said. I turned and sat up. "You and Salt are safe too. Myles and Shad are dead."

"Deddy killed them?" She nodded. "What did he say?"

"He was too shaken up about Big John to say more than he'd killed them and was on his way back with Cookie."

"Is she okay?"

"Roughed up, but she'll be all right."

I'd been afraid, more than afraid, of losing Big John, Deddy, and Cookie in the same day. Two of those three had survived. Part of me wanted to jump on the bed and sing my favorite songs. The other wanted to hide under the bed and never come out.

I stood. "Can I see Big John now?"

"Sam's calling the hospital to let Victry know. Then he'll take you."

"Won't you come?"

"Slide, this morning was the first time I've set foot in a hospital since my daddy died from lung cancer. But there's more to it this go-round. Cookie has a bad cut and hasn't eaten or changed clothes in days. Cash wanted me at our house in case they needed to stop by on their way to the hospital."

I gave Momma a hug and headed for Sam's Buick.

———— ✶ ✶ ✶ ————

I FOLLOWED SAM THROUGH THE HOSPITAL lobby and down a long hall which led to another hall and Big John's room. Sam turned the corner and froze. I did the same.

Victry, standing outside Big John's door, was breathing hard and staring at the tile floor. He didn't look up as we ran his way. He didn't blink when Sam draped an arm across his shoulder.

"What is it?" Sam asked.

Victry shook his head, trying to catch his breath while I answered Sam's question in my mind—Big John was dead.

"Sam, I've been standing here since you called," Victry finally said. "No joy or relief over Cookie and Cash. No sorrow for Big John. I don't know what's wrong with me."

This isn't about you! I wanted to shout.

"There's nothing wrong with you," Sam said, holding Victry at arm's length. "You're torn in so many directions you can't feel a thing."

Victry nodded, closed his eyes, and wept as Sam pulled him in for a long hug.

For the next hour, Victry and I took turns holding Big John's hand while Sam stood at the foot of the bed. Nobody cried. Sam didn't pray.

I hadn't prayed since Humphrey busted into our tent. I'd hoped for the best the best I could, but doubt had beaten the hell out of hope.

I wanted to cry but couldn't. Too numb, I figured, like Victry before Sam took him into his arms. "Think about something else," Momma said when enduring another bout with a man on a bottle. The man I didn't know.

Who is my deddy? I asked myself. He wasn't a cook who couldn't get over a kitchen fire. That said, I still felt like I was crawling through a dark room searching for a switch.

I asked my deddy's only friend. Sam didn't answer. I turned and faced the one who'd known Deddy the longest.

Victry shifted in his seat. "What do you mean, Slide?"

"Big John was choking on blood and barely able to talk when he told Deddy to find Cookie and kill Myles and Shad. He said it like the matter was already settled."

"I guess it was."

"What do you know, Victry?"

"Very little. I think you should ask your father."

"He's never told me shit. I'm asking you."

"I only know what I've heard from Big John and Cookie and others in our family."

"What have you heard?"

"Let me think on it a minute."

"We have an hour or so before Deddy and Cookie get here."

"Slide, your father was a decorated soldier in Vietnam, though I doubt any of us know exactly what he did."

"What do you know?"

"From what I've gathered, Myles and Shad had no chance against your father. None whatsoever. He was a sniper of some sort. A hunter of men. An army unto himself."

I could've busted through every brick in the hospital when Victry called Deddy "an army unto himself." Instead, I busted through the door and raced down the hall to the bathroom. I locked the door behind me, rested my hands on the sink, and cried for a long time.

I rinsed my eyes and stared at the boy in the mirror. I still didn't know much of what Deddy had done in Vietnam. But for the first time, I felt like I knew my deddy.

— ✳ ✳ ✳ —

WHEN THE DOOR OPENED, I FIGURED it was a doctor with bad news until Victry bolted up and yelled Cookie's name. Her eyes told him to sit down and shut up.

I'd never seen a wrinkle in Cookie's clothes, never imagined a hair out of place. Now her long black hair was caked across her head, and her dress was tattered and filthy. A cut on her nose was held together by dried blood instead of skin. Only her eyes looked the same.

Sam reached for a hug but didn't get one.

"Get Cash," she told him. "He's in the hall."

As Deddy walked to the bed and studied what was left of his brother, I wanted to hide. Was it the eyes? The grinding teeth? The hand that kept making a fist, holding for maybe a second, and exploding as if every finger was on a mission to kill? I wouldn't know, but I had no doubt he wanted Myles and Shad close by his side. Alive, so he could kill them again.

A doctor opened the door and hurried our way. He glanced at the monitor next to Big John's bed, held his wrist, and looked him over.

"His condition continues to decline," the doctor said. "Pulse is on a steady decline. Breaths are strained and further apart."

"What exactly are you saying?" Deddy asked.

"I'll be surprised if he lasts through the night," the doctor said. "I'm sorry."

"Big John needs our prayers," Cookie said. "Needs 'em now."

She glared at the doctor until he left.

Sam stepped closer to the bed. "I'll say a word."

"Not now," Deddy said. "I'd like to be alone with my brother."

"We all need to be lifting him up to the Lawd," Cookie said.

"You heard me," Deddy said.

"We got a right to be with this man when he goes on to glory," she said.

Deddy bowed his head. "Please. Please go. I need to be alone with my big brother."

She nodded. "I see where you coming from, Cash."

I couldn't remember what car we took from the hospital. Or who drove. Did I eat supper or dash straight to my room? Did I sleep?

I knew that answer.

48

I TRUDGED DOWN THE HALL TOWARD THE SPOT I'd been dreading all night. I stopped at the door. Again and again, I reached for the knob but pulled away like it was a hot skillet.

Finally I opened the door, stepped in, and knew right off I'd missed my hero's last breath. Sam stood at the foot of the bed. His bowed head and hunched shoulders told me Big John had died. Deddy, Cookie, and Victry sat next to the bed with faces that said the same. I was staring at my feet when a hand gripped my arm.

"Come join us," Sam said.

"When did he die?" I asked.

"He's alive," Sam said. "Doctors can't explain how he made it through the night, but it won't be long now."

"If God's so good, why can't He save Big John?" I asked.

"Slide, come sit next to me," Deddy said. "I need you."

I didn't notice the doctor until he lifted Big John's hand and checked his pulse. He studied the lines on a screen.

"How long?" Cookie asked.

"Maybe an hour," the doctor said. "Should I leave?"

Cookie nodded, then waited for the door to close.

"For Big John's sake, I wanted him to pass when Myles dragged him over the barbed-wire fence," she said. "I told the Lawd to take Big John home after they left him in that shed. Told Him again yesterday when I walked into this room and saw this fine man. Now I'm seeing something else."

She stood. Her eyes raced across the ceiling and settled on a spot over the bed.

"Laaaawwwwdd!" she called out. "Lawd, You know this man means the world to every person in this room. Course I'll be all right. Sam'll make it. I'm not sure about Cash. But Slide and Victry gotta have their rock until they learn that *You*, and You alone, are their rock. Amen."

She held her long arms over the bed until they shook. She reached down, touching the only part of Big John's cheek that wasn't covered in bandages.

"Lawd, don't You know we've had enough death in this place? Yes, Lawd, You know. Heal this man and be done with it. Amen."

With that Cookie marched to the door. She stopped and turned back.

"Everybody out," she said. "Time for Big John to be alone with his Lawd. Come on, Cash, I need a ride."

—✳ ✳ ✳—

MOMMA MADE COUNTRY-FRIED STEAK FOR SUPPER that night. It was tougher than the oldest saddle in Big John's barn. The gravy reminded me of what Annabelle threw up when she ate grass. I chewed and chewed but didn't taste a thing.

We were clearing the table when the phone rang.

"The hospital," Deddy said, slouching over his full plate. "My brother died."

Momma picked up, sighed, and said "Hello."

"Mr. Hood," she said. She listened. "You're very kind, Mr. Hood, but we'll have someone meet her at the airport. Thank you so much."

She hung up and looked our way. "Pearl's flying into Memphis early in the morning. Mr. Hood offered to pick her up and drive her to the hospital, but I thought one of the family oughta get her."

"I guess I can," Deddy said.

"I was thinking Victry," she said. "You could use some rest."

"I can't rest."

I put my hand on his shoulder. "I'll go with you, Deddy."

Momma reached for the phone. "I'll call Cookie, in case she wants Victry to ride with y'all."

The ceiling fan made circle after circle as I lay in bed. I pondered Shine and heaven, Myles and hell. I smiled, remembering what Victry had said about Deddy. Cookie's prayer for Big John came to mind, and I smiled no more.

Think about something else, I told myself for the second time in two days. Big John's birthday dinner. The redneck at the bait shop. The crowbar. Myles, the man I'd wanted to be. Myles, the scourge that strangled our homeland. The twisted white strands of Victry's rope. The day Victry had surprised Big John, then cried in his arms.

Cried in his arms? Yesterday Victry stood in the hall at Big John's door, staring down and breathing hard and looking every bit as confused as he'd been after Big John had cut the rope. Again, an older man ran to my cousin, offered words of comfort, and met Victry's tears with a long hug. Only this time, Sam was standing in Big John's place.

In Big John's place. I cried and cried, for I knew Cookie's prayer hadn't worked. My hero was going to die.

49

Cookie

THE DOCTOR AND THOSE NURSES ACTED LIKE MOSES had parted the Red Sea as they told Cookie that Big John had made it through the night and woken up asking for coffee. Fact was, the crazy looks on those white faces reminded her of the nuthouse at Whitfield. They were so rattled she didn't tell them it was the Lawd just doing His job—He'd been holding out long enough and decided to get on back to work.

Cookie did ask for a rundown on what Big John had in store. She held back a laugh when the doctor said her guess was as good as his. The man finally got himself together and said a bad limp and scarred-up face made the worst of what Big John had to look forward to.

Cookie chuckled to herself. If the doctor only knew that a stout cane would mosey Big John's rump from the kitchen or porch to the truck without a hitch. As for his face, nobody ever called Big John a handsome man. Not even Shine.

"One more question," Cookie said. "I'm sure y'all heard some of what's gone down over the past few days. What does Big John know?"

"Everything we do," the doctor said. "That you and the boy and his father have been here and must be okay. We keep telling him we don't know where his daughter is."

She thanked the doctor and turned for Big John's room.

─ ✳ ✳ ✳ ─

BIG JOHN WAS SITTING UP WHEN Cookie walked in and took a seat next to the bed. She smiled, wondering how the Lawd had worked this miracle. The dying man of yesterday was not only breathing but had no pain on his face. Well, the breathing part was true.

"They say you a new man," she said.

"Where's Pearl?" he asked with a frown.

"She'll be here before long."

"Thank You, Lord," he said, closing his eyes. He rested his head on the pillow. "Thank You."

"Some things we're not meant to understand."

Big John tilted his head. "I'm surprised to hear you say that, Cookie."

"You ain't the only one."

"What do you not understand?"

"Myles would be one."

"How many are out there?"

"I ain't got a clue. Only the Lawd knows, I reckon."

He nodded, leaned back, and drifted off to sleep.

He woke up when the door shut. Pearl had come home, and this daddy would've had his girl five feet off the ground before she'd made it halfway across the room if he'd been able to. He reached out with his good arm, blubbering too much to say her name.

Pearl never had been much for crying. She hugged, pulled back, and looked her daddy over. He didn't seem to notice the bump on her belly.

Cookie patted the seat next to hers. "Pearl, tell us what plans you got."

She sat. "First off, I need to tell you both how sorry I am." She stared as if counting the stitches on Cookie's nose. "None of this would've happened if I'd listened to you. You warned me." She turned. "Daddy, I had no right to blame you. *I* made the decision to marry Myles."

"Darling, you don't have to say any of this," he said.

"Victry came with Uncle Cash and Slide to pick me up at the airport and bring me—"

"Where they at?" Cookie asked, wondering why they hadn't come to check on Big John.

"I asked them to give me some time alone with Daddy. But I'm glad you're here, Cookie. Thank God you're safe."

"Thank Cash while you're at it," Cookie said.

Pearl nodded. "Victry told me Cash found you in the shed where they'd left Holly to die. And that Myles is dead."

"That's right," Cookie said, trying to read the girl's face. "Cash took care of him and Shad."

"They never had a chance, did they?" Pearl asked, staring at her knees.

"Nope. Yo daddy was right about his little brother."

A minute passed, maybe two.

"I'm proud of Uncle Cash," Pearl said in a way that made Cookie proud.

"Me too," Cookie said. "Now tell us what you got in mind."

"Well, I'll be moving back home, if Daddy will have me."

"For good this time?" Cookie asked.

"I'll never marry again. Now I know why you never trusted anyone after Billy."

"Billy was no Myles," Cookie said. She nodded at Pearl's belly. "The Lawd might have other plans for you anyhow."

Pearl eyed her daddy. "I'm pregnant."

Big John didn't look happy or sad. Just lost. Cookie did the math on Pearl's bump while he came to his senses.

"Pearl," he whispered, reaching her way. "You and your baby will stay with me."

Cookie let them hug as long as she could. "Have a seat, Pearl. Yo daddy's heart is liable to bust. No use him dying this late in the game."

Pearl kissed the top of his head and sat.

"So, who's the daddy?" Cookie asked.

"Myles."

"Like hell he is," Cookie said.

"You think I'd let a man touch me after all this? I haven't slept with anybody since Myles."

"You damn sure have," Cookie said. "Fact is, you slept with a passel of men."

"Cookie, what are you talking about?" Big John asked.

The daddy was still lost, but his girl started nodding in the right direction.

"This whole county will know Myles was more than a bad man," Cookie said. "No chile oughta carry that load."

Pearl took a deep breath, sat up in her chair, and faced her daddy. "Cookie's right. I've slept with more men than I can count. Too many to guess who the real father is."

"But folks are bound to talk," he said, thinking of his own baby and not hers.

"Who cares about talk right now?" Cookie asked.

"There's no going back, Daddy."

He rested his head on the pillow. "No going back," he kept mumbling to himself. He met Pearl's eyes.

"You're right, darling," he said. "And you're tough. We'll make it."

"We'll more than make it," Pearl said. "My baby will have a momma who'll do whatever it takes to make up for the blood a father left behind. Not to mention the best granddaddy a kid could hope for."

Big John looked his girl over. He smiled. Tears streamed around stitches and into cuts that had been too small to sew up.

"And I can't wait to be a granddeddy," he said.

The End

Author's Note

WHILE *GO TO HELL OLE MISS* is a work of fiction, I've made every effort to accurately portray the history that often builds its plot, themes, and characters.

The late-born son of a former B-24 pilot in WWII, I grew up around old-timers from the South who knew how to tell a story. The title is based on a true story from my father's experience as a POW. As with Big John in this novel, the words carved in that lonely German shed gave my father hope in the midst of serious hardship.

I hope they do the same for you.

Acknowledgments

THE EIGHT-YEAR JOURNEY OF WRITING THIS book has been a passion if not a calling, but I wouldn't have made it alone. I owe so many for their kindness and support.

Special thanks to the veteran authors who've graciously given their time and advice—Hampton Sides, Jamie Kornegay, Ron Hall, Neil White, Richard Grant, Jeffrey Blount, Lisa Patton, Molly Crosby, Jamie Quatro, Harrison Scott Key, Matthew Guinn, Courtney Santo, Tim Johnston, and David Magee, whose advice eventually led me to my wonderful publisher, Greenleaf Book Group. The team at Greenleaf has been patient, professional, and a pleasure to work with every step of the way.

Many thanks to Amy Collins, a renowned literary agent who's treated this stranger like an old friend. Thanks also to the editors who've provided such spot-on feedback on various rewrites through the years: Shari Lopatin, Alexandra Shelley, Joe Maxwell, Maggie Riggs, Laurie Chittenden, Elizabeth Waffler, and Christine Pride.

I've also been blessed with a gifted and supportive team of beta readers. Thanks so much to James, Sue, Shea, Sarah, Kelley, L, OCB, Mary Dudley, E Wood, Allison, Lauren, Liz, David, Amee, Peter, Nick, Maria, Jason, and Elizabeth.

Special friends have advised and encouraged me through what can be a lonely journey. To Joey, Randy, Tricia, Kelley, Murray, Dan, Room, Scotty, Carl, Gabe, Leslie, Joel, and too many others to name—I can't thank you enough for your support.

To Pops, Dot Dot, Beverly, and Alice. Your lives nurtured and inspired so many of us. There wouldn't be a *Go to Hell Ole Miss* without you.

And to my beloved four—Amy, Kate, Hall, and Ellie. Where would this novel, where would I, be without you? I love you so much.

About the Author

JEFF BARRY IS A NATIVE MEMPHIAN with deep Mississippi roots. After graduate school, he lived on a small cattle farm like the one featured in *Go to Hell Ole Miss*. Over the past twenty years, Jeff has worked in the farmland business in the Mississippi Delta, taught English in Peru, and advised farmers in northern Uganda. He now lives in Tennessee with his wife and three children. He enjoys hiking and camping, loves Hazel, his yellow Lab, and likes one of his wife's three cats.